The Deadly Bride

The Deadly Bride

And 21 of the Year's Finest Crime and Mystery Stories

Including complete coverage of the year in mystery and crime fiction

EDITED BY

Ed Gorman

AND **Martin H. Greenberg**

CARROLL & GRAF PUBLISHERS

NEW YORK

THE DEADLY BRIDE
And 21 of the Year's Finest Crime and Mystery Stories

Carroll & Graf Publishers
An Imprint of Avalon Publishing Group, Inc.
245 West 17th Street
11th Floor
New York, NY 10011

AVALON
publishing group incorporated

Copyright © 2007 Ed Gorman and Martin H. Greenberg

Library of Congress Cataloging-in-Publication Data is available.

ISBN-10: 0-7867-1917-6
ISBN-13: 978-0-78671-917-4

9 8 7 6 5 4 3 2 1

Book design by Maria E. Torres

Printed in the United States of America
Distributed by Publishers Group West

Contents

The Mystery in 2005 and 2006
Jon L. Breen   1

A 2005 Yearbook of Crime and Mystery
Edward D. Hoch   35

Online Mystery Fiction in 2005 and 2006
Sarah Weinman   65

The Catch
James W. Hall   71

There Is No Crime on Easter Island
Nancy Pickard   .   95

Born Bad
Jeffery Deaver   125

The Deadly Bride
Sharan Newman   149

Highest, Best Use
J. A. Jance   171

Interlude at Duane's
F. Paul Wilson   197

The Abelard Sanction
David Morrell   217

Lightning Rider
Rick Mofina   237

Driven to Distraction
Marcia Talley   265

Little Sins
Mike MacLean   279

Dust Up
Wendy Hornsby   291

Why'd You Bring Me Here?
Stanley Cohen   313

Chapter 82: Myrna Lloyd Is Missing
Robert S. Levinson   329

Down and Out in Brentwood
Neal Marks   357

Cain Was Innocent
Simon Brett   373

A Temporary Crown
Sue Pike   403

Sanctuary!
Peter Tremayne   421

A Matter of Honor
Jeremiah Healy   443

Low Drama
Kim Harrington   469

Jury Duty
Kristine Kathryn Rusch   477

The Last Interview
Craig McDonald   505

Lost Causes
Anne Perry   525

Permissions   551

The Mystery in 2005 and 2006

Jon L. Breen

2005 was a Year of Milestones and Commemorations. The centenary of the Ellery Queen team of Frederic Dannay (1905-1982) and Manfred B. Lee (1905-1971) was recognized by a full-day symposium at Columbia University, a volume of their radio plays (*The Adventure of the Murdered Moths* [Crippen & Landru]), and a year's worth of special features in *Ellery Queen's Mystery Magazine*. The 60th anniversary of the founding of Mystery Writers of America was celebrated at the annual Edgar Awards, whose own 60th birthday would be marked a year later. On a sadder note, 2005 saw the passing of two of the most prolific, influential, versatile, and multiple-bylined crime writers in the history of the form.

Evan Hunter (1926-2005), who also wrote as Curt Cannon, Richard Marsten, Hunt Collins, Ezra Hannon, and (most famously) Ed McBain, was certainly the most durable and probably the greatest literary practitioner of the police procedural, while also exploring virtually every other mystery subgenre and producing mainstream bestsellers, first and most notably *The Blackboard Jungle* (1954). As Lawrence Block pointed out in a tribute, Hunter/McBain demonstrated his unquenchable optimism when he began in his last days an alphabet-coded series of suspense novels. Only *Alice in Jeopardy* (2005) has been published, but *Bianca in Jeopardy* was announced as forthcoming.

Dennis Lynds (1924-2005) was best known to mystery readers as Michael Collins, the creator of one-armed private eye Dan Fortune, but he also wrote as William Arden, Mark Sadler, John Crowe, and Carl Dekker, plus numerous house names. Combining social consciousness and serious literary ambition with unerring craftsmanship, he was revered by his fellow professionals.

The most controversial book of 2005 was Stephen King's *The Colorado Kid* (Hard Case). The publisher specializes in hardboiled noir of the type found in the best '50s paperback originals, but (despite the sexy cover) King's novel wasn't that. It set up a seemingly impossible problem and examined it from all angles, suggesting a classical deductive detective novel, but it wasn't that either: King perversely refused to provide a solution. For the style, the characters, and the theme of the role of media, I found it worthwhile, but I can't claim those readers who were disappointed, or even angry, reacted unreasonably.

2006 demands to be designated the Year of the Thriller. The band of writers who in 2004 organized into International

Thriller Writers, Inc. held their first annual ThrillerFest in Scottsdale, Arizona; gave out their first Thriller Awards; and published an anthology to benefit and publicize their organization, logically called *Thriller* (Mira), edited by James Patterson.

Thriller in its current usage is primarily a commercial designation. It has a specific definition (per Patterson's introduction, "what gives the variety of thrillers a common ground is the intensity of emotions they create, particularly those of apprehension and exhilaration, of excitement and breathlessness") but has often been employed as loosely or inexactly as mystery or suspense. The term has sometimes, especially in Britain, designated the whole broad genre whose most nearly accurate umbrella label is crime fiction.

Some proponents seem determined to differentiate the thriller from the stodgy and predictable old mystery. Sara Weinman wrote in a May 15 *Publishers Weekly* article, "Although it's hard to say what would qualify as the first thriller (it was probably a movie), one might point to Ian Fleming's James Bond series or John le Carré's George Smiley titles as instances of storytelling with a sweep and nuance that just didn't feel like a mystery." This is a puzzling statement on several scores. What were John Buchan, Sax Rohmer, Eric Ambler, Edgar Wallace, Manning Coles, Ethel Lina White, Cornell Woolrich, and Charlotte Armstrong writing if not thrillers? And some of the recent bestsellers Weinman touts as examples—e.g., Michael Connelly's *The Poet* and Dan Brown's *The Da Vinci Code*—are clearly just as much mystery and detective novels. In fairness, a listing of "Must-Read Thrillers," introduced by David Morrell on the organization's website, takes a broader historical view, listing seventy cornerstones from Edgar Allan Poe's *The Narrative of Arthur Gordon Pym* (1838) to David Baldacci's *Absolute Power* (1995).

Inevitably, 2006 was another year of loss. One of the most widely known and commercially successful writers of detective fiction, Mickey Spillane, died at age 88. Controversial as he was in literary terms, he was a kind and generous man well liked even by detractors. Marilyn Wallace (1941-2006) is remembered as writer, friend to writers, and influential anthologist, editor of the five-volume *Sisters in Crime* series, for which her original title (per Judy Greber a.k.a. Gillian Roberts writing in MWA's newsletter, *The Third Degree*) was *Bitches' Brew*.

2006 also marked a centenary, but the hundredth anniversary of John Dickson Carr's birth was surprisingly even less widely commemorated than the EQ occasion of the year before. Slated for publication late in the year from Crippen & Landru was *Thirteen to the Gallows and Other Plays*, a collection of four stage works by Carr and Val Gielgud. The fiftieth anniversary of crime fiction's second most venerable periodical was celebrated by the anthology *Alfred Hitchcock's Mystery Magazine Presents Fifty Years of Crime and Suspense* (Pegasus), edited by Linda Landrigan.

Fans of wise Asian sleuths played by Caucasian actors in 1930s movies could celebrate DVD sets from Fox Video devoted to Charlie Chan (Warner Oland) and Mr. Moto (Peter Lorre).

Finally, both 2005 and 2006 saw a heartening increase in the volume of crime fiction translated into English from other languages, a trend that is reflected on the lists below.

BEST NOVELS OF THE YEAR 2005

The following fifteen were the most impressive crime novels I read and reviewed in 2005. The standard disclaimer applies: I don't pretend to cover the whole field—no single reviewer does—but try to find fifteen better.

Peter Abrahams: *Down the Rabbit Hole* (Laura Geringer/HarperCollins). Though aimed at children ten and up, the story of thirteen-year-old sleuth Ingrid Levin-Hill is like all the best juvenile fiction in appealing also to adults.

Sally Beauman: *The Sisters Mortland* (Warner). Set at an ancient Suffolk abbey that is the family home of the titular sisters, this delicate balance of the supernatural and psychological is notable for excellent writing, complex structure, and unconventional mystery.

Gabriel Brownstein: *The Man from Beyond* (Norton). Though far from the first work of fiction about Houdini and Conan Doyle, it must rank close to the best.

Lee Child: *One Shot* (Delacorte). In his Jack Reacher novels, Child is the writer most likely to satisfy equally the thriller buff and the advocate of pure detection.

Max Allan Collins: *Road to Paradise* (Morrow). The third of the gangster trilogy that began with the graphic novel (and later great film) *Road to Perdition* is arguably the best of the three.

Michael Connelly: *The Closers* (Little, Brown). Harry Bosch is back where he belongs with the LAPD after a wrong turn as private eye. Connolly did two excellent novels in the year, the other being the Edgar nominee *The Lincoln Lawyer* (Little, Brown).

Thomas H. Cook: *Red Leaves* (Harcourt/Penzler). Past Edgar winner Cook had another nominee in this fine novel about the effect on a family of suspicion directed at one of its members.

Tess Gerritsen: *Vanish* (Ballantine). The Edgar judges made another smart choice for nomination in this first-rate entry from the Boston-based series about medical examiner Maura Isles and police detective Jane Rizzoli, still very pregnant as the curtain rises.

P.D. James: *The Lighthouse* (Knopf). The latest Adam Dalgliesh novel finds James, now in her middle-eighties, at the height of her powers.

Ed McBain: *Fiddlers* (Harcourt/Penzler). Sadly, this is the final novel in the 87th Precinct's fifty-year run; happily, it ranks with the best of the series.

Walter Mosley: *Cinnamon Kiss* (Little, Brown). Sixties L.A. private eye Easy Rawlins almost turns to crime in the latest from an exceptional series.

Leonardo Padura: *Havana Red*, translated from the Spanish by Peter Bush (Bitter Lemon). This extraordinary Cuban novel, first published in Spanish in 1997, was my book of the year. Also featuring Havana cop Mario Conde and nearly as outstanding was *Adiós Hemingway*, translated from the Spanish by John King (Canongate), published as by Leonardo Padura Fuentes.

Rebecca Pawel: *The Watcher in the Pine* (Soho). The third novel about Carlos Tejada, Guardia officer of World-War-II era Fascist Spain, is well up to expectations.

George Pelecanos: *Drama City* (Little, Brown). In this Washington, D.C.-based Edgar nominee, one of the best writers around brings to life a gang-connected ex-con working for the Humane Society and his female parole officer, both heartwarmingly decent, both with heavy baggage.

Luis Fernando Verissimo: *Borges and the Eternal Orangutans*, translated from the Portuguese by Margaret Jull Costa (New Directions). Casting the Argentine Nobel Prize winner as amateur detective when murder strikes an Edgar Allan Poe conference in Buenos Aires, this Brazilian novella was the most Queenian work published in the year of the Ellery Queen centenary.

BEST NOVELS OF THE YEAR 2006

I won't repeat the disclaimer, except to add that some late-year books were not seen before this article's deadline.

Robert Barnard: *Dying Flames* (Scribner). The account of a novelist revisiting a past relationship ranks with the best by a writer who is always worth reading.

Poppy Z. Brite: *Soul Kitchen* (Three Rivers). Be warned the crime and mystery content is slight, but this is a superb novel about the restaurant business in New Orleans.

Gianrico Carofiglio: *A Walk in the Dark*, translated from the Italian by Howard Curtis (Bitter Lemon). The second novel to be published in English about Italian attorney Guido Guerrieri is even better than the first.

Tony Dunbar: *Tubby Meets Katrina* (NewSouth). Here is the best suspense novel so far to depict New Orleans before, during, and after Hurricane Katrina.

Howard Engel: *Memory Book*, with an afterword by Oliver Sacks, M.D. (Carroll & Graf). The brain injury that robs private eye Benny Cooperman of his ability to read (though not to write) and causes other tricks of memory parallels that suffered by Engel in a 2000 stroke. One of the most unusual detective novels of the year is also among the most fairly clued.

Loren D. Estleman: *Nicotine Kiss* (Forge). Detroit private eye Amos Walker hobbles through this one, but his creator's singing prose doesn't.

Brent Hartinger: *Grand & Humble* (HarperTempest). Two high school students—one a jock insider, the other a geeky outsider—share the stage in a small masterpiece of trick construction.

Margaret Maron: *Winter's Child* (Mysterious). The novels about North Carolina Judge Deborah Knott, now married to Sheriff's Deputy Dwight Bryant, are so consistently excellent, it's easy to take them for granted.

Leonardo Padura: *Havana Black*, translated from the Spanish by Peter Bush (Bitter Lemon). Another book about Havana cop Mario Conde (see above), whose cases may become a fixture on these lists if the translator keeps busy.

Nancy Pickard: *The Virgin of Small Plains* (Ballantine). Few books get their readers in a tighter grip than this combination of romantic suspense and small-town family intrigue, with a hint of the supernatural cum spiritual.

Bill Pronzini: *The Crimes of Jordan Wise* (Walker). Recalling the best of James M. Cain and the 1950s paperback original writers, this story of an ordinary man turned daring criminal (complete with femme fatale) is a great reading experience.

Lisa Scottoline: *Dirty Blonde* (HarperCollins). A federal judge's double life gets her in trouble in one of the best from a master of the legal thriller.

Gerald Seymour: *Traitor's Kiss* (Overlook). An espionage veteran shows us how spycraft has changed in a post-Cold War world.

Richard Stark: *Ask the Parrot* (Mysterious). The latest

about career criminal Parker, forty-four years after his first appearance, is my book of the year, a model of pace, professionalism, and oddball wisdom. Stark is the best-known pseudonym of Donald E. Westlake.

Kjell Westö: *Lang*, translated from the Swedish by Ebba Segerberg (Carroll & Graf). This darkly lively account of a Finnish talk-show host's involvement with a young mother and her abusive ex-husband suggests some trends in media and popular culture are universal.

SUB-GENRES

Private eyes. The most offbeat novel of this kind I read in 2005 was Rick Dewhurst's satirical *Bye Bye, Bertie* (Broadman & Holman), about Christian private eye Joe LaFlam. Series sleuths for hire in good form, along with Mosley's Rawlins on my list of fifteen, included Bill Pronzini's San Franciscan Nameless in *Nightcrawlers* (Forge); and Terence Faherty's '40s Hollywood sleuth Scott Elliott in the novella-length *In a Teapot* (Mystery Company/Crum Creek). In 2006, another private eye of '40's Hollywood, John Ray Horn, has a case involving the Communist hunt in Edward Wright's *Red Sky Lament* (Orion/Trafalgar Square). Also in commendable action was Marcia Muller's Sharon McCone in the unusual whydunit *Vanishing Point* (Mysterious).

Amateur sleuths. Two writers who feature police sleuths produced 2005 books in which amateurs are more prominent: Robert Barnard with *The Graveyard Position* (Scribner), an unusual variation on the claimant novel, and Peter Lovesey with the classical puzzle *The Circle* (Soho), in which the Chichester Writers' Circle carry the ball for half the distance before giving way to Inspector Henrietta Mallin. Publisher John M. Daniel introduced publisher Guy Mallon in the book-world satire *The Poet's Funeral* (Poisoned Pen). Established characters in good form included Maddy Hunter's travel escort Emily Andrew in *Hula Done It?* (Pocket), Eleanor Sullivan's nursing sleuth Monika Everhardt in *Deadly Diversion* (Hilliard Harris), Katherine Hall Page's caterer Faith Fairchild in *The Body in the Snowdrift* (Morrow), Lyn Hamilton's antique dealer Lara McClintoch in *The Moai Murders* (Berkley), Deborah Donnelly's wedding planner Carnegie Kincaid in *Death Takes a Honeymoon* (Dell), Parnell Hall's faux crossword expert Cora Felton in *Stalking the Puzzle Lady* (Bantam); Jude and Carole of the English village of Fethering in Simon Brett's *The Witness at the Wedding* (Berkley); and John R. Corrigan's PGA golfer Jack Austin in *Bad Lie* (Hardscrabble/University Press of New England). From the 2006 crop, I can recommend Jonathan Kellerman's psychologist Alex Delaware in *Gone* (Ballantine); Barbara Colley's New Orleans cleaning entrepreneur Charlotte LaRue in *Married to the Mop* (Kensington); Harlan Coben's sports agent Myron Bolitor in *Promise Me* (Dutton); and a new character, small-town Iowa's Brandy Borne in *Antiques Roadkill* (Kensington) by Barbara Allan (joint pseudonym of Barbara and Max Allan Collins).

Police. In 2005, Anne Argula's *Homicide My Own* (Pleasure Boat Studio) featured two Spokane cops in an offbeat paranormal mystery; Ben Elton's *Past Mortem* (Transworld UK/Trafalgar) involved a Scotland Yard detective with a website that reunites old school friends; and Tokyo police did the honors in Miyuki Miyabe's highly unusual

Internet-centered mystery *Shadow Family* (Kodansha), translated from the Japanese by Juliet Winters Carpenter. Series cops walking their beats effectively included Mat Coward's London team of Packham and Mitchell in *Open and Closed* (Five Star); Andrea Camilleri's Sicilian Inspector Montalbano in *Excursion to Tindari* (Penguin), translated from the Italian by Stephen Sartarelli; Yasmina Khadra's Algerian Superintendent Llob in *Double Blank* (Toby Press), translated from the French by Aubrey Botsford; and Baantjer's long-running Amsterdam cop in DeKok and *Murder by Melody* (Speck), translated from the Dutch by H.G. Smittenaar. Lest I seem to be neglecting American police, 2006 brought James Lee Burke's Louisiana cop Dave Robicheuax in *Pegasus Descending* (Simon and Schuster); Stuart M. Kaminsky's Chicagoan Abe Lieberman in *Terror Town* (Forge); and Laurie R. King's San Franciscan Kate Martinelli, investigating a Sherlockian mystery in *The Art of Detection* (Bantam). International police sleuths were busy as well, notably Deon Meyer's Cape Town cop Mat Joubert in *Dead Before Dying* (Little, Brown), translated from the Afrikaans by Medelaine van Biljon; Anne Holt's Oslo detective Adam Stubo in *What is Mine* (Warner), translated from the Norwegian by Kari Dickson; and Camilleri's Montalbano in *Rounding the Bend* (Penguin), again translated by Sartarelli. British colleagues included Ken Bruen's McBain-fan London cop Brant in *Calibre* (St. Martin's Minotaur); and Katherine John's Trevor Joseph in the novella *The Corpse's Tale* (Accent/Dufour), intended for new readers but worth the time of others as well.

Lawyers. In 2005, Italian defender Guido Guerrieri, of

Gianrico Carofiglio's *Involuntary Witness* (Bitter Lemon), translated from the Italian by Patrick Creagh, was a welcome addition to the ranks. (He scored even better on his second appearance. See my best of the following year.) Among those presenting persuasive arguments in 2006 were William Bernhardt's Ben Kincaid in *Capitol Murder* (Ballantine) and Linda Fairstein's Alex Cooper in *Death Dance* (Scribner).

Crooks. Steve Brewer's 2005 car-theft epic *Boost* (Speck) may remind you of Donald E. Westlake, either as himself or as Richard Stark. Another specialist in automotive crime is the getaway car driver of James Sallis's *Drive* (Poisoned Pen). Loren D. Estleman's retired killer for hire Peter Macklin continues to fail to escape his past in *Little Black Dress* (Forge). Moving to 2006, no less lovable central character is likely to come your way than Giorgio Pellegrini in Massimo Carlotto's darkly compelling *The Goodbye Kiss* (Europa), translated from the Italian by Lawrence Venuti. Even Max Allan Collins's retired hitman character in *The Last Quarry* (Hard Case) is a pussycat by comparison.

Historicals. In 2005, Rupert Holmes's *Swing* (Random) captured the 1940s popular music scene in fine style, including an original CD of period-style songs with each book, while Max Allan Collins revisited the 1938 Orson Welles radio hoax in *The War of the Worlds Murder* (Berkley). Laurie R. King's *Locked Rooms* (Bantam) brought Sherlock Holmes and wife Mary Russell to 1924 San Francisco, while Mitch Cullin's *A Slight Trick of the Mind* (Talese/Doubleday), with its moving account of a nonagenarian Holmes, is more a fine study of old age than a mystery or crime novel. Among historical series sleuths in good form were Michael Jecks's Sir Baldwin Furnshill and Bailiff Simon Puttock in *The Chapel of Bones* and *The Butcher of St. Peter's* (both Headline/Trafalgar); Kathy Lynn Emerson's sixteenth-century herbalist sleuth Susanna, Lady Appleton in *Face Down Below the Banqueting House* (Perseverance); Boris Akunin's ninteenth-century Russian Erast Fandorin in *The Turkish Gambit* (Random), translated from the Russian by Andrew Bromfield; and Laura Joh Rowland's seventeenth-century Japanese Sano Ichiro in *The Assassin's Touch* (St. Martin's Minotaur) In 2006, Steve Hockensmith's 1890s cowboy sleuth Old Red appeared for the first time at novel length in *Holmes on the Range* (St. Martin's Minotaur). Others making history come alive were Bernard Knight's twelfth-century coroner Crowner John in *The Elixir of Death* (Simon & Schuster UK/Trafalgar Square); David Fulmer's pre-World War I New Orleans private detective Valentin St. Cyr in *Rampart Street* (Harcourt); Hal Glatzer's 1940s musician Katy Green in *The Last Full Measure* (Perseverance); and Kerry Greenwood's 1920s flapper sleuth Phryne Fisher in her debut case *Cocaine Blues* (Poisoned Pen), first published in Australia in 1989.

Thrillers. In line with the discussion above, I will define thriller as any book that doesn't fit the other categories. Some good 2005 examples included Robert S. Levinson's Hitchcockian *Ask a Dead Man* (Five Star), Brian Pinkerton's wildly plotted *Vengeance* (Leisure), Marcia Muller's *Cape Perdido* (Mysterious) from her Soldedad County series; Dean Koontz's delightfully over the top *Velocity* (Bantam); Steven Owad's hockey tale *Bodycheck* (Rendezvous Crime), and several good horse racing thrillers: John McEvoy's *Blind Switch* (Poisoned Pen), John Francome's *Dead Weight* (St. Martin's Minotaur), Lyndon Stacey's *Outside Chance* (Hutchinson/Trafalgar Square), and the final novel of the late William Murray, *Dead Heat* (Eclipse Press). (Admirers of those last four will undoubtedly celebrate the 2006 comeback of Dick Francis in *Under Orders* [Putnam], which I have not yet read.) Some 2006 highlights were Stephen King's science fictional mobile phone nightmare, *Cell* (Scribner); Walter Mosley's also science fictional *The Wave* (Warner); Paul Malmont's *The Chinatown Death Cloud Peril* (Simon and Schuster), putting a bunch of 1930s pulp writers into something resembling one of their own stories; Dean Koontz's over-the-top-once-more *The Husband* (Bantam); and two fine novels set in the art world: New Zealander Chad Taylor's *Departure Lounge* (Europa) and *Blood Mask* (Ecco) by Lauren Kelly (Joyce Carol Oates).

Juveniles. Apart from Peter Abrahams on my list of fifteen, writers doing their best to nurture a new generation of mystery readers in 2005 included Laura J. Burns and Melinda Metz with *The Case of the Prank That Stank* (Sleuth/Razorbill), for ten and up; and Walter Sorrells with *Fake I.D.* (Sleuth/Dutton), for young adults. In 2006, I had a look at some kids' books with Sherlockian connections and can recommend two that focus on Holmes's young street-wise helpers, Alex Simmons and Bill McCay's *The Raven League* (Sleuth/Razorbill) and Tracy Mack and Michael Citrin's *Sherlock Holmes and the Baker Street Irregulars: The Fall of the Amazing Zalindas* (Orchard/Scholastic). Recommended slightly less enthusiastically are Dave Keane's *The Haunted Toolshed* and *The Neighborhood*

Stink (HarperCollins), first two in the Joe Sherlock, Kid Detective series. Yes, they're funny, but the trend to indulging children in their love for fart jokes even in the pages of their books is somewhat dubious.

SHORT STORIES

The traffic in single-author collections remained hearteningly brisk. Highlights from specialist publisher Crippen & Landru in 2005 gathered stories by Terence Faherty, Margaret Millar, Edward Marston, Gladys Mitchell, and others. Another independent press, Wildside, collected Rob Kantner's Ben Perkins stories and Johnston McCulley's vintage pulp tales about Thubway Tham. Five Star, which rarely publishes collections anymore, had a winner in Benjamin M. Schutz's *Mary, Mary, Shut the Door and Other Stories*. Notable from the New York majors was Cornell Woolrich's *Tonight, Somewhere in New York* (Carroll & Graf), edited by Francis M. Nevins. See Edward D. Hoch's yearbook feature for the full story on 2005 collections.

In 2006, the riches continued. Those who treasure locked rooms and impossible crimes especially welcomed two late-year volumes: Hoch's *More Things Impossible: The Second Casebook of Dr. Sam Hawthorne* (Crippen & Landru), and Paul Halter's *The Night of the Wolf* (Wildside), translated from the French by John Pugmire and Robert Adey. Crippen & Landru also published Dennis Lynds's *Slot-Machine Kelly: The Collected Private Eye Cases of the One-Armed Bandit*, Erle Stanley Gardner's *The Casebook of Sidney Zoom*, Rafael Sabatini's *The Evidence of the Sword and Other Mysteries*, Ellis Peters's *The Trinity Cat and Other Mysteries*, and Amy Myers's *Murder, 'Orrible*

Murder, while Wildside collected O'Neil DeNoux's stories about a '40 private eye in *New Orleans Confidential*. Twilight Tales brought us *My Lolita Complex and Other Tales of Sex and Violence*, collaborations of Max Allan Collins and Matthew V. Clemens. Imported from Australia was Peter Corris's *Taking Care of Business* (Allen & Unwin), about private eye Cliff Hardy. From the New York "bigs" came Peter Tremayne's *An Ensuing Evil and Others* (St. Martin's Minotaur), Perri O'Shaughnessy's *Sinister Shorts* (Delacorte), Faye Kellerman's *The Garden of Eden and Other Criminal Delights* (Warner), Lawrence Block's third Keller collection-disguised-as-a-novel *Hit Parade* (Morrow), Joyce Carol Oates's *The Female of the Species: Tales of Mystery and Suspense* (Harcourt), and Dennis Lehane's *Coronado: Stories* (Morrow).

Anthologies by multiple authors continued the trend of recent years: usually original stories, often with inventive themes. Among the most unusual of 2005 was *Meeting Across the River* (Bloomsbury), edited by Jessica Kaye and Richard Brewer, a score of stories inspired by the titular Bruce Springsteen song; and 2006 also had a musically-themed collection, *A Merry Band of Murderers* (Poisoned Pen), edited by Claudia Bishop and Don Bruns—this one came with a CD! The Medieval Murderers, a British group of five historical specialists (Michael Jecks, Susanna Gregory, Bernard Knight, Ian Morson, and Philip Gooden) produced two collections of connected stories, *The Tainted Relic* (2005) and *The Sword of Shame* (2006)(both Simon & Schuster UK/Trafalgar). Prolific editor Mike Ashley continued to gather original historicals in 2005's *The Mammoth Book of New Historical Whodunnits* and 2006's *The Mammoth Book of Jacobean Whodunnits* (both Carroll & Graf).

Other notable 2005 anthologies included a monumental novella collection, *Transgressions* (Forge), edited by Ed McBain; the crafts-themed *Murder Most Crafty* (Berkley), edited by Maggie Bruce, pseudonym of Marilyn Wallace; *Murder in Vegas* (Forge), edited by Michael Connelly for the International Association of Crime Writers; a pair from busy editor Otto Penzler, *Dangerous Women* and *Murder is My Racquet* (both Mysterious); the Biblically-themed *Thou Shalt Not Kill* (Carroll & Graf), edited by Anne Perry; *The Cocaine Chronicles* (Akashic), edited by Gary Phillips and Jervey Tervalon; the hitman-themed *Greatest Hits* (Carroll & Graf), edited by Robert J. Randisi; and *Plots with Guns: A Noir Anthology* (Dennis McMillan), edited by Anthony Neil Smith. Among the burgeoning crop of regional anthologies were *Tar Heel Dead* (University of North Carolina Press), edited by Sarah R. Shaber, and *Manhattan Mysteries* (KS Publishing)—Manhattan, Kansas, that is—winners of a contest judged by Jeanne M. Dams, Eileen Dreyer, Nancy Pickard, Marcia Talley, and Carolyn Wheat. Again, for the full story on 2005, see Ed Hoch's bibliography.

In 2006, Otto Penzler brought forth no less than three more volumes in his sports-themed series, *Murder at the Foul Line*, *Murder at the Racetrack*, and *Murder in the Rough* (all Mysterious). Akashic Books' noir series, which seems determined to cover every major American city plus a few outside, added *Manhattan Noir*, edited by Lawrence Block; *D.C. Noir*, edited by George Pelecanos; and *Dublin Noir*, edited by Ken Bruen. In a similar vein and drawing on many of the same authors was *Hardboiled Brooklyn*

(Bleak House), edited by Reed Farrel Coleman. Other orig-
inal anthologies of note included the Mystery Writers of
America's *Death Us Do Part: New Stories About Love, Lust,
and Murder* (Little, Brown), edited by Harlan Coben; the
Detection Club's *The Detection Collection* (St. Martin's
Minotaur), edited by Simon Brett; *Women of Mystery* (Har-
rington Park), edited by Katherine V. Forrest; *Murder
Through the Ages* (iBooks), edited by Maxim Jakubowski;
and another hitman anthology, *These Guns for Hire* (Bleak
House), edited by J.A. Konrath.

Among the reprint collections, Tony Hillerman and
Rosemary Herbert essayed a new version of an antholog-
ical classic in *A New Omnibus of Crime* (Oxford University
Press) in 2005. Commemorating the best stories of 2004
were *The Best American Mystery Stories 2005* (Houghton
Mifflin, 2005), credited to guest editor Joyce Carol Oates
and series editor Otto Penzler; and the present volume's
predecessor, *The Adventure of the Missing Detective and 19
of the Year's Finest Crime and Mystery Stories* (Carroll &
Graf, 2006), edited by Ed Gorman and Martin H. Green-
berg, who also offered a companion volume, *The Widow of
Slane and Six More of the Best Crime and Mystery Novellas
of the Year* (Carroll & Graf, 2006). Oates/Penzler and
Gorman/Greenberg had only one story in common: Laura
Lippman's "The Shoeshine Man's Regrets." *The Best British
Mysteries 2005* (Allison & Busby), edited by Maxim
Jakubowski, perversely enough, consisted of stories first
published in 2003, but *Best British Mysteries 2006* (Allison
& Busby) covers 2004 and has Anne Perry's "A Tale of One
City" in common with *Widow of Slane*.

Scott Turow served as Penzler's guest editor for *The Best*

American Mystery Stories 2006 (Houghton Mifflin), gathering highlights of 2005. And the most unusual retrospective anthology of 2006 was surely *The Best of 10 Story Book: From Harry Stephen Keeler's Spicy Magazine 1919-1940* (Ramble House), edited by Chris Mikul, in which writers as well-known as Carroll John Daly, Theodore Pratt, Kenneth Fearing, Jack Woodford, Len Zinberg (later known as Ed Lacy), Zora Neale Hurston, August Derleth, Vincent Starrett, Harold Q. Masur, and Keeler himself share the pages with period nudes.

Reference Books and Secondary Sources

Book of the year in this category in 2005 was Melanie Rehak's Edgar and Agatha winning *Girl Sleuth: Nancy Drew and the Women Who Created Her* (Harcourt). Leslie S. Klinger completed *The New Annotated Sherlock Holmes* (Norton) with a third volume covering the four novels, while Hallie Ephron produced one of the most valuable how-to manuals I have ever seen, *Writing and Selling Your Mystery Novel: How to Knock 'em Dead with Style* (Writer's Digest). Jess Nevins's remarkable *The Encyclopedia of Fantastic Victoriana* (MonkeyBrain) had a wider scope but included more intelligent, knowledgeable, and sometimes iconoclastic history and criticism of 19th-century detective fiction than any book in memory. Also of special note were Marvin Lachman's authoritative *The Heirs of Anthony Boucher: A History of Mystery Fandom* (Poisoned Pen); Michael Kreyling's *The Novels of Ross Macdonald* (Columbia: University of South Carolina Press); Michael Burgess and Jill H. Vassilakos's *Murder in Retrospect: A Selective Guide to Historical Mystery Fiction* (Libraries Unlimited); Drewey

Wayne Gunn's *The Gay Male Sleuth in Print and Film* (Scarecrow); Judith A. Markowitz's *The Gay Detective Novel* (McFarland); and Stuart Kaminsky and Laurie Roberts's excellent (though miserably proof-read) interview collection, *Behind the Mystery: Top Mystery Writers* (Hot House). For the full story, see Ed Hoch's bibliography.

The 2006 crop included Mitzi M. Brunsdale's error-prone but useful *Gumshoes: A Dictionary of Fictional Detectives* (Greenwood); Dana Martin Batory's *Sherlock Holmes: A Baker Street Dozen: 14 Excursions into the Sherlockian Mythos* (Gryphon); Terry J. Erdman and Paula W. Block's *Monk: The Official Episode Guide* (St. Martin's Griffin); *Mystery Muses: 100 Classics That Inspire Today's Mystery Writers* (Crum Creek), edited by Jim Huang and Austin Lugar; Daniel Stashower's *The Beautiful Cigar Girl: Mary Rogers, Edgar Allan Poe, and the Invention of Murder* (Dutton); Chris Roerden's *Don't Murder Your Mystery: 24 Fiction-Writing Techniques to Save Your Manuscript From Turning Up D.O.A.* (Bella Rosa); and several more from the prolific mystery buffs at McFarland: Thomas C. Renzi's *Cornell Woolrich from Pulp Noir to Film Noir*; Barbara Bogue's *James Lee Burke and the Soul of Dave Robicheaux: A Critical Study of the Crime Fiction Series*; Phyllis M. Betz's *Lesbian Detective Fiction: Woman as Author, Subject and Reader*; M. Ray Lott's *Police on Screen: Hollywood Cops, Detectives, Marshals and Rangers*; Carla T. Kungl's *Creating the Fictional Female Detective: The Sleuth Heroines of British Women Writers, 1890-1940*; Lewis D. Moore's *Cracking the Hard-Boiled Detective: A Critical History from the 1920s to the Present*; and *Hispanic and Luso-Brazilian Detective Fic-*

tion: Essays on the Genero Negro Tradition, edited by Renée W. Craig-Odders, Jacky Collins, and Glen S. Close.

A Sense of History

Perhaps the most unexpected revival of 2005, viewed in terms both of quality and political correctness, was G.G. Fickling's sexy male-wish-fulfillment private eye Honey West with the 1957 novel *This Girl for Hire* (Overlook). Of more solid merit were Rue Morgue's rediscoveries (continuing into 2006) of writers like Dorothy Bowers, Gladys Mitchell, Kelley Roos, and Margaret Scherf. Otto Penzler's line of past Edgar winners for Forge included new editions of books by William Bayer, Joe Gores, and the team of Warren Murphy and Molly Cochran; while Stark House produced two-novels-to-a-volume reprints of such writers as Elizabeth Sanxay Holding, Day Keene, Vin Packer, and Peter Rabe; and Walker, which now publishes regrettably little crime fiction, offered a new edition of John Le Carré's 1963 classic, *The Spy Who Came in From the Cold*. The increased interest in hardboiled fiction noir brought new editions of Martin M. Goldsmith's 1939 novel *Detour* (O'Bryan), source of an iconic 1945 B-movie, and books from Hard Case Crime by Donald E. Westlake, Wade Miller, Day Keene, and others. Crippen & Landru departed from its usual short stories only policy to revive the work of the first African-American mystery writer, Philip S. Warne's *Who Was Guilty?: Two Dime Novels*, originally published in 1872 and 1881. Wilkie Collins's 1874 novella *The Dead Alive* had a new edition (Northwestern University Press) with additional material by Rob Warden about its source case and the general subject of wrongful conviction.

A number of foreign landmarks were published in English translation for the first time. In 2005 came Swedish pioneer Aurora Ljungstedt's *The Hastfordian Escutcheon* (The Battered Silicon Dispatch Box), translated by Bertil Falk; and the following year brought Japanese trailblazer Edogawa Rampo's *The Black Lizard and Beast in the Shadows* (Kurodahan), translated by Ian Hughes, and German icon Friedrich Glauser's *In Matto's Realm* (Bitter Lemon), translated by Mike Mitchell.

In 2006, Stark House added to its twofer stable Benjamin Appel, Malcolm Braly, Stephen Marlowe, Harry Whittington, and Margaret Millar, a particularly important inclusion given her stature in the American mystery field; Rue Morgue reintroduced Pamela Branch, three of whose four novels appeared in the U.S. for the first time; and Penguin launched a reprinting of early Maigret novels by Georges Simenon. A new imprint specializing in psychological dark suspense, Millipede Press, offered handsome editions of Theodore Sturgeon's *Some of Your Blood* (1961), Ramsey Campbell's *The Face That Must Die* (1979), and Fredric Brown's *Here Comes a Candle* (1950). Pegasus had a new edition of Cornell Woolrich's transitional 1932 novel *Manhattan Love Song*, while Ramble House revived an even obscurer piece of early Woolrich, 1930's *A Young Man's Heart*, not a suspense novel but notable for its autobiographical interest.

At the Movies

The MWA members judging the best motion picture category had a rare opportunity in 2005: they could have awarded an Edgar to a movie about the writing of an Edgar-winning book. But in an exceptionally strong year for crime and mystery films, the excellent *Capote*, directed by Bennett Miller from Dan Futterman's script based on Gerald Clarke's 1988 biography, wasn't even nominated. The "origin" saga of the true-crime classic *In Cold Blood* was a nominee for best-picture Oscar and the remarkable Philip Seymour Hoffman a winner for best actor.

While I enjoyed the Edgar winner, Steven Gaghan's big-canvas international thriller on oil-industry corruption *Syriana*, based on the book by Robert Baer, I preferred three of the other nominees, all more intimate in scope. Woody Allen's British-based and intricately plotted *Match Point*, was widely heralded as a return to top form for the prolific writer-director. *The Ice Harvest*, a black comedy directed by Harold Ramis from a script by Richard Russo and Robert Benton, based on Scott Phillips's novel, rein-forced the niche of Billy Bob Thornton, star of 2003's *Bad Santa*, as the screen's leading specialist in Christmas noir. *A History of Violence*, directed by David Cronenberg from Josh Olson's screenplay, followed *Road to Perdition* as a superb crime film with its origins in a graphic novel, this one by John Wagner and Vince Locke.

The Oscar winner for Best Picture, Paul Haggis's *Crash*, with screenplay by Haggis and Bobby Moresco from Haggis's story, was also an Edgar nominee. This film was even more polarizing than its main Oscar competition, *Brokeback Mountain*. The gay cowboy saga merely divided those who saw it from those who refused to see it, while *Crash* generated pro and con camps from its actual audi-ence. Some found it a masterpiece, others vastly overrated and the worst top Oscar winner since 1952's *The Greatest Show on Earth*. Put me in the second group.

Some of the many 2005 crime films I preferred to *Crash* included the oddly controversial fictionalization of the Israeli response to the terrorist attack on their athletes at the 1972 Olympics, *Munich*, directed by Stephen Spielberg and scripted by Tony Kushner and Eric Roth from George Jonas's *Vengeance: The True Story of an Israeli Counter-Terrorist Team*; the first film to be directed by Tommy Lee Jones, *The Three Burials of Melquiades Estrada*, from the screenplay of Guillermo Arriaga; the New York action drama *16 Blocks*, directed by Richard Donner from Richard Wenk's script; Atom Egoyan's show-biz whodunit *Where the Truth Lies*, adapted from Rupert Holmes's novel; the screen adaptation of John le Carré's *The Constant Gardener*, directed by Fernando Meirelles from Jeffrey Caine's screenplay; and one of those films that keep you guessing *after* you see it, Austrian director Michael Haneke's French-language study in voyeurism, *Caché*.

Most surprising past author to be adapted for the big screen in 2005 had to be Michael Shayne's creator, Brett Halliday, whose 1941 novel *Bodies are Where You Find Them* was the basis for Shane Black's semi-spoof *Kiss, Kiss, Bang, Bang*.

2006 appears a much weaker year for big-screen crime, at least through its first three quarters. It's tempting to nominate for top honors Chris Payne's documentary *Who Killed the Electric Car?*, while noting that it is true crime rather than fiction. I can also recommend *Inside Man*, a fine heist-cum-hostage thriller directed by Spike Lee from Russell Gewirtz's script; *The Sentinel*, an effective Secret Service thriller directed by Clark Johnson from George Nolfi's script, based on Gerald Petievich's novel; and Neil

Burger's tricky and visually stunning spiritualism historical *The Illusionist*, from Steven Millhauser's short story
"Eisenheim the Illusionist." *The Night Listener*, directed by
Patrick Stettner, who shared screenplay credit with Armis-
tead Maupin and Terry Johnson, from Maupin's novel, is a
suspenseful example of the what's-going-on-here mystery
genre, highlighted by a wonderfully creepy performance
from Toni Collette. Some rightly complained, however, that
it didn't play fair with the viewer—and it easily could have
with a slightly different approach to one early scene.

Not viewed in time for this article but eagerly anticipated
were two late-year L.A.-based mysteries, *Hollywoodland*,
directed by Allen Coulter from Paul Bernbaum's script, about
the suicide (or was it murder?) of TV's Superman, George
Reeves, and the movie version of James Ellroy's novel *The
Black Dahlia*, directed by Brian DiPalma and written by Josh
Friedman. Also promising is an adaptation of Ruth Rendell's
novel *The Bridesmaid*, directed by the French master Claude
Chabrol. Finally, there's another film about Truman Capote
and the writing of *On Cold Blood* on the horizon: Douglas
McGrath's *Infamous*, based on George Plimpton's oral history
Truman Capote. Capote this time is played by Toby Jones, a
better physical match for his subject than Hoffman.

Award Winners

Awards tied to publishers' contests, those limited to a geo-
graphical region smaller than a country, those awarded for
works in languages other than English (with the exception
of Crime Writers of Canada's nod to their French members), and those confined to works from a single periodical
have been omitted.

Awarded in 2006 for Material Published in 2005

EDGAR ALLAN POE AWARDS
(Mystery Writers of America)
BEST NOVEL: Jess Walter, *Citizen Vince* (Regan Books)
BEST FIRST NOVEL BY AN AMERICAN AUTHOR: Theresa Schwegel,
Officer Down (St. Martin's Minotaur)
BEST ORIGINAL PAPERBACK: Jeffrey Ford, *Girl in the Glass* (Dark
Alley)
BEST FACT CRIME BOOK: Edward Dolnick, *Rescue Artist: A True
Story of Art, Thieves, and the Hunt for a Missing Masterpiece*
(HarperCollins)
BEST CRITICAL/BIOGRAPHICAL WORK: Melanie Rehak, *Girl Sleuth:
Nancy Drew and the Women Who Created Her* (Harcourt)
BEST SHORT STORY: James W. Hall, "The Catch" (*Greatest Hits*,
Carroll & Graf)
BEST YOUNG ADULT MYSTERY: John Feinstein, *Last Shot* (Knopf)
BEST JUVENILE MYSTERY: D. James Smith, *The Boys of San
Joaquin* (Simon & Schuster)
BEST PLAY: Gary Earl Ross, *Matter of Intent* (Theater Loft)
BEST TELEVISION EPISODE TELEPLAY: Ed Whitmore, "Amulet"
(*Sea of Souls*)
BEST MOTION PICTURE SCREENPLAY: *Syriana*, screenplay by
Stephen Gaghan, based on the book by Robert Baer
(Warner Brothers)
GRAND MASTER: Stuart Kaminsky
ROBERT L. FISH AWARD (BEST FIRST STORY): Eddie Newton, "Home"
(*Ellery Queen's Mystery Magazine*, May)
ELLERY QUEEN AWARD: Brian Skupin and Kate Stine
(*Mystery Scene*)
RAVEN: Black Orchid Bookshop (Bonnie Claeson & Joe

Gugliemelli, owners); Men of Mystery Conference (Joan Hansen, creator)

MARY HIGGINS CLARK AWARD: Karen Harper, *Dark Angel* (MIRA)

AGATHA AWARDS

(Malice Domestic Mystery Convention)

BEST NOVEL: Katherine Hall Page, *The Body in the Snowdrift* (Morrow)

BEST FIRST NOVEL: Laura Durham, *Better Off Wed* (HarperCollins)

BEST SHORT STORY: Marcia Talley, "Driven to Distraction" (*Chesapeake Crime 2*, Quiet Storm)

BEST NON-FICTION: Melanie Rehak, *Girl Sleuth: Nancy Drew and the Women Who Created Her* (Harcourt)

BEST CHILDREN'S/YOUNG ADULT (TIE): Peter Abrahams, *Down the Rabbit Hole* (HarperCollins); Carl Hiaasen, *Flush* (Knopf)

LIFETIME ACHIEVEMENT AWARD: Robert Barnard

POIROT AWARD: Douglas G. Greene

DAGGER AWARDS

(Crime Writers' Association, Great Britain)

DUNCAN LAWRIE DAGGER: Ann Cleeves, *Raven Black* (Macmillan)

INTERNATIONAL DAGGER: Fred Vargas, *The Three Evangelists*, translated from the French by Sian Reynolds (Harvill)

IAN FLEMING STEEL DAGGER: Nick Stone, *Mr. Clarinet* (Penguin)

GOLD DAGGER FOR NON-FICTION: Linda Rhodes, Lee Sheldon and Kathryn Abnett, *The Dagenham Murders* (The Borough of Barking and Dagenham)

BEST SHORT STORY: to be announced

NEW BLOOD DAGGER: Louise Penny, *Still Life* (Headline)

DIAMOND DAGGER: Elmore Leonard

ELLIS PETERS HISTORICAL DAGGER: to be announced

DAGGER IN THE LIBRARY (VOTED BY LIBRARIANS FOR A BODY OF
WORK): Jim Kelly
DEBUT DAGGER (FOR UNPUBLISHED WRITERS): Otis Twelve (D. V.
Wesselmann), *Imp*

ARTHUR ELLIS AWARDS
(Crime Writers of Canada)
BEST NOVEL: William Deverell, *April Fool* (McClelland & Stewart)
BEST FIRST NOVEL: Louise Penny, *Still Life* (McArthur & Company)
BEST NON-FICTION: Rebecca Godfrey, *Under the Bridge: The True
Story of the Murder of Reena Virk* (HarperCollins Canada)
BEST JUVENILE NOVEL: Vicki Grant, *Quid Pro Quo* (Orca Book
Publishers)
BEST SHORT STORY: Rick Mofina, "Lightning Rider" (*Murder in
Vegas*, Forge)
BEST CRIME WRITING IN FRENCH: Gerald Galarneau, *Motel Riviera*
(Les Editions JCL)
DERRICK MURDOCH AWARD FOR LIFETIME ACHIEVEMENT:
Mary Jane Maffini

NED KELLY AWARDS
(Crime Writers' Association of Australia)
BEST NOVEL: (tie) Peter Temple, *The Broken Shore* (Text) and
Chris Nyst, *Crooks as Rookwood* (HarperCollins)
BEST FIRST NOVEL: Wendy James, *Out of Silence: A Story of Love,
Betrayal, Politics and Murder* (Random House)
BEST TRUE CRIME: Lachlan McCulloch, *Packing Death* (Sly Ink)
LIFETIME ACHIEVEMENT: Andrew Rule and John Sylvester

HAMMETT PRIZE
(International Crime Writers)
Joseph Kanon, *Alibi* (Holt)

DILYS AWARD

(Independent Mystery Booksellers Association)

Colin Cotterill, *Thirty Three Teeth* (Soho)

LEFTY AWARD

(Left Coast Crime)

(best humorous mystery novel in the English language)

Peter Guttridge, *Cast Adrift* (Allison & Busby, UK)

BRUCE ALEXANDER AWARD

(Left Coast Crime)

(best historical mystery novel)

Tony Broadbent, *Spectres in the Smoke* (St. Martin's)

THRILLER AWARDS

(International Thriller Writers, Inc.)

BEST NOVEL: Christopher Reich, *The Patriots Club* (Delacorte)

BEST FIRST NOVEL: Adam Fawer, *Improbable* (Morrow)

BEST PAPERBACK ORIGINAL: R. Cameron Cooke,

Pride Runs Deep (Jove)

BEST SCREENPLAY: Michael Haneke, *Caché (Hidden)*

THRILLERMASTER AWARD: Clive Cussler

Awarded in 2005 for Material Published in 2004

ANTHONY AWARDS

(Bouchercon World Mystery Convention)

BEST NOVEL: Willliam Kent Krueger, *Blood Hollow* (Atria)

BEST FIRST NOVEL: Harley Jane Kozak, *Dating Dead Men*

(Doubleday)

BEST PAPERBACK ORIGINAL: Jason Starr, *Twisted City* (Vintage Crime)

BEST SHORT STORY: Elaine Viets, "Wedding Knife" (*Chesapeake Crimes*, Quiet Storm)

BEST CRITICAL/BIOGRAPHICAL: Max Allan Collins, George Hagenauer, and Steven Heller, *Men's Adventure Magazines in Postwar America: The Rich Oberg Collection* (Taschen)

BEST COVER ART: *Brooklyn Noir*, designed by Sohrab Habibiom, edited by Tim McLoughlin (Akashic Press)

SHAMUS AWARDS

(Private Eye Writers of America)

BEST NOVEL: Ed Wright, *While I Disappear* (Putnam)

BEST FIRST NOVEL: Ingrid Black, *The Dead* (St. Martin's)

BEST ORIGINAL PAPERBACK NOVEL: Max Phillips, *Fade to Blonde* (Hard Case Crime)

BEST SHORT STORY: Pearl Abraham, "Hasidic Noir" (*Brooklyn Noir*, Akashic Press)

THE EYE (LIFE ACHIEVEMENT): Sara Paretsky

DAGGER AWARDS

(Crime Writers' Association, Great Britain)

GOLD DAGGER: Arnaldur Indridason, *Silence of the Grave* (Harvill Press)

SILVER DAGGER: Barbara Nadel, *Deadly Web* (Headline)

JOHN CREASEY MEMORIAL DAGGER (BEST FIRST NOVEL): Dreda Say Mitchell, *Running Hot* (Maia Press)

SHORT STORY DAGGER: Danuta Reah (Carla Banks), "No Flies on Frank" (*Sherlock Magazine*, issue 64)

GOLD DAGGER FOR NON-FICTION: Greg and Gina Hill, *On the Run* (Hutchinson)

DIAMOND DAGGER: Ian Rankin

ELLIS PETERS HISTORICAL DAGGER: C. J. Sansom, *Dark Fire* (Macmillan)

IAN FLEMING STEEL DAGGER: Henry Porter, *Brandenburg* (Orion)

DAGGER IN THE LIBRARY (VOTED BY LIBRARIANS FOR A BODY OF WORK): Jake Arnott

DEBUT DAGGER (FOR UNPUBLISHED WRITERS): Ruth Dugdall, *The Woman Before Me*

LEO HARRIS AWARD: Prof. Bernard Knight, for the best contribution to the CWA monthly bulletin, *Red Herrings*

DAGGER OF DAGGERS: John le Carré *The Spy Who Came in from the Cold* (1963)

MACAVITY AWARDS

(Mystery Readers International)

BEST NOVEL: Ken Bruen, *The Killing of the Tinkers* (St. Martin's Minotaur)

BEST FIRST NOVEL: Harley Jane Kozak, *Dating Dead Men* (Doubleday)

BEST NON-FICTION: D. P. Lyle, *Forensics for Dummies, M.D.* (Wiley)

BEST SHORT STORY: Terence Faherty, "The Widow of Slane" (*Ellery Queen's Mystery Magazine*, March/April)

ARTHUR ELLIS AWARDS

(Crime Writers of Canada)

BEST NOVEL: Barbara Fradkin, *Fifth Son* (RendezVous)

BEST FIRST NOVEL: Jon Evans, *Dark Places* (HarperCollins Canada)

BEST NONFICTION: Matthew Hart, *The Irish Game* (Viking Canada)

BEST JUVENILE NOVEL: Carrie Mac, *The Beckoners* (Orca)

BEST SHORT STORY: Leslie Watts, "Crocodile Tears" (*Revenge*,
Insomniac)
BEST CRIME WRITING IN FRENCH: Ann Lamontagne, *Les Douze
Pierres* (Vents d'Ouest)
DERRICK MURDOCH AWARD FOR LIFETIME ACHIEVEMENT: Max Haines

NED KELLY AWARDS

(Crime Writers' Association of Australia)
BEST NOVEL: Michael Robotham, *Lost*
BEST FIRST NOVEL: Malcolm Knox, *A Private Man*
BEST TRUE CRIME: (tie) Tony Reeves, *Mr Big*; Helen Garner, *Jo
Cinque's Consolation*
LIFETIME ACHIEVEMENT: Stuart Coupe
Note: Information on publishers unavailable

BARRY AWARDS

(*Deadly Pleasures* magazine)
BEST NOVEL: Lee Child, *The Enemy* (Delacorte)
BEST FIRST NOVEL: Carlos Ruiz Zafon, *The Shadow of the Wind*
(Penguin)
BEST BRITISH NOVEL: John Harvey, *Flesh and Blood* (Heinemann)
BEST PAPERBACK ORIGINAL: Elaine Flinn, *Tagged for Murder* (Avon)
BEST THRILLER: Barry Eisler, *Rain Storm* (Putnam)
BEST SHORT STORY: Edward D. Hoch, "The War in Wonderland"
(*Green for Danger*, Do-Not Press)
DON SANDSTROM MEMORIAL AWARD FOR LIFETIME ACHIEVEMENT IN
MYSTERY FANDOM: Bill Crider

NERO WOLFE AWARD

(Wolfe Pack)
Lee Child, *The Enemy* (Delacorte)

DILYS AWARD

(Independent Mystery Booksellers Association)

Jeff Lindsay, *Darkly Dreaming Dexter* (Doubleday)

HAMMETT PRIZE

(International Crime Writers)

Chuck Hogan, *Prince of Thieves* (Scribner)

ELLEN NEHR AWARD

(for excellence in mystery reviewing)

(The American Crime Writers League)

Hallie Ephron, *The Boston Globe*

A 2005 Yearbook of Crime and Mystery

Compiled by Edward D. Hoch

Collections and Single Stories

Bellem, Robert Leslie. *Dan Turner, Hollywood Detective*. Rialto, CA: Pulpville Press. Eight stories and a comic strip from Spicy Detective and Speed Detective, 1935-46. Edited by Jerry L. Schneider. (Not to be confused with the 1983 collection from Bowling Green State U. Popular Press.)

_____. *Dan Turner, Hollywood Detective 2*. Rialto, CA: Pulpville Press. Nine stories from Hollywood Detective, 1943. Edited by Jerry L. Schneider.

_____. *Killer's Ruse*. Rialto, CA: Pulphouse Press. Six non-series stories from Fifth Column Stories, Private Detective and Super-Detective, 1940-49. Edited by Jerry L. Schneider.

_____. *Knife in the Dark and Other Stories*. Rialto, CA:

Pulphouse Press. Thirteen non-series stories from the pulps, 1931-49, some detective stories. Edited by Jerry L. Schneider.

Bodkin, M. McDonnell. *The Beck-Myre Family Omnibus Set*. Shelburne, Ont., Canada: The Battered Silicon Dispatch Box. All seven volumes of the stories (and two novels) about Paul Beck, Dora Myrl and their son. Introduction by Geoff Bradley.

Box, C. J. *Dull Knife*. Mission Viejo, CA: A.S.A.P. Publishing. A single short story about Joe Pickett. Introduction by Ken Bruen.

Bracken, Michael. *Yesterday in Blood and Bone*. Rockville, MD: Wildside Press. A new novella and nineteen stories, one new.

Burke, James Lee. *Molester*. Amazon.com. A new twenty-page story sold and delivered electronically in a series of Amazon Shorts.

Chesbro, George. *Strange Prey and Other Tales of the Hunt*. Apache Beach Publications. Eleven stories from various sources.

Chesterton, G.K. *Father Brown: The Essential Tales*. New York: Modern Library. A new selection of fifteen stories from the first two Father Brown collections. Introduction by P.D. James.

Christie, Agatha. *Masterpieces in Miniature: The Detectives*, New York: St. Martin's. Thirty-nine stories featuring Parker Pyne, Harley Quin, Poirot and Miss Marple.

Coben, Harlan. *The Innocent*. New York: Dutton. A novel accompanied by a new basketball short story featuring the author's series sleuth Myron Bolitar.

Coel, Margaret. *Day of Rest.* Mission Viejo, CA: A.S.A.P. Publishing. Latest story in her Arapaho Ten Commandments series. Introduction by C.J. Box.

Cummings, Ray. *Thrilling Mystery Stories.* Rialto, CA: Pulphouse Press. Nine weird-menace stories from Thrilling Mystery, 1939-41, one with a private eye. Edited by Jerry L. Schneider.

Faherty, Terence. *The Confessions of Owen Keane.* Norfolk, VA: Crippen & Landru. Seven stories and novelettes about an amateur sleuth, two new, four from *EQMM*.

_____. *Good Night, Dr. Kobel.* Norfolk, VA: Crippen & Landru. An unpublished non-series story included with the limited edition of *The Confessions of Owen Keane.*

Farley, Ralph Milne. *The Ralph Milne Farley Collection Book 1.* Rialto, CA: Pulphouse Press. Three novelettes, one a detective story from Five-Novels Monthly, 1936. Edited by Jerry L. Schneider.

Fleming-Roberts, G. T. *Compleat Adventures of the Green Ghost.* Shelbourne, Ont., Canada. Battered Silicon Dispatch Box. A two-volume edition of all the Green Ghost pulp stories.

Gorman, Ed. *Different Kinds of Dead and Other Tales.* Waterville, ME: Five Star. A mixed collection of fifteen stories, 1968-2004, five previously collected, some mystery.

Greene, Graham. *Complete Short Stories.* New York: Penguin. All fifty-three of Greene's short stories, several crime and suspense.

_____. *No Man's Land.* London: Hesperus Press. Two

15,000-word novelettes, written as film treatments
and not included in the *Complete Short Stories.*

Hammett, Dashiell. *Lost Stories.* San Francisco: Vince
Emery Productions. Twenty-one "lost" stories, with a
short biography of Hammett. Introduction by Joe
Gores.

_____. *Vintage Hammett.* New York: Vintage Books.
Episodes from all five novels plus three Continental
Op stories and the non-series story "Nightshade."

Holmes, Rupert. *The Long Winter's Nap.* New York: The
Mysterious Bookshop. A single new story in a
Christmas chapbook from a Manhattan bookstore.

Jeffers, H. Paul. *The Forgotten Adventures of Sherlock
Holmes.* New York: Carroll & Graf. Thirteen stories
based on the 1940s radio plays by Anthony Boucher
and Denis Green.

Kantner, Rob. *Trouble Is What I Do.* Rockville, MD: Point
Blank/Wildside. Eighteen stories, one new.

Ljungstedt, Aurora. *The Hastfordian Escutcheon.* Shel-
bourne, Ont., Canada: Battered Silicon Dispatch Box.
Two 1870 mystery novelettes, translated from the
Swedish and introduced by Bertil Faulk.

Lynds, Dennis, writing as Michael Collins. *Slot-Machine
Kelly: The Collected Private Eye Cases of the "One-
Armed Bandit."* Norfolk, VA: Crippen & Landru. Thir-
teen stories, 1962-66, mainly from *Mike Shayne
Mystery Magazine.* Introduction by Robert J. Randisi.

Marston, Edward. *Murder, Ancient and Modern.* Norfolk,
VA: Crippen & Landru. Eighteen mysteries through
history, two new, from biblical times to the present.

_____. *The End of the Line.* Norfolk, VA: Crippen & Landru.

A single new story to accompany the limited edition of *Murder, Ancient and Modern.*

McCulley, Johnston. *Tales of Thubway Tham.* Holicong, PA: Wildside Press. Exploits of a pickpocket, from 1920s issues of *Detective Story Magazine.*

McDermid, V. L. *Stranded.* East Fourstones, England: Flambard. Nineteen stories, one new, almost all crime and suspense.

Mitchell, Gladys. *Sleuth's Alchemy: Cases of Mrs. Bradley and Others.* Norfolk, VA: Crippen & Landru. Thirty-one brief stories mainly from the Evening Standard newspaper, 1936-56. Edited by Nicholas Fuller. A Lost Classics volume.

Oates, Joyce Carol. *The Female of the Species: Tales of Mystery and Suspense.* New York: Otto Penzler/Harcourt. Nine stories and novelettes, 2001-04, some fantasy, three from EQMM, one from AHMM.

Queen, Ellery. *The Adventure of the Murdered Moths and other radio mysteries.* Norfolk, VA: Crippen & Landru. Fourteen radio plays, 1939-45, most previously unpublished.

_____. *The Case of the Three Macklins.* Norfolk, VA: Crippen & Landru. A six-page radio play included with the limited edition of *Murdered Moths.*

Robinson, Peter. *Blue Christmas.* Norfolk, VA: Crippen & Landru. A single new Inspector Banks story in a Christmas chapbook.

Sallis, James. *The James Sallis Reader.* Rockville, MD: Point Blank/Wildside. Stories, essays, poetry and two novels.

Sayers, Dorothy L. *The Travelling Rug.* Altadena, CA:

Mythopoeic Press. A previously unpublished short story, with a complete checklist of her short fiction. Introduction by Joe R. Christopher, with annotations by Janet Brennan Croft.

Saylor, Steven. *A Gladiator Dies Only Once.* New York: St. Martin's. Eight novelettes.

Schutz, Benjamin M. *Mary, Mary, Shut the Door and Other Stories.* Waterville, ME: Five Star. Twelve stories, mainly from 1988-2001.

Tremayne, Peter. *An Ensuing Evil and Others: Fourteen Historical Mysteries.* New York: St. Martin's. More Sister Fidelma stories.

Wolven, Scott. *Controlled Burn: Stories of Prison, Crime and Men.* New York: Scribner. Thirteen stories, three previously reprinted in *Best American Mystery Stories* anthologies.

Warne, Philip S. & Howard W. Macy. *Who Was Guilty?* Norfolk, VA: Crippen & Landru. Two "Dime Novels," 1873-81, by early black writers. The editor, Marlena E. Bremseth, presents a strong case that "Warne" was a pseudonym of Macy.

Anthologies

Alexander, Skye, Kate Flora & Susan Oleksiw, eds. *Riptide: Crime Stories by New England Writers.* Prides Crossing, MA: Level Best Books. The second in an annual series of new stories.

Andrews, Donna, foreword by. *Chesapeake Crime II.* Martinsburg, WV: Quiet Storm Publishing. Fifteen stories in the second of a series.

Ashley, Mike, ed. *The Mammoth Book of New Historical*

Whodunnits. New York: Carroll & Graf. Twenty-six stories, fifteen new, in the third volume of a series.

Batonne, Eva & Jeffrey Marks, eds. *Techno-Noir*. Austin, TX: Zumaya Publications. Short stories, new and old, on the dark side of technology.

Brett, Simon, ed. *The Detection Collection*. London: Orion. Eleven new stories by members of Britain's famed Detection Club, celebrating its 75th anniversary, plus a brief history of the Club by the editor.

Bruce, Maggie, ed. *Murder Most Crafty*. New York: Berkley. Fifteen new stories about handicrafts.

Bruen, Ken, ed. *Dublin Noir*. Brooklyn: Akashic. Nineteen new stories.

Connelly, Michael, ed. *Murder in Vegas*. New York: Forge. Twenty-two new stories in an anthology from the International Association of Crime Writers.

Edwards, Martin, ed. *Crime on the Move*. London: Do-Not Press. Twenty-two stories, all but three new, in an annual anthology from Britain's Crime Writers Association.

Gilbert, Jim & Gail Waller, eds. *A Kudzu Christmas*. Montgomery, AL: River City Publishing. Twelve Christmas mysteries by southern writers, some fantasy. Introduction by Julia Spencer-Fleming.

Gorman, Ed & Martin H. Greenberg, eds. *The Adventure of the Missing Detective and 19 of the Year's Finest Crime and Mystery Stories*. New York: Carroll & Graf. Twenty stories from various sources plus five articles on the 2004 mystery scene.

Greenberg, Martin H., Jon Lellenberg & Daniel Stashower, eds. *Ghosts in Baker Street*. New York:

Carroll & Graf. Ten new Sherlockian pastiches with possible supernatural overtones, plus three essays by Caleb Carr, Barbara Roden and Loren D. Estleman.

Hillerman, Tony & Rosemary Herbert, eds. *A New Omnibus of Crime.* Oxford: Oxford University Press. Twenty-seven stories, 1924-2005, three new. Contributing editors: Sue Grafton & Jeffery Deaver.

Jakubowski, Maxim, ed. *The Best British Mysteries 2006.* London: Allison & Busby. Twenty-nine stories published during 2004.

_____. *The Mammoth Book of Vintage Whodunnits.* New York: Carroll & Graf. Twenty-seven stories, 1834-1935.

Ladies Killing Circle. *When Boomers Go Bad.* Canada: RendeVous Press. New Stories in a continuing series from Canadian mystery writers.

Maravelis, Peter, ed. *San Francisco Noir,* Brooklyn: Akashic. Fifteen new stories.

Massey, Ellen Gray, ed. *Mysteries of the Ozarks, Volume I.* Dallas: Skyward. A mixed collection of mystery and horror stories.

McBain, Ed, ed. *Transgressions.* New York: Forge. Ten new novellas by leading mystery writers.

McLoughlin, Tim, ed. *Brooklyn Noir 2: The Classics.* Brooklyn: Akashic. Fourteen stories with Brooklyn settings, 1927-2004, mainly crime.

Morgan, Jill M., ed. *Creature Cozies.* New York: Berkley. Eleven new stories about cats and dogs with crime-solving instincts.

Oates, Joyce Carol, ed. *The Best American Mystery Stories 2005.* Boston: Houghton Mifflin. Twenty stories from various sources. Series editor: Otto Penzler.

Pelecanos, George, ed. *D.C. Noir.* Brooklyn: Akashic. Sixteen new stories set in the nation's capital.

Penzler, Otto, ed. *Murder Is My Racquet.* New York: Mysterious Press. Fourteen new stories about tennis.

Perry, Anne, ed. *Thou Shalt Not Kill: Biblical Mystery Stories.* New York: Carroll & Graf. Fifteen new biblically-based mysteries.

Pollack, Neal, ed. *Chicago Noir.* Brooklyn: Akashic. Eighteen new stories.

Randisi, Robert J., ed. *Greatest Hits: Original Stories of Assassins, Hitmen, and Hired Guns.* New York: Carroll & Graf. Fifteen new stories.

Shaber, Sarah R., ed. *Tar Heel Dead: Tales of Mystery and Mayhem from North Carolina.* University of North Carolina Press. Eighteen stories from EQMM, AHMM and elsewhere.

Smith, Anthony Neil, ed. *Plots With Guns: A Noir Anthology.* Tucson: Dennis McMillan. Twenty-four new stories, some from an online magazine of the same name.

Tervalon, Jervey & Gary Phillips, eds. *The Cocaine Chronicles.* New York: Akashic. Seventeen new stories about the cocaine lifestyle, mainly crime.

Non-Fiction

Burgree, Michael & Jill H. Vassilakos. *Murder in Retrospect: A Selective Guide to Historical Mystery Fiction.* Westport, CT: Libraries Unlimited. Alphabetical entries with critical summaries and lists of works.

Carr, John Dickson. *Helmsmen of Atlantis and other poems.* Karlskrona, Sweden: Psilander Grafiska. A

100-copy limited edition of a pamphlet containing Carr's teenage poetry. Introduction by Douglas G. Greene.

Chandler, Charlotte. *It's Only a Movie: Alfred Hitchcock, a Personal Biography.* New York: Simon & Schuster. A new biography of the film director.

Chandler, Raymond. *Philip Marlowe's Guide to Life.* New York: Knopf. An A-Z compendium of Marlowe's observations on life, taken from his novels and stories. Edited by Martin Asher.

Childs, Peter. *The Fiction of Ian McEwan.* London: Palgrave. Study of a leading British writer whose novels often contain criminal elements.

Comentale, Edward P., Stephen Watt & Skip Willman, eds. *Ian Fleming & James Bond: The Cultural Politics of 007.* Bloomington, IN: Indiana University Press. A collection of essays and reviews.

Cox, J. Randolph & David S. Siegel. *Flashgun Casey, Crime Photographer: From the Pulps to Radio and Beyond.* Yorktown Heights: Book Hunter. A brief biography of George Harmon Coxe and summary of his Casey series, including the first Casey story and two radio scripts. Introduction by William F. Nolan.

Cypert, Rick. *America's Agatha Christie: Mignon Good Eberhart, Her Life and Works.* Susquehanna University Press. A critical biography.

Eames, Andrew. *The 8:55 to Baghdad: From London to Iraq on the Trail of Agatha Christie.* New York: Overlook. Following Christie's travels.

Ephron, Hallie. *Writing and Selling Your Mystery Novel: How to Knock 'Em Dead With Style.* Cincinnati: Writers Digest Books. A guide for new writers.

Feole, Glenn L. & Don Lasseter. *The Complete Patricia Cornwell Companion.* New York: Berkley. A brief biography, tribute and annotated bibliography, with character profiles, chronologies, medical terms and a list of characters and settings.

Fowles, John. *The Journals, Volume One: 1949-1965.* New York: Knopf. Journals by the author of *The Collector* and *The Magus.* Edited by Charles Drazin.

Gunn, Drewey Wayne. *The Gay Male Sleuth in Print and Film: A History and Annotated Bibliography.* Lanham, MD: Scarecrow Press.

Harmon, Claire. *Myself and the Other Fellow: A Life of Robert Louis Stevenson.* New York: HarperCollins. A new biography of the author of *Dr. Jekyll and Mr. Hyde* and several crime short stories.

Horsley, Lee. *Twentieth Century Crime Fiction.* New York: Oxford University Press. A history and analysis.

James, Dean & Elizabeth Foxwell. *The Robert B. Parker Companion.* New York: Berkley. An interview, plot synopses and notes on screen adaptations.

Kaminsky, Stuart. *Behind the Mystery.* Cohasset, MA: Hot House Press. Interviews with eighteen American mystery writers, photos by Laurie Rober.

Klinger, Leslie S. *The New Annotated Sherlock Holmes: The Novels.* New York: Norton. Completes the three-volume set begun in 2004.

Kreyling. Michael. *The Novels of Ross Macdonald.* Columbia, SC: U. of South Carolina. A critical biography.

Lachman, Marvin. *The Heirs of Anthony Boucher: A History of Mystery Fandom.* Scottsdale, AZ: Poisoned Pen

Press. A detailed account of fan organizations, mystery conventions, fanzines and Internet websites. Introduction by Edward D. Hoch.

Layman, Richard, ed. *Discovering The Maltese Falcon and Sam Spade: The Evolution of Dashiell Hammett's Masterpiece, Including John Huston's Movie with Humphrey Bogart.* San Francisco: Vince Emery Productions. Hundreds of essays, reviews, documents and illustrations about Hammett and his most famous novel. Revised version of a 2003 volume published by Gale.

Lord, Graham. *John Mortimer: The Devil's Advocate.* London: Orion. A biography of Rumpole's creator.

Markowitz, Judith A. *The Gay Detective Novel: Lesbian and Gay Main Characters and Themes in Mystery Fiction.* Jefferson, NC: McFarland. A study of some one hundred characters, with bibliography.

Marrs, Suzanne. *Eudora Welty: A Biography.* New York: Harcourt Brace. The life of a famed southern author whose writing occasionally touched on crime, and who carried on a lengthy correspondence and friendship with Ross Macdonald.

Pappas, Charles. *It's a Bitter Little World.* Cincinnati: Writer's Digest Books. A collection of quotes from classic and contemporary film noir.

Pauly, Thomas H. *Zane Grey: His Life, His Adventures, His Women.* Chicago: University of Illinois Press. Biography of the famed western writer whose work included a dozen novels about Sgt. King of the Mounties.

Penzler, Otto & Thomas H. Cook, eds. *The Best American*

Crime Writing 2005. New York: Harper. Fifteen true crime articles, with an introduction and an original essay by James Ellroy.

Perriam, Geraldine, ed. *Josephine Tey: A Celebration.* Glasgow: Black Rock Press. A seventy-seven-page festschrift of essays on Tey's life and work. Consultant editor: Catherine Aird.

Rehak, Melanie. *Girl Sleuth: Nancy Drew and the Women Who Created Her.* New York: Harcourt. The early days of the popular juvenile series.

Renzi, Thomas C. *Cornell Woolrich from Pulp Noir to Film Noir.* Jefferson, NC: McFarland. A survey of Woolrich's life and work.

Rodriguez, Ralph. *Brown Gumshoes: Detective Fiction and the Search for Chicano/a Identity*, University of Texas Press. The first comprehensive study of the subject.

Scaggs, John. *Crime Fiction.* Oxford: Routledge. A volume in the New Critical Idiom series.

Sheldon, Sidney. *The Other Side of Me: A Memoir.* New York: Warner. Memoir of the best-selling film producer and thriller writer.

Shimeld, Thomas J. *Walter B. Gibson and the Shadow.* Jefferson, NC: McFarland. Study of Gibson and his most popular creation.

Sotelo, Susan Baker. *Chicano Detective Fiction.* Jefferson, NC: McFarland. A critical study of five mystery novelists.

Terdoslavich, William. *The Jack Ryan Agenda: Policy and Politics in the Novels of Tom Clancy: An Unauthorized Analysis.* New York: Forge. Political attitudes in the Clancy books.

Thompson, George J. "Rhino." *Hammett's Moral Vision.*

San Francisco: Vince Emery Productions. A study of Hammett's novels, originally published in seven issues of *The Armchair Detective.*

Wagstaff, Vanessa & Stephen Poole. *Agatha Christie: A Reader's Companion.* London: Aurum Press. An illustrated compendium.

Weller, Sam. *The Bradbury Chronicles: The Life of Ray Bradbury.* New York: Morrow. A tribute to the fantasy writer who sometimes ventures into mysteries.

Yanal, Robert J. *Hitchcock as Philosopher.* Jefferson, NC: McFarland. A discussion of twelve Hitchcock films.

Obituaries

Ted Allbeury (1917-2005). Well-known British author of some fifty spy and intrigue novels, including a few as by "Richard Butler" and "Patrick Kelly," starting with *A Choice of Enemies* (1972). Sixteen short stories collected in *Other Kinds of Treason* (1990).

Norma Ames (1920-2005). Pseudonym of Ames Norman, author of two paperback mysteries, 1970-72.

Mary Hayley Bell (1917-2005). Widow of British actor John Mills who authored a number of suspense plays and novels including *Duet for Two Hands* and *Whistle Down the Wind.*

George Bernau (1945-2005). Author of three suspense novels, 1988-94, starting with *Promises to Keep.*

John (Raymond) Brosnan (1947-2005). Australian/ British science fiction writer whose books include one crime novel, *Skyship* (1981), one collaboration as "Harry Adam Knight," and five police procedurals as "John Raymond," 1985-87.

William J. Buchanan (1926-2005). Author of a single suspense novel, *Present Danger* (1986).

Kenneth Bulmer (1921-2005). Science fiction writer who also authored some fifteen suspense novels, 1968-83, some as by "Ken Blake" and some in collaboration.

Edward Bunker (1933-2005). Author of five crime novels starting with *No Beast So Fierce* (1973), based on his prison experiences.

F. M. Busby (1921-2005). Science fiction writer who published one suspense novel, *The Singularity Project* (1993).

Glyn Carr (1908-2005). Pseudonym of British author Showell Styles who published fifteen popular mountain-climbing mysteries, 1951-69, notably *Death Finds a Foothold* (1961).

Bruce Cassiday (1920-2005). Author of scores of novels and non-fiction books including a dozen mysteries under his own name and others as by "Carson Bingham," "Nick Carter," "Mary Anne Drew," "Lee Falk," "C.K. Fong," "Annie Laurie McAllister," "Annie Laurie McMurdie" and "Michael Stratford." Fiction editor of *Argosy*, *Adventure* and other magazines. Former executive vice-president of MWA. Eight pulp stories collected as *None But The Vengeful* (2000).

Jack L. Chalker (1944-2005). Science fiction writer who published five mystery novels, 1976-2000, three about Sam and Brandy Horowitz.

Larry Collins (1929-2005). Best-selling co-author of *Is Paris Burning?* who also published six suspense and intrigue novels, 1980-99, one in collaboration.

Michael G. Coney (1932-2005) British/Canadian science

fiction writer whose work included two novels and several short stories with crime elements.

N(orman) J(ames) Crisp (1923-2005). British TV writer who also authored four suspense novels, 1976-87.

Andre Delmonico (1911-2005). Pseudonym of Eula Atwood Morrison, author of two suspense novels, 1968-69, starting with *Chateau Chaumond.*

Eugenia Desmond (1921-2005). Author of *Shadow at Dunster Hall* (1965).

Leslie John Duxbury (1926-2005). Co-author of *Angels* (1975), a collection of short stories, some criminous, based on a British TV series.

Alice Thomas Ellis (1932-2005). Pseudonym of Anna Haycraft, author of *Pillars of Gold* (1992).

Charlotte Epstein (1921-2005). Author of two mystery novels starting with *Murder in China* (1986).

Harry Farrell (1924-2005). Journalist and winner of MWA's Fact Crime Edgar for *Swift Justice: Murder and Vengeance in a California Town* (1992).

Sue Feder (?-2005). Mystery reviewer and editor/publisher of the fanzine "Murder: Past Tense."

Shelby Foote (1916-2005). Noted historian who published two suspense novels, *Follow Me Down* (1950) and *September September* (1978).

John Fowles (1926-2005). Well-known British author of *The Collector* (1963) and *The Magus* (1965).

Christopher Fry (1907-2005). Well-known playwright whose work included the borderline crime drama *The Lady's Not For Burning* (1949).

Martin Garaway (1913-2005). Author of *The Theft of the Anasazi Pots* (1999).

Elmer Grape (1929-2005). Former co-owner, with his wife mystery writer Jan Grape, of Austin's Mystery & More bookstore and co-chair of the 1993 Southwest Mystery/Suspense Convention.

Batya Gur (1947-2005). Leading Israeli mystery writer and author of the Inspector Michael Ohayon novels, starting with *The Saturday Morning Murder* (1992).

Colonel David H. Hackworth (1930-2005). Author of *The Price of Honor* (1999).

Willis Hall (1929-2005). British TV and fantasy writer, author of *The Fuzz* (1977).

Sylvian Hamilton (?-2005). British author of three historical mysteries, starting with *The Bone-Pedlar* (2000).

Charles L. Harness (1915-2005). Science fiction writer whose work included two futuristic suspense novels, *The Venetian Court* (1982) and *Lunar Justice* (1991).

Reynolds H. Hayden (1911-2005). Author of *Splendid Murder* (1977).

Theda O. Henle (1918-2005). Author of *Death Files for Congress* (1971).

Mantle Hood (1918-2005). Author of three suspense novels, 1998-2000, starting with *The Keeper*.

Edwin Palmer Hoyt (1923-2005). Author of two suspense novels, 1966-71, starting with *A Matter of Conscience*.

David Hughes (1930-2005). British author whose works included a single suspense novel, *The Pork Butcher* (1984).

Alan Hunter (1922-2005). British author of nearly fifty novels about Inspector George Gently, starting with *Gently Does It* (1955) and ending with *Gently Mistaken* (1999).

Evan Hunter (1926-2005). Famed author of *The Blackboard Jungle* (1954) and many other novels, who achieved even greater renown as "Ed McBain" with fifty-five novels about the detectives of the 87th Precinct, notably *Cop Hater* (1956), *Fuzz* (1968), *Sadie, When She Died* (1972), *Ice* (1983) and *Widows* (1991). Also published thirteen McBain novels about Florida lawyer Matthew Hope, and other novels and stories as by "John Abbott," "Curt Cannon," "Hunt Collins," "Ezra Hannon" and "Richard Marsten." Recipient of MWA Grand Master Award and CWA Diamond Dagger. His numerous story collections include *The Empty Hours* (1962), *The McBain Brief* (1982) and *Learning to Kill* (2006).

Grace Ingoldby (1949-2005). Irish/British author of borderline crime novels who won the *Sunday Times* Crime Writer's prize in 1990 with a story under the name "Colin Gray."

Derek Karton (1919-2005). British author of six intrigue novels, 1983-93, one co-written.

Marjorie Kellogg (ca.1920-2005). Mainstream author of *Tell Me That You Love Me, Junie Moon*, who wrote the screenplay for a suspense film "Rosebud" (1975).

Michael Kilian (1919-2005). *Chicago Tribune* columnist who authored more than a dozen suspense novels under his own name and as by "Rex Dancer," starting with *The Valkyrie Project* (1981).

Perry Lafferty (1917-2005). Author of four mystery novels, 1990-92, three featuring Jack Jablonski.

Gavin Lambert (ca.1925-2005). Mainstream author and screenwriter who published an Edgar-nominated collection of essays on nine suspense writers, *The Dangerous Edge* (1976).

Edwin Leather (1919-2005). British author of three thrillers, 1978-80, starting with *The Vienna Elephant.*

Ernest Lehman (1915-2005). Noted screenwriter of Hitchcock's *North by Northwest* and other films, who also published two suspense novels, 1977-82.

Barbara Levy (ca. 1921-2005). Winner of the Fact Crime Edgar for *Legacy of Death* (1973).

Ann Loring (1915-2005). Author of *The Mark of Satan* (1969) and *The 13th Doll* (1970).

Dennis Lynds (1924-2005), Author of more than twenty Dan Fortune novels as by "Michael Collins," beginning with his Edgar-winning *Act of Fear* (1967). Also published mainstream fiction under his own name, and mysteries as by "William Arden," "John Crowe," "Carl Dekker," Sheila McErlean" and "Mark Sadler," as well as the house names "Nick Carter" and "Maxwell Grant." The Collins short stories were collected in *Crime, Punishment and Resurrection* (1992), *Fortune's World* (2000), *Spies and Thieves, Cops and Killers, etc.* (2002) and *Slot-Machine Kelly* (2005).

Charlotte MacLeod (1922-2005). Author of twenty-five mystery novels, several about Professor Peter Shandy, notably *Rest You Merry* (1978) and *The Corpse Oozak's Pond* (1987), as well as two collections of short stories, *Grab Bag* (1987) and *It Was an Awful Shame* (2002), and a biography of Mary Roberts Rinehart, *Had She But Known* (1994). Also published eleven mysteries with Canadian settings as by "Alisa Craig."

Gary Madderom (1937-2005). Author of two mystery

novels, 1971-73, starting with *The Four Chambered Villain.*

Glenn Mahan (1929-2005). Author of *Death Shadows* (2000).

Paule Mason (1923-2005). Swiss/American actress, author of two suspense novels, 1967-69, starting with *The Dark Mirror.*

Harold Q. Masur (1909-2005). Well-known author of thirteen mystery novels, 1947-83, including eleven about lawyer detective Scott Jordan, notably *Bury Me Deep* (1947), *So Rich, So Lovely, and So Dead* (1952) and a story collection *The Name Is Jordan* (1962). Also ghosted a mystery novel by opera singer Helen Traubel and edited some hardcover anthologies credited to Alfred Hitchcock. Long active in Mystery Writers of America, he served as its president in 1973.

Paul (Stewart) Meskil (1923-2005). Author of *Sin Pit* (1954).

Arthur Miller (1915-2005). Noted playwright, a few of whose plays and screenplays contain criminous elements.

M(arion) E. Morris (1926-2005). Author of at least seven suspense novels, starting with *Alpha Bug* (1986).

William Murray (1926-2005). Author of fifteen mystery novels, 1960-2005, several about horse racing, one as by "Max Daniels" and one in collaboration with Chuck Scarborough.

Andre Norton (1912-2005). Well-known fantasy writer whose work included eight suspense novels, one a collaboration as by "Allen Weston," another in collaboration with Robert Bloch.

Warren Norwood (1945-2005). Author of three science fiction mysteries featuring the Time Police, starting with *Vanished* (1988).

Philip Oakes (1928-2005). British crime fiction critic who authored a single suspense novel of his own, *Experiment at Proto* (1973).

Veneiro A. Octavian (1930-2005), Author of *The Pianist* (1993).

Roger Ormerod (1920-2005). British author of nearly fifty mystery novels, 1974-97, notably *The Silence of the Night* (1974), *Full Fury* (1975) and *More Dead Than Alive* (1980).

Ronald Pearsall (1927-2005). Author of *The Belvedere* (1977) and a 1989 Sherlockian pastiche.

M. Scott Peck (1936-2005). Mainstream author who published a single crime novel, *A Bed by the Window* (1990).

Robin (L.) Perry (1917-2005). Author of *Welcome For the Hero* (1975).

Kin Platt (1911-2003). Author of ten crime novels under his own name, 1970-86, plus eight more as "Kirby Carr," 1974-76. Also published juvenile mysteries including *Sinbad and Me* (1966), an Edgar winner.

Ted Pollock (1929-2005). Author of *The Rainbow Man* (1979).

Byron Preiss (1953-2005). Publisher, book packager and editor of an anthology of original pastiches, *Raymond Chandler's Philip Marlowe: A Centennial Celebration* (1988). Also authored two graphic crime novels.

Raymond Joseph Prost (1913-2005). Author of *Murder Matters* (2000), containing two novelettes.

A. J. Quinnell (1941-2005). Pseudonym of Philip Nicholson, author of *Man on Fire* (1987).

Fritzen (H.) Ravenswood (1925-2005). She authored a single suspense novel, *The Witching* (1980).

Sidney Rosen (1916-2005). Co-author, with Dorothy Rosen, of *Death and Blintzes* (1985) and *Death and Strudel* (2000).

Judith Rossner (1935-2005). Author of *Looking for Mister Goodbar* (1973).

Leonard Sanders (1929-2005). Author of two suspense novels, 1982-90, starting with *Act of War*.

Lily K. Scott (1913-2005). Author of *A House of Women* (1966).

Mary Lee Settle (1918-2005). Mainstream writer who authored a single crime novel, *Blood Tie* (1977).

Alfred James Shaughnessy (1916-2005). Screenwriter who authored a suspense play *Double Cut* (1985) based on an earlier British film.

Robert Sheckley (1928-2005). Well-known science fiction writer who authored some fifteen suspense novels, notably *The Tenth Victim* (1965).

Edwin S. Sinaiko (1910-2005). Author of *Rite of Passage* (1999).

Kurt Singer (1911-2005). Editor of *World's Greatest Spy Stories* (1954).

Barbara Burnett Smith (1947-2005). Author of seven mystery novels starting with *Writers of the Purple Sage* (1994).

Larry D. Soderquist (1944-2005), author of ten books including two mysteries featuring Eric Berg, *The Lab Coat* (1998) and *The Iraqi Provocation* (2003).

Arnold C. Stream (1918-2005). Author of two suspense novels, 1986-91, starting with *The Third Bullet.*

Val Thiessen (1917-2005). Author of *My Brother Cain* (1964).

Geri Trotta (1914-2005). Author of two mysteries, 1952-56, starting with *Veronica Died Monday.*

Robert Tylander (1918-2005). Author of *Mystery at Manatee Creek* (1999).

Arkadii Vainer (1931-2005). Russian co-author, with his brother, of a single crime novel, *Twenty-four Hours With the Moscow Police* (1980/translation 1990).

Vladimir Volkoff (1932-2005). Award-winning French spy novelist who authored *The Turn-Around* (1981) and *The Set-Up* (1984).

Max Weatherly (1921-2005). Author of *The Mantis and the Moth* (1964).

David Westheimer (1917-2005). Author of *Von Ryan's Express* who also published a 1963 suspense novel as "Z.Z. Smith" and five intrigue novels, 1972-82, the final one a collaboration.

Elizabeth (L.) Wetzel (1930-2005). Author of *Deadly Arts* (1997).

Rodney Whitaker (1931-2005). Author of the popular "Trevanian" novels starting with *The Eiger Sanction* (1972) and *The Loo Sanction* (1973), and editor of a mystery anthology *Death Dance* (2002). He also wrote as "Nicholas Seare," "Benat LeCagot" and "Edoard Moran."

Richard Whittingham (1939-2005). Author of two novels about Sgt. Joe Morrison, starting with *State Street* (1991).

J. N. Williamson (1932-2005). Author of four suspense novels, one in collaboration, as well as four story collections, some from EQMM under this name and as Jerry Neal Williamson.

Helen York (1927-2005). Author of four mystery novels, 1974-78, starting with *Malverne Manor.*

Obituaries 2006

Jay Presson Allen (1922-2006). Well-known screenwriter, her works included *Marnie* (1964), *Travels With My Aunt* (1971) and *Deathtrap* (1982).

James (Jim) Baen (1941-2006). Well-known SF editor and publisher who co-authored a single futuristic crime novel, *The Taking of Satcon Station* (1982).

Lisa A. Barnett (1958-2006). Fantasy writer, collaborator with Melissa Scott on an SF mystery *Point of Hopes* (1995).

Peter Benchley (1940-2006). Best-selling author of *Jaws* who also published four suspense novels, 1976-89.

Ted Berkman (1914-2006). Co-author of two crime screenplays, 1957-58.

Flonet Biltgen Bonaventure (1945-2006). Pen name of SF writer and fan Flonet Biltgen, She published a single short mystery in AHMM, September 1998.

Herbert Burkholz (1932-2006). Author of six mystery-suspense novels, 1975-92, two in collaboration with Clifford Irving, and one of these as by "John Luckless."

Frederick Busch (1941-2006). Mainstream novelist who authored at least three suspense novels, notably *The Night Inspector* (1999).

Otis Carney (1922-2006). Author of *The Paper Bullet* (1966).

Robert Colby (1919-2006). Author of some twenty mystery novels, notably *The Captain Must Die* (1959), and at least one under the "Nick Carter" house name. Several stories were gathered in *The Devil's Collector* (1998) and *The Last Witness* (2002).

Scott Corbett (c.1913-2006). Author of nonfiction and juveniles, winner of the MWA Edgar Award for best juvenile mystery, *Cutlass Island* (1962).

Ernest Dudley (1908-2006). Best-known pseudonym of Vivian Ernest Coltman-Allen, who also wrote as "J. J. Lydecker." British author of some thirty novels, notably *Dr. Morelle and the Drummer Girl* (1950) and *Nightmare for Dr. Morelle* (1960), along with several volumes of short stories.

Henry Farrell (1920-2006). Best-known pseudonym of Charles Myers, screenwriter and author of six suspense novels, notably *Whatever Happened to Baby Jane?* (1960).

Michael Gilbert (1912-2006). Major British mystery writer, recipient of MWA's Grand Master Award and CWA's Diamond Dagger, author of over fifty novels and short story collections, notably *Close Quarters* (1947), *Smallbone Deceased* (1950), *Death Has Deep Roots* (1952), *The Country-House Burglar* (1955), *Blood and Judgement* (1959), *The Ninety-Second Tiger* (1973) and the short story collections *Game Without Rules* (1967), *Petrella at Q* (1977), *The Man Who Hated Banks* (1997) and *The Curious Conspiracy* (2002).

John Godey (1912-2006). Pseudonym of Morton Freedgood,

author of nearly twenty suspense novels, notably *The Taking of Pelham One Two Three* (1973).

Val Guest (1911-2006). Director and screenwriter who authored a dozen crime screenplays, 1938-80.

Patricia Guiver (c.1929-2006). British/American author six pet mysteries, starting with *Delilah Doolittle and the Purloined Pooch* (1997).

John Haase (1923-2006). Mainstream novelist who authored a single borderline suspense novel, *The Noon Balloon to Rangoon* (1967).

Ross Harding (1948-2006). Pseudonym of fantasy writer David Gemmell who authored a single suspense novel, *White Knight Black Swan* (1993).

Stanislaw Lem (1921-2006). Well-known Polish science fiction writer who published two suspense novels, *The Investigation* (1974) and *The Chain of Chance* (1978).

Roderick (Rod) MacLeish (1926-2006). Former CBS News commentator who authored two suspense novels, 1976-90, starting with *The Man Who Wasn't There*.

Naguib Mahfouz (1911-2006). Nobel Prize-winning author of *The Cairo Trilogy*, who published a single suspense novel, *The Search* (1964).

James McClure (1939-2006). South African/British author of a dozen mystery novels, 1971-91, most featuring South African detectives Kramer & Zondi, starting with *The Steam Pig*, a CWA Gold Dagger winner. His 1976 non-series novel *Rogue Eagle* won the CWA Silver Dagger.

Frank Orenstein (1919-2006). Author of seven mystery novels, 1983-94, most about sleuths Ev Franklin or

Hugh Morrison, both of whom appear in *The Man in the Gray Flannel Shroud* 1984).

Arthur Porges (1915-2006). Fantasy and mystery writer whose hundreds of short stories included Sherlockian adventures of "Stately Homes," collected in *Three Parodies and a Pastiche* (1988). *The Mirror and Other Strange Reflections* (2002), collects twenty-eight stories, mainly fantasy, six from AHMM.

Allan Prior (1922-2006). British screenwriter and author of eleven suspense novels, 1951-87, notably *The Interrogators* (1965).

Peter Rawlinson (1919-2006). Former British government official who authored five crime novels, 1991-98, notably *Hatred and Contempt* (1992).

Katherine Shepherd (?-2006). Author of two romantic suspense novels, *Fraternity of Silence* (2003) and *Betrayed by Silence* (2004).

Gilbert Sorrentino (1929-2006). Mainstream poet and novelist who published two crime novels, notably *Mulligan Stew* (1979).

Muriel Spark (1918-2006). Well-known British author of *The Prime of Miss Jean* Brodie whose mainstream novels included at least ten with criminal elements, notably *Memento Mori* (1959), *The Driver's Seat* (1970) and *The Only Problem* (1984).

Mickey Spillane (1918-2006). Famed author of twenty-two novels, 1947-96, thirteen of them bestsellers about hardboiled private eye Mike Hammer, starting with *I, the Jury*. He also published several collections, including *Byline: Mickey Spillane* (2004), and received the MWA Grand Master award in 1995.

Scott Stone (1932-2006). Author of twenty-nine books including four suspense novels, starting with *The Dragon's Eye* (1969), MWA Edgar winner for Best Paperback Original.

Frank Thomas (1921-2006). Actor who authored six Sherlockian pastiches, 1973-86, the first in collaboration with George Gooden.

Gerald Tomlinson (1933-2006). Author of a historical mystery novel, *On a Field of Black* (1980), plus a true crime book, *Murdered in Jersey* (1994), and several short stories in EQMM and AHMM.

Dorothy Uhnak (1930-2006). Former policewoman and mystery writer who authored a memoir and nine novels (1968-97), notably *The Bait*, MWA Edgar winner for best first novel, and the best-seller *Law and Order* (1973).

Richard Usborne (1910-2006). British author of *Clubland Heroes* (1953), a study of Dornford Yates, John Buchan, "Sapper," and other adventure/suspense writers of the early 20th century.

Justo Vasco (c.1942-2006). Cuban/Spanish mystery writer, active in the International Association of Crime Writers.

Marilyn Wallace (1941-2006). Author of at least seven mystery novels, 1986-98, starting with *A Case of Loyalties*. She also edited five *Sisters in Crime* anthologies, 1989-92, and in 2005 published a novel and short story as by "Maggie Bruce."

Elizabeth M. Walter (c.1927-2006). British writer and editor, four of whose ghost story collections, 1965-75, include criminous tales. She also edited books for the Collins Crime Club, 1961-93.

Angus Wells (1943-2006). British author of three suspense novels, 1976-84, two of them under the name of Joseph Hedges.

Akira Yoshimura (1927-2006). Well-known Japanese mystery writer, at least one of whose novels, *On Parole* (2000), has been translated into English.

Online Mystery Fiction in 2005 and 2006

Sarah Weinman

Last time out, I wrote about why online short story markets are a viable alternative for writers whose voices didn't quite fit the *Ellery Queen* and *Alfred Hitchcock* mold. Because those voices needed to be heard—and still do. As for what's transpired since the previous edition of *Year's Finest,* many talented newcomers have gained exposure and an audience over the last two years, but the online world has had its bittersweet moments, too. Some of the best known markets, like *Thrilling Detective, SHOTS* and *Shred of Evidence*, have slowed their outputs down, while others had to pack up their shingles before they ever really got underway. And we had to say goodbye to *Plots with Guns,* the venerable magazine that gave homes to the new generation of noir fiction (though the zine will live on forever in a handsome collection released in late 2005 by the boutique publisher Dennis McMillan.)

But the good news far outweighs the bad thanks to new markets, more awards and continued praise. The most notable new names in online fiction? Todd Robinson's *ThugLit* (www.thuglit.com), which placed a story in the upcoming edition of *Best American Mystery Stories* only months after its Fall 2005 launch; Bryon Quertermous's *Demolition* (www.demolitionmag.com), an outgrowth of his Blog Short Story Project, has had three successful themed issues to date (with one devoted to the "Ladies of Noir" including yours truly, in full disclosure); And Tribe's *Flashing with the Gutters* (http://tribe.textdriven. net/flash), devoted to the succinct art of writing a quality story in 600 words or less.

Aside from commendations by *Best American Mystery Stories,* online mystery stories featured prominently in StorySouth's Million Writers Award. Tales originally published at *Thrilling Detective, Thuglit, SHOTS* and *Shred of Evidence* made the notable list, and *Crime Scene Scotland* figured in the top ten. Though StorySouth's award focuses primarily on literary journals, their lists show that genre is hardly being ignored—rather, it's thriving and considered to be of quality. And let's not forget about those writers primarily known for their online writing who've found success in other quarters. Iain Rowan was a finalist in the Crime Writers Association Debut Dagger Competition for 2006. Ray Banks has taken his short story PI protagonist Callum Innes and given him life in several novels. *Saturday's Child* and *Donkey Punch* are published in the UK by Polygon and soon by Harcourt in the US.

What of those whose online work graced the pages of the previous *Year's Finest?* The good news abounds with them, too. Martyn Waites, after years writing strictly for the UK market, found favor with an upstart American publisher who made his newest novel, *The Mercy Seat*, their launch title in April 2006. Aliya Whiteley made her UK debut in July 2006 with *Three Things about Me*, one of the first titles released by Macmillan as part of their New Writing Initiative. And the third member of the trio is perhaps the best example of online success translating into print recognition. Derringer Award winner David White's stories appeared exclusively in online markets for years. But after his appearance in *Year's Finest*, he scored the opening story in *Damn Near Dead: An Anthology of Geezer Noir* (Busted Flush Press, July 2006) and the sum of his work no doubt helped secure his next project: a book deal with Three Rivers Press for the first two novels featuring New Jersey PI Jackson Donne. Look for *When One Man Dies* in September 2007, with the next to follow a year later.

This brings me to the four stories—two from 2005, two from 2006—I've selected for inclusion in this volume. The process took great care and time, and many fine stories just missed making the cut. But in the end, the four I chose were the ones that stuck with me the longest, whose writers display breadth and talent that will no doubt translate into years of success.

Neal Marks' "Down and Out in Brentwood" was the aforementioned story shortlisted for the Million Writers Award. It's easy to see why: wonderful writing, a tremendous sense of place and time and momentum that builds and builds.

I devoured Craig McDonald's "The Last Interview" as soon as it was published, and read it several times afterward. His rendering of a desiccated writer who still believes he has something worthwhile to say is not just chilling, but reeks of verisimilitude thanks to his own prior experience interviewing notable crime writers.

Mike MacLean now has the double honor of being featured in *Best American Mystery Stories* and *Year's Finest*—for completely different stories. "Little Sins" continues the story of an amoral, nameless PI who has no need for any normal code, but stays true to the idiosyncratic one of his own.

And Kim Harrington's "Low Drama," which rounds out the online selection, works for many reasons. It has a killer twist of an ending, sharp-edged dialogue and best of all, it's peopled with characters who behave in ways we know to be true.

Just like last year, consider these stories as a taste of what's out there in the online fiction realm. Once you've partaken, you'll be back for more.

Links to Chosen Stories

"Down and Out in Brentwood" by Neal Marks
Crime Scene Scotland, January/February 2005
http://www.crimescenescotland.com/fiction_down_and_o
ut_in_Brentwood_jan_feb_2005.htm

"The Last Interview" by Craig McDonald
Mississippi Review, January 2005
http://www.mississippireview.com/2005/Vol11No1-
Jan05/1101-010805-mcdonald.html

"Low Drama" by Kim Harrington
Demolition, Spring 2006
http://www.demolitionmag.com/IssueTwo/demolition-harrington.htm

"Little Sins" by Mike MacLean
Thrilling Detective, January 2006
http://www.thrillingdetective.com/fiction/05_12_03.html

The Catch

James W. Hall

James W. Hall is a Florida writer who pens poetry and non-fiction works as well as his fiction. Hall's most recent release, *Forests of the Night,* features Charlotte and Parker Monroe, a police officer and defense attorney, and their daughter Gracey, who live in Coral Gables, FL, but it's Hall's character, a man named Thorn (an almost modern-day Travis McGee whose adventures began in *Under Cover of Daylight*), who has snagged the lion's share of Hall's published works. Hall was honored with a 2005 Edgar Award from the Mystery Writers of America in the short story category for "The Catch." He was previously nominated for "Crack" in 2000, which was also reprinted in that year's *Best Crime and Mystery Stories* anthology.

"Two hundred bucks? You're kidding, right?"

"A hundred now, the rest when it's done."

"You can't be serious."

"You're asking me to charge more?"

"I always heard it was like five thousand or something."

"Yeah? Where'd you hear that?"

"The movies, I guess. Somewhere."

Mason took a second to appraise the guy—shoulders pulled back, trim waist, the look of command. Wearing a dark blue corporate suit, oxblood cordovans polished to a deep gleam. Gray hair clipped in a military style. Ice blue eyes clicking here and there, but a little pouchy underneath them like he wasn't getting his full eight hours. Fifty-nine, sixty years old. Stock broker, he said. Probably pulled down half a million a year. Manicured and massaged with a leased Porsche and slinky girlfriends, a third his age. An apartment with a ten mile ocean view, decorated with furniture too chrome and weird-angled to sit in. To this guy two hundred bucks was tip money for a valet parker.

"Some get five thousand, some get more," Mason said. "The rip-off artists. The hotshots. How hard it is to pull a trigger? Two hundred dollars. I been getting that for forty years. It's my rate."

"But the chances you take. Prison, the death penalty. I don't know, it just sounds cut-rate."

"Think of me as the generic alternative. Same drug, lower price."

"Weird," the guy said. "Very weird."

"You want to pay more, I got some phone numbers, guys'll be glad to take your cash."

On his prehistoric Motorola *Jeopardy* was playing. Some red-haired twerp was getting everything right, been winning for a solid month, like they were feeding him the answers. Trying to draw in a larger audience. Mason wouldn't put it past the TV assholes. That's how it worked. Couldn't trust anything that came out of that box. Which didn't keep him from having it on twenty-four hours a day. Playing in the background like Muzak with pictures. Kept him company, kept him from drifting off into memories, bad dreams, regrets or worse.

Mason sat in his green corduroy chair. One lamp on. Lighting up the over-sized oil painting of Jesus with his hands upraised like he was calling a heavenly touchdown.

The painting belonged to his wife, long dead. He kept it as a reminder of her and her ridiculous faith.

"Do they know what you do, your relations?" The guy motioned toward the front house where his son lived with his anorexic wife and three brats.

Mason shrugged, and the guy took a deep breath and blew it out.

"So how'm I doing so far?" Mason said.

"I'm sorry, what?"

"You're interviewing me, how'm I doing?"

"Hey, I'm just trying to get a feel for this thing. Who you are, what I'm getting into. How much danger I'm putting myself in. You're so nonchalant, cause yeah, you do this all the time. But this is a big deal for me."

"I just told you," said Mason. "I never been in jail. Never arrested, or seen the inside of a courtroom. Nothing like that. If that isn't good enough, take a hike."

"But I found you. A normal guy like me. What's to keep the cops from doing the same thing? Sniffing you out."

Mason just smiled. The people Mason got rid of, shit almighty, the cops should give him the keys to the city.

"All I'm saying, the kind of reputation you've got, if I were you, I'd charge more." The executive dug his hands in the pockets of his nicely tailored trousers. "I'd raise it to two, three thousand at least."

"So buy a gun," Mason said. "Hang out a shingle."

The guy turned away from Mason, glanced at Jesus, at the TV, at the empty bird cage. The cage was another left-over from his wife. Mason hated birds. How could anybody love a bird? Like loving a radish with feathers. But his wife had adored the thing. Broke her heart when the chirping, shitting, pecking creature died. Wept for weeks, stayed in bed. Mason kept the cage for the same reason he held onto the Jesus picture. Something from that other time, that life when she fussed over that bird, fussed over Mason, fussed over their boy. The boy who now lived in the ten thousand square foot mansion and let Mason stay rent free in the pool house.

"Just so you know," the executive said. "I got your name from a shoe shine guy in the lobby of my building downtown."

"I'm supposed to be surprised? That's how it works."

"It's amazing," the guy said. "I sort of hinted around I wanted a person removed, made it sound like a joke. Just said it to this one guy, kind of a shady character. Made it sound like I was fooling around. Then yesterday he gives me your name and address. Whispers it while he's putting a shine on."

"Word of mouth," Mason said. "A killer's best friend."

"So I guess you want to know who I want dead."

"Either that, or I go shoot somebody at random."

The guy tried a smile but after a nervous second it curdled

and slipped off his lips. He lowered his butt to the arm of a chair and watched *Jeopardy* for a minute. The executive had a name, Arnold Chalmers, an old-fashioned moniker like the name of some loser from a black and white Bogart movie.

In the backyard one of the brats, his grandson, was playing with a neighbor kid. They were passing a football back and forth, getting pissed off over something. Squawking at each other. Always with the squawking. His son and the anorexic, not the greatest parents.

Truth be told, Mason hadn't been either. A downright shitty father. Moody and irritable. Feeling low a good percentage of the time. Nothing much to celebrate, a professional hitter with a busy schedule. Leaving the child rearing to his wife, giving her something to do while Mason flew in and out of Miami all the time. Two hundred bucks plus expenses. Which had been a decent wage in the early sixties when he started out.

But Chalmers was right. Mason should ask a thousand at least, more likely five or ten. But he stuck with the two hundred out of stubborn habit. Funny thing was, these days since it was such a ridiculous amount, and since Mason was such a withered up old fart, an oddity in this age of bleached blond punks from Odessa and Gdansk, covered in tattoos and flashing their chrome nine millimeters, Mason had acquired a certain status. A retro celebrity. His name getting around in circles he'd never cracked before. Becoming a minor legend. Funny. A thing like he did, requiring no skills whatsoever, all of a sudden people treating him like he's Babe Ruth.

Not that he was ever a second-rater. Back in the old

days when Miami Beach was the mob's winter playground, Mason had more business than he could handle. Things getting so routine at one point, he even had a regular commute. Up and back to New York. Some Goomba wanted his son-in-law whacked, guy had been cheating on the Goomba's daughter or maybe it was a bookie skimming receipts. Next week a Miami dog track boss calls up and gives Mason the address of somebody to clip in Long Island—retaliation and more retaliation. Back and forth, back and forth, Miami International to Newark or LaGuardia. Mason working both sides. Though he had to admit, he got more of a zing from doing the New York assholes. Their loud-mouth arrogance annoyed him. The way they treated Miami like a bumpkin patch. Their bus station urinal. Miami was Mason's town. Had been since birth. As bad as it was turning out with the Cubans and the Nicaraguans and the Haitians and the Russians crowding the roads and stinking up the evening news, he'd take Miami over New York any day of the week. A paradise. As good a place as there was to get old and wait to die.

Chalmers dug out his wallet. He fingered through the bills and extracted two fifties. Held them out to Mason.

"On top of the TV," Mason said.

He aimed the remote and flicked through the channels, looking for what he watched after *Jeopardy*. Lately he'd been on a *Seinfeld* binge. Reruns. Those four kooks hanging out in Jerry's apartment or the diner downstairs. The goofball with the big hair always sliding into Jerry's apartment like it was an ice rink. The goony faces he made. And the fat little schmuck who reminded Mason of his own son. Such a loser he was actually funny.

"So there it is," Chalmers said. "Aren't you going to count it?"

The guy smirked at him. Proud of his stupid joke.

When Mason didn't smile back, Chalmers walked over to the bird cage and peered inside the bars. Everything was still exactly like the day the bird died. Same newspaper on the floor. Hulls, bird shit, little plastic swing.

"Okay," the guy said. "There's the money. Now what's the catch?"

"The catch," Mason said.

"There is one, isn't there?"

Mason watched Jerry spooning cereal into his smug New Yorker mouth while Elaine yakked about some new boyfriend. George on the couch clipping his toenails. Gross and as annoying as usual. Annoying and oblivious. He could picture shooting them, one by one, make the remaining ones watch what was coming. They made him laugh though. Funny but irritating.

Mason said, "Well, I wouldn't call it a catch exactly."

"Christ, I knew it," Chalmers said. "Two hundred dollars, there had to be a catch."

"I'm not a sociopath," Mason said. "That's the catch."

"Yeah, okay? What's that supposed to mean?"

"I got a sense of shame. I'm not some robot, wind him up, he goes and shoots a guy, then comes home makes a plate of spaghetti and sleeps his eight hours. I used to be that guy, but I'm not anymore."

"I still don't get it."

Seinfeld's latest girlfriend comes strutting out of the back bedroom, making a grand entrance. She's tall and wearing a super tight low cut blouse which naturally shows off her mammoth boobs. Jerry introduces her to Elaine and Elaine looks at her and slips up and says something about knockers. She can't help herself. For the next minute everything out of her mouth is about tits. All tasteful enough for TV, but still a little on the raunchy side. *Seinfeld* was a TV show his wife would never sit still for. The morals of America were in steep decline, that was her view. From the time she was born in some redneck coal town in West Virginia, American morals had been sliding downhill. For seventy-two years, everywhere the woman looked, everything she saw confirmed it. America was going to hell. Their entire married life the woman thought Mason sold medical supplies.

"Okay, so you got a conscience. How's that change things?"

"It means you gotta convince me."

"Convince you to murder this person?"

"Something like that. I gotta hear what he did. I got to see this from your point of view, be converted."

"Jesus Christ."

"You don't like the rules, take your money and go."

"You want me to plead with you, grovel, is that it? Get on my knees."

"What I'm saying is, I got scruples. Only way I can do what I do, I gotta be convinced it's necessary."

The executive stared at Mason for half a minute then sighed and walked to the door. He opened it, gave Mason a parting look, and headed out into the dusky light and shut the door behind him.

Todd, the bratty grandson, screamed at his little brat friend and the two of them came whooping over to the pool house. A few seconds later, Todd threw open the door, stuck his fat sweaty head inside and screeched for a full five seconds then slammed the door and ran back into the yard. His little game. Scream at the boogeyman. That's what he called his grandfather. Not Granddad. Not some cute goo-goo name left over from when he couldn't pronounce. No, Mason was boogeyman.

A minute later Mason was back with *Seinfeld*. The show was almost over and he'd only caught the basic outline. The bosomy girlfriend, Elaine's breast jokes. George and Kramer in awe of the woman, falling all over themselves as she approached. Not the funniest one Mason had seen.

As the final commercial came on, the door opened again and Chalmers walked back in. He was shaking his head like he couldn't believe he'd returned to this nut house.

"It's my son," the guy said. "I want you to kill my son."

"Okay, that's a start."

The man's neat haircut look rumpled now. Like he'd been grinding his head in his hands. Giving him a wretched look.

"You're not shocked. A man wanting his own son dead."

"Wouldn't be my first," Mason said. "Wouldn't be my second or third."

The brats were practicing their banshee yells outside Mason's bathroom window. Cranking up the volume, trying to outdo each other. Hateful little turds.

"Here's a picture," Chalmers said.

He dug a snapshot out of his jacket pocket and held it out. Mason told him to put it on the arm of his chair. Not like he was obsessive compulsive about fingerprints or any of that DNA bullshit. He just didn't want to touch things if he didn't have to.

Chalmers set the photo on the chair arm, nudged it around so Mason had a good view, then he stepped back.

Chalmers was wearing bathing trunks and had his arm around the shoulder of the boy. There was a lake behind them, other swimmers. The boy was maybe thirty, thirty-three. Wearing shorts and a Budweiser T-shirt that fit tight enough to show the hump of his belly. Wide simple face, bad haircut, blunt features, too much forehead.

"Retarded?" Mason said.

"Learning disabled." Chalmers turned his back on Mason and watched the commercials jabbering on and on.

"So cause he's dumb, he's got to die?"

Chalmers came around slowly. A look forming on his face, going from the gloomy dread he'd been wearing to something with more edge. His business face. Take it or leave it, that's my best offer. A bully boy look.

"You trying to piss me off?"

Mason reached into the crack of the cushion and extracted Ruger .22 auto with the long silencer cylinder.

He lay the pistol on his lap and watched Chalmers' face drain of hardass. The same effect the Ruger usually had—making the lungs tighter, the eyes more focused.

"He's retarded," Mason said. "For thirty years you put up with it, now enough's enough. Is that it? He's cramping your style. Your bachelor ambitions. The girls find out about him, it turns them off?"

"Fuck this," Chalmers said and headed for the door again. Then remembered the photo and about-faced and came over and plucked it off the chair.

"So help me," Mason said. "What changed? What made it suddenly intolerable to live with this pitiful creature? Your son."

"He raped a girl."

Mason gave it a few seconds' thought then nodded.

"Okay. That would change things."

"Raped her and then threw her off a bridge."

"Here in Miami?"

"In Lauderdale."

"I didn't see it on the news," Mason said. "I watch the news and there wasn't anything about a rape and a girl off a bridge."

"I got there in time," Chalmers said.

"And you covered it up," said Mason. "You buried the girl."

Chalmers took a deep breath and looked at the photo, at himself and his son. Same blood bumping through their veins. But Mason knew that didn't count for shit. Look at his own flesh and blood son. Look at his grandson. They might as well be from Gdansk themselves, for all he knew them, understood them, cared about them. Or vice versa.

"His name is Julius," Chalmers said. "I call him Jules."

"And you buried the girl. The two of you."

"I did it," Chalmers said. "I dug a hole and put her in it and Jules stood there the whole time complaining about his pecker. How it itched. He raped this girl, killed her and he's grumbling about how she gave him some disease. Crabs or something. While I was digging out in the dark, he's going on about feeling prickly between his legs."

"You wanted to hit him with the shovel. Smack him in the face."

Chalmers raised his eyes and gave Mason a level look.

"Is this some kind of game you play?"

Mason said, "Yeah, it's a game. That's right. You enjoying it?"

He picked up the Ruger, unscrewed the suppressor a couple of turns then tightened it back down.

"Okay, so we're at the bridge. You're digging and Jules is whining about crabs."

"That's all," Chalmers said.

Mason shook his head.

"I said that's all. That's all there is. He killed a girl. And, I don't know, maybe he knew what he was doing, maybe he didn't. Maybe he has a guilty conscience. But I don't think so. I'm afraid he found out he liked it, raping girls and killing them, and he's going to do it again and then again after that, and one of those times I won't be able to cover it up."

"So?" Mason lay the Ruger across his lap. "So the kid gets caught, goes to jail, problem solved. You save two hundred bucks, don't have to live with the guilt you killed your own boy."

Out in the yard the brats were splashing in the pool. School night, but they might be going at it till ten, eleven o'clock before the anorexic or Mason's fat, sloppy son called them in to bed.

Already dark out there, but the floodlights from the rear patio were on. Sometimes his son and the anorexic forgot and left the floodlights on all night, blasting into Mason's bedroom. Penetrating the slats in his worthless mini-blinds. Mason would lie there and stare at the slits of light and he'd think of what his wife would say. She wouldn't complain about there being too much light to sleep. No, that old woman would be blathering about the wasted money. Ten dollars at least, all those lights running through the night. You know how hard people in her generation had to work for ten dollars, the things she had to do. Take in sewing, baby-sit, all the pennies she put away, and look at that waste, those big fancy lights burning for no good reason.

Mason didn't miss his wife. He didn't miss her bird and if something happened to his own son and the grandchil-dren, hell, he wouldn't miss them either. All three of them were brats. Screaming in the pool, going out of their way to raise the volume. And did his fat, lazy son put down his cocktail for a second to go out and see what they were screaming about? Never. Not once. They could be drowning, or being molested by a passing pervert.

"I don't want my son going to jail."

"You don't mind killing him," Mason said, "but what is it, you don't want some big black guy bulldozing your baby's butt. That it?"

"You're a crude man."

"I don't get paid for my refinement and urbanity."

Chalmers watched a few seconds of the TV show, another sitcom set in New York City. *Friends*. A bunch of do-nothing twenty-year-olds who could spend half an hour whining about an ingrown toenail or a soufflé that collapsed. Mason usually switched over to CNN after *Seinfeld*, spent the evening catching up on all the ways the world was going to hell. Something the dead wife would appreciate. See there. See there. See there. Gloom, gloom, and more gloom.

Chalmers sat down in the chair beneath the Jesus pic-ture. He raised both hands and finger combed his hair, raking it back into place.

"I don't want my boy going to jail."

"Yeah, we established that. We just haven't figured out why that's worse than him being dead."

"Don't you have what you wanted? Isn't it enough he killed this girl?"

"That's a start, yeah. I'm getting into your head a little, seeing your misery. Yeah. Digging a hole, rolling a dead girl into it, son scratching his nuts the whole time. I'm warming up to it, I'm just not quite there yet."

"I'll give you five hundred dollars. Shit, I'll give you ten thousand. I don't care. Just no more questions, okay?"

"That's a good sign, resisting like that. Means we're getting closer, a layer or two more, we might have a deal."

"Look, maybe you should just shoot me. Just shoot me now. Right here, right now. Do it. Take all my money, get rid of my corpse. Nobody knows I'm here. You could get away with it."

"That what you want?"

"I don't know. Maybe it is."

"Do me a favor, Chalmers. Before we go any farther with this, get up, take down that picture."

Chalmers looked at Mason for a few seconds then turned his head and looked up at Jesus.

"That?"

"That."

Chalmers rose and lifted the painting off its hook. Grunted a little. The thing was heavier than it looked.

He set it down, propped it against the TV.

"So?"

"The wall," Mason said.

Chalmers looked back at the wall. Chunks missing in

the dry wall, fist-sized holes, dried blood, some fragments of bone and hair.

"Fuck."

Chalmers swung back, giving Mason a wild stare.

Expecting the Ruger to be aimed his way. But it lay on Mason's lap.

"What is this?"

Chalmer's mouth was open, a ribbon of drool showing at the corner.

"You execute people in here? This is a murder chamber?"

"That makes it sound creepy."

"You shoot people. Clients coming in to hire you. You kill them instead."

"Right where you're standing. Ten, twelve. I don't keep a total."

"Why?"

"They ask me to. Sometimes they beg."

"Jesus, this is fucking crazy. You're a crazy man."

"Some guys, they come in, tell their story, I bully till it's all out, last bit of puke from their guts, then bingo, they ask me to do it. They plead. Well, sometimes they plead, not always. Different people, it works different ways."

"And how's it working with me?"

"Don't know yet. We're not there. Not at the end. We're sort of stuck on why you'd rather your son be dead than go to jail."

"I'm out of here," Chalmers said.

"No one's stopping you."

Chalmers stared at the wall again as if counting the holes. That wasn't a reliable way to figure out how many had died because sometimes it took two shots, sometimes, Mason hated to admit, he missed with the first one, sometimes the second one too. So there had to be a few more holes than victims.

"What were you wearing?"

"Wearing?"

"We're back at the hole, the grave for this girl. What'd you have on?"

"Hell, I don't know. Why's that matter?"

"I'm trying to get a picture. I'm trying to put myself there, inside your skin. Get the feel."

"A suit," Chalmers said. "A black suit."

"Armani, that's what you wear?"

Chalmers swallowed.

"How'd you know that?"

"I got an eye for tailoring. I'm not a clothes horse myself, but some of the guys I associated with in my younger days, they dressed nice. I made it a hobby. So you're in your black Armani, five, six thousand dollar coat and pants. You're sweating like a pig. Your son is all cranky about his itchy dick. I bet there were mosquitoes out there too."

"A few, but I wasn't feeling much."

"Too focused on the inner turmoil. Cleaning up after your son's murder. A guy wouldn't feel a few mosquito bites."

"I got blisters on my hands from the shovel. I remember that."

"Bleed a little, did you?"

"Where's this going?"

"Hey, you were there, not me," Mason said. "I don't know where it's going."

On the TV the good looking blond girl who is also the resident airhead is trying to cook something for Thanksgiving dinner. But she'd read the recipe wrong. That was supposed to be funny? Maybe his wife had a point. The world was going to hell. Men wanted to hire other men to kill their retarded sons while there were all those people in an audience laughing at a girl who couldn't cook.

"I buried the girl then Jules and I drove back to my apartment and we took showers and changed clothes and I ordered a pizza."

"A pizza."

"Jules has a very limited range of foods he'll eat."

"Picky boy."

"It's part of his disability. He gets stuck in ruts."

"Happens to the best of us," Mason said.

Chalmers glanced back at the wall behind him.

"What do you do with the bodies?" Chalmers said it, then he swung around to face Mason and said, "Never mind, that's none of my business."

"I use a wheelbarrow," Mason said. "Roll 'em out to my car, put them in the trunk. I got a canal I like out in the Glades. Shovels, no way, I'm too old for shovels. This canal, though, it has gators."

"No one's ever been found?"

"Not that I heard."

Chalmers sat down in the chair again. His body seemed heavier than it had a few minutes earlier.

"So you and Jules are eating pizza. How's his itch doing?"

"Still there," Chalmers said.

One of the girl brats, fourteen, fifteen, Mason could never

remember, she turns on the music in her bedroom. Window open, this ghetto rap, hip-hop bullshit starts booming. The boys in the pool yell for her to turn it down. It turns into a war out there. Girl screeches and little boy screeches, and the volume of the music gets higher. And where's Daddy and anorexic Mommy? No fucking where to be found.

"I told Jules he had to go see a psychiatrist. He had to get this new lustfulness under control."

"Lustfulness? That's what you think?"

"Whatever the right word is. I'm no shrink."

"So this just started? Came out of the blue, did it. He's thirty, all of a sudden he's horny?"

"As far as I know."

"Nothing set it off?"

"What're you saying?"

"I'm asking questions. I'm not saying anything."

"You're suggesting something I did might've set it off. That I'm responsible for what my son does. My adult son. My dating habits influenced him to go out and rape a girl."

Mason looked across at the holes in his wall. Seeing a little fragment of a blouse wedged into one of the ragged craters. Mason remembered that one. She was one of the pleaders. Yeah, down on her knees. Begging with her hands pressed together like Mason was the Pope. Pretty woman. Mason made her stand up. Made her look him in the eye. Made her stop crying. Made her stand up straight. Then that was that.

"If Jules went to jail, it would all go public. It would be a major story. The people I represent, they're the movers and shakers in this community. Names you'd know. Owners of the sports franchise, the cruise ship company.

You know who I mean. I'd be ruined. My business is built on trust and confidence. How's anybody going to give me their life savings to manage if they know what's in my family's bloodstream?"

"So, your boy's got to die to protect your net worth."

"He could rape and kill again. Another innocent girl. That's my number one concern. But, yeah, to be completely honest, the money's an issue too. I've got obligations."

"Mortgage, things like that."

"Alimony payment, mortgage, I've got obligations like everybody else."

"So Jules gets two in the brain."

"Oh, fuck it. Forget this. I'm out of here. Go ahead, try to shoot me. I'm gone."

But Chalmers didn't get up from the chair. They usually didn't.

"Pizza is over, you had some ice cream, whatever, and what then?"

"I don't remember."

"Sure you do. That's a night you're not going to forget."

"I had an appointment. I went out."

"Left your boy in your condo, blood on his hands, while you went out on a date."

"Where'd you get 'date?' I went out."

"With a woman."

"Okay, okay. I had a date. It was important to me. I was in love with this woman."

"Not anymore though."

Chalmers shook his head. Watched a little of the end of *Friends*. Everyone laughing their heads off about the fucked up recipe. Poor air headed blonde.

"Jules," Chalmers spoke softly, watching the TV show. "He followed me that night. He waited till I was gone from Sheila's condo, and he broke in and raped her."

"Yeah, okay. But there's a topper. Something worse."

"How do you know that?"

"There's a topper. What is it?"

"Sheila had a security video. She runs it to make sure her Nanny isn't abusing her kid while she's off at work."

"Okay," Mason said. "So she's got the whole rape thing on tape. Now she's blackmailing you. Or she goes to the police and there goes your career."

Chalmers stared at Mason.

"Jesus, where do you get this stuff?"

"I'm an old man. There's only so many ways people can treat each other badly."

"I been sending her ten thousand a month."

Mason nodded.

"Ten thousand's a bargain."

"It's pinching me. That and everything else. The alimony. All of it, the market dipping, it's making life difficult."

"So killing Jules, how does that fix anything?"

He rocked forward, settled his elbows on his knees, giving Mason an earnest look. Salesman's eyes, man to man.

"I thought if Jules turns up dead, clearly a murder, it would scare her off. Show her what I'm capable of."

Mason shrugged, picked up the remote and cut to CNN. People starving somewhere in Africa. Their bellies swollen, flies all around their eyes. Little kids who looked two hundred years old. Bones showing through.

"Yeah, I guess, a certain woman, that could work."

"It's to scare her away, but it's also because I'm worried what that boy'll do next. I don't see any other choice."

"So two hundred bucks, that's a bargain. Saves you a fortune."

"It's not the money."

"It's never the money."

The little brat, his grandson, came screeching one more time at Mason's door, swung it open, stuck his blocky head through, closed his beady eyes and wailed for five seconds, then slammed the door and ran off to the big house where the anorexic and Mason's sad, unhappy son were burying themselves alive.

Chalmers looked over his shoulder at the wall.

"I don't want to die."

Mason said, "I'm not trying to convince you of anything."

"I got things I want to do, places I want to see. I've got appetites. I'm not suicidal."

"That's good. Everyone needs something to live for."

The starving kids in Africa were living in camps behind barbed wire. Their mothers pressed them to their breasts. Dying faster themselves so their kids could live a few more days. No men anywhere. All of them had been macheted or machine-gunned by another tribe. One tribe versus another tribe. Women nursing kids. People starving. Babies dying. Flies everywhere.

"You can put Jesus back on the wall."

Chalmers's frown relaxed and his eyes lingered on Mason.

Chalmers rose and hung the Jesus picture on the wall. Covering up the gashes and bloody streaks.

He adjusted the angle of the painting, stepping back to make sure he'd gotten it lined up.

"You're a religious man?" Chalmers said.

"Water to wine. People coming back to life? Yeah, right."

Chalmers looked away from Christ and stared at the empty birdcage.

"Your bird died."

"I hated that bird. It was a fucking nuisance. The old woman liked it. I was glad to see it fall off its perch."

. Mason watched Chalmers draw a hard breath. A quick glance at the painting to see if he had it straight.

"If you hate a bird," Chalmers said, "it's simple to break its neck, be done with it."

"I look like a guy who murders parakeets?"

Chalmers turned and eyed Mason. He drew a long breath.

Then he clenched his face into a tight scrunch like he'd stepped on a tack. When his features relaxed, he looked different. Not any smarter, not any richer or happier, but his suit fit better. His eyes were a quieter shade of blue.

One more slow look around Mason's pathetic pool house apartment, then Chalmers dug out his wallet and fingered through the bills and came out with two more fifties and set them on the television.

Mason was quiet. Some did it this way. You never knew how it would play out. It was what kept him interested, these conversations, these surprises at the end.

"Keep it," Chalmers said. "You earned it."

"I didn't kill anybody."

"That's what I mean."

"Two hundred for an hour of talk," Mason said. "They'll bust me for practicing without a license."

The commercial was on. That dark-haired woman with the pouty lips, lounging in a doorway making eyes at her husband who has finally taken the right drug and gotten his pecker working again. Modern science. Too bad they couldn't find a pill for those starving babies with the flies all over them.

"Hey, listen," Chalmers said. "How would it be if I brought Jules over sometime? Just for some talk, nothing more than that."

Chalmers heard his own words, then shook his head. A preposterous idea. Sorry he'd mentioned it.

He headed for the door.

Was halfway out when Mason said, "Sure, why not? Bring the kid over. Let's hear his side."

~~~~~~~~~~

There Is No Crime
on Easter Island

Nancy Pickard

~~~~~~~~~~

Considered one of today's best mystery writers, Nancy Pickard
has published dozens of short stories and more than a dozen
novels. Pickard juggles three series: Jenny Cain, Maries Light-
foot, and Eugenia Potter (originally created by Virginia Rich). Her
writing has earned her numerous awards including the Agatha,
Anthony, Macavity, and Shamus awards, as well as nominations
for the Edgar Allen Poe and Mary Higgins Clark awards. Pickard
has also been honored with a Lifetime Achievement award for
suspense fiction, from *Romantic Times*.

As the five-hour flight from Santiago came within sight of
its destination, the man in the window seat said to
Katharine Peters, "Have you ever been to Easter Island
before?"

A little embarrassed, realizing she was practically

leaning over him to look out, Katharine pulled back and said, "No. It's our first trip." With a gesture of her hand, she indicated that by "our" she was including her husband, on the other side of her, as well as the couple seated in front of them.

The man beside her pushed his seat back so that Katharine could see better.

Although they had sat beside each other for hours, they hadn't conversed, except to utter the usual courtesies of "Hello" and "Is my bag in your way?" and "Sorry to bother you, but I need to get into the aisle." He had slept or read for most of the trip, making conversation impossible anyway. Now Katharine heard more distinctly the Spanish accent she had noticed in his brief earlier words. When they boarded, she had seen him use a Chilean passport for his identification. He was a carmel-skinned man of late middle-age, tall enough to look even more cramped than most people would be in the small space allotted to him. Feeling sympathetic, Katharine had left him the armrest they shared, but now she leaned her elbow on it as she looked out the tiny window. She saw her own face in the glass, superimposed on the clouds: a red-haired woman in her worried forties, with a high, lined forehead and a long, thin nose.

The man pointed to the patch of land their plane was circling.

"See the volcanos?" he asked her. "The big one at the top of the island is Terevaka. But the one you really want to climb is Rano Kau. That's where the quarry is. That's where all the famous statues were carved, right out of the rock walls of the crater. I always tell people, think of Mount

Rushmore, only imagine if the sculptor had cut the presidents loose from the mountain and then set them up on platforms."

"It doesn't look like there's much there," Katharine said, meaning on the island.

"There isn't," he agreed with a slight smile, "except for history. Everybody lives in that one town you see down there, and except for the army base, the rest of the island is essentially one big public park."

It was a funny-looking island, Katharine thought; it was shaped like a soft triangle with the big volcano at the apex, smaller volcanos holding down the other corners, and a bottom edge that curved in and out, as if it were rippling. Its odd configuration brought to her mind a Halloween ghost costume—a small child with a sheet draped over him.

"I don't see any statues," she said, squinting.

"You will," the man told her, "when you get closer."

There was something about the way he said it, and perhaps combined with the impression she had of the island looking ghostlike, that gave Katharine a shudder of unease. To hide it, she said, "Are you visiting, too?"

It came out sounding stilted, overpolite.

"No." He took his time answering, as if the question had prompted him to think of something else. "I used to live in Santiago, but I retired here." He glanced at her. "You might not believe it, but at one time there may have been as many as thirty thousand people living down there. Now there are about a tenth that number, mostly Polynesians, and some Chileans, like me. At the worst of it, back around the late nineteenth century, there were barely a hundred people still alive on the whole island."

The man in front of them had turned around to listen in on their conversation. Katharine and Michael's friend, Lon Reynolds, was a big blond man with a receding hairline and a booming voice. Now, in a manner that suggested he already knew it all, he said: "They killed each other. They cut down all the trees and ruined the soil. They killed the birds and depleted their fisheries. There never had been much water, and they fought over that. Maybe there was also a climate change, or maybe not. But the formerly peaceful clans who had cooperated with each other for centuries got desperate. They turned on each other in a vicious civil war." He was rising what Katharine's husband, Michael, called "Lon's lecturing voice." As was often the case, it was loud enough to attract attention, including that of Michael, who glanced over with an exasperated expression. Other passengers also looked over and listened to him. Lon noticed his extra audience and said, "At which point, the inhabitants began to eat the only protein they had left . . ."

Each other, Katharine knew Lon meant, and hoped he wouldn't say.

The man with the Spanish accent interrupted, but graciously. "You're right." His voice took on a dry edge, and his smile turned wry. "There's a taunt we still use on the island: *Your mother is stuck in my teeth. . . .*"

"Ew!" said a female voice in front of them.

Katharine smiled to hear her friend Nadia's predictable reaction to the cannibal joke. Lon's wife could be counted on to puncture her husband's more pompous moments.

". . . but it's also true," the Chilean man continued, in the same dry tone, "that the slave traders didn't help, nor did the smallpox they brought with them."

Michael Peters spoke up on the other side of Katharine. He was several inches shorter and about fifty pounds lighter than his friend Lon, but as he liked to joke, "At least I still have my hair." In fact, he had it in quantity and in length, and wore it tied back in a long, now-graying ponytail at the nape of his neck.

"Don't worry," Michael said with a laugh, "we're only bringing money."

The wry look in the Chilean's eyes deepened. "As deadly as any disease," he murmured, though Katharine was the only one who heard him, just as a recorded voice announced their final approach to landing.

The four friends walked single file down the steps from the aircraft onto the runway at Mataveri airport. Slim, dark-haired Nadia Reynolds led the way, followed by her husband Lon, both in crisp, colorful designer resort attire, and then Katharine and Michael Peters, who looked more as if they'd plucked their jeans and T-shirts off the top of a laundry pile.

"This is it?" Nadia asked at the bottom. She stared around, looking and sounding disappointed. Two Polynesian men slowly pushed luggage carts toward the LAN CHILE Boeing 757 on which the friends had just flown in. Beyond the one-story terminal, the land was flat and brown, sparsely populated, rising to cliffs in the distance. "There's nobody here! This looks like the middle of nowhere."

"What did you expect, Nadia?" Lon was sarcastic. "O'Hare? LaGuardia? There are only two flights here a week." He held up a pair of fingers in front of her face. "Two. We're not in Chicago anymore. You do realize, Nadia," he lectured, "that we're two thousand miles from South America. Why do you think it took us five hours to get here? This is literally the most remote inhabited spot on earth."

"Well, yeah," Nadia said, "but I didn't know it would *feel* like it."

"Yes!" Michael Peters made a fist and pumped it triumphantly in the tropical air. "We did it! We have finally come to the ends of the earth!"

"My purse!" Katharine's face blanched and her eyes widened in panic. The foursome had picked up their luggage and were now walking toward the front doors leading onto the island proper. Because the island was a Chilean territory and they had come from Santiago, they hadn't even had to go through customs. Their arrival had been disarmingly casual. But now, Katharine frantically checked her other bags. "I've left my purse somewhere! It's got my passport, and our money . . ."

"Well, *that's* gone," Nadia said, "you'll never see *that* again."

"Michael, did I give it to you?" Katharine pleaded with her husband.

"No, I don't have it—" He looked stunned, then panicked.

"Come with me!" she begged all of them. "We have to find it!"

With Katharine running in the lead, the other three walked rapidly behind her toward the "*No Entrada*/Do Not Enter" sign on the door through which they had come only moments earlier. Before they could get there, however, Katharine's seatmate, the tall Chilean man, pushed it open. Seeing them rushing toward him, he smiled broadly and held up a large straw object, for them to see.

"My purse!" Katharine exclaimed, running up to him. "Oh, thank you!"

"You left it on your seat," he told her kindly.

Michael shook the stranger's hand with as much vigor as if he'd saved their lives. "Thank you very much. *Muchas gracias.* I can't believe we got it back. I was sure it was long gone."

"On Easter Island?" The man's eyebrows rose. "Oh, no. There was no way you weren't going to get it back."

"Why not?" Nadia demanded.

He smiled at her. "Because there is no crime on Easter Island."

"Right," Nadia said, and laughed.

"No, really," he told her earnestly. "There isn't."

"You must have one hell of a police force," she said cynically.

"We don't have a police force."

"You're kidding," Lon Reynolds exclaimed, for once having been taken by surprise. "Why not?"

The tall man in the bright floral shirt and khaki trousers smiled again. "Because there is no crime on Easter Island."

His name, he told them, was Manuel Noriega. "Just like the former dictator of Panama," he said, flashing his charming smile. When he learned they had no hotel reservations—because they'd heard it wasn't necessary during low tourist season—he helped them select a *residencia* from among the several offered, in person, on the spot, in the airport—and then he hitched a ride with them in the *residencia*'s van.

"What's a *residencia?*" Nadia asked, mispronouncing it.

"Didn't you read any of those travel books I gave you?" Lon asked her, sounding annoyed.

"That's your job," she retorted.

Katharine, in the van's middle seat in front of them, turned around. "A *residencia* is a private home, Nadia. We'd probably call it a bed and breakfast."

"Oh, well, I love B and B's," Nadia said, sounding pleased.

"It's a good thing," her husband said sarcastically, "that the rest of us know what you like so we can always provide it."

"Yes," Nadia said, with a contented-cat grin that she directed to Katharine and Michael. "It is." But as she stared at the scenery passing by, her expression turned sour again. "You didn't do a very good job of it this time, though. Where are the beaches? Where's the shopping? What in the world are we supposed to *do* here? At least Machu Picchu was beautiful, and there were markets. And Egypt was fabulous, even with all those little kids constantly begging us for stuff all the time. And Stonehenge was okay, 'cause we could go back to London. But this place is like . . . nothing."

"Nadia!" her husband whispered in reproof. Lon cast a telling glance toward Noriega and the *residencia* owner who was driving the van. But in the seat between, Michael Peters burst out laughing. "What are we going to *do* here, Nadia? Gee, I dunno. What can there possibly be to do in a place with so much history and mystery?"

"I know, I know," she said grumpily. "Look at dumb ol' statues and stuff."

Her husband rolled his eyes and shook his head. "Dumb old statues," he muttered. "Dumb old statues!"

Katharine Peters, feeling embarrassed, glanced at the

front seat to see if the driver and their helpful new friend were hearing and understanding what was being said in back. She was relieved when she thought she caught Manuel Noriega with a fleeting grin on his face. It was typical of Nadia Reynolds, Katharine thought, to be able to say even the most superficial, insulting, or outrageous things, and the very people she should have offended would only smile or laugh. It was, Katharine figured, a perk of beauty. Nadia always got away with things, and always would get away with things, because she was so pretty. Even now, Katharine saw Manuel Noriega glance in the rearview mirror at the beautiful, sulky, dark-haired woman in the backseat, and there was admiration in his eyes. But then his gaze shifted so that suddenly he was gazing directly into Katharine's eyes.

Quickly, she lowered hers, and turned to look at the scenery.

She hated to admit it, but Nadia was right: there wasn't much to see so far. Once, this island had been a thickly forested paradise; now, she didn't see a single tree, save for a few scraggly palms near the seashore. When people said the original inhabitants had cut down all the trees, apparently they really meant *all* the trees. The landscape that stretched up from the road on which they were traveling looked as spare and barren as a Midwestern prairie. Katharine shot a glance at their helpful stranger again, and was relieved to see that he was busy conversing with the driver, instead of paying attention to them. She wondered why anybody would choose to leave a country as lush and beautiful as mainland Chile, and a city as exciting as Santiago, and come to live on an island as haunted,

plain, and isolated as this one, even if the ocean that surrounded it was lovely.

The two men up front stopped talking.

"What do you do here, Mr. Noriega?" Katharine blurted
into the silence.

He propped his left arm on the seat back and turned
around to answer her with his charming smile. "Manuel.
Please call me Manuel. What do I do? I'm afraid I do what
everybody else does on Easter Island, Señora Peters. I wait
for the airplanes to deliver tourists. And then I offer my
services as a guide around the island. If you want me to, I
can show you the statues, the volcanos, the quarry, the
caves . . ."

"No wonder you know so much," Nadia said.

"The caves!" Her husband leaned toward the front seat.
"You can show us the caves?"

But Katharine thought, with a start: *He called me
Señora Peters.* When they had all introduced themselves,
in the terminal, they had given him only their first names,
since there were four of them and only one of him. But he
had just then called her by her last name. She looked
around to see if any of the others had noticed—and found
Nadia looking back at her, one eyebrow elevated.

Nadia leaned forward and whispered, "How does he
know your name? You'd better check your purse, Katy."

When Katharine reached for her straw bag, Nadia provided cover by exclaiming, "What caves? I hate caves! You
all know how claustrophobic I am. You didn't get me into
the pyramids, and you're not getting me into any caves."

On the pretext of getting her sunglasses, Katharine
examined her purse.

As far as she could tell, everything that was supposed to be there was there. Nothing seemed disturbed, including the personal mail she had brought with her on the trip, intending to find time to pay bills, among other things. She was slipping on her sunglasses just as Manuel turned around again and said, "Pyramids? Stonehenge, Machu Picchu? It sounds as if the four of you travel together a lot, and you go to—"

"The world's weirdest places," Nadia interrupted. "My husband just wants to be able to brag that he's been there, and Michael always thinks he's going to have some mystical experience, and Katy likes the scenery, and I—"

"Yes," Michael broke in, with a grin. "Why do you come with us, Nadia?"

"And I," she repeated, emphasizing the pronoun, "come because I can't talk them into going someplace easy, like Florida, and I don't want them to leave me home alone." She gave them all a half-serious, half-angry stare. "But that does *not* mean you're getting me into any cave."

When they alighted from the van, in the driveway of the sprawling house where they were going to rent rooms, Katy whispered to Nadia, "It's okay. Nothing's missing. I feel bad for being suspicious. He's been so nice to us—"

"Maybe too nice?" Nadia's tone was cynical again. "Maybe he just knows how to glom onto rich tourists when he sees us."

"Rich?" Katharine's grin was rueful. "Speak for yourself."

She immediately regretted saying it, because Nadia grasped her wrist and gave it a sympathetic squeeze. "Listen, if you ever need anything . . ."

She left the rest unsaid, but it was all there in the warmth of her eyes.

Katharine felt her face get hot. She shook her head. She felt touched, but also mortified. It was hard to be getting broker instead of getting better off in life. They all knew— though so far not even Lon had said it out loud—that this was probably their last exotic trip together, because it was the last one that the Peterses could pretend to afford, and even this was stretching an already-strained budget to its breaking point.

"We're fine," Katharine assured her friend.

Nadia's gaze was steady and sceptical, but she didn't say anything more.

Before they could go to the caves, their new acquaintance and newly hired guide insisted they see the most famous lineup of *moai* on the island: fifteen upright statues of varying heights, all in a single line with their distinctive sway backs to the sea, and one fallen *moai* lying with its face to the sky.

"They represent chiefs," Manuel explained, "and members of ruling families."

"How *did* they move such huge statues?" Katharine asked him.

Lon laughed. "Mike, here, thinks it was aliens."

Michael shot him an unfriendly look. "I'm not an idiot."

Manuel grinned at him. "Don't worry. If you did think that, you'd have lots of company. And then there are the people who swear that the statues got up and walked here by themselves, by magic. But the most likely explanation is also the explanation for the disappearance of the trees. They used ropes and logs to pull and roll the statues. As they built more and more statues, they needed more and more rope and logs from the trees. Add that to a growing population who needed ever more firewood, harpoons, and boats, and something had to give."

Lon took over the lecture. "Then, when things finally did fall apart on the island, the warriors ran around knocking over each other's statues, until there wasn't a single one standing. These have all been re-erected, right, Manny?"

Their guide overlooked the familiarity and simply nodded.

"Why did they make them to begin with?" Michael asked, turning pointedly to Manuel.

"Competition," Lon said loudly. "Just like guys building skyscrapers today. Only back then, it was the one with the biggest statue wins."

"How many are there?" Michael inquired, and even more pointedly added, *"Manuel?"*

"How many statues, you mean?" Again, it was Lon who answered. "Hundreds. Maybe eight hundred, all together."

Michael's mouth dropped open, though he still didn't acknowledge that it was Lon who'd been speaking. "And they knocked them *all* down?"

"Yes," Manuel said, but Lon said, "Every damn one of them," at the same time, and drowned him out.

"You'd think," Nadia said, "that the statues would be facing out to sea."

"They all face inland," Lon informed her. "No one really knows why."

"I think I do," Katharine said, and when the others looked over at her, she blushed. "Well, I mean, I don't really know why they did it, but I know why I'd do it this way." Her voice grew quiet, seeming to compel their attention, so that even Lon didn't interrupt her as she said, "If I lived here in the middle of nowhere, where there was never anything on the horizon and ships never arrived from anywhere, I'd line the whole island with statues and turn them to face me, so it wouldn't feel so lonely. . . ."

The wind picked up at that moment, whistling around the statues and the living humans who had turned to stare at them.

The next morning, they traveled to the caves.

"Aren't you coming in with us, Manny?"

Lon stopped at the wide mouth of the first cave and called back to their guide. But Manuel shook his head. "No. You'll be fine going in alone."

He had arrived at their guesthouse to pick them up in a four-wheel-drive vehicle loaded with bottled water and snacks, because there was nowhere on the island to buy supplies outside of town.

"Why won't you go in the cave?" Nadia wanted to know. "Scared?"

He smiled at her. "No, just traditional . . . and cautious."

"Cautious?" Michael looked suddenly sceptical of the excursion. "What's there to be cautious about for you, but not for us?"

Manuel explained, "There's a taboo against going into these caves."

"Well, then, why are *they* going?" Nadia demanded of him.

"It's only those of us who live on the island who observe the taboo," he explained. "Visitors don't have to."

"Why not?" Katharine asked him.

He looked straight at her. "Because you'll be leaving soon."

There was a moment's silence while they took in the implication of that, and then they all laughed nervously. "You mean," Lon said, "we'll be okay just so long as we don't stick around long enough for the taboo to get us?"

Their guide smiled in a way that got across the idea that he knew what he was saying was anachronistic and amusing, but that he was sticking to it anyway. "More or less. Yes."

Nadia stepped close to her husband, looked up into his face, and said: "Boo!"

That broke up the tension and made them laugh.

"Go ahead," Manuel urged them. "I think you'll find it surprising."

"Does this cave have a name?" Lon wanted to know before be stepped into it.

"It's called the Cave of the Virgins," Manuel answered.

"Cave of the Virgins?" Nadia laughed. "Obviously, *I've* got no business going in there. You'd better watch it, Katy, or it'll spit you out, too."

Fifteen minutes later, when Katharine stumbled out of the cave looking pale and ill, Nadia glanced up in surprise and said, "Hey, I didn't think it would really happen!" When Katharine put out a hand to support herself on the exterior cave wall, and then bent over at the waist as if she was going to vomit, Nadia sprang to her feet.

"What's the matter, Katy?"

Katharine waved for her to sit back down. "Dizzy." After a moment, she straightened back up and then looked over to where Nadia was once again seated on the grass with Manuel. "There are human skulls in there."

"Skulls!'"

Manuel smiled apologetically. "I warned you to expect surprises."

"You could have warned her to expect skulls!"

He shrugged. "I never know whether to tell people ahead of time. If I don't tell them, it may upset them . . . like you, Señora. But most of the time they get a thrill out of it, and they kind of enjoy the shock."

"Katharine doesn't look as if she liked the shock."

Katharine walked over toward them on unsteady legs. "There were two of them, Nadia. Just . . . heads . . . and there may have been a few other bones—"

"Yes," Manuel said, "there are."

"It was just—" Katharine sat down near them. "Scary. Grotesque."

"And the boys loved it, I'll bet," her friend said.

"Of course. They're still in there, looking for more bones."

Manuel had warned them earlier not to touch or disturb any artifacts on the island.

"I'll have to remember to show them the finger bone," he murmured now.

"Finger bone?" Katharine asked weakly. He nodded. "A finger bone was found beneath one of the statues that were knocked over all those years ago. Somebody must not have moved fast enough to get out of the way."

"Gross," Nadia said.

Katharine shuddered. "It's no wonder there's no crime here."

Their guide looked surprised. "Why do you say that?"

She looked at him with eyes that still registered the shock she'd felt at seeing human skulls inside the cave.

"Because there has already been enough crime on this island to last forever."

Two hours later, Katharine and Manuel stood on a slight rise, just inside a dormant volcano, watching Nadia and Lon snipe at each other. The married couple were standing in front of a partially completed statue that towered over them. All around them lay the remains of the single basalt quarry where all the sculpting work had been achieved. Workmen from ancient days appeared to have dropped their tools and walked off the job, leaving behind them tools on the ground and several hundred statues in various stages of completion.

"These are the ugliest statues I've ever seen," Nadia said, starting it.

"How can you call them ugly?" Lon shot back. "Nadia, these are the most famous statues in the world."

"Well, Mick Jagger is famous, too, but that doesn't make him pretty."

"My God, Nadia, do you have to judge everything by modern standards?"

"Do I look like a first-century art critic, Lon?" she retorted, and then she waved a dismissive hand at all the statues and pieces of statues around her. "I've seen garden gnomes that looked better than these things."

Standing beside Katharine, several yards away, Manuel said quietly, "Why does she do that?"

Katharine glanced at him. "Why does she act like an idiot, you mean? To annoy Lon, I think. He can be a little full of himself . . ." She smiled apologetically. ". . . as you may have noticed. He didn't used to be so obnoxious. When we first knew him, he was lots of fun."

"What happened?"

She shrugged. "Money. Success. Security. But Nadia's not really an idiot, you know."

"I know," the guide said, and then he added, when he saw she looked surprised, "I had a chance to talk to her alone when the rest of you were in the cave. Even in that short time, I could tell that she is quite intelligent. And that it isn't true that she hadn't read a lot before coming here. She was telling me things about it before I could even tell her."

"Yeah, she always does that. We go on these trips and she pretends to be a twit, and she really knows more than the rest of us do. She holds a very high-powered job in a huge insurance corporation," Katharine told him. "So does Lon, that's how they met. But when she says that all she really wants to do on vacation is veg in the sun, she means it."

"Does she ever get to do that?"

"Does she ever get her way, you mean? Not very often."

"Which is why she does this to annoy him," Manuel observed.

"Exactly."

He turned to her. "And what do you and your husband do when you're not traveling to mystical places?" He smiled at her, which dragged a smile out of her, too. "I've got to say the two of you don't exactly strike me as corporate types, but maybe that's only because you're on vacation."

"No," she said. "We're not like that. Michael's an artist. I'm a freelance writer."

Manuel looked as if he was about to follow up that piece of information with a question, but then he closed his mouth again, as if he had decided that whatever he was going to ask might be tactless.

She said it for him: "How can we afford this, you're wondering? Since artists and writers usually don't make much money?" A little grimly, Katharine patted the straw purse that hung over her shoulder, the purse where the unopened bills still lay. "Funny thing, but I've been asking myself the same question lately."

"Then why—?"

"Do we keep coming? Because Michael and Lon have been friends since they were in college. They've always egged each other on." Her expression turned a little bitter. "And now, even though the price of eggs has gotten way too high, we just keep buying them." She broke off and laughed, sounding embarrassed. "I'm sorry. That was even dumber than Nadia makes herself sound. I'd better go look at those 'ugly old statues' that I keep hearing so much about."

She started to move away from him, but he stopped her by asking, "Was it really the skulls that made you sick this morning?"

Katharine turned to look up at him. "No." She looked distressed again. "The men were being ugly to each other. Lon was bragging about how well he's doing, and Michael was giving him a hard time. I hate it. It upsets me."

She turned away, and hurried off to see the statues that many people considered to be one of the wonders of the world.

Off in a corner of the quarry, Nadia pulled Katharine aside and said, "I asked Manuel what he did for a living in Chile, before he came here, but he wouldn't tell me."

"Wouldn't tell you? What do you mean?"

"I mean he fudged. He said, 'Oh, this and that, one thing and another.'" Nadia had the suspicious look in her eyes again. "So I said, what does that mean, and he said, 'It was a long time ago.'"

"Well, he doesn't *have* to tell us anything."

"No, but I like to know who I'm hiring."

Katharine grinned. "Next time we hire a guide, we'll make him submit a resume to your personnel department."

Nadia laughed at that. "Damn right. But really, Katy, we should watch him. He could be a crook, he could steal us blind. Hang on to your purse, girl."

"He already had a chance at my purse," Katharine reminded her, and then couldn't help but tease. "You're the one who'd better be careful with her purse. It would be much better pickings."

Unfortunately, it came out sounding harsh and bitter, which she hadn't intended.

When Katharine saw her friend's eyes widen in surprise and what looked like hurt, she rushed to say, "I didn't mean that the way it sounded, truly."

Before Nadia could respond, their husbands came hurrying up to them. Lon threw an arm around Nadia's shoulders and then pointed to the top of the crater with his free hand. "I want to hike around the rim of this volcano tomorrow. Who's coming with me?"

Under his arm, his wife shuddered. "Not me, not heights."

"How high is it?" Michael inquired of Manuel.

"On the other side, there's a four-hundred-foot sheer drop to the ocean. It's spectacular, but it's not recommended for anybody except the most experienced climbers."

Michael looked disappointed. "That lets me out."

"Oh, come on," Lon scoffed at him. "You never know, you might have one of your mystical epiphanies up there."

"I've already had my epiphany for this trip," Michael said in a tight voice.

"Oh yeah, and what was it?"

"I had a revelation that you're a jerk, Lon."

Nadia laughed, relieving some of the tension. "Well, *that's* not news!"

"I don't care if nobody goes with me," Lon said aggressively. "I'll hike it by myself."

But their guide stared across at him with a serious expression. "I wish you wouldn't, Señor Reynolds. It's the most dangerous hike on the island. If you do it, you should definitely have a partner."

Lon looked at his three mates, and when none of them volunteered, he shrugged.

"No problem," he said, with a definite bite to his words, "I'll just do it the next time we come to Easter Island." It was clear to all of them that what he really meant was, *We'll never be back here again. Thanks a lot for spoiling my fun.*

It seemed that Lon still hadn't gotten over it by the time the friends went to dinner that night. The restaurant they chose, at Manuel's suggestion, was basically just tables and chairs set on top of a concrete slab painted green, with a thatched roof overhead. Even the kitchen was open-air, so they could watch the chef broiling their shrimp and boiling the pasta.

Lon's words grew more snappish with every refill of his glass of wine.

Over salad, he seemed merely baffled and annoyed, saying, "I don't know what's the matter with you pansies. It doesn't look like such a difficult hike to me. Hell, we've walked all over England together—"

"Yeah, over grass and gentle hills," Michael reminded him.

"We've walked in the desert—"

"Which is, you may recall, *flat*," Nadia said, which made the others laugh.

Her husband's face flushed. He took a swig from his wineglass, and did not join their laughter. "I just think it would be a highlight of our lives to be up there on that ridge as the sun comes up tomorrow. We could leave the *residencia* while it's still dark, and be on top in time for the sunrise—"

"Oh, even smarter," his wife said. "You want to hike up there in the *dark*."

"Don't make such a big deal out of everything, Nadia." Lon's eyes were hot with anger. "The only reason Manuel warned us away was to keep from getting sued if one of us did fall, which is not going to happen."

"Ha! And why would I sue *him,* if *you* act like a fool and break your neck?"

Lon's face flushed an even deeper red. "Hell, we've only *got* tomorrow, and then we're gone, and we'll never be back again. I'm telling you, you'll regret it if you don't go with me."

Katharine looked alarmed. "You're still going, Lon?"

"I might," he said aggressively.

"I can't *believe* you!" Nadia picked up her napkin from her lap and threw it at him.

He glared at her. "It's my neck."

"And a shame there's no brain on top of it!"

By the time they finished the appetizers, he had come back to the subject, only by then he'd had more wine and his tongue was even looser. "Maybe I'll hire Manuel to go with me." He nodded his head in the direction of a long bar where their guide sat on a stool, in conversation with the Polynesian bartender. Lon glared at Michael across the table. "Just because you can't afford him, doesn't mean I shouldn't get to go."

Nadia darted a glance at him, and Katharine gasped a little.

"We can afford it, Lon," she told him.

"Really? Then why did you need me to pay for all of us today?"

Katharine looked bewildered. "We didn't—"

Michael put a hand on top of hers. "I told him we'd pay him back—"

"Out of what?" Lon sneered. "It's finally coming home to roost, isn't it? After all these years, we're finally seeing who has been the smart one, after all. For so many years, ever since we graduated from college, you've mocked me for being a corporate guy. You and your free spirit, right? Never going to be tied down, always just delighted to go to your own work every day, never reporting to any boss . . ."

"Where did this come from?" Michael said, looking stunned.

"Where did it come from? It came from all these years of you being so smug about being a stupid artist . . ." He glanced at Katharine. ". . . and writer. Like either of you is ever going to have any real success! You draw the equivalent of box tops, for God's sake." Again he glanced at Katharine. "And you, you write ad copy for chewing gum. Yeah, there's so much integrity in that, right? You're both such *artists*. And now, guess what? After thirty years of actually getting out of bed and going to work every day, after working our tails off and earning every penny, Nadia and I get to retire with several million bucks apiece. And what do you get to retire on, Michael? Katharine? Oh, that's right, you don't ever get to retire, do you? You'll still be drawing your stupid box tops when you're eighty years old. Katharine will still be trying to find ad copy to write when you're both senile and she can't string two words together. . . ."

"Lon, stop it!" Nadia tried to take one of his hands, but he jerked out of her grasp.

"Nadia and I will still be taking any trips we want to take," he plunged on, ignoring her. "And what will you be doing, Michael? You'll be walking from one end of the hall in the Medicaid nursing home to the other end of the hall . . ."

Katharine pushed her chair back and stood up.

Michael shook his head, as if to clear it, and then he stood up, too. In a voice that trembled with emotion, he stared across the table at his best friend and said, "Go on up on that ridge, Lon. Take all the chances you want, buddy. You want to take a hike, Lon? Fine! Take a hike, buddy. Take a long walk off a short ridge. Go see your sunset. I hope it's the last one you ever get to *buy*."

He put an arm around his wife and pushed her ahead of him.

They were gone by the time the entrées were placed on the table. At the far end of the bar, Manuel Noriega exchanged glances with the bartender. Lon's voice had easily carried over to them. The bartender, a Polynesian, smiled slightly, as if to say, "Tourists!" Manuel shook his head, as if in agreement, but he paid for his drinks soon after that and left without ordering dinner.

Manuel found Katharine Peters sitting alone on a side patio of the *residencia*.

"Is everything all right, Señora?"

When she looked up at him, her face was in shadow so he couldn't see her expression clearly, but there was unhappiness in her voice. "Some things never change, do they?"

"What do you mean?" he asked her.

"From one century to the next, we pretty much behave just the same. Everybody gets along fine, and then before you know it, we're knocking each other down. Did we make fools of ourselves back in the restaurant, Manuel?"

His face was shadowed, too, so she couldn't see his smile. "Not all of you."

When she didn't respond, he turned quietly and walked away.

The noise of a car engine woke Katharine up with a start that set her heart pounding. Instinctively, she turned toward the other side of the bed to touch Michael, but when she put her hand where his chest should be, he wasn't there.

Katharine turned on a lamp on her side of the bed. Their travel clock said: 4:00 A.M. Her husband's side of the bed was empty, the sheets pulled back.

She got up and turned on more lights. They revealed that the clothes he had taken off to come to bed were gone. It appeared to her that some time after she fell asleep,

Michael had slipped out of bed, gotten dressed again, and then left their room without waking her, or telling her where he was going.

Katharine looked around for a note from him, but didn't find one.

She opened the door and looked out into the darkness of the backyard of the guesthouse. Michael wasn't on the back porch. After she had walked all around the house in her nightgown, she knew he wasn't on any of the patios, either. She saw that the big van was not in the driveway, and one of the bicycles the home kept for its guests was gone as well.

There is no crime on Easter Island . . .

Katharine decided to believe that, and to believe that Michael had gone out—safely—for a walk along the safe, deserted streets of the town. Maybe he had indigestion, either from some of the food they'd had that day, or from the things that Lon had said to them.

She went back to bed, but didn't get back to sleep.

Shortly after dawn, the door to the room quietly opened.

Katharine shut her eyes.

She heard someone come in and slip off clothing. Then the bed covers next to her stirred and her husband lay down beside her. She realized that if the sound of the van's engine had not awakened her, she would never have known that he had come and gone.

"Where have you been, Michael?"

She could feel how startled he was to hear her voice.

"Oh, I'm sorry. Did I wake you?"

"Where'd you go?"

"I couldn't sleep, so I went for a walk."

Usually, Katharine could tell the minute he dropped off to sleep, because Michael snored. But although she lay with her eyes open for another hour, she never heard him make a sound until the sun was high enough to stream in through the windows.

At breakfast in the *residencia*'s dining room, Nadia told them that Lon had taken the van out during the night in order to drive himself back to the volcano.

"I couldn't stop him."

She sounded more angry than worried, even though she said he had left at four in the morning, and it was by then already eight A.M.

Katharine didn't want to ask the obvious: *Shouldn't he be back by now?*

When Lon Reynolds still had not returned with the van by ten, and the owner of the *residencia* needed it to make an airport run, he called his friend Manuel Noriega for assistance. "Can you drive out there and look for him?" he asked. "And if you find him, tell him to bring my van back as soon as possible."

By eleven A.M., when neither Manuel nor Lon had appeared, Nadia was frantic.

"I'd call the police," she said, "if this godforsaken island had any!"

Upon hearing that, Katharine Peters burst into tears.

Ten minutes later, Lon Reynolds drove up to the guest-house in the van, got out, and walked casually over to the frightened little band of people on the back porch.

"You all look as if you've just seen a ghost," he said. And then, "You missed a hell of a show. I walked the entire rim of that crater and saw the most spectacular sunrise I'll ever see in my life."

"Where have you *been?*" his wife screamed at him.

He looked at her as if she had lost her marbles, and shrugged. "Since I already had the van, I drove all the way around the island to see the rest of it. Why? Is there a problem?"

Manuel Noriega stood at the airport fence watching the LAN CHILE jet take off for Santiago, taking "his" tourists with it. There was a fresh check for $1,000 in his pocket, to match the one he had taken from Katharine Peters's handbag when she had "accidentally" left it behind in the airplane on the day of their arrival. She was a nice, caring, efficient woman, he thought. When he had gone up to the LAN CHILE ticket counter at the airport in Santiago, his prepaid ticket to Easter Island was there for him, just as she had e-mailed that it would be.

They had conducted their business entirely by e-mail.

She had been looking for a private investigator.

He wasn't that, but he had been a cop.

A friend passed his name along to the American woman who was privately looking for a bodyguard. "I would like you to keep a close watch on our friend Lon Reynolds," were her e-mail instructions. "Don't let anything happen to him."

She had not told him what that "anything" might be.

Maybe she had not even known for sure, herself, exactly what the danger might be, but he was pretty sure that she feared it might come from her own husband, if he was pushed too far.

Easter Island was a land of extremes, Manuel believed, a land at the end of the earth, a place where nothing ever happened and even if it did, there was nothing to be done about it afterward. When he had watched the acrimony grow between the two old friends, he had believed he was witnessing the possibility that something very bad, something irrevocable was about to happen.

Lon Reynolds was an obnoxious, stubborn man.

Michael Peters was a defeated, humiliated one.

After their argument in the restaurant, Manuel had driven out to the volcano, parked his car where no one could see it, and then he had hiked up to the rim to wait. The first of them to arrive had been Michael Peters, bicycling quietly up the dirt roads, and also hiking up to wait. But when he arrived at the top of the precipitous ridge he had found not his old friend Lon but their "guide," Manuel.

They had stared at each other, the two men from different cultures.

No words had been exchanged until Michael had said, "So you're going to walk with him, to make sure he doesn't fall off."

"Yes."

"Then I'll go back. There's no reason for me to be here, then."

The words could have meant anything. They hung in the tropical air.

Michael Peters turned, and carefully made his way back down, vanishing into the darkness for a while. When the headlights of the van appeared, and that door opened and then slammed, it was only by looking through binoculars that Manuel was able to see Michael take the bicycle out of hiding, get on it, and peddle away unobserved by his friend.

"You're here!" were Lon's first words when he reached the top.

"I thought it safer this way," Manuel told him. "I won't charge you."

"That's good," Lon said ungraciously, "since I never asked you to do this."

I won't charge you for saving your life, Manuel thought, as he led the way along the ridge above the sea, *because I've already been paid.* Lon Reynolds would never know that Katharine had used money she couldn't afford to spend in order to keep two old friends from destroying each other like primitive men in a battle for supremacy. Manuel wondered if Michael really would have pushed his old friend off the cliff, like one of the ancient islanders shoving a statue down. And he wondered what would happen to all of them when they returned home. Maybe this strange, charged episode between them would defuse things, maybe they would safely drift apart. There was only one thing Manuel knew for sure as the jet shrank to a dot in the sky and he turned around to leave the airport: Thanks to himself and to Katharine Peters, there was no crime on Easter Island.

Born Bad

Jeffery Deaver

Best-selling novelist Jeffrey Deaver has been honored a number of times for his writing. He is a three-time recipient of the Ellery Queen Reader's Award for Best Short Story of the Year. He's won the W.H. Smith Thumping Good Read Award for his Lincoln Rhyme novel *The Empty Chair,* and the Crime Writers Association of Great Britain's Ian Fleming Steel Dagger Award for *Garden Of Beasts* and the Short Story Dagger for "The Weekender." Additionally, Deaver has been nominated for six Edgar Awards, an Anthony Award, a Gumshoe Award. The author of twenty-one novels, Deaver's work has been translated into thirty-five languages. *The Bone Collector* was a feature release from Universal Pictures and *A Maiden's Grave* was made into an HBO film *Dead Silence.* His latest novel is *The Cold Moon.*

Sleep, my child and peace attend thee, all through the night. . . .

The words of the lullaby looped relentlessly through her mind, as persistent as the clattering Oregon rain on the roof and window.

The song that she'd sung to Beth Anne when the girl was three or four seated itself in her head and wouldn't stop echoing. Twenty-five years ago, the two of them: mother and daughter, sitting in the kitchen of the family's home outside Detroit. Liz Polemus, hunching over the Formica table, the frugal young mother and wife, working hard to stretch the dollars.

Singing to her daughter, who sat across from her, fascinated with the woman's deft hands.

I who love you shall be near you, all through the night.
Soft the drowsy hours are creeping.
Hill and vale in slumber sleeping.

Liz felt a cramp in her right arm—the one that had never healed properly—and realized she was still gripping the receiver fiercely at the news she'd just received. That her daughter was on her way to the house.

The daughter she hadn't spoken with in more than three years.

I my loving vigil keeping, all through the night.

Liz finally replaced the telephone and felt blood surge into her arm, itching, stinging. She sat down on the embroidered couch that had been in the family for years and massaged her throbbing forearm. She felt light-headed, confused, as if she wasn't sure the phone call had been real or a wispy scene from a dream.

Only the woman wasn't lost in the peace of sleep. No, Beth Anne was on her way. A half-hour and she'd be at Liz's door.

Outside, the rain continued to fall steadily, tumbling into the pines that filled Liz's yard. She'd lived in this house for nearly a year, a small place miles from the nearest suburb. Most people would've thought it too small, too remote. But to Liz it was an oasis. The slim widow, midfifties, had a busy life and little time for housekeeping. She could clean the place quickly and get back to work. And while hardly a recluse, she preferred the buffer zone of forest that separated her from her neighbors. The minuscule size also discouraged suggestions by any male friends that, hey, got an idea, how 'bout I move in? The woman would merely look around the one-bedroom home and explain that two people would go crazy in such cramped quarters; after her husband's death she'd resolved she'd never remarry or live with another man.

Her thoughts now drifted to Jim. Their daughter had left home and cut off all contact with the family before he died. It had always stung her that the girl hadn't even called after his death, let alone attended his funeral. Anger at this instance of the girl's callousness shivered within Liz but she pushed it aside, reminding herself that whatever the young woman's purpose tonight there wouldn't be enough time to exhume even a fraction of the painful memories that lay between mother and daughter like wreckage from a plane crash.

A glance at the clock. Nearly ten minutes had sped by since the call, Liz realized with a start.

Anxious, she walked into her sewing room. This, the largest room in the house, was decorated with needlepoints of her own and her mother's and a dozen racks of spools—some dating back to the fifties and sixties. Every shade of God's palette was represented in those threads. Boxes full of

Vogue and Butterick patterns too. The centerpiece of the room was an old electric Singer. It had none of the fancy stitch cams of the new machines, no lights or complex gauges or knobs. The machine was a forty-year-old, black-enameled workhorse, identical to the one that her mother had used.

Liz had sewed since she was twelve and in difficult times the craft sustained her. She loved every part of the process: buying the fabric—hearing the *thud thud thud* as the clerk would turn the flat bolts of cloth over and over, unwinding the yardage (Liz could tell the women with near-prefect precision when a particular amount had been unfolded). Pinning the crisp, translucent paper onto the cloth. Cutting with the heavy pinking shears, which left a dragon-tooth edge on the fabric. Readying the machine, winding the bobbin, threading the needle . . .

There was something so completely soothing about sewing: taking these substances—cotton from the land, wool from animals—and blending them into something altogether new. The worst aspect of the injury several years ago was the damage to her right arm, which kept her off the Singer for three unbearable months.

Sewing was therapeutic for Liz, yes, but more than that, it was a part of her profession and had helped her become a well-to-do woman; nearby were racks of designer gowns, awaiting her skillful touch.

Her eyes rose to the clock. Fifteen minutes. Another breathless slug of panic.

Picturing so clearly that day twenty-five years ago—Beth Anne in her flannel 'jammies, sitting at the rickety kitchen table and watching her mother's quick fingers with fascination as Liz sang to her.

Sleep, my child, and peace attend thee . . .

This memory gave birth to dozens of others and the agitation rose in Liz's heart like the water level of the rain-swollen stream behind her house. Well, she told herself now firmly, don't just sit here . . . do something. Keep busy. She found a navy-blue jacket in her closet, walked to her sewing table, then dug through a basket until she found a matching remnant of wool. She'd use this to make a pocket for the garment. Liz went to work, smoothing the cloth, marking it with tailor's chalk, finding the scissors, cutting carefully. She focused on her task but the distraction wasn't enough to take her mind off the impending visit—and memories from years ago.

The shoplifting incident, for instance. When the girl was twelve.

Liz recalled the phone ringing, answering it. The head of security at a nearby department store was reporting—to Liz's and Jim's shock—that Beth Anne had been caught with nearly a thousand dollars' worth of jewelry hidden in a paper bag.

The parents had pleaded with the manager not to press charges. They'd said there must've been some mistake.

"Well," the security chief said skeptically, "we found her with five watches. A necklace too. Wrapped up in this grocery bag. I mean, that don't sound like any mistake to me."

Finally, after much reassurance that this was a fluke and promises she'd never come into the store again, the manager agreed to keep the police out of the matter.

Outside the store, once the family was alone, Liz turned to Beth Anne furiously. "Why on earth did you do that?"

"Why not?" was the girl's singsong response, a snide smile on her face.

"It was stupid."

"Like, I care."

"Beth Anne . . . why're you acting this way?"

"What way?" the girl'd asked in mock confusion.

Her mother had tried to engage her in a dialogue—the way the talk shows and psychologists said you should do with your kids—but Beth Anne remained bored and distracted. Liz had delivered a vague, and obviously futile, warning and had given up.

Thinking now: You put a certain amount of effort into stitching a jacket or dress and you get the garment you expect. There's no mystery. But you put a thousand times *more* effort into raising your child and the result is the opposite of what you hope and dream for. This seemed so unfair.

Liz's keen gray eyes examined the wool jacket, making sure the pocket lay flat and was pinned correctly into position. She paused, looking up, out the window toward the black spikes of the pine, but what she was seeing were more hard memories of Beth Anne. What a mouth on that girl! Beth Anne would look her mother or father in the eye and say, "There is no Goddamn way you're going to make me go with you." Or, "Do you have *any* fucking clue at all?"

Maybe they should've been stricter in their upbringing. In Liz's family you got whipped for cursing or talking back to adults or for not doing what your parents asked you to do. She and Jim had never spanked Beth Anne; maybe they *should've* swatted her once or twice.

One time, somebody had called in sick at the family

business—a warehouse Jim had inherited—and he needed Beth Anne to help out. She'd snapped at him, "I'd rather be dead than go back inside that shithole with you."

Her father had backed down sheepishly but Liz stormed up to her daughter. "Don't talk to your father that way."

"Oh?" the girl asked in a sarcastic voice. "How *should* I talk to him? Like some obedient little daughter who does everything he wants? Maybe that's what he wanted but it's not who he got." She'd grabbed her purse, heading for the door.

"Where are you going?"

"To see some friends."

"You are not. Get back here this minute!"

Her reply was a slamming door. Jim started after her but in an instant she was gone, crunching through two-month-old gray Michigan snow.

And those "friends"?

Trish and Eric and Sean . . . Kids from families with totally different values from Liz's and Jim's. They tried to forbid her from seeing them. But that, of course, had no effect.

"Don't tell me who I can hang out with," Beth Anne had said furiously. The girl was eighteen then and as tall as her mother. As she walked forward with a glower, Liz retreated uneasily. The girl continued, "And what do you know about them anyway?"

"They don't like your father and me—that's all I need to know. What's wrong with Todd and Joan's kids? Or Brad's? Your father and I've known them for years."

"What's *wrong* with them?" the girl muttered sarcastically. "Try, they're losers." This time grabbing both her purse and the cigarettes she'd started smoking, she made another dramatic exit.

With her right foot Liz pressed the pedal of the Singer and the motor gave its distinctive grind, then broke into *clatta clatta clatta* as the needle sped up and down, vanishing into the cloth, leaving a neat row of stitches around the pocket.

Clatta, clatta, clatta . . .

In middle school the girl would never get home until seven or eight and in high school she'd arrive much later. Sometimes she'd stay away all night. Weekends too she just disappeared and had nothing to do with the family.

Clatta clatta clatta. The rhythmic grind of the Singer soothed Liz somewhat but couldn't keep her from panicking again when she looked at the clock. Her daughter could be here at any minute.

Her girl, her little baby . . .

Sleep, my child . . .

And the question that had plagued Liz for years returned now: What had gone wrong? For hours and hours she'd replay the girl's early years, trying to see what Liz had done to make Beth Anne reject her so completely. She'd been an attentive, involved mother, been consistent and fair, made meals for the family every day, washed and ironed the girl's clothes, bought her whatever she needed. All she could think of was that she'd been too strong-minded, too unyielding in her approach to raising the girl, too stern sometimes.

But this hardly seemed like much of a crime. Besides, Beth Anne had been equally mad at her father—the softie of the parents. Easygoing, doting to the point of spoiling the girl, Jim was the perfect father. He'd help Beth Anne and her friends with their homework, drive them to school himself when Liz was working, read her bedtime stories and tuck her in at night. He made up "special games" for him and Beth Anne to play. It was just the sort of parental bond that most children would love.

But the girl would fly into rages at him too and go out of her way to avoid spending time with him.

No, Liz could think of no dark incidents in the past, no traumas, no tragedies that could have turned Beth Anne into a renegade. She returned to the conclusion that she'd come to years ago: that—as unfair and cruel as it seemed—her daughter had simply been born fundamentally different from Liz; something had happened in the wiring to make the girl the rebel she was.

And looking at the cloth, smoothing it under her long, smooth fingers, Liz considered something else: rebellious, yes, but was she a *threat* too?

Liz now admitted that part of the ill ease she felt tonight wasn't only from the impending confrontation with her wayward child; it was that the young woman scared her.

She looked up from her jacket and stared at the rain spattering her window. Her right arm tingling painfully, she recalled that terrible day several years ago—the day that drove her permanently from Detroit and still gave her breathless nightmares. Liz had walked into a jewelry store and stopped in shock, gasping as she saw a pistol swinging toward her. She could still see the yellow flash as the man pulled the trigger, hear the stunning explosion, feel the numbing shock as the bullet slammed into her arm, sending her sprawling on the tile floor, crying out in pain and confusion.

Her daughter, of course, had nothing to do with that

tragedy. Yet Liz had realized that Beth Anne was just as willing and capable of pulling the trigger as that man had done during the robbery; she had proof her daughter was a dangerous woman. A few years ago, after Beth Anne had left home, Liz had gone to visit Jim's grave. The day was foggy as cotton and she was nearly to the tombstone when she realized that somebody was standing over it. To her shock she realized it was Beth Anne. Liz eased back into the mist, heart pounding fiercely. She debated for a long moment but finally decided that she didn't have the courage to confront the girl and decided to leave a note on her car's windshield.

But as she stepped to the Chevy, fishing in her handbag for a pen and some paper, she glanced inside and her heart shivered at the sight: a jacket, a clutter of papers and half-hidden beneath them a pistol and some plastic bags, which contained white powder—drugs, Liz assumed.

Oh, yes, she now thought, her daughter, little Beth Anne Polemus, was very capable of killing.

Liz's foot rose from the pedal and the Singer fell silent. She lifted the clamp and cut the dangling threads. She pulled it on and slipped a few things into the pocket, examined herself in the mirror and decided that she was satisfied with the work.

Then she stared at her dim reflection. Leave! a voice in her head said. She's a threat! Get out now before Beth Anne arrives.

But after a moment of debate Liz sighed. One of the reasons she'd moved here in the first place was that she'd learned her daughter had relocated to the Northwest. Liz had been meaning to try to track the girl down but had found herself oddly reluctant to do so. No, she'd stay, she'd meet with Beth Anne. But she wasn't going to be stupid, not after the robbery. Liz now hung the jacket on a hanger and walked to the closet. She pulled down a box from the top shelf and looked inside. There sat a small pistol. "A ladies' gun," Jim had called it when he gave it to her years ago. She took it out and stared at the weapon.

Sleep, my child . . . All through the night.

Then she shuddered in disgust. No, she couldn't possibly use a weapon against her daughter. Of course not.

The idea of putting the girl to sleep forever was inconceivable.

And yet . . . what if it were a choice between her life and her daughter's? What if the hatred within the girl had pushed her over the edge?

Could she kill Beth Anne to save her own life?

No mother should ever have to make a choice like this one.

She hesitated for a long moment, then started to put the gun back. But a flash of light stopped her. Headlights filled the front yard and cast bright yellow cat's eyes on the sewing room wall beside Liz.

The woman glanced once more at the gun and, rather than put it away in the closet, set it on a dresser near the door and covered it with a doily. She walked into the living room and stared out the window at the car in her driveway, which sat motionless, lights still on, wipers whipping back and forth fast, her daughter hesitating to climb out; Liz suspected it wasn't the bad weather that kept the girl inside.

A long, long moment later the headlights went dark.

Well, think positive, Liz told herself. Maybe her daughter had changed. Maybe the point of the visit was reaching out to make amends for all the betrayal over the years. They could finally begin to work on having a normal relationship.

Still, she glanced back at the sewing room, where the gun sat on the dresser, and told herself: Take it. Keep it in your pocket.

Then: No, put it back in the closet.

Liz did neither. Leaving the gun on the dresser, she strode to the front door of her house and opened it, feeling cold mist coat her face.

She stood back from the approaching silhouetted form of the slim young woman as Beth Anne walked through the doorway and stopped. A pause, then she swung the door shut behind her.

Liz remained in the middle of the living room, pressing her hands together nervously.

Pulling back the hood of her windbreaker, Beth Anne wiped rain off her face. The young woman's face was weathered, ruddy. She wore no makeup. She'd be twenty-eight, Liz knew, but she looked older. Her hair was now short, revealing tiny earrings. For some reason, Liz wondered if someone had given them to the girl or if she'd bought them for herself.

"Well, hello, honey."

"Mother."

A hesitation then a brief, humorless laugh from Liz. "You used to call me 'Mom.' "

"Did I?"

"Yes. Don't you remember?"

A shake of the head. But Liz thought that in fact she did remember but was reluctant to acknowledge the memory. She looked her daughter over carefully.

Beth Anne glanced around the small living room. Her eye settled on a picture of herself and her father together— they were on the boat dock near the family home in Michigan. Liz asked, "When you called you said somebody told you I was here. Who?"

"It doesn't matter. Just somebody. You've been living here since . . ." Her voice faded.

"A couple of years. Do you want a drink?"

"No."

Liz remembered that she'd found the girl sneaking some beer when she was sixteen and wondered if she'd continued to drink and now had a problem with alcohol.

"Tea, then? Coffee?"

"No."

"You knew I moved to the Northwest?" Beth Anne asked.

"You always talked about the area, getting away from . . . well, getting out of Michigan and coming here. Then after you moved out you got some mail at the house. From somebody in Seattle."

Beth Anne nodded. Was there a slight grimace too? As if she was angry with herself for carelessly leaving a clue to her whereabouts. "And you moved to Portland to be near me?"

Liz smiled. "I guess I did. I started to look you up but I lost the nerve." Liz felt tears welling in her eyes as her daughter continued her examination of the room. The house was small, yes, but the furniture, electronics and appointments were the best—the rewards of Liz's hard work in recent years. Two feelings vied within the woman: She half-hoped the girl would be tempted to reconnect with her mother when she saw how much money Liz had but, simultaneously, she was ashamed of the opulence; her daughter's clothes and cheap costume jewelry suggested she was struggling.

The silence was like fire. It burned Liz's skin and heart.

Beth Anne unclenched her left hand and her mother noticed a minuscule engagement ring and a simple gold band. The tears now rolled from her eyes. "You—?"

The young woman followed her mother's gaze to the ring. She nodded.

Liz wondered what sort of man her son-in-law was. Would he be someone soft like Jim, someone who could temper the girl's wayward personality? Or would he be hard? Like Beth Anne herself?

"You have children?" Liz asked.

"That's not for you to know."

"Are you working?"

"Are you asking if I've changed, Mother?"

Liz didn't want to hear the answer to this question and continued quickly, pitching her case. "I was thinking," she said, desperation creeping into her voice, "that maybe I could go up to Seattle. We could see each other . . . We could even work together. We could be partners. Fifty-fifty. We'd have so much fun. I always thought we'd be great together. I always dreamed—"

"You and me working together, Mother?" She glanced into the sewing room, nodded toward the machine, the racks of dresses. "That's not my life. It never was. It never could be. After all these years, you really don't understand that, do you?" The words and their cold tone answered Liz's question firmly: No, the girl hadn't changed one bit.

Her voice went harsh. "Then why're you here? What's your point in coming?"

"I think you know, don't you?"

"No, Beth Anne, I *don't* know. Some kind of psycho revenge?"

"You could say that, I guess." She looked around the room again. "Let's go."

Liz's breath was coming fast. "Why? Everything we ever did was for you."

"I'd say you did it *to* me." A gun appeared in her daughter's hand and the black muzzle lolled in Liz's direction. "Outside," she whispered.

"My God! No!" She inhaled a gasp, as the memory of the shooting in the jewelry store came back to her hard. Her arm tingled and tears streaked down her cheeks.

She pictured the gun on the dresser.

Sleep, my child . . .

"I'm not going anywhere!" Liz said, wiping her eyes.

"Yes, you are. Outside."

"What are you going to do?" she asked desperately.

"What I should've done a long time ago."

Liz leaned against a chair for support. Her daughter noticed the woman's left hand, which had eased to within inches of the telephone.

"No!" the girl barked. "Get away from it."

Liz gave a hopeless glance at the receiver and then did as she was told.

"Come with me."

"Now? In the rain."

The girl nodded.

"Let me get a coat."

"There's one by the door."

"It's not warm enough."

The girl hesitated, as if she was going to say that the warmth of her mother's coat was irrelevant, considering what was about to happen. But then she nodded. "But don't try to use the phone. I'll be watching."

Stepping into the doorway of the sewing room, Liz picked up the blue jacket she'd just been working on. She slowly put it on, her eyes riveted to the doily and the hump of the pistol beneath it. She glanced back into the living room. Her daughter was staring at a framed snapshot of herself at eleven or twelve standing next to her father and mother.

Quickly she reached down and picked up the gun. She could turn fast, point it at her daughter. Scream to her to throw away her own gun.

Mother, I can feel you near me, all through the night . . .

Father, I know you can hear me, all through the night . . .

But what if Beth Anne *didn't* give up the gun?

What if she raised it, intending to shoot?

What would Liz do then?

To save her own life could she kill her daughter?

Sleep, my child . . .

Beth Anne was still turned away, examining the picture. Liz would be able to do it—turn, one fast shot. She felt the pistol, its weight tugging at her throbbing arm.

But then she sighed.

The answer was no. A deafening no. She'd never hurt her daughter. Whatever was going to happen next, outside in the rain, she could never hurt the girl.

Replacing the gun, Liz joined Beth Anne.

"Let's go," her daughter said and, shoving her own pistol into the waistband of her jeans, she led the woman outside, gripping her mother roughly by the arm. This was, Liz realized, the first physical contact in at least four years.

They stopped on the porch and Liz spun around to face her daughter. "If you do this, you'll regret it for the rest of your life."

"No," the girl said. "I'd regret *not* doing it."

Liz felt a spatter of rain join the tears on her cheeks. She glanced at her daughter. The young woman's face was wet and red too, but this was, her mother knew, solely from the rain; her eyes were completely tearless. In a whisper she asked, "What've I ever done to make you hate me?"

This question went unanswered as the first of the squad cars pulled into the yard, red and blue and white lights igniting the fat raindrops around them like sparks at a Fourth of July celebration. A man in his thirties, wearing a dark wind-breaker and a badge around his neck, climbed out of the first car and walked toward the house, two uniformed state troopers behind him. He nodded to Beth Anne. "I'm Dan Fleath, Oregon State Police."

The young woman shook his hand. "Detective Beth Anne Polemus, Seattle PD."

"Welcome to Portland," he said.

She gave an ironic shrug, took the handcuffs he held and cuffed her mother's hands securely.

Numb from the cold rain—and from the emotional fusion of the meeting—Beth Anne listened as Heath recited to the older woman, "Elizabeth Polemus, you're under arrest for murder, attempted murder, assault, armed robbery and dealing in stolen goods." He read her her rights and explained that she'd be arraigned in Oregon on local charges but was subject to an extradition order back to Michigan on a number of outstanding warrants there, including capital murder.

Beth Anne gestured to the young OSP officer who'd met her at the airport. She hadn't had time to do the paperwork that'd allow her to bring her own service weapon into another state so the trooper had loaned her one of theirs. She returned it to him now and turned back to watch a trooper search her mother.

"Honey," her mother began, the voice miserable, pleading.

Beth Anne ignored her and Heath nodded to the young uniformed trooper, who led the woman toward a squad car. But Beth Anne stopped him and called, "Hold on. Frisk her better."

The uniformed trooper blinked, looking over the slim, slight captive, who seemed as unthreatening as a child. But, with a nod from Heath, he motioned over a policewoman, who expertly patted her down. The officer frowned when she came to the small of Liz's back. The mother gave a piercing glance to her daughter as the officer pulled up the woman's navy-blue jacket, revealing a small pocket sewn into the inside back of the garment. Inside was a small switchblade knife and a universal handcuff key.

"Jesus," whispered the officer. He nodded to the policewoman, who searched her again. No other surprises were found.

Beth Anne said, "That was a trick I remember from the old days. She'd sew secret pockets into her clothes. For shoplifting and hiding weapons." A cold laugh from the young woman. "Sewing and robbery. Those're her talents." The smile faded. "Killing too, of course."

"How could you do this to your mother?" Liz snapped viciously. "You Judas."

Beth Anne watched, detached, as the woman was led to a squad car.

Heath and Beth Anne stepped into the living room of the house. As the policewoman again surveyed the hundreds of thousands of dollars of stolen property filling the bungalow, Heath said, "Thanks, Detective. I know this was hard for you. But we were desperate to collar her without anybody else getting hurt."

Capturing Liz Polemus could indeed have turned into a bloodbath. It had happened before. Several years ago, when her mother and her lover, Brad Selbit, had tried to knock over a jewelry store in Ann Arbor, Liz had been surprised by the security guard. He'd shot her in the arm. But that hadn't stopped her from grabbing her pistol with her other hand and killing him and a customer and then later shooting one of the responding police officers. She'd managed to escape. She'd left Michigan for Portland, where she and Brad had started up her operation again, sticking with her forte—knocking over jewelry stores and boutiques selling designer clothes, which she'd use her skills as a seamstress to alter and then would sell to fences in other states.

An informant had told the Oregon State Police that Liz Polemus was the one behind the string of recent robberies in the Northwest and was living under a fake name in a bungalow here. The OSP detectives on the case had learned that her daughter was a detective with the Seattle police department and had helicoptered Beth Anne to Portland airport. She'd driven here alone to get her mother to surrender peacefully.

"She was on two states' ten-most-wanted lists. And I heard she was making a name for herself in California too. Imagine that—your own mother." Heath's voice faded, thinking this might be indelicate.

But Beth Anne didn't care. She mused, "That was my childhood—armed robbery, burglary, money laundering . . . My father owned a warehouse where they fenced the stuff. That was their front—they'd inherited it from his father. Who was in the business too, by the way."

"Your *grandfather?*"

She nodded. "That warehouse . . . I can still see it so clear. Smell it. Feel the cold. And I was only there once. When I was about eight, I guess. It was full of perped merch. My father left me in the office alone for a few minutes and I peeked out the door and saw him and one of his buddies beating the hell out of this guy. Nearly killed him."

"Doesn't sound like they tried to keep anything very secret from you."

"Secret? Hell, they did everything they could to get me *into* the business. My father had these special games, he called them. Oh, I was supposed to go over to friends' houses and scope out if they had valuables and where they were. Or check out TVs and VCRs at school and let him know where they kept them and what kind of locks were on the doors."

Heath shook his head in astonishment. Then he asked, "But you never had any run-ins with the law?"

She laughed. "Actually, yeah—I got busted once for shoplifting."

Heath nodded. "I copped a pack of cigarettes when I was fourteen. I can still feel my daddy's belt on my butt for that one."

"No, no," Beth Anne said. "I got busted *returning* some crap my mother stole."

"You what?"

"She took me to the store as cover. You know, a mother and daughter wouldn't be as suspicious as a woman by herself. I saw her pocket some watches and a necklace. When we got home I put the merch in a bag and took it back to the store. The guard saw me looking guilty, I guess, and he nailed me before I could replace anything. I took the rap. I mean, I wasn't going to drop a dime on my parents, was I? . . . My mother was so mad . . . They honestly couldn't figure out why I didn't want to follow in their footsteps."

"You need some time with Dr. Phil or somebody."

"Been there. Still am."

She nodded as memories came back to her. "From, like, twelve or thirteen on, I tried to stay as far away from home as I could. I did every after-school activity I could. Volunteered at a hospital on weekends. My friends really helped me out. They were the best . . . I probably picked them because they were one-eighty from my parents' criminal crowd. I'd hang with the National Merit scholars, the debate team, Latin club. Anybody who was decent and normal. I wasn't a great student but I spent so much time at the library or studying at friends' houses I got a full scholarship and put myself through college."

"Where'd you go?"

"Ann Arbor. Criminal justice major. I took the CS exam and landed a spot on Detroit PD. Worked there for a while. Narcotics mostly. Then moved out here and joined the force in Seattle."

"And you've got your gold shield. You made detective

fast." Heath looked over the house. "She lived here by herself? Where's your father?"

"Dead," Beth Anne said matter-of-factly. "She killed him."

"What?"

"Wait'll you read the extradition order from Michigan.
Nobody knew it at the time, of course. The original coroner's
report was an accident. But a few months ago this guy in
prison in Michigan confessed that he'd helped her. Mother
found out my father was skimming money from their operation and sharing it with some girlfriend. She hired this guy
to kill him and make it look like an accidental drowning."

"I'm sorry, Detective."

Beth Anne shrugged. "I always wondered if I could forgive
them. I remember once, I was still working Narc in Detroit. I'd
just run a big bust out on Six Mile. Confiscated a bunch of
smack. I was on my way to log the stuff into Evidence back at
the station and I saw I was driving past the cemetery where
my father was buried. I'd never been there. I pulled in and
walked up to the grave and tried to forgive him. But I
couldn't. I realized then that I never could—not him or my
mother. That's when I decided I had to leave Michigan."

"Your mother ever remarry?"

"She took up with Selbit a few years ago but she never
married him. You collared him yet?"

"No. He's around here somewhere but he's gone to
ground."

Beth Anne gave a nod toward the phone. "Mother tried
to grab the phone when I came in tonight. She might've
been trying to get a message to him. I'd check out the
phone records. That might lead you to him."

"Good idea, Detective. I'll get a warrant tonight."

Beth Anne stared through the rain, toward where the squad car bearing her mother had vanished some minutes ago. "The weird part was that she believed she was doing the right thing for me, trying to get me into the business. Being a crook was her nature; she thought it was my nature too. She and Dad were born bad. They couldn't figure out why I was born good and wouldn't change."

"You have a family?" Heath asked.

"My husband's a sergeant in Juvenile." Then Beth Anne smiled. "And we're expecting. Our first."

"Hey, very cool."

"I'm on the job until June. Then I'm taking an LOA for a couple of years to be a mom." She felt an urge to add, "Because children come first before anything." But, under the circumstances, she didn't think she needed to elaborate.

"Crime Scene's going to seal the place," Heath said. "But if you want to take a look around, that'd be okay. Maybe there's some pictures or something you want. Nobody'd care if you took some personal effects."

Beth Anne tapped her head. "I got more mementos up here than I need."

"Got it."

She zipped up her wind-breaker, pulled the hood up. Another hollow laugh.

Heath lifted an eyebrow.

"You know my earliest memory?" she asked.

"What's that?"

"In the kitchen of my parents' first house outside of Detroit. I was sitting at the table. I must've been three. My mother was singing to me."

"Singing? Just like a real mother."

Beth Anne mused, "I don't know what song it was. I just remember her singing to keep me distracted. So I wouldn't play with what she was working on at the table."

"What was she doing, sewing?" Heath nodded toward the room containing a sewing machine and racks of stolen dresses.

"Nope," the woman answered. "She was reloading ammunition."

"You serious?"

A nod. "I figured out when I was older what she was doing. My folks didn't have much money then and they'd buy empty brass cartridges at gun shows and reload them. All I remember is the bullets were shiny and I wanted to play with them. She said if I didn't touch them she'd sing to me."

This story brought the conversation to a halt. The two officers listened to the rain falling on the roof.

Born bad . . .

"All right," Beth Anne finally said, "I'm going home."

Heath walked her outside and they said their good-byes. Beth Anne started the rental car and drove up the muddy, winding road toward the state highway.

Suddenly, from somewhere in the folds of her memory, a melody came into her head. She hummed a few bars out loud but couldn't place the tune. It left her vaguely unsettled. So Beth Anne flicked the radio on and found Jammin' 95.5, filling your night with solid-gold hits, party on, Portland . . . She turned the volume up high and, thumping the steering wheel in time to the music, headed north toward the airport.

The Deadly Bride

Sharan Newman

Sharan Newman's Guinevere trilogy—*Guinevere, The Chessboard Queen,* and *Guinevere Evermore*—found seed from a graduate school research project and Newman's interest in Arthurian legend. Besides her fiction which includes short stories and *The Real History Behind the Da Vinci Code.* Newman is the author of a ten-book award-winning series featuring a twelfth-century inquisitive heroine, Catherine LeVendeur, *Death Comes as Epiphany* was the winner of the Macavity Best First Novel award in 1994, and *Cursed in Blood* was honored with the first Herodotus Award in 1999.

July 1140

The summer sun was setting on Paris. The air was full of the sound of mothers calling children home, of bells summoning monks to prayer and of beer casks being tapped for workers thirsty from a day in the heat.

Solomon ben Jacob stretched his legs out into the narrow street, and balanced his drinking bowl on the wooden bench next to him. A stray dog sniffed at the contents and Solomon growled at it, but without energy. The evening was too hot to begrudge a fellow creature a swallow of beer.

The benches were becoming crowded but no one took the seat next to him. Jews were tolerated in Paris, but few people wanted to associate with them. Solomon closed his eyes and leaned back against the tavern wall, grateful to be left alone.

A moment later he was alarmed to feel the shadow of someone standing above him. He sat up, alert at once. The slanting rays of the sun outlined a slightly-built man with a heavy beard. He exhaled in relief. It was his old friend, Tobias.

"Solomon! Rejoice with me!" Tobias sat down with a thump that rocked the bench. "I'm getting married!"

"*Mazel tov!*" Solomon lifted his bowl and drank. "Better you than me. Who is she? Did your mother find her for you?"

"No," Tobias said proudly. "I arranged the marriage myself."

Solomon blinked in surprise. "And your families don't mind? Amazing! Who is she? Do I know her?"

"Probably not," Tobias answered. "She lives in Rouen."

"I don't go there much," Solomon admitted. "You couldn't find a girl closer to home?"

Tobias's stricken look made Solomon wish he'd held his tongue. A poor man with a blind father and aging mother to care for had little chance for a suitable bride.

"Well, I wish you a long and happy life with her," he said quickly, signaling the pot boy for another bowl of beer. "Are you moving there or bringing her back here to Paris?"

Tobias wiggled uncomfortably on the bench.

Solomon put the bowl down. He turned to look at his friend.

"Tobias," he sighed. "I know what you're going to ask. I'm not going with you all the way to Rouen to pick up your bride."

"Why not?" Tobias bristled. "You're my best friend. Who else would I want to witness my wedding?"

"I have to be in Toulouse then," Solomon said, it being the first thing he could think of.

"No you don't," Tobias countered. "I already asked your uncle. And I didn't tell you when it would be."

He put his arm around Solomon's shoulder, "Please come with me. Meet my Sarah. Dance at the wedding feast. Who knows, you may find a wife of your own among her friends."

Solomon gave a snort. "My Aunt Johanna has already combed all of Normandy, France, and Champagne searching for a bride for me."

He closed his eyes. Sarah of Rouen, the name stirred something in his memory.

"*Adonai!* Tobias, you can't mean the daughter of Raguel the linen merchant?"

Tobias lifted his chin. "As a matter of fact, yes. She's beautiful, pious, intelligent, and kind. I'm fortunate that her parents have allowed the match."

Solomon was aghast. "Beautiful, pious, intelligent, and cursed, Tobias! Has no one told you about her? You'll not live out your wedding night."

Tobias pulled away from Solomon. "I thought you were more rational than that," he said. "How can you believe the slanders about her?"

"Slanders?" Solomon's voice rose. "Three times her father has married her off and three men have died before bedding her. That's not rumor; it's fact."

"Solomon, quiet!" Tobias looked nervously at the men drinking and talking around them.

He moved closer to Solomon and spoke in a tense whisper.

"I don't believe Sarah is cursed," he said. "And I don't believe she killed those men as some say."

"And what is your explanation?" Solomon asked with a cynical grimace. "Her husbands all expired from anticipation?"

"No," Tobias answered seriously. "I believe that the Lord, blessed be he, laid his hand upon them so that she might be saved for me."

Solomon's jaw dropped.

"You see yourself as a divinely appointed husband?" He snorted his opinion of that.

Tobias smiled. "How else could I have become betrothed to her? Since my father lost his sight, my mother and I have been hard pressed to survive and care for him. I am a man without money or prospects. Sarah's father is rich. She is his only child. If not for their belief in this curse, many men would be begging for her hand."

"You're mad," Solomon observed.

Tobias hung his head. "This is my only chance. I must care for my parents in their last years. Sarah's father will support them as well as us," he said. "I'm honored that he has even considered my request. Why aren't you willing to celebrate with me?"

The idea of being happy for Tobias's imminent death was so ridiculous that Solomon refused to continue the discussion. He finished his beer and left his friend to his dreams of matrimony.

But the young man wasn't so quickly discouraged. The next morning he appeared at the door of the house where Solomon lived with his Aunt Johanna and Uncle Eleazar.

"May the Lord bless all here," he greeted them.

"Thank you, Tobias," Eleazar smiled. "May He keep you and your parents in good health. Come, sit down."

Johanna made a place for him and handed him a bowl to wash his hands from before passing him the platter of soft cheese covered in fruit.

"Solomon told us your news," she said. "Your parents are happy with this match?"

Tobias nodded, his mouth full. "Sarah's mother is a cousin on my father's side. I know she has been unfortunate in her marriages, but it's nothing more. Why should she be cursed?"

"Being good and pious can't protect one from the evil in the world," Johanna said. "Look at your poor father. He didn't deserve blindness. It is not our place to ask why the Holy One, blessed be He, allows such things to happen."

"Exactly," Tobias answered. "Why should we assume a curse?"

He turned to Solomon. "Whatever you think of the marriage, won't you come with me for the sake of friendship?"

Eleazar coughed. "I do have a small task that you might do for me in Rouen, if you wouldn't mind."

Solomon gave him a sour look. He sighed and threw up his hands.

"Very well," he said. "I suppose I should go to the shops and look for a bridal gift. I only hope you survive to enjoy it."

Tobias left to prepare. Solomon went down to sit at the riverbank, chewing on a blade of grass. His thoughts were sour. Everything he had heard seemed to support the belief that some otherworldly hand had struck down Sarah's first three husbands. If that were so then there was no way to keep Tobias from death. Solomon knew that the scholars would say it was the height of pride to assume that man can understand Divine judgments. But he had lived too long among the questioning students of Paris, both Jewish and Christian. They accepted a supernatural reason only when all the natural ones had been eliminated.

Had anyone bothered to seek a human hand in all this?

Solomon gave a deep sigh. It appeared that he had been divinely pointed to find out.

In the study hall of the synagogue in the town of Rouen, there was equal consternation.

"Raguel has bethrothed Sarah yet again?" Peretz nearly blotted the scroll he was copying. "What man would be so rash?"

"I don't know," his fellow student, Shemariah, answered. "Don't tip over the inkpot. Master Samuel is unhappy enough with your work as it is."

Peretz set the pot to one side and carefully covered the scroll to dry.

"Now, tell me," he demanded. "Who would marry Sarah

after she was thrice widowed? More importantly, will there be another wedding feast?"

Shemariah laughed. "Always ready to fill your belly!"

"Raguel has good wine and sets a fine table," Peretz answered, laughing too. "Why shouldn't I enjoy it, as long as I'm not the groom?"

"Shh!" Shemariah cautioned.

Another man had just entered the house of study. He was in his late thirties and his dark hair was deciding whether to turn gray or just finish falling out. The beard was decidedly gray and these things together made him seem a generation older than his years.

"Samuel!" Peretz greeted him. "Is it true that your cousin Sarah will again be a bride?"

"So my uncle tells me," Samuel shook his head. "How he can keep doing this to the poor girl, I don't know. It's clear that the Holy One, blessed be He, does not intend for Sarah to marry."

"I've heard it said that a demon comes into the chamber and strangles her husbands as soon as they approach the bed," Peretz commented.

"That's nonsense!" Samuel rounded on him. "My family does not harbor demons."

"Of course not," Peretz apologized quickly, seeing his chance for an invitation slipping away. "It was only idle gossip, I'm sure. She must have been cursed by someone with a grudge against her father. When will the wedding be?"

"As soon as the groom arrives from Paris," Samuel told them. "If reason doesn't prevail. When I've finished here, I'm going to go see if I can convince Uncle Raguel not to put Sarah through this again."

"What does she think about it?" Shemariah asked quietly.

Peretz glanced at him. He had forgotten that Shemariah had been one of Sarah's earliest suitors. Raguel had rejected him as not being of good enough family. Did he still have hopes for her?

Samuel shrugged. "I haven't seen her. But she doesn't have much choice, after all. It's not as if she could be sent off to a convent like the Christians do with their unwanted women."

Shemariah tensed at this depiction of Sarah, but said nothing. Soon after, both he and Samuel left. Peretz rolled up the now dry scroll. His face was unusually serious. Even after the mysterious deaths of Sarah's husbands, Shemariah had renewed his offer for her. Peretz saw the anguish in his eyes and wondered just what lengths a man would go to have the woman he loved.

Tobias and Solomon had taken the River Seine all the way to Rouen. Despite his worry over the fate of his friend, Solomon had enjoyed the voyage, doing nothing but lie out of the way on the barge as it took wine casks down to the coast to put on a ship for England. They reached the town late on a Friday afternoon. Tobias had fretted the last few bends of the river, fearing that they wouldn't arrive before the start of Shabbat. But there had been time to unload their baggage and take it to the home of Bonnevie, the wealthiest Jew in town, who had agreed to put them up until the wedding.

Solomon was happy to have the Sabbath meal with them but not so enthusiastic about accompanying Tobias and Bonnevie to the synagogue for prayers first. Fortunately, there were enough men in the community that he had only to try to stay awake and keep his stomach from rumbling until the end.

He took the time to observe the other men of the minyin. The two students, Peretz and Shemariah, prayed with closed eyes, apparently interested in nothing but their devotions. The cousin of Raguel, Samuel, seemed distracted. Well, Solomon thought, not everyone could shed his worries upon entering the house of prayer. The bride's father, Raguel, also had difficulty concentrating. His eyes darted around the room as if expecting something to jump out of the corners. Bonnevie read the portion in tones as rich as his purse. He seemed to have no thoughts other than impressing the Lord with his piety. The other men were much like those of Paris. Solomon had a hard time imagining that any of them were concealing murder in his heart.

That evening, Bonnevie took Solomon aside.

"Tobias is a good man," he stated.

"Yes," Solomon said. "Devoted to his parents."

"An only son," Bonnevie said sadly. "How can they send him to this?"

"I don't know," Solomon answered. "Perhaps they don't believe he is in danger. This curse seems to be assumed by everyone, but why? How exactly did the other men die?"

Bonnevie's usually genial expression changed. "They simply stopped breathing," he said, "At least, that's all we can tell. The first time the man was a great deal older than Sarah." He gave an embarrassed grin. "We all assumed that the prospect of a young bride was too much for him. The second man was about your age. A scholar from a good family. He collapsed on the way to the bridal chamber. His limbs seemed to freeze. He died before morning."

"After that, I'm surprised there was a third," Solomon commented.

Bonnevie shrugged. "Raguel is very rich and his daughter very beautiful. More than that. Sarah is kind and pious. She doesn't deserve to endure such horror."

He shook his head and sighed, then continued. "The third marriage was about three years ago. A man from London. I don't know much about him. He seemed fine, although he drank more at the wedding supper than a bridegroom should. That was the worst. He and Sarah were alone. She says that he started to reach for her, then stopped as if struck. She screamed. He was dead before she could bring help. His expression was of a man in a nightmare, twisted in shock. That was when the rumors began."

"Well, if she isn't murdering them herself, I don't see how anyone else could be," Solomon concluded. "Curse or human hands, Tobias shouldn't be allowed to marry her until we know how it happened."

Bonnevie agreed. "Excellent!" he smiled. "And how do you propose we do that?"

Solomon had no idea. "I'll sleep on the matter," he told his host. "Perhaps the Holy One will send me the answer in a dream."

The object of all this concern was the one most upset about the prospect of marriage, Sarah, daughter of Raguel and Edna, still a virgin and likely to remain one, was trying to think of a way out. "Mother," she said, "I am not going to be a widow again. How can you continue to try to marry me off? It's clear that the Lord doesn't wish me to be any man's wife."

The two women were sitting in the enclosed garden behind their home. Sarah's mother took great pride in the arrangement of the flower beds and the fact that she had managed to get a pomegranate to survive in Normandy. But neither Sarah nor Edna was taking any joy in the fragrant roses or the struggling little tree.

Edna leaned over and cupped Sarah's face in her hands.

"My exquisite child," she smiled sadly. "We cannot know the desires of the Holy One. It may be, as Tobias believes, that He was guarding you for him alone. In that case, everything will be fine."

Sarah pulled away. "And I am simply to have faith that I won't have to watch Tobias die, too? Mother, listen to your words! If Father weren't so respected in the community, we'd have been driven out by now. I am Sarah the thrice-cursed and that's only what they say when I'm there to overhear. I'm not going to risk Tobias's life on a foolish hope."

She stood and turned her back to her mother. Edna sighed. Everything Sarah said was true. Perhaps in her eagerness to see her daughter married she was going against the Divine plan. How was one to know?

Sarah turned around.

"Mother, have you ever asked yourself why this is happening?" she demanded. "Who could hate me this much? Who could care so little about the lives of three men?"

"I'm not a fool, daughter!" Edna snapped back. "Your father and I have searched our lives for anyone we might have wronged. We would gladly make amends if this evil could be removed from you. But we can think of nothing. It's as if a demon has been loosed upon us."

Sarah knelt next to Edna and wrapped her arms about her.

"Mother, we must not put Tobias in the way of this demon," her voice shook.

Edna tilted Sarah's face up. What she saw made her heart shudder.

"Oh, my dearest!" she cried. "Don't tell me that you have fallen in love with this man? You mustn't let anyone know. If someone has laid a curse upon you, this will only make them more determined to destroy us."

Sarah burst into sobs. "I know. I know! Mother, please, you must stop my wedding!"

Edna stroked her hair. "It's too late, my darling. The *ketuba* has been signed. We can't cancel it now."

Three days in Rouen had convinced Solomon that Raguel was widely envied for his wealth and despised for his flaunting of it. More than one person had confided that Sarah was too much prized by her parents. "She's their idol," one woman sneered. "The way they bedeck her, you'd think she was Queen Esther, herself."

Only Bonnevie had nothing bad to say of him. "Raguel is an honest man, for all he drives a hard bargain."

"Is there anyone who may have been ruined by one of these bargains?" Solomon persisted.

"No one I know of," Bonnevie answered. "Even so, what point would there be in killing three men? Why not just kill Raguel, if you have a grudge against him? And there's still the problem of how it was done. Until you can explain that, people will prefer to believe in a curse."

Solomon had no answer. He decided to take his concerns directly to Tobias' prospective in-laws.

• • •

Raguel greeted him with quiet cheer.

"You are Tobias's friend," he said. "We are delighted that you could come. I only wish his parents had been well enough to make the journey."

"Yes, so do I," Solomon answered. He tried to think of a way to introduce the subject of murder without committing a social blunder. "They are happy to welcome Sarah into their family and hope she and Tobias will soon return to Paris."

"Papa, who is our guest?"

Solomon turned to look. Sarah stood in the doorway to the garden. Her arms were full of flowers. She smiled.

"Ah," Solomon inhaled sharply. Now he understood. Sarah was more than beautiful. She was radiant. Even without a dowry, she would be a prize for any man. It was also clear why people preferred to blame the deaths on a curse. No one could see her gentle, sad face and believe her a murderer.

Raguel introduced Solomon.

"Have you come to tell us that Tobias wishes to be released?" she asked. "If so, I shall gladly agree, for his sake."

This took Solomon aback.

"He doesn't know I'm here," he explained. "I only came to . . . to . . . I'm sorry."

He bowed to take his leave. Sarah held up a hand to stop him.

"I understand," she said. "You're his friend. It's your duty to try to save him from this fate."

"I see now why he rushes to embrace it," Solomon took her outstretched hand. "Do you think you are cursed?"

"Oh, yes," Sarah answered. "What other answer is there?"

She looked up at him. He had never seen such an expression of despair. His heart sank. If Sarah and her family didn't know why this was happening, there seemed to be no way to find out.

Now he had to face Tobias and admit he had failed.

Tobias was stubborn in his refusal to break his betrothal.

"Tobias, they are offering to release you from the marriage contract," Solomon told his friend. "You will lose no honor. Do it. Tear up the *ketuba* and let's go home."

Tobias drew himself up proudly. "I would never do that!" he stated. "What kind of a man would I be if I abandoned Sarah?"

"A live one?" Solomon was losing patience. "I'll grant you she's a great marriage prize. After Bonnevie, Raguel is the richest man in town. But how many times must I remind you that you won't enjoy it if you're dead?"

They were standing near the wharf, watching people and goods being unloaded. There was a cool breeze blowing from the water. It brought a smell of fish and rotting plants. It reminded Solomon that he could be sitting on a log next to the Seine in Paris swilling wine with his friends, instead of in Rouen trying to knock sense into Tobias.

Tobias had answered him but Solomon's mind was far upriver.

"What?" he asked.

"I said that the men from the yeshiva, Peretz and Shemariah, are giving a dinner for me tonight, since I have no family here," Tobias repeated. "Will you come with me?"

"If I must," Solomon replied, still staring at the river. Suddenly, he had a thought. "Tobias," he asked. "Did all the other bridegrooms have a dinner the night before the wedding?"

Tobias lifted his shoulders. "I don't know. It's traditional. Why?" "Nothing," Solomon answered, "just promise that you won't start without me."

"That's better!" Tobias grinned. "Just don't make me wait."

Solomon walked back to the home of Raguel and Edna. He needed to get more information.

Raguel was annoyed by Solomon's question.

"Of course we considered poison," he said. "We're not credulous peasants. But the men didn't become ill. They didn't vomit or clutch their stomachs. They simply stopped breathing as if frozen. And, even if it were poison, who could have given it to those men?" Raguel continued. "How could it have been done?"

"At the dinner the night before the wedding or at the wedding supper," Solomon explained.

Edna disagreed. "That would be impossible. The food at the dinner is served from common platters and shared. On the wedding night, the bride and groom sip from the same wine cup and share a trencher. You aren't suggesting anything that hasn't been considered."

"Oh," Solomon shook his head. He should have known it wasn't that simple. "Very well. I know you say you have wronged no one intentionally. But there is no one without enemies."

Raguel admitted this. "Of course there are those who

say I took trade from them but they were not asked to
Sarah's weddings. Without sorcery, they could not have
harmed anyone there. And how can we prove such a
thing?"

Once again defeated, Solomon went back to Bonnevie's
home to prepare for the dinner. He wondered how soon
he'd be preparing for a funeral.

Under the circumstances, the feast for the bridegroom
didn't have the ribald tone of others that Solomon had
attended. But the wine pitcher went around with greater
frequency and the water pitcher rarely followed it. As the
evening progressed, the tension began to release itself in
bursts of maudlin poetry and song. Solomon realized that
the men, unable to celebrate the wedding, had switched to
Spanish songs of love lost, of Israel lost. Tobias was
singing and weeping along with them. A cheerful gathering, indeed.

Solomon had let the pitcher pass him by, a sacrifice that
he hoped Tobias would appreciate. He watched the others
with the clarity and repugnance of the sober. The students,
Peretz and Shamariah, were gulping down tears. Bonnevie
had fallen asleep, his head on his arms like a child at a
seder. Raguel and his nephew, Samuel, were sitting on
either side of Tobias, all three staring into a wine cup as if
at an oracle.

Shamariah pushed himself off his stool and staggered
over to Tobias.

"Yrrr a good man," he said with a hiccough. "Go home
and frrrget Sarrrah. The Holy One . . ."

"Blessed be He," Bonnevie murmured from the tabletop.

"Blessssssed be He," Shamariah agreed. "He doesn't want our Sarrrah to wed. It's cleeerrrr. Go home, Tobias."

He slowly folded to the ground at Tobias's feet.

Samuel stared at the crumpled form, shaking his head.

"Never mind him, Tobias," he said, "Shamariah just wants her for himself. It would never happen."

Raguel was now weeping on Samuel's shoulder.

"My sweet Sarah," he burbled. "My only child. The light of my house. And Tobias, the only son of his good parents. What a joy it would be to share a grandson with Tobit! How can we keep tragedy from them?"

"There, there, Uncle," Samuel patted him. "Whatever comes, I shall see that Sarah is taken care of."

"And I," came Shamariah's voice from the floor.

Raguel sniffed back tears. "Thank you, my friends."

Solomon stared at them. Ordinarily, he would have been just as drunk, seeing the world through a soft haze. Now suddenly, everything came into focus. They had been asking the wrong questions all along. There was really only one reason for each one of Sarah's husbands to die before the marriage could be consummated. And, when he knew why, he knew who. It was the how that still eluded him.

One thing he was certain of, Tobias was still in great danger.

The wedding day was cloudy with a cool breeze. In the house of Bonnevie, only Solomon was awake to eat the bread and fruit the servants had left for them. He paced the hall until his host finally appeared, bleary-eyed and disheveled.

"Bonnevie!" Solomon greeted him. "I need to ask you something at once."

Bonnevie gave him a poisonous glance. "Only if you lower your voice," he said.

Solomon apologized. "I only need to know something about Raguel's finances. What happens to his money if Sarah dies childless?"

"It would go to his wife, Edna, and then to the children of his brothers." Bonnevie winced. "You could have figured that out for yourself."

"Yes," Solomon said. "I just wanted to be sure. I need to go out for a while. Don't let anyone near Tobias until I return, please."

"Anything," Bonnevie waved him away. "Just remove your all too energetic self from my sight."

He sat down and rested his head in his hands as Solomon tiptoed out.

Solomon spent the day asking more questions as delicately as he could. It was one thing to think a man a murderer, another to prove it. His inquiries led him finally to a Christian apothecary, who remembered both the man and the remedy he had purchased.

"I warned him that only a small pinch is necessary," the apothecary explained. "In wine is best; it kills the flavor. The whole packet could kill but I'm sure the buyer was very careful. He's been back four times in the past six years or so. So the concoction must have given satisfaction."

"What is the herb that can harm?" Solomon asked.

"Ah, good old hemlock," the man smiled. "The plant grows everywhere. Sometimes people mistake it for parsley, but a bite or two and they know their mistake. A small dose makes one ill but no more. But it's only in combination with my secret ingredient that the desired effect occurs."

Solomon thanked him and hurried back to find Tobias. He wondered why the murderer hadn't made the poisonous compound himself. Then it occurred to him that if the deed had been discovered the murderer could blame the Christian. Although going back to him four times would be harder to explain.

Tobias was relieved to see him.

"It's almost time for the wedding," he exclaimed. "Hurry and change. I can't let Sarah think I'm reluctant."

"Yes, in a minute," Solomon answered. "Tobias, has anyone given you something to take, just in case you have trouble, um, with the consummation?"

"How did you guess?" Tobias laughed, holding up a small bag. "Can you imagine? I've done nothing but dream of this night for months. I've no intention of taking it, of course. I'll need no help from anyone but Sarah. Don't say anything, though. I don't want to hurt his feelings. It was a generous thought."

Solomon promised.

The wedding, though subdued, went smoothly. Sarah and Tobias sat together at the dinner afterward looking at each other in a way that gave Solomon a pang of jealousy. He prayed that he was right and that no harm would come to Tobias in the night.

The new couple were led to their chamber and told to bolt

the door on the inside. The windows were small and high in the wall. At least Solomon felt certain no one could enter.

The next morning, half the community was outside Raguel's house.

"Are they awake yet?" Shemariah asked when Edna came to the door. "Is Sarah all right?"

"Has the curse been broken?" Samuel was next to him.

Solomon worked his way through to stand just behind the two men.

"Shame on you all for wanting to awaken a newly married couple at dawn," Edna said, "The door is still shut and I've heard no sound this morning. But in this case, perhaps we should check. If we knock and hear Tobias's voice, will you all go home?"

Solomon grabbed Shemariah and Samuel and volunteered to go with her.

The three men approached the door.

"I feel very awkward doing this," Shemariah said.

"Sarah may need your support if the curse has struck again," Samuel reminded him.

Solomon raised his hand to knock. The door flew open. In the threshold stood Tobias and Sarah, both radiantly alive.

Samuel stepped back. "That can't be!" He pointed at Tobias. "It must have been you who killed the others! This proves it!"

Solomon caught Samuel's outstretched hand and twisted it behind his back.

"It proves nothing except that Tobias didn't feel the need of your potion to enjoy his wedding night," he announced to the people who were now crowding into the hall.

"What are you talking about?" Raguel demanded. "Samuel is Sarah's cousin."

"Exactly," Solomon answered. "And he has a wife and children, but not much money. It was only when I stopped seeing this as a crime of revenge or passion that I saw the obvious. Sarah is the only child. If she dies too soon, then Raguel might do anything with his wealth. But if she were convinced never to marry, then her inheritance would go to Samuel's family."

"That's ridiculous!" Samuel cried. "I would never have anything to do with demons. I didn't curse her."

"Demons, no," Solomon said. "There was never a curse, just a nice aphrodisiac for a nervous groom."

He produced the packet.

"Only I wasn't nervous," Tobias grinned. "Was I, Sarah?" Sarah blushed agreement and Tobias continued. "Samuel gave me the herbs. He told me to pour wine over them and drink the whole mess down. It was really clever. I wouldn't have guessed if Solomon hadn't explained it to me. If you can't put poison into a man's cup, get him to put it there himself."

"Lies! All of it!" Samuel screamed. "I only wanted to help. That Christian must have tainted it. They don't care if we die."

"What Christian?" Raguel asked. "You don't mean Silas down by the bridge? I think we should have a word with him. Solomon, you can release my nephew now. The community will decide if he is guilty and, if so, see to it that he is punished."

"Gladly." Solomon pushed Samuel into the arms of the crowd. "My only care was to see that Tobias didn't meet the same fate as the other bridegrooms."

Tobias grinned at him. "You will always be welcome in our home, my friend."

Sarah stepped forward. "I don't know how to thank you," she said. "I only wish you could be as happy as we are. I have a friend—"

Solomon held up both hands in horror. "Please! I wish you every happiness but I have had enough of weddings for now."

"Perhaps in Paris then." Sarah gave him a smile that made Solomon waver, just for a moment. That was enough to tell him it was time to go.

The next morning he boarded a barge working its way up the river and was soon on his way home, far from marriage arrangements and deadly brides.

Highest, Best Use

J. A. Jance

New York Times best-selling author J. A. Jance is best known for her novels which offer the adventures of Seattle police detective J. P. Beaumont (*Long Time Gone* was the seventeenth in the series) and Arizona sheriff Joanna Brady (the 2006 release of *Dead Wrong* is the twelfth in the series). Though initially steered away from writing fiction by her college professor, Jance eventually found her way into publishing and was honored with the American Mystery Award in 1991.

For years ours was a three-dog family with two elderly golden retrievers, Nikki and Tess, and an ugly but honest mutt named Boney, who was half German shepherd and half Irish wolfhound. When Nikki and Tess were finally called home to heaven at ages eleven and twelve, respectively, a grieving Mr. Bone (who makes cameo appearances in my two thrillers Hour of the Hunter *and* Kiss of the Bees*)* went into a great decline. Deciding he was lonely, we went in search of a companion for him. We intended to come home with one puppy, but of course, being softhearted ninnies, we arrived instead with two equally adorable—in our minds, anyway—red-dog golden retrievers.

It's six years ago now since those two tiny balls of fluff tumbled into our lives. In our view, they were virtually identical. For a while, the only way we could tell them apart was by the color of their collars—Aggie's was green and Daphne's, pink. Boney, however, had no difficulty at all in telling them apart. He looked at Daph and said to himself, "Hey, you're a little cutie." From then on, Daphne could do no wrong. She could pull Bone's ears and tail and all she would elicit from him was a long-suffering sigh. Aggie was a different story altogether. Boney took one look at her and said to himself, "You are the Devil's spawn!" From that moment on, it never changed. If Aggie came too close to Mr. Bone, she was greeted with a low-throated growl and a puppy-eye-level view of his two-inch long and very sharp fangs.

Four years ago, we lost Boney, too—after eleven short years. Like Maddy Watkins in the story, I'm greedy and think dogs should all live much longer. While Bone was around, he was definitely top dog, and he enforced an artificial pack hierarchy with Daphne in the middle and Aggie on the bottom. Once Boney was gone, the two girls had to settle the top-dog question to their own satisfaction. They did it by way of a bloody battle that sent them both to the vet. My daughter, who was dogsitting at the time of the fight, broke it up by throwing a full Brita water pitcher into the fray. She, understandably, refers to the Girls as "hooligans." My husband calls them "Angel Dogs."

I won't say which of those two names they answer to, but I will say that these wonderful little sixty-pound dogs have added immeasurably to our quality of life. I can only hope we do the same for them.

—J. A. JANCE

The first day of school. Maddy Watkins sighed at the very thought of it. After all those years of teaching kindergarten and loving it, school was starting without her. Again. It was six years now since she had stopped teaching for good. It surprised her to realize that the first day of school still had the power to leave her feeling blue. *Oh well,* she thought. *No use sitting around feeling sorry for myself.*

Finishing the last of her breakfast coffee, she set the dainty china cup down on its saucer. Instantly her red-dog golden retrievers, Daphne and Agatha, went on full alert, watching her intently, to see if Maddy's next move would have something to do with them—an after-breakfast treat, perhaps, or maybe, if they were lucky, a walk on the beach. Both dogs sat without moving while Maddy cleared and rinsed the breakfast dishes and put the milk carton back into the refrigerator.

"So what is it then, girls?" she asked. "A walk?"

After sprinting to the door, their toenails snapping and skidding on the hardwood floor, the two nearly identical dogs stood side by side with their tails wagging in unison while Maddy slipped a light sweater over her shoulders and gathered her walking stick and whistle.

"Now wait," she told them. Obligingly, the two dogs stepped aside while Maddy went first. Only when she said, "Okay," did they come gamboling and frolicking through the door, across the porch, and down through the yard where they stopped again, waiting expectantly, for Maddy to open the gate that allowed access onto the long stretch of private beach that Maddy Watkins shared with other homeowners whose property bordered Race Lagoon.

By the time Maddy made her way to the gate, the dogs were literally dancing back and forth with excitement. "All right, girls, all right," Maddy grumbled good-naturedly. "Hold your horses."

Once she opened the gate, the dogs raced headlong toward the beach and the water where there might be dead crabs or rotting starfish for rolling on and dead twigs suitable for chasing. Just watching the dogs run side by side, leaping over logs and sprinting through the knee-high grass, made Maddy feel better. Their happiness was so utterly uncomplicated and honest, and it was almost always catching. As they reached the water's edge, she gave a short blast on her whistle. Immediately Aggie and Daph whirled around and raced back, tongues lolling, faces smiling. "Okay," Maddy said as soon as they reached her, then she sent them galloping away once again, back toward the water.

Watching the joyful dogs running at breakneck speed, Maddy couldn't help but remember that snotty young woman at the animal shelter. It had been a year after Bud, Maddy's husband, had died of kidney failure, and six months after Maddy's eleven-year-old dog, Sarah, had died unexpectedly in her sleep. Maddy had gone to her local animal shelter thinking she'd come home with some nice puppy—one of those sad, abandoned creatures that the ads always describe as "free to good home."

"But you're seventy years old," the young woman had objected archly while scanning the information on Maddy's application. She made it sound as though Maddy were actually older than God. From the young woman's point of view, maybe that was true.

"So?" Maddy had demanded.

"But it says here you want a puppy."

"That's exactly what I want—a puppy that hasn't already been wrecked by someone else. A puppy I can train to do things the way I want them done."

"But wouldn't you rather have a nice sedate older dog? We have several of them here right now, ready for adoption."

Maddy didn't feel like explaining that she had done that once—taken in an older dog. Sarah had been at least six when someone had left her—sick, dirty, underfed, and barely able to walk—in a ditch alongside the road. That had meant that there were only five short years between Sarah's arrival in Maddy's home and the terrible hurt of losing her. Maddy Watkins was tired of loving and losing. She was greedy and wanted more time. "I said I want a puppy," she insisted.

"But puppies are so much hard work," the young woman said, speaking clearly and slowly as though Maddy were both deaf and developmentally disabled. "With house training and exercising. Puppies can be *very* demanding."

Maddy gave another short blast on the whistle. Again, Aggie and Daph tore back to her, running at breakneck speed. While Maddy took her own sweet time getting down to the pebbly stretch of beach, the girls would have run the entire distance six full times. So much for them not getting enough exercise!

"Young lady," an exasperated Maddy had responded. "I taught kindergarten for forty years, so I have some dim idea of what's involved in potty training. Kids or puppies—it's all pretty much the same."

"Still," the young woman had replied. "Our guidelines won't allow us to send animals to unsuitable homes—ones where we don't think they'll receive the proper kind of care."

"Care!" Maddy had exploded. "You're looking at my *age* and my cane and you think that gives you the right to judge whether or not I'm qualified to have a dog? I'll tell you what you can do then. You can take your animal shelter and go straight to hell, and don't expect any more donations of dog food from me, either!"

With that, Maddy had flounced out of the shelter, although flouncing was difficult to achieve with her cane as well as her newly remodeled hip. Within days she had gone from the shelter to a dog breeder where she had blown the better part of one month's worth of retirement income on two lovable full sisters from a litter of eleven fuzzy golden puppies. And then, because she had always loved murder mysteries, Maddy had named the two puppies after her two favorite authors, Agatha Christie and Daphne DuMaurier.

Maybe all those years of dealing with kindergarteners had shielded Maddy from what was going on outside the walls of her classroom and her home, but that confrontation at the shelter had been her first eyeball-to-eyeball encounter with age discrimination as it applied to Maddy Watkins. The unfortunate experience hadn't turned her into a raging Gray Panther on the spot, but it had certainly raised her consciousness. From then on, wherever she encountered it, she fought back as best she could.

Of course, her friends and her son had been as universally disapproving as the little twit at the pound. "Why on earth did you get two of them?" Tess McKnight had asked over their weekly bridge game. "Why not just one? Wouldn't it be easier for someone your age to take care of one dog instead of two?"

"Because two puppies will keep each other company," Maddy had returned. "And both of them will be good company for someone *my* age."

Rex, her middle-aged son the real estate developer, and his fashion plate wife, Gina, hadn't been any happier about the situation than Tess was. "You're getting up there, Mom," Rex had hinted darkly. "You shouldn't be out here all by yourself. It's dangerous. You never know who or what might come wandering by. There are all kinds of nuts running around loose these days, even out here in the country."

"I have your father's gun for protection," Maddy had told him. "I'll bet when it comes to target practice, I can still shoot circles around you."

Knowing she was right, Rex nodded in grudging agreement. Bud Watkins had been a lifelong member of the National Rifle Association. To Bud's dismay, his son had always been far more interested in shooting hoops than in shooting guns. Now Rex didn't bother arguing the point with his mother.

"Still," he continued, "one of these days, you're going to have to get out of this big old place and move into town. What will you do with two dogs then?"

Of course, the house wasn't big at all, not by modern

standards. And Maddy knew what Rex really wanted—a huge waterfront lot where he could build some big rambling monstrosity on spec, one he'd be able to sell for a fortune to some willing Microsoft millionaire from Seattle.

"I'll cross that bridge when I get to it," Maddy had told her son crossly. "Besides," she added, "Ag and Daph are both a lot better behaved than you were at their age." *Or even now,* she thought, but she didn't say it aloud. Rex hadn't liked her parting comment very much, but it had served him right. He had some nerve, trying to force his mother out of her own home long before she was ready.

Maddy reached the beach and took up her favorite position—a seat on a worn old driftwood log. Later in the lull, once the rains and high tides came, that narrow strip of beach would virtually disappear under water, but for now, she sat high and dry. Early morning mist and fog had burned off, giving way to bright September sunlight. Maddy sat with warmth washing over her body while the dogs played a madcap game of tag up and down the beach and in and out of the water. Tiring of that, Aggie pounced eagerly on a piece of driftwood and brought it over to Maddy where she deposited it just within reach in a none-too-subtle hint.

This, too, was part of the morning ritual. It was Maddy's job to hurl the chosen piece of wood into the water as far as possible so the dogs could swim out, grab it in their mouths, and bring it back. After all, that's what they were—retrievers—and Maddy loved to watch them do their chosen work. Of the two, Aggie was by far the better swimmer. She was usually the one who swam out far enough to grasp the stick, but as soon as she brought it within range, Daphne would latch on to one end. Then, together, the two dogs would bring the stick out of the water, looking for all the world like a team of very wee, miniature plow horses.

The last time Maddy threw the stick, however, she noticed that Aggie was the only one bringing it back for a change. Instead of lunging in to steal a piece of the prize, Daphne seemed to have lost interest in the game and was intent on something else. After a moment's hesitation, Aggie, too, abandoned the stick. When they came out of the water, what they dropped at Maddy Watkins's feet wasn't the stick at all. Instead, it was a purse—a woman's large leather purse, complete with a long shoulder strap trailing a skirt of seaweed.

"What in the world is this?" Maddy demanded, picking it up.

The dogs raced off, expecting Maddy to make another throw. When she didn't, they paused long enough to shake off excess water.

Maddy unclasped the purse and emptied it. Along with water and more seaweed, a clutch of items fell out onto the gravel. Included were several tubes of lipstick, three different pens, a compact, and a soggy passport. Maddy had to be quick in order to scoop up the booty before the dogs beat her to it. Once upright again, Maddy couldn't help but marvel. Dr. Mason had told her that after surgery, her hip would be as good as new. Two years later, it still wasn't quite perfect, but it was far better than it had been. Before the surgery, bending down to pick up anything would have caused her impossible agony. Now it was more of a serious twinge, unpleasant but not unbearable.

"Okay, girls," she said. "Enough. We'd better go back to the house and see if we can find the nice lady who lost her purse. It looks valuable. I'm sure she's going to want it back." Aggie and Daphne may have been disappointed at having their outing cut short, but they raced up the path with the same uncompromising enthusiasm they had shown coming down to the beach. Back at the house, Maddy toweled off the wet dogs and ordered them onto their rugs to dry. By then Maddy had completely forgotten about this being the first day of school. She poured herself another cup of coffee, then she covered the Formica kitchen table with towels and laid out the wet purse and its contents so she could examine them more closely.

Maddy was no expert in purses; she usually bought hers from the bargain table at Ross Dress For Less, but this one looked expensive. It was made of fine-grained leather with what looked like a brass medallion hanging over the clasp. With the help of her best reading glasses, Maddy was just able to make out the words written there in raised letters. "Brahmin, Fairehaven, Massachusetts."

She used dish towels to dry what she could. The powder in the compact had dissolved and disappeared entirely, but the tubes of lipstick were still pretty much intact. Years of being an Avon Lady on the side had made Maddy a whiz when it came to women's cosmetics. The labels may have all been illegible, but she recognized the distinctive cases. These were expensive items—ones that came from upscale counters at Nordstrom and The Bon or from exclusive spa-type places, not from your neighborhood Bartell Drugs.

Putting a towel inside the purse to blot up more of the water, she noticed a zippered compartment at the back.

Opening that, she pulled out a sodden mass of paper and gasped in surprise when she realized it was a thick wad of money. Bud had never been one for cleaning out his pockets, and Maddy hadn't been much better. Over the years, she had washed his wallet countless times. She had learned through trial and error the best remedy for repairing water damaged currency had been her trusty clothes dryer—turned to the DELICATE setting, of course. So that's what she did now. She put the fistful of money as well as the soggy passport into the dryer and turned it on. Then, feeling like a modern-day Miss Marple, she turned her attention to the contents of the small zippered wallet.

She hit paydirt almost immediately. The plastic cards inside the wallet were all impervious to water. Laurel Riggins was the woman's name. Age 43. Blond hair; blue eyes. Her address was listed as Double Bluff Road on the far end of Whidbey Island. The official Department of Licensing photo showed an attractive woman with what looked like a shy smile. "Now we're getting someplace, girls," Maddy said as she got up to go in search of the phone book.

Lying on their rugs, the damp dogs thumped their tails in grateful acknowledgment of that morsel of attention. Moments later, again with the help of her reading glasses— why did they insist on using such fine print in phone books these days?—Maddy had located the number for Hadley M. Riggins on Double Bluff Road. Her call to the Riggins residence was answered by the voice of a middle-aged male. "Is Laurel there, please?" she asked.

"Not right now," the man said. "This is her husband. Is there something I can do for you?"

"My name is Maddy Watkins. My dogs and I were down

playing on the beach this morning," Maddy explained. "I live on Race Inlet. And Ag and Daph—those are my dogs— seem to have found your wife's purse. I have it here now. It's water damaged, of course. I doubt she'll be able to use it again, but I thought she'd want the contents back at least."

"How very kind of you!" Hadley Riggins exclaimed. "Laurel lost it a number of weeks ago. We thought maybe it had fallen out of the car when she was taking the ferry. As I said, she's not here right now. She's in town at the moment, but she'll be thrilled to have it back. She's replaced her driver's license and so forth, but still, it'll be a relief to have it back. I could come over right now and pick it up—if that wouldn't be too inconvenient."

"Not at all," Maddy said. "That will be fine." She gave him directions to the house. It wasn't until after she got off the phone that she realized he had made no mention of the money. The better part of an hour passed before Hadley Riggins drove into the yard in a white Lincoln. Leaving the dogs inside the house, Maddy went out to meet him, carrying the purse and its contents stowed in a plastic grocery bag.

"I hope you don't mind," she said. "I put the money in the dryer. But it's all there."

"Money?" he asked with a frown.

"Yes," Maddy said. "The eight thousand dollars that was in your wife's purse. It was in a zippered compartment. I dried it in the dryer just like I used to do when my husband's wallet went though the wash."

Hadley Riggins nodded. "Oh, that's right," he said. "I forgot about that."

But Maddy Watkins had been a kindergarten teacher for too many years not to recognize a lie when she heard it.

Hadley Riggins had known nothing at all about the small fortune in cash that had been concealed in his wife's purse. And that seemed odd. If Maddy had ever had occasion to carry that much money around in her own purse, you can bet Bud Watkins would have known all about it. Losing eight thousand dollars didn't seem like the kind of thing that would simply slip a person's mind.

"I'm sure Laurel would want me to give you something for your trouble . . ." Hadley Riggins began as he reached belatedly for his wallet.

"You'll do nothing of the kind," Maddy declared, waving aside his tentative offer of compensation. "Honesty is its own reward," she added, hoping that he got her disapproving message all the same. It seemed to her that the least he could have done was act moderately grateful, even if he wasn't.

That was on Tuesday morning. For the next several days, Maddy busied herself with looking after the dogs, caring for her jungle of houseplants, reading her Bible, and letting the warm September days slip over her like a soft, warm blanket. She had said she wanted no reward, and she had meant it. Hadley Riggins's unconvincing offer of monetary compensation hadn't set well with her. Maddy certainly didn't want money, but she did expect to receive a gracious thank-you note for her trouble. Her parents had brought up Maddy with a strict sense of right and wrong. Her mother had insisted that one of the hallmarks of good breeding was the prompt sending of thank-you notes. A full week passed during which no thank-you note was forthcoming. By then, Maddy was growing suspicious.

First there was the presence of all that money—a sum Maddy Watkins was convinced Hadley Riggins had known nothing about. And then there was the passport. Maddy had a passport of her own. She and Bud had gotten passports when they had taken a Caribbean cruise years ago. Maddy's passport was still valid, but she certainly didn't carry it around with her or put it in her purse whenever she planned to take a ferry off the island. The only time the document had been in her purse was when she and Bud were actually on their cruise. The rest of the time she kept it in the strong box upstairs along with the rest of her important papers. Had Laurel Riggins been running away from something with all that money and her passport? Her husband, perhaps? That might explain why Hadley Riggins had known nothing about his wife's eight thousand dollars.

Finally, on Wednesday of the following week, Maddy stopped off at the sheriff's substation in Oak Harbor when she went into town to buy groceries. The young officer at the desk, Deputy Pete Harris, couldn't have been more polite. "How can I be of service?" he asked.

Maddy had been considering what to say and how best to say it all the way into town. "I think I'd like to report someone missing," she said.

Deputy Harris sat forward in his chair. "You *think* you want to report someone missing?" he asked. "Does that mean you don't know if they're really missing or you don't know whether or not you should report it?"

"I *believe* a woman named Laurel Riggins is missing," Maddy said. "But I don't know for sure." She went on to tell the whole story. In the beginning, Deputy Harris took copious notes on what appeared to be an official piece of paper, but by the time Maddy finished, he had put down his pen and was actually grinning at her.

"You're filing this report based entirely on the fact that a woman you've never met hasn't bothered to send a thank-you note?" He made no effort to hide his mirth. Maddy, on the other hand, was not amused.

"So you don't think thank-you notes are important?" she demanded.

Deputy Harris sobered. "Of course they're important ma'am," he said. "But not a matter of life and death. It just doesn't sound to me as though there's enough here to warrant an official investigation. We haven't had any other complaints about this. I think it's possible Laurel Riggins just didn't have the benefit of the kind of upbringing you did. I'm sure she's fine."

It was the snotty young woman at the animal shelter all over again, only Deputy Harris was more polite.

"I'm sure she is, too," Maddy said. She got up and headed for the door.

Deputy Harris beat her to it and held the door open for her. "If there's anything else we can do . . ."

"Don't bother," she replied curtly, jabbing the sidewalk with her cane as she walked past him. "You've done quite enough."

Aggie and Daphne were waiting in the back seat of Maddy's Buick. They wanted to kiss her hello when she came back to the car, but Maddy wasn't interested. She was too provoked. "Not a matter of life and death," she grumbled to the dogs. "Well, we'll just see about that."

She went home and put on her Avon Lady vest, the one with all her sales awards pinned to it. Then after walking and watering the dogs, she loaded them and her cosmetics sample case back in the car and headed for Double Bluff Road. She avoided the Riggins's place, but she called on houses up and down the road. At several places there was no one at home. But when someone did come to the door, there was little reluctance when they saw a white haired little old lady standing on the doorstep leaning heavily on a cane. Usually she was asked in and invited to sit down and even offered something to drink. At each house she explained that she was in the neighborhood because she had come to deliver an order to Laurel Riggins. Finding no one home, she hadn't wanted to waste the trip. In the process, she did her sales pitch and managed to pick up an order or two along the way, probably because people felt sorry for her.

It was at the fourth house that she hit the jackpot. "Why, Laurel's in New Zealand," Tammy Wyndham told her. "She left about a month ago—to visit her daughter. Chrissy's a missionary, you know, working for some outfit that's headquartered in Auckland."

Laurel didn't go to New Zealand without her passport, Maddy thought, but she kept her face perfectly composed. "Oh, that's right," she said. "Now I remember her saying something about a trip. It's just that what she wanted has been back-ordered so many times that I completely forgot about her being out of town."

Maddy smoothed things over as best she could, sold Tammy Wyndham some lipstick, some foundation, and a bottle of perfume, and then headed back to Oak Harbor. When she returned to the sheriff's substation, Deputy Harris was still on duty. "Still no thank-you note?" he asked with a small smirk.

Maddy did not smile. "Her neighbors say she went to New Zealand."

"No wonder then," he said. "The mail from there probably takes a little longer."

"If Laurel Riggins left the country, she didn't have her passport," Maddy responded sternly. "It was still in her purse when I dragged it out of the water. The passport was there along with eight thousand dollars. I know because I counted the money myself. Not only that, when I called, her husband told me she wasn't home. He said it in a way that sounded as though she'd just that minute walked out the door to go to the store and would be back in an hour or so."

Deputy Harris grimaced. "All right," he said. "I'll send an officer out, but I still think it's a wild goose chase."

Relieved, Maddy went home. A fierce squall was blowing in off the water. The huge evergreen trees at the back of the house were shedding pieces of limbs around them as she and the dogs ran into the house. With the wind blowing the rain sideways against the windows, Maddy couldn't help being grateful for the hours of careful craftsmanship she and Bud had put into the building of their snug little house. Safe and warm, she made her evening meal—a small bowl of chicken-noodle soup, a slice of buttered bread, half an apple, and a single glass of Chardonnay. Then, with the two dogs at her side, she settled in for a quiet evening, sitting in front of the fire in Bud's old easy chair, rereading Agatha Christie's fascinating autobiography, and listening to classical music on KING-FM.

The hours slipped by. The living room with its handsome river-rock fireplace was the part of the house that reminded her the most of Bud and made her feel close to him. He had laid the fireplace himself. He had crafted the sturdy andirons in his machine shop/foundry. He had also made the little pair of bronze baby shoes that sat on a plaque on the mantel. Rex, of course, had never been the least bit interested in working with his hands, and he had been ashamed of his father for doing so. That was one of the reasons Maddy kept his baby shoes right there in plain sight—to serve as a reminder to both of them.

All her life, Maddy Watkins had been a night owl. Her propensity to stay up late had been the bane of her existence all those years when she'd had to get up the next morning or even later that *same* morning and go to school to face a classroom of exuberant five-year-olds. Now though, staying up as late as she liked and rising only when she was ready were some of the most worthwhile benefits of being retired. Unaware of time passing, she glanced at the clock and was surprised to see that it was already after twelve. There were only two pages left in the chapter she was reading, so she decided to finish those before letting the dogs out and making her way into the bedroom.

It was halfway through the first of those two pages when Aggie raised her head. Ears pricked and hackles up, she let out a long, low growl. The ferocity in the growl was enough to make the hair on the back of Maddy's neck stand on end. At once Daphne, too, was on full alert. Before the dogs could bark, Maddy stifled them. "Enough!" she ordered. "Quiet." It was something she had taught Sarah when Bud had been so sick and needed his sleep. When the girls had come along, she had taught them the same thing. Now they didn't bark, but Aggie was still growling.

Maddy reached over and switched off her reading lamp. Then she turned off the music as well. The fire had burned down to mere coals that left a dim, ruddy glow in the room. Maddy was sitting and holding her breath when she heard the tinkle of breaking glass coming from the direction of her bedroom. The tinkle of glass was followed by a huge *whump*. At once she smelled smoke.

She reached for the phone, thinking to dial 9-1-1, but the line was dead. Another breaking window and another *whump* told her a second firebomb had been thrown, this one into the guest bedrooms upstairs. If whoever was doing this was systematically working his way around the house, the living room would be next, followed by the kitchen. There was no chance of getting to Bud's gun. That was in the bedroom in the nightstand drawer. Maddy's only hope lay in making it out the back door without being seen.

Grabbing her cane, she hustled to the back door. "Come," she said to the dogs. "Right here."

They came at once, astonished at their good fortune that she would consider going for a walk with them so late at night. Her slicker hung on a peg beside the door—another piece of Bud's thoughtful handiwork. She grabbed the slicker and shrugged her way into it as she crossed the porch. Outside, the night was black. Rain still fell in pelting sheets, but that was good. It would make her more difficult to see—and hear. More breaking glass. This time from the living room. Her attacker was still around the corner of the house, but he wouldn't be for long.

With her heart pounding in her throat, Maddy did what she hoped her attacker wouldn't expect. Instead of heading for her nearest neighbors and help, she and the dogs made

for the gate and for the windswept strip of beach beyond it.
Afraid her attacker might catch sight of movement as he
came around to the kitchen side of the house, Maddy hurried through the gate at the end of the yard and then
ducked behind the massive gate post. Sure enough, she had
barely hidden herself away when a shadowy figure
emerged from behind the corner of the house. While he
knelt with his back to her, Maddy turned and fled down
the path toward the beach.

In the dark and rain, the narrow path was slick and
steep. Once Maddy slipped and almost fell, imagining what
would happen if she dislodged that incredibly expensive
artificial hip. But somehow, scrambling desperately with
her cane, she managed to right herself and go on. She
knew that as soon as she finished descending the bluff,
she would be out of sight of someone standing next to the
house, but if he came to the edge of the yard or as far as
the gate, he'd still be able to spot her.

The dogs, pulled by the lure of the water, threatened to
dash on ahead. "Right here," Maddy commanded in an
urgent whisper. And then, when they did as they were told
and stayed at her heels, she added a grateful, "Good dogs.
Good right here."

It seemed to take forever to reach the narrow strip of
gravelly beach. Ducking down behind the driftwood log,
Maddy grabbed the dogs and held them close. Panting, they
lapped happily at her face with their long smooth tongues.
Shaken as she was, it was all Maddy could do to hang on to
them, but she didn't dare set them loose for fear her attacker
would see them moving and come after them.

Huddling in the cold and wet, Maddy struggled to come

to terms with what had happened. Someone had actually tried to kill her. But just when she had almost managed to convince herself that perhaps she was mistaken and had dreamed the whole thing—that it was nothing but a waking nightmare—a tongue of vivid orange flame shot high into the air. From her home. From the house Bud and she had built with their own hands and backbreaking labor and hard-earned cash.

No, it wasn't a dream at all. Someone *had* tried to kill her—someone who had thought a little old lady in her seventies would be safely in bed and sound asleep by midnight. And she knew without question who that someone was—Hadley Riggins. Maddy knew it in the same intuitive way Miss Marple must have known things. Hadley Riggins had murdered his wife, and he was willing to kill again in order to cover up that first crime.

Chilled, wet, and miserable, Maddy clutched the dogs to her and refused to move while her home on the bluff turned to ashes. Because of the metal roof, most of the flames were invisible from the place where Maddy huddled on the beach, but the dark clouds overhead turned orange in the reflected glow of the fierce flames. She didn't cry. There was no point. She and the dogs were alive and safe. That's what counted. Nothing else mattered.

After what seemed like an eternity and only when Maddy heard the sound of approaching sirens did she struggle to her feet and start back toward the house, toward the place where her house had once been but would be no more. She pushed open the gate at the top of the path and saw a small group of people huddled in the far corner of her backyard, far enough to be out of the way of the firemen swarming like so many ants around what was left of her house. Fanny Baxter, Maddy's next-door neighbor, was the first to spot Maddy and her dogs.

"Oh my God!" she exclaimed as though she'd seen a ghost. "Where were you? We all thought you were dead!"

"I was supposed to be," Maddy told her, and then let herself and the dogs be enveloped in the welcome comfort of her neighbors' outstretched arms.

By four o'clock the next morning, Maddy and the dogs were back at the substation. This time, however, instead of being left outside in the car, the dogs had been ushered into the office itself. A young officer who wasn't Deputy Harris had led Aggie and Daphne into a coffee room area where he promised them water and a few oatmeal cookies. Meanwhile, Lieutenant Caldwell, the supervisor who was taking Maddy's statement, listened carefully to everything Maddy said. And again, unlike Deputy Harris, Lieutenant Caldwell wrote it all down.

"So you didn't *see* anyone there in the yard?"

"No," Maddy replied. "Not at first. I heard glass breaking and the first fire start. It made a terrible noise—a huge *whoosh* kind of thing. I took the dogs and my cane and made for the beach. Later, I caught a glimpse of someone, a man I think, from the gate, but I was too far away to make out any details." She paused. "Have you sent anyone to check on Hadley Riggins?" she asked.

Lieutenant Caldwell nodded. "I did. No one seems to be home at the moment."

"He killed his wife," Maddy declared. "I'm sure of it. And now he's tried to kill me as well."

"You say his daughter is a missionary in New Zealand?"

Maddy nodded. "In Auckland. At least, that's what I was told."

"Do you have an address for her?"

"No," Maddy replied, "but you might check with the Riggins's neighbor, Tammy Wyndham. She lives on Double Bluff Road. She may be able to tell you."

"We've already done some checking," Lieutenant Caldwell said. "With the State Department. No one has been able to find any record that Laurel Riggins ever left the country."

"See there?" Maddy said. "I didn't think she had."

"We've put up roadblocks," Lieutenant Caldwell added. "Wherever Hadley Riggins is right now, I can assure you he won't be able to get off the island."

Behind Maddy, the outside door opened and closed. "Mother?"

Maddy turned to see Rex standing just inside the doorway. She hadn't called him, but someone must have— one of the neighbors, no doubt. It had taken him this long to drive from Seattle. The last ferry had already left Edmonds. He'd had to drive all the way around, through Mt. Vernon and down the length of the island.

"Hello, Rex," she said.

"Are you all right?"

"I'm fine."

"And the dogs?" he asked.

It gladdened her heart to think that he had actually asked about Aggie and Daph, that he'd gone so far as to inquire after their welfare.

"They're both fine, too," Maddy said. "They're out in the kitchen caging cookies from somebody's lunch."

Rex stumbled over to Maddy's chair. He pulled her upright and drew her into a heartfelt hug. Maddy could tell he was relieved and frightened, too.

"What happened?" he demanded.

"Somebody tried to kill me," she said calmly. "But I got away."

"Who?" he said.

Maddy shrugged. "It doesn't matter. This nice man, Lieutenant Caldwell, is going to catch him."

Rex looked at the man seated behind the desk. "Is that true?" he asked. "Somebody really did try to kill her?"

Lieutenant Caldwell nodded. "But don't worry," he said. "We *will* catch him."

Rex turned back to Maddy. "But what about you?" he asked. "Dennis Baxter called and told me about the house. He says it looks like it's a complete loss. What will you do? Where will you go?"

"Don't be silly," Maddy said. "The girls and I will be fine. I'll take whatever I get from the insurance company and buy myself a little place in town, maybe right here in Oak Harbor, someplace that's close enough to the beach that the girls will still be able to play in the water. And then you'll have your wish, too, Rex. You can build some humongous house on my old lot, sell it, and make yourself a fortune."

"But what are you going to do tonight?" Rex asked. "Do you want to come into the city with me? I'll be glad to take you. That's why I'm here."

"Certainly not," Maddy replied primly. "I wouldn't think of it. What would Gina say? There must be a motel around here someplace. When you call for a reservation, though, make sure they take dogs."

For a change Rex did come through. That night he found a room at the Seafarers Inn. It was there, in a shabby motel room with dingy wallpaper and bedding that reeked of cigarette smoke, that Maddy Watkins finally let herself think of all she had lost. She pulled the dogs up onto the grimy plaid bedspread and held them tight while she wept for her lost home, for her fireplace, for that plaque with its tiny bronze shoes.

The next day, Rex and Gina managed to locate a quaint little B and B called The Oakdale, which was within easy walking distance of the beach. The B and B owner, upon hearing what had happened, allowed as how Aggie and Daphne would be welcome to stay despite the fact that hers was usually a no-dogs-allowed establishment.

A week later, on an autumn afternoon dripping with hazy, golden sunshine, Maddy and the girls returned to the B and B to find a patrol car parked near the front gate. When she saw the waiting officer was none other than Deputy Harris, Maddy was less than thrilled.

"What is it?" she asked.

"I thought you'd want to know," Deputy Harris said warily. "We found Hadley Riggins this afternoon."

"Where?" Maddy asked.

"In his car out in the woods. It was parked on a deserted road out by Coupeville."

"He's dead?"

Harris nodded.

"Suicide?"

"Yes."

"Was there a note?"

Deputy Harris nodded again. "It seems Hadley Riggins

let his twenty-year-old daughter run off to New Zealand to marry an old duffer who's at least fifty years older than she is. The old man's a missionary of some sort. Hadley Riggins was all for it. He said he thought it was his daughter's highest, best use. Laurel Riggins evidently disagreed with her husband. She made plans to go to New Zealand on her own in hopes of bringing the daughter back. We know that's where she planned on going because she'd gotten herself a visa."

"Hadley found out and kept her from leaving," Maddy breathed.

Deputy Harris sighed. "According to the note, he pushed her off a ferry the night she was supposed to leave, and no one saw her go overboard. He must have figured the body would never be found. Then, he pretended that she'd gone off to New Zealand just the way she'd planned. Everybody pretty much believed him, except for you, Mrs. Watkins." Harris shook his head then. "If it weren't for you and that missing thank-you note, ma'am, it probably would have taken us a whole lot longer to figure out something was wrong."

"Well," Maddy said, relenting enough to give him a faint smile. "My mother always told me thank-you notes were frightfully important."

"Yes," Deputy Harris replied sheepishly. "You might say they really can be a matter of life and death."

Interlude at Duane's

F. Paul Wilson

F. Paul Wilson, a practicing osteopathic family physician, is the author of more than thirty books, including science fiction novels (*The Tery, Sims, An Enemy of the State*), horror thrillers (*The Keep, The Tomb, Sibs, Midnight Mass*), contemporary thrillers (*Implant, Deep as the Marrow*), as well as several collaborations. He is more closely associated with one Repairman Jack, an anti-hero character in Wilson's *Harbingers, Crisscross, Gateways,* and five other titles. Wilson has also written for stage, screen, and interactive media with his original teleplay "Glim-Glim" aired on Monsters in 1989, an adaptation of his short story "Menage a Trois" was part of the pilot for *The Hunger* series that debuted on Showtime in July 1997, and *The Touch* is being developed for a TV series. *The Keep* was developed into a film by Michael Mann. He won the first Prometheus Award in 1979 for his novel *Wheels Within Wheels* and another in 2004 for *Sims*. He has also been honored with a Bram Stoker Award and nominations for the World Fantasy Award and the Nebula Award.

"Lemme tell you, Jack," Loretta said as they chugged along West Fifty-eighth, "these changes gots me in a baaaad mood. Real bad. My feets killin me, too. Nobody better hassle me afore I'm home and on the outside of a big ol glass of Jimmy."

Jack nodded, paying just enough attention to be polite. He was more interested in the passersby and was thinking how a day without your carry was like a day without clothes.

He felt naked. He'd had to leave his trusty Glock and backup home today because of his annual trip to the Empire State Building. He'd designated April 19th King Kong Day. Every year he made a pilgrimage to the observation deck to leave a little wreath in memory of the Big Guy. The major drawback to the outing was the metal detector everyone had to pass through before heading upstairs. That meant no heat.

Jack didn't think he was being paranoid. Okay, maybe a little, but he'd pissed off his share of people in this city and didn't care to run into them naked.

After the wreath-laying ceremony, he decided to walk back to his place on the West Side and ran into Loretta along the way.

They went back a dozen or so years to when both waited tables at a long-extinct trattoria on West Fourth. She'd been fresh up from Mississippi then, and he only a few years out of Jersey. Agewise, Loretta had a good decade on Jack, maybe more—might even be knocking on the door to fifty. Had a good hundred pounds on him as well. She'd dyed her Chia Pet hair orange and sheathed herself in some shapeless, green-and-yellow thing that made her look like a brown manatee in a muumuu.

She stopped and stared at a black cocktail dress in a boutique window.

"Ain't that pretty. 'Course I'll have to wait till I'm cremated afore I fits into it."

They continued to Sixth Avenue. As they stopped on the corner and waited for the walking green, two Asian women came up to her.

The taller one said, "You know where Saks Fifth Avenue is?"

Loretta scowled. "On Fifth Avenue, fool." Then she took a breath and jerked a thumb over her shoulder. "That way."

Jack looked at her. "You weren't kidding about the bad mood."

"You ever know me to kid, Jack?" She glanced around. "Sweet Jesus, I need me some comfort food. Like some chocolate-peanut-butter-swirl ice cream." She pointed to the Duane Reade on the opposite corner. "There."

"That's a drugstore."

"Honey, you know better'n that. Duane's got everything. Shoot, if mine had a butcher section I wouldn't have to shop nowheres else. Come on."

Before he could opt out, she grabbed his arm and started hauling him across the street.

"I specially like their makeup. Some places just carry Cover Girl, y'know, which is fine if you a Wonder bread blonde. Don't know if you noticed, but white ain't zackly a big color in these parts. Everybody's darker. Cept you, a course. I know you don't like attention, Jack, but if you had a smidge of coffee in your cream you'd be *really* invisible."

Jack expended a lot of effort on being invisible. He'd inherited a good start with his average height, average build, average brown hair and nondescript face. Today he'd accessorized with a Mets cap, flannel shirt, worn Levi's and battered work boots. Just another guy, maybe a construction worker, ambling along the streets of Zoo York.

Jack slowed as they approached the door.

"I think I'll take a rain check, Lo."

She tightened her grip on his arm. "Hell you will. I need some company. I'll even buy you a Dew. Caffeine still your drug of choice?"

"Yeah. Until it's time for a beer." He eased his arm free. "Okay, I'll spring for five minutes, but after that, I'm gone. Got things to do."

"Five minutes ain't nuthin, but okay."

"You go ahead. I'll be right with you."

He slowed in her wake so he could check out the entrance. He spotted a camera just inside the door, trained on the comers and goers.

He tugged down the brim of his hat and lowered his head. He was catching up to Loretta when he heard a loud, heavily accented voice.

"*Mira! Mira! Mira!* Look at the fine ass on you!"

Jack hoped that wasn't meant for him. He raised his head far enough to see a grinning, mustachioed Latino leaning on the building wall outside the doorway. A maroon gym bag sat at his feet. He had glossy, slicked-back hair and prison tats on the backs of his hands.

Loretta stopped and stared at him. "You better not be talkin a me!"

His grin widened. "But *señorita,* in my country it is a privilege for a woman to be praised by someone like me."

"And just where is this country of yours?"

"Ecuador."

"Well, you in New York now, honey, and I'm a bitch from the Bronx. Talk to me like that again and I'm gonna Bruce Lee yo ass."

"But I know you would like to sit on my face."

"Why? Yo nose bigger'n yo dick?"

This cracked up a couple of teenage girls leaving the store. Mr. Ecuador's face darkened. He didn't seem to appreciate the joke.

Head down, Jack crowded close behind Loretta as she entered the store.

She said, "Told you I was in a bad mood."

"That you did, that you did. Five minutes, Loretta, okay?"

"I hear you."

He glanced over his shoulder and saw Mr. Ecuador pick up his gym bag and follow them inside.

Jack paused as Loretta veered off toward one of the cosmetic aisles. He watched to see if Ecuador was going to hassle her, but he kept on going, heading toward the rear.

Duane Reade drugstores are a staple of New York life. The city has hundreds of them. Only the hoity-toitiest Upper East Siders hadn't been in one dozens if not hundreds of times. Their most consistent feature was their lack of consistency. No two were the same size or laid out alike. Okay, they all kept the cosmetics near the front, but after that it became anyone's guess where something might be hiding. Jack could see the method to that madness: The more time people had to spend looking for what they'd come for, the greater their chances of picking up things they hadn't.

This one seemed fairly empty and Jack assigned himself the task of finding the ice cream to speed their departure.

He set off through the aisles and quickly became disoriented. The overall space was L-shaped, but instead of running in parallel paths to the rear, the aisles zigged and
zagged. Whoever laid out this place was either a devotee of
chaos theory or a crop-circle designer.

He was wandering among the six-foot-high shelves and
passing the hemorrhoid treatments when he heard a harsh
voice behind him.

"Keep movin, yo. Alla way to the back."

Jack looked and saw a big, steroidal black guy in a red
tank top. The overhead fluorescents gleamed off his
shaven scalp. He had a fat scar running through his left
eyebrow, glassy eyes and held a snub-nose .38-caliber
revolver—the classic Saturday night special.

Jack kept his cool and held his ground. "What's up?"

The guy raised the gun, holding it sideways like in the
movies, the way no one who knew squat about pistols
would hold it.

"Ay yo, get yo ass in gear fore I bust one in yo face."

Jack waited a couple more seconds to see if the guy
would move closer and put the pistol within reach. But he
didn't. Too experienced maybe.

Not good. The big question was whether this was personal or not. When he saw the gaggle of frightened-looking
people—the white-coated ones obviously pharmacists—
kneeling before the pharmacy counter with their hands
behind their necks, he figured it wasn't.

A relief . . . sort of.

He spotted Mr. Ecuador standing over them with a
gleaming nickel-plated .357 revolver.

Robbery.

Okay, just keep your head down to stay off the cameras and off these bozos' radar, and you'll walk away with the rest of them.

The black guy pushed him from behind.

"Assume the position, asshole."

Jack spotted two cameras trained on the pharmacy area. He knelt at the left end of the line, intertwined his fingers behind his neck and kept his eyes on the floor.

He glanced up when he heard a commotion to his left. A scrawny little Sammy Davis-size Rasta man with his hair packed into a red-yellow-and-green-striped knit cap showed up packing a sawed-off pump-action twelve and driving another half a dozen people before him. A frightened-looking Loretta was among them.

And then a fourth—Christ, how many were there? This one had dirty, sloppy, light brown dreads, piercings up the wazoo, and was humping the whole hip-hop catalog: wide baggy jeans, huge New York Giants jersey, peak-askew cap.

He pointed another special as he propelled a dark-skinned, middle-aged—Indian? Pakistani?—by the neck.

Both the newcomers had glazed eyes, too. All stoned. Maybe it would make them mellow.

What a crew. Probably met in Rikers. Or maybe the Tombs.

"Got Mr. Manager," the white guy singsonged.

Ecuador looked at him. "You lock the front door?"

Whitey jangled a crowded key chain and tossed it on the counter.

"Yep. All locked in safe and sound."

"*Bueno*. Get back up there and watch in case we miss somebody. Don't wan nobody getting out."

"Yeah, in a minute. Somethin I gotta do first."

He shoved the manager forward, then slipped behind the counter and disappeared into the pharmacy shelves.

"Wilkins! I tol you, get up front!"

Wilkins reappeared, carrying three large plastic stock bottles. He plopped them down on the counter. Jack spotted Percocet and Oxy-Contin on the labels.

"These babies are mine. Don't nobody touch em."

Ecuador spoke through his teeth. *"Up front!"*

"I'm gone," Wilkins said, and headed away.

Scarbrow grabbed the manager by the jacket and shook him.

"The combination, mofo—give it up."

Jack noticed the guy's name tag: J. Patel. His dark skin went a couple of shades lighter. The poor guy looked ready to faint.

"I do not know it!"

Rasta man raised his shotgun and pressed the muzzle against Patel's quaking throat.

"You tell de mon what he want to know. You tell him *now!*"

Jack saw a wet stain spreading from Patel's crotch.

"The manager's ou-out. I d-don't know the combination."

Ecuador stepped forward. "Then you not much use to us, eh?"

Patel sagged to his knees and held up his hands. "Please! I have a wife, children!"

"You wan see them again, you tell me. I know you got armored-car pickup every Tuesday. I been watchin. Today is Tuesday, so give."

"But I do not—!"

Ecuador slammed his pistol barrel against the side of Patel's head, knocking him down.

"You wan die to save you boss's money? You wan see what happen when you get shot inna head? Here. I show you." He turned and looked at his prisoners. "Where that big bitch with the big mouth?" He smiled as he spotted Loretta. "There you are."

Shit.

Ecuador grabbed her by the front of her dress and pulled, making her knee-walk out from the rest. When she'd moved half a dozen feet he released her.

"Turn roun, bitch."

Without getting off her knees, she swiveled to face her fellow captives. Her lower lip quivered with terror. She made eye contact with Jack, silently pleading for him to do something, anything, *please!*

Couldn't let this happen.

His mind raced through scenarios, moves he might make to save her, but none of them worked.

As Ecuador raised the .357 and pointed it at the back of Loretta's head, Jack remembered the security cameras.

He raised his voice. "You really want to do that on TV?"

Ecuador swung the pistol toward Jack. "What the fuck?"

Without looking around, Jack pointed toward the pharmacy security cameras. "You're on *Candid Camera*."

"The fuck you care?"

Jack put on a sheepish grin. "Nothing. Just thought I'd share. Done some boosting in my day and caught a jolt in Riker's for not noticing one of them things. Now I notice—believe me, I *notice*."

Ecuador looked up at the cameras and said, "Fuck."

He turned to Rasta man and pointed. Rasta smiled, revealing a row of gold-framed teeth, and raised his shotgun.

Jack started moving with the first booming report, when all eyes were on the exploding camera. With the second boom he reached cover and streaked down an aisle.

Behind him he heard Ecuador shout, "Ay! Where the fuck he go? Wilkins! Somebody comin you way!"

The white guy's voice called back, "I'm ready, dog!"

Jack had hoped to surprise Wilkins and grab his pistol, but that wasn't going to happen now. Christ! On any other day he'd have a couple dozen 9mm hollowpoints loaded and ready.

He'd have to improvise.

As he zigged and zagged along the aisles, he sent out a silent thank-you to the maniac who'd laid out these shelves. If they'd run straight, front to back, he wouldn't last a minute. He felt like a mouse hunting for cheese, but this weird, mazelike configuration gave him a chance.

He hurried along, looking for something, anything, to use against them. Didn't even have his knife, dammit.

Batteries . . . notebooks . . . markers . . . pens . . . gum . . . greeting cards . . .

No help.

He saw a comb with a pointed handle and grabbed it. Without stopping, he ripped it open and stuck it in his back pocket.

He heard Ecuador yelling about how he was going this way and Jamal should go that way, and Demont should stay with the people.

Band-Aids . . . ice cream . . . curling iron—could he use that? Nah.

Hair color . . . humidifiers . . . Cheetos . . . beef jerky—
Come on!

He turned a corner and came to a summer-cookout section. Chairs—no help. Umbrella—no help. Heavy-duty
spatula—grabbed it and hefted it. Nice weight, stainless-
steel blade, serrated on one edge. Might be able to do a
little damage with this. Spotted a grouping of butane
matches. Grabbed one. Never hurt to have fire.

Fire . . . he looked up and saw the sprinkler system.
Every store in New York had to have one. A fire would set
off the sprinklers, sending an alert to the NYFD.

Do it.

He grabbed a can of lighter fluid and began spraying
the shelves. When he'd emptied half of it and the fluid
was puddling on the floor, he reached for the butane
match—

A shot. A *whizzz!* past his head. A quick glance down
the aisle to where Scarbrow—who had to be the "Jamal"
Ecuador had called to—stood ten yards away, leveling his
.38 for another go.

"Ay yo, I found him! Over here!"

Jack ducked and ran around a corner as the second
bullet sailed past, way wide. Typical of this sort of oxygen
waster, he couldn't shoot. Junk guns like his were good for
close-up damage and little else.

With footsteps behind him. Jack paused at the shelf's
endcap and took a quick peek at the neighboring aisle.
No one in sight. He dashed across to the next aisle and
found himself facing a wall. Ten feet down to his right—
a door.

EMPLOYEES ONLY

He pulled it open and stuck his head inside. Empty except for a table and some sandwich wrappers. And no goddamn exit.

Feet pounded his way from behind to the left. He slammed the door hard and ran right. He stopped at the first endcap and dared a peek.

Jamal rounded the bend and slid to a halt before the door, a big grin on his face.

"Gotcha now, asshole."

In a crouch, gun ready, he yanked open the door. After a few heartbeats he stepped into the room.

Here was Jack's chance. He squeezed his wrist through the leather thong in the barbecue spatula's handle, then raised it to vertical in a two-handed samurai grip, serrated edge forward.

Then he moved, gliding in behind Jamal and swinging at his head. Maybe the guy heard something, maybe he saw a shadow, maybe he had a sixth sense. Whatever the reason, he ducked to the side and the chop landed wide. Jamal howled as the edge bit into his meaty shoulder. Jack raised the spatula for a backhand strike, but the big guy proved more agile than he looked. He rolled and raised his pistol.

Jack swung the spatula at it, made contact, but the blade bounced off without knocking the gun free.

Time to go.

He was in motion before Jamal could aim. The first shot splintered the door frame a couple of inches to the left of his head as he dived for the opening. He hit the floor and rolled as the second went high.

Four shots. That left two—unless Jamal had brought extras. Somehow he couldn't imagine a guy like Jamal thinking that far ahead.

On his way toward the rear, switching aisles at every opportunity, he heard Ecuador shouting from the far side of the store.

"Jamal! You get him? You get him?"

"No, Fucker almost got me! I catch him I'm gonna skin him alive."

"Ain't got time for that! The truck be here soon! We gotta get inna the safe! Wilkins! Get back here and start lookin!"

"Who's gonna watch the front?"

"Fuck the front! We're locked in, ain't we?"

"Yeah, but—"

"Find him!"

"A'ight. Guess I'll have to show you guys how it's done."

Jack now had a pretty good idea where Ecuador and Jamal were—too near the barbecue section to risk going back. So he moved ahead. Toward Wilkins. He sensed that if this chain had a weak link, Wilkins was it.

Along the way he scanned the shelves. He still had the spatula, the comb and the butane match but needed something flammable.

Antibiotic ointments . . . laxatives . . . marshmallows . . . Shit.

He zigged and zagged until he found the hair-care aisle. Possibilities here. Needed a spray can.

What the—?

Every goddamn bottle was pump action. He needed fluorocarbons. Where were the fluorocarbons when you needed them?

He ran down to the deodorant section. Everything here was either a roll-on or a smear-on. Whatever happened to Right Guard?

He spotted a green can on a bottom shelf, half hidden behind a Mitchum's floor display. Brut. He grabbed it and scanned the label.

DANGER: *Contents under pressure . . . flammable . . .*

Yes!

Then he heard Wilkins ambling along the neighboring aisle, calling in a high, singsong tone.

"Hello, Mr. Silly Man. Where aaaare youuu? Jimmy's got a present for you." He giggled. "No, wait. Jimmy's got six— count em—six presents for you. Come and get em."

High as the space station.

Jack decided to take him up on his offer.

He removed the Brut cap as he edged to the end of the aisle and flattened against the shelf section separating him from Wilkins. He raised the can and held the tip of the match next to it. As soon as Wilkins's face came into view, Jack reached forward, pressing the nozzle and triggering the match. A ten-inch jet of flame engulfed Wilkins's eyes and nose.

He howled and dropped the gun, lurched away, kicking and screaming. His dreads had caught fire.

Jack followed him. He used the spatula to knock off the can's nozzle. Deodorant sprayed a couple of feet into the air. He shoved the can down the back of Wilkins's oversize jeans and struck the match. His seat exploded in flame. Jack grabbed the pistol and trotted into an aisle. Screams followed him toward the back.

One down, three to go.

He checked the pistol as he moved. An old .38 revolver with most of its bluing rubbed off. He opened the cylinder. Six hardball rounds. A piece of crap, but at least it was his piece of crap.

The odds had just become a little better.

A couple of pairs of feet started pounding toward the front. As he'd hoped, the screams were drawing a crowd.

He heard cries of "Oh, shit" and "Oh, fuck!" and "What he *do* to you, bro?"

Wilkins wailed in a glass-breaking pitch. "Pepe! Help me, man! I'm dyin'!"

Pepe . . . now Ecuador had a name.

"Si," Pepe said. "You are."

Wilkins screamed, "No!"

A booming gunshot—had to come from the .357.

"Fuck!" Jamal cried. "I don't believe you *did* that!"

A voice called from the back. "What goin on dere, mon? What hoppening?"

"S'okay, Demont!" Pepe called back. "Jus stay where you are!" Then, in a lower voice to Jamal: "Wilkins jus slow us down. Now find that fuck fore he find a phone!"

Jack looked back and saw a plume of white smoke rising toward the ceiling. He waited for the alarm, the sprinklers. Nothing.

What did he have to do—set a bonfire?

He slowed as he came upon the employee lounge again. Nah. That wasn't going to work twice. He kept going. He was passing the ice-cream freezer when something boomed to his right and a glass door shattered to his left. Ice-cream sandwiches and cones flew, gallons rolled.

Jack spotted Demont three aisles away, saw him

pumping another shell into the chamber. He ducked back as the top of the nearest shelf exploded in a cloud of shredded tampons.

"Back here! I have him!"

Jack hung at the opposite endcap until he heard Demont's feet crunch on broken glass in the aisle he'd just left. He eased down the neighboring lane, listening, stopping at the feminine-hygiene area as he waited for Demont to come even.

As he raised his pistol and held it two inches from the flimsy metal of the shelving unit's rear wall, he noticed a "personal" douche-bag box sitting at eye level. Was there a community model?

When he heard Demont arrive opposite him, he fired two shots. He wanted to fire four but the crappy pistol jammed. On the far side Demont grunted. His shotgun went off, punching a hole in the dropped ceiling.

Jack tossed the pistol. Demont would be down but not out. He needed something else. Douche bags had hoses, didn't they? He opened the box. Yep—red and ribbed. He pulled it out.

Footsteps pounded his way from the far side of the store as he peeked around and spotted Demont clutching his right shoulder. He'd dropped the shotgun but was making for it again.

Jack ran up and kicked it away, then looped the douche hose twice around Demont's scrawny neck and dragged him back to the ruined ice-cream door. He strung the hose over the top of the metal frame and pulled Demont off his feet. As the little man kicked and gagged, Jack slammed the door, trapping the hose. He tied two quick knots to make sure it didn't slip, then dived through the empty frame for the shotgun. He pumped out the spent shell, chambered a new one and pulled the trigger just as Jamal and Pepe rounded the corner.

Pepe caught a few pellets, but Jamal, leading the charge, took the brunt of the blast. His shirtfront dissolved as the double-ought did a pulled-pork thing on his overdeveloped pecs. Pepe was gone by the time Jack chambered another shell. Looked back: Demont's face had gone pruney, his kicks feeble. Ahead: Jamal lay spread-eagle, staring at the ceiling with unblinking eyes.

Now what? Go after Pepe or start that fire?

Fire. Start a big one. Get those red trucks rolling.

But which way to the barbecue section? He was disoriented. He remembered it being somewhere near the middle.

Three aisles later he found it—and Pepe, too, who was looking back over his shoulder as he passed it. Jack raised the shotgun and fired, but Pepe went down just before the double-ought arrived. Not on purpose. He'd slipped in the spilled lighter fluid. The shot went over his head and hit the barbecue supplies. Bags of briquettes and tins of lighter fluid exploded. Punctured cans of Raid whirlygigged in all directions, fogging the air with bug killer.

Pepe slipped and slid as he tried to regain his feet— would have been funny if he hadn't been holding a .357. Jack pumped again, aimed, and pulled the trigger.

Clink.

The hammer fell on an empty chamber.

Pepe was on his knees. He smiled as he raised his pistol. Jack ducked back and dived for the floor as one bullet after another slammed through the shelving of the cough and cold products, smashing bottles, drenching him with Robitussin and NyQuil and who knew what else.

He counted six shots. He didn't know if Pepe had a speed loader and didn't want to find out. He yanked the butane match from his back pocket and lit her up. He jammed a Sucrets pack into the trigger guard, locking the flame on, then tossed it over the shelf. He heard no *whoomp!* like gasoline going up, but he did hear Pepe cry out in alarm. The cry turned to screams of pain and terror as the spewing Raid cans caught.

Jack crept back and peeked around the corner.

Pepe was aflame. He had his arms over his eyes, covering them against the flying, flaming pinwheels of Raid as he rolled in the burning puddle, making matters worse. Black smoke roiled toward the ceiling.

And then it happened. Clanging bells and a deluge of cold water.

Yes.

Jack saw the .357 on the floor. He sprinted by, kicking it ahead of him as he raced through the downpour to the pharmacy section. After dancing through an obstacle course of ice pops and gallons of ice cream, he found Loretta and the others cowering behind the counter. He picked up the key ring and tossed it to Patel.

"Out! Get everybody out!"

As the stampede began, he heard Loretta yelling.

"Hey, y'all! This man just saved our lives. You wanna pay him back, you say you never seen him. He don't exist. You say these gangstas got inna fight and killed each other. Y'hear me? Y'hear?"

She blew Jack a kiss and joined the exodus. Jack was about to follow when a shot smashed a bottle of mouthwash near his head. He ducked back as a second shot narrowly missed. He dived behind the pharmacy counter and peeked over the top.

A scorched, steaming, sodden Pepe shuffled Jack's way through the rain with a small semiauto clutched in his outstretched hand. Jack hadn't counted on him having a backup. Hell, he hadn't counted on him doing anything but burning. The sprinkler system had saved him.

Pepe said nothing as he approached. Didn't have to. He had murder in his eyes. And he had Jack cornered.

He fired again. The bullet hit the counter six inches to jack's right, showering him with splinters as he ducked.

Trapped. Had to find a way to run out Pepe's magazine. How? A lot of those baby semis held ten shots.

He peeked up again. Pepe's slow progress had brought him within six feet. Jack was about to duck again when he saw a blur of bright green and yellow flash into view.

Loretta, moving faster than Jack ever would have thought possible, charged with a gallon container of ice cream held high over her head in a two-handed grip. Pepe might have heard her without the hiss and splatter of the sprinklers. But he remained oblivious until she streaked up behind him and smashed the container against the back of his head.

Jack saw his eyes bulge with shock and pain as he pitched toward the floor. Probably felt like he'd been hit with a cinder block. As he landed face-first, Loretta stayed on him—really on him. She jumped, landing knees first on the middle of his back.

The air rushed out of him with an agonized groan as his ribs shattered like glass.

But Loretta wasn't finished. Shouting, she started slamming the rock-hard container against his head and neck, matching the rhythm of her words to the blows.

"NOW you ain't NEVER gonna point no GUN to my HEAD ever aGAIN!"

Jack moved up beside her and touched her arm.

"I think he's got the message."

Loretta looked up at him, then back down at Pepe. His face was flattened against the floor, his head canted at an unnatural angle. He wasn't breathing.

She nodded. "I do believe you right."

Jack pulled her to her feet and pushed her toward the front.

"Go!"

But Loretta wasn't finished. She turned and kicked Pepe in the ribs.

"Told you I was a bitch!"

"Loretta—come on!"

As they hustled toward the front, she said, "We even, Jack?"

"Even Steven."

"Did I happen to mention my bad mood?"

"Yes, you did, Loretta. But sometimes a bad mood can be a good thing."

The Abelard Sanction

David Morrell

David Morrell is a bestselling and award-winning author. The creator of Rambo (in *First Blood*) served as an instructor of writing at the University of Iowa for sixteen years. After the success of his first novel, Morrell penned a number of national bestsellers, including *The Brotherhood of the Rose* (the basis for a highly rated NBC miniseries starring Robert Mitchum), *Black Evening, Long Lost, The Protector,* and others. Morrell's current release is *Creepers.* Morrell received a Distinguished Recognition Award from the Friends of American Writers in 1972 for *First Blood.* He has been nominated twice for the World Fantasy Award for best novella and has won the Horror Writers Association's Bram Stoker Awards in 1988 for "Orange is for Anguish, Blue is for Insanity" and in 1991 for "Beautiful Uncut Hair of Graves" for Long Fiction, and in 2005 for his novel, *Creepers.* Besides his novels, Morrell has written a book for writers called *Lessons from a Lifetime of*

Writing: A Novelist Looks at His Craft. Along with Gayle Linds and others, Morrell helped found the International Thriller Writers organization.

At the start, Abelard safe houses existed in only a half-dozen cities: Potsdam, Oslo, Lisbon, Buenos Aires, Alexandria and Montreal. That was in 1938, when representatives of the world's major intelligence communities met in Berlin and agreed to strive for a modicum of order in the inevitable upcoming war by establishing the principle of the Abelard sanction. The reference was to Peter Abelard, the poet and theologian of the Dark Ages, who seduced his beautiful student Heloise and was subsequently castrated in family retaliation. Afraid for his life, Abelard took refuge in a church near Paris and eventually established a sanctuary called The Paraclete, in reference to the Holy Spirit's role as advocate and intercessor. Anyone who came for help was guaranteed protection.

The modern framers of the Abelard sanction reasoned that the chaos of another world war would place unusual stress on the intelligence operatives within their agencies. While each agency had conventional safe houses, those sanctuaries designated "Abelard" would embody a major extension of the safe house concept. There, in extreme situations, any member of any agency would be guaranteed immunity from harm. These protected areas would have the added benefit of functioning as neutral meeting grounds in which alliances between agencies could be safely negotiated and intrigues formulated. The sanctuaries would provide a chance for any operative, no matter his or her allegiance, to rest, to heal and to consider the wisdom of tactics and choices. Anyone speaking frankly in one of these refuges need not fear that his or her words would be used as weapons outside the protected walls.

The penalty for violating the Abelard sanction was ultimate. If any operative harmed any other operative in an Abelard safe house, the violator was immediately declared a rogue. All members of all agencies would hunt the outcast and kill him or her at the first opportunity, regardless if the transgressor belonged to one's own organization. Because Abelard's original sanctuary was in a church, the framers of the Abelard sanction decided to continue that tradition. They felt that, in a time of weakening moral values, the religious connection would reinforce the gravity of the compact. Of course, the representative from the NKVD was skeptical in this regard, religion having been outlawed in the USSR, but he saw no harm in allowing the English and the Americans to believe in the opiate of the masses.

During the Second World War and the escalating tensions of the subsequent cold war, Abelard sanctuaries proved so useful that new ones were established in Bangkok, Singapore, Florence, Melbourne, Ferlach, Austria and Santa Fe, New Mexico. The latter was of special note because the United States representative to the 1938 Abelard meeting doubted that the sanction could be maintained. He insisted that none of these politically sensitive, potentially violent sites would be on American soil. But he turned out to be wrong. In an ever more dangerous world, the need for a temporary refuge became greater. In a cynical profession, the honor and strength of the sanction remained inviolate.

Santa Fe means Holy Faith. Abelard would approve, Saul Grisman thought as he guided a nondescript rented car along a dusk-shadowed road made darker by a sudden rainstorm. Although outsiders imagined that Santa Fe was a sun-blistered, lowland, desert city similar to Phoenix, the truth was that it had four seasons and was situated at an altitude of seven thousand feet in the foothills of a range of the Rocky Mountains known as Sangre de Cristo (so called because Spanish explorers had compared the glow of sunset on them to what they imagined was the blood of Christ). Saul's destination was toward a ridge northeast of this artistic community of fifty thousand people. Occasional lightning flashes silhouetted the mountains. Directions and a map lay next to him, but he had studied them thoroughly during his urgent flight to New Mexico and needed to stop only once to refresh his memory of landmarks that he'd encountered on a mission in Santa Fe years earlier. His headlights revealed a sign shrouded by rain: Camino de la Cruz, the street of the cross. Fingers tense, he steered to the right along the isolated road.

There were many reasons for an Abelard safe house to have been established near Santa Fe. Los Alamos, where the atomic bomb was invented, was perched on a mountain across the valley to the west. Sandia National Laboratories, a similar research facility important to U.S. security, occupied the core of a mountain an hour's drive south near Albuquerque. Double agent Edward Lee Howard eluded FBI agents at a sharp curve on Corrales Street here and escaped to the Soviet Union. Espionage was as much a part of the territory as the countless art galleries on Canyon Road. Many of the intelligence operatives stationed in the area fell in love with the Land of Enchantment, as the locals called it, and remained in Santa Fe after they retired.

The shadows of piñon trees and junipers lined the pot-holed road. After a quarter mile, Saul reached a dead end of hills. Through flapping windshield wipers, he squinted from the glare of lightning that illuminated a church steeple. Thunder shook the car as he studied the long, low building next to the church. Like most structures in Santa Fe, its roof was flat. Its corners were rounded, its thick, earth-colored walls made from stuccoed adobe. A sign said, Monastery of the Sun and the Moon. Saul, who was Jewish, gathered that the name had relevance to the nearby mountains called Sun and Moon. He also assumed that in keeping with Santa Fe's reputation as a New Age, crystal-and-fung-shui community, the name indicated this was not a traditional Catholic institution.

Only one car, as dark and nondescript as Saul's, was in the parking lot. He stopped next to it, shut off his engine and headlights, and took a deep breath, holding it for a count of three, exhaling for a count of three. Then he grabbed his over-the-shoulder travel bag, got out, locked the car and hurried through the cold downpour toward the monastery's entrance.

Sheltered beneath an overhang, he tried both heavy-looking wooden doors but neither budged. He pressed a button and looked up at a security camera. A buzzer freed the lock. When he opened the door on the right, he faced a well-lit lobby with a brick floor. As he shut the door, a strong breeze shoved past him, rousing flames in a fire-place to the left. The hearth was a foot above the floor, its opening oval in a style known as kiva, the crackling wood leaning upright against the back of the firebox. The aromatic scent of piñon wood reminded Saul of incense.

He turned toward a counter on the right, behind which a young man in a priest's robe studied him. The man had ascetic, sunken features. His scalp was shaved bare. "How may I help you?"

"I need a place to stay." Saul felt water trickle from his wet hair onto his neck.

"Perhaps you were misinformed. This isn't a hotel."

"I was told to ask for Mr. Abelard."

The priest's eyes changed focus slightly, becoming more intense. "I'll summon the housekeeper." His accent sounded European but was otherwise hard to identify. He pressed a button. "Are you armed?"

"Yes."

The priest frowned toward monitors that showed various green-tinted night-vision images of the rain-swept area outside the building: the two cars in the parking lot, the lonely road, the juniper-studded hills in back. "Are you here because you're threatened?"

"No one's pursuing me," Saul answered.

"You've stayed with us before?"

"In Melbourne."

"Then you know the rules. I must see your pistol."

Saul reached under his leather jacket and carefully withdrew a Heckler & Koch 9mm handgun. He set it on the counter, the barrel toward a wall, and waited while the priest made a note of the pistol's model number (P2000) and serial number.

The priest considered the ambidextrous magazine and

slide release mechanisms, then set the gun in a metal box. "Any other weapons?"

"A HideAway knife." Modeled after a Bengal tiger's claw, the HideAway was only four inches long. Saul raised the left side of his jacket. The blade's small black grip was almost invisible in a black sheath parallel to his black belt. He set it on the counter.

The priest made another note and set the knife in the box. "Anything else?"

"No." Saul knew that a scanner built into the counter would tell the priest if he was lying.

"My name is Father Chen," a voice said from across the lobby.

As thunder rumbled, Saul turned toward another man in a priest's robe. But this man was in his forties, Chinese, with an ample stomach, a round face and a shaved scalp that made him resemble Buddha. His accent, though, seemed to have been nurtured at a New England Ivy League university.

"I'm the Abelard housekeeper here." The priest motioned for Saul to accompany him. "Your name?"

"Saul Grisman."

"I meant your code name."

"Romulus."

Father Chen considered him a moment. In the corridor, they entered an office on the right, where the priest took a seat behind a desk and typed on a computer keyboard. He read the screen for a minute, then again looked at Saul, appearing to see him differently. "Romulus was one of the twins who founded Rome. Do *you* have a twin?"

Saul knew he was being tested. "Had. Not a twin. A

brother of sorts. His name was . . ." Emotion made Saul hesitate. "Chris."

"Christopher Kilmoonie. Irish." Father Chen gestured toward the computer screen. "Code name Remus. Both of you were raised in an orphanage in Philadelphia. The Benjamin Franklin School for Boys. A military school."

Saul knew he was expected to elaborate. "We wore uniforms. We marched with toy rifles. All our classes—history, trigonometry, literature, et cetera—were related to the military. All the movies we saw and the games we played were about war."

"What is the motto of that school?"

" 'Teach them politics and war so their sons may study medicine and mathematics in order to give their children a right to study painting, poetry, music and architecture.' "

"But that quotation is not from Benjamin Franklin."

"No. It's from John Adams."

"You were trained by Edward Franciscus Eliot," Father Chen said.

Again, Saul concealed his emotions. Eliot had been the CIA's director for counterespionage, but Saul hadn't known that until years later. "When we were five, he came to the school and befriended us. Over the years, he became . . . guess you'd call him our foster father, just as Chris and I were foster brothers. Eliot got permission to take us from the school on weekends—to baseball games, to barbecues at his house in Falls Church, Virginia, to dojos where we learned martial arts. Basically, he recruited us to be his personal operatives. We wanted to serve our father."

"And you killed him."

Saul didn't answer for a moment. "That's right. It turned

out the son of a bitch had other orphans who were his personal operatives, who loved him like a father and would do
anything for him. But in the end he used all of us, and
Chris died because of him, and I got an Uzi and emptied a
magazine into the bastard's black heart."

Father Chen's eyes narrowed. Saul knew where this was
going. "In the process, you violated the Abelard sanction."

"Not true. Eliot was off the grounds. I didn't kill him in
a sanctuary."

Father Chen continued staring.

"It's all in my file," Saul explained. "Yes, I raised hell in
a refuge. Eventually Eliot and I were ordered to leave. They
let him have a twenty-four-hour head start. But I caught
up to him."

Father Chen tapped thick fingers on his desk. "The
arbiters of the sanction decided that the rules had been
bent but not broken. In exchange for information about
how Eliot was himself a mole, you were given unofficial
immunity as long as you went into exile. You've been helping
to build a settlement in Israel. Why didn't you stay there?
For God's sake, given your destructive history, how can you
expect me to welcome you to an Abelard safe house?"

"I'm looking for a woman."

Father Chen's cheeks flared with indignation. "Now you
take for granted I'll supply you with a prostitute?"

"You don't understand. The woman I'm searching for is
my wife."

Father Chen scowled toward an item on the computer
screen. "Erika Bernstein. A former operative for Mossad."

"The car in the parking lot. Is it hers?"

"No. You said you're *searching* for her?"

"I haven't seen her in three weeks. Does the car belong to Yusuf Habib?"

As thunder again rumbled, Father Chen nodded. "He is a guest."

"Then I expect Erika to arrive very soon, and I'm not here to cause trouble. I'm trying to stop it."

A buzzer sounded. Frowning, Father Chen pressed a button. The image on the monitor changed to a view of the lobby. Saul felt blood rush to his heart as a camera showed Erika stepping from the rain into the lobby. Even in black and white, she was gorgeous, her long dark hair tied back in a ponytail, her cheekbones strong but elegant. Like him, she wore running shoes and jeans, but in place of his leather coat, she had a rain slicker, water dripping from it.

Saul was out of the office before Father Chen could rise from his chair. In the brightly lit lobby, Erika heard Saul's urgently approaching footsteps on the brick floor and swung protectively, hardly relaxing when she saw who it was.

She pointed angrily. "I told you not to come after me."

"I didn't."

"Then what the hell are you doing here?"

"I didn't follow you. I followed *Habib*." Saul turned toward Father Chen. "My wife and I need a place where we can talk."

"The refectory is empty." The priest indicated the corridor behind them and a door on the left, opposite his office.

Saul and Erika stared at one another. Impatient, she marched past him and through the doorway.

Following, Saul turned on the overhead fluorescent lights. The fixtures hummed. The refectory had four long tables arranged in rows of two. It felt cold. The fish smell of the evening meal lingered. At the back was a counter behind which stood a restaurant-size refrigerator and stainless-steel stove. Next to containers of knives, forks and spoons, there were cups and a half pot of coffee on a warmer. As rain lashed at the dark windows, Saul went over and poured two cups, adding nondairy creamer and the sugarless sweetener Erika used.

He sat at the table nearest her. Reluctant, she joined him.

"Are you all right?" he asked.

"Of course I'm *not* all right. How can you ask that?"

"I meant, are you injured?"

"Oh." Erika looked away. "Fine. I'm fine."

"Except that you're not."

She didn't reply.

"It's not just *your* son who's dead." Saul peered down at his untasted coffee. "He was *my* son, too."

Again, no reply.

"I hate Habib as much as you do," Saul said. "I want to squeeze my hands around his throat and—"

"Bullshit. Otherwise, *you'd* do what *I'm* doing."

"We lost our boy. I'll go crazy if I lose you, also. You know you're as good as dead if you kill Habib here. For breaking the sanction, you won't live another day."

"If I don't kill Habib, I don't *want* to live another day. Is he here?"

Saul hesitated. "So I'm told."

"Then I'll never get a better chance."

"We can go to neutral ground and wait for him to leave. I'll help you," Saul said. "The hills around here make perfect vantage points. Will a shot from a sniper's rifle give you the same satisfaction as seeing Habib die face-to-face?"

"As long as he's dead. As long as he stops insulting me by breathing the same air I breathe."

"Then let's do it."

Erika shook her head from side to side. "In Cairo, I nearly got him. He has a bullet hole in his arm to remind him. For two weeks, he ran from refuge to refuge as cleverly as he could. Then six days ago, his tactics changed. His trail became easier to follow. I told myself that he was getting tired, that I was wearing him down. But when he shifted through Mexico into the southwestern United States, I realized what he was doing. In the Mideast, he could blend. In Santa Fe, for God's sake, Mideasterners are rarely seen. Why would he leave his natural cover? He lured me. He *wants* me to find him here. I'm sure his men are waiting for me outside right now, closing the trap. Habib can't imagine that I'd readily break the sanction, that I'd gladly be killed just so I could take him with me. He expects me to do the logical thing and hide among the trees outside, ready to make a move when he leaves. If I do, his men will attack. *I'll* be the target. Dammit, why didn't you listen to me and stay out of this? Now you can't get out of here alive any more than I can."

"I love you," Saul said.

Erika stared down at her clenched hands. Her angry features softened somewhat. "The only person I love more than you is . . . was . . . our son."

A voice said, "Both of you must leave."

Saul and Erika turned toward the now-open doorway, where Father Chen stood with his hands behind his robe. Saul had no doubt that the priest concealed a weapon.

A door farther along the refectory wall opened. The ascetic-looking priest from the reception counter stepped into the doorway. He, too, had his hands behind his robe.

Saul took for granted that the refectory had hidden microphones. "You heard Erika. Habib has a trap arranged out there."

"A theory," Father Chen replied. "Not proven. Perhaps she invented the theory to try to force me to let the two of you stay."

"Habib's an organizer for Hamas," Erika said.

"Who or what he works for isn't my concern. Everyone is guaranteed safety here."

"The bastard's a psychologist who recruits suicide bombers." Erika glared. "He runs the damn training centers. He convinces the bombers they'll go to paradise and fuck an endless supply of virgins if they blow themselves up along with any Jews they get near."

"I'm aware of how suicide bombers are programmed," Father Chen said. "But the sanctity of this Abelard safe house is all that matters to me."

"Sanctity?" Saul's voice rose. "What about the sanctity of our *home?* Four weeks ago, one of Habib's maniacs snuck into our settlement and blew himself up in the market. Our home's near the market. Our son . . ." Saul couldn't make himself continue.

"Our son," Erika said in a fury, "was killed by a piece of shrapnel that almost cut off his head."

"You have my sincerest and deepest sympathy," Father Chen said. "But I cannot allow you to violate the sanction because of your grief. Take your anger outside."

"I will if Habib calls off his men," Erika said. "I don't care what happens to me, but I need to make sure nothing happens to Saul."

Thunder rumbled.

"I'll convey your request," Father Chen said.

"No need." The words came from a shadow in the corridor.

Saul felt his muscles tighten as a sallow face appeared behind Father Chen. Habib was heavyset, with thick dark hair, in his forties, with somber eyebrows and intelligent features. He wore dark slacks and a thick sweater. His left arm was in a sling.

Keeping the priest in front of him, Habib said, "I, too, am sorry about your son. I think of victims as statistics. Anonymous casualties. How else can war be waged? To personalize the enemy is to invite defeat. But it always troubles me when I read about individuals, children, who die in the bombings. *They* didn't take away our land. *They* didn't institute laws that treat us as inferiors."

"Your sympathy almost sounds convincing," Erika said.

"When I was a child, my parents lived in Jerusalem's old city. Israeli soldiers patrolled the top of the wall that enclosed the area. Every day, they pissed down onto our vegetable garden. Your politicians have continued to piss on us ever since."

"Not me," Erika said. "I didn't piss on anybody."

"Change conditions, give us back our land, and the bombing will stop," Habib said. "That way, the lives of other children will be saved."

"I don't care about those other children." Erika stepped toward him.

"Careful." Father Chen stiffened, about to pull his hands from behind his robe.

Erika stopped. "All I care about is my son. *He* didn't piss on your vegetables, but you killed him anyhow, just as surely as if you'd set off the bomb yourself."

Habib studied her as a psychologist might assess a

disturbed patient. "And now you're ready to sacrifice the lives of both you and your husband in order to get revenge?"

"No." Erika swelled with anger. "Not Saul. He wasn't supposed to be part of this. Contact your men. Disarm the trap."

"But if you leave here safely, you'll take their place," Habib said. "You'll wait for me to come outside. You'll attack me."

"I'll give you the same terms my husband gave his foster father. I'll give you a twenty-four-hour head start."

"Listen to yourself. You're on the losing side, but somehow you expect me to surrender my position of strength."

"Strength?" Erika pulled down the zipper on her rain slicker. "How's this for strength?"

Habib gasped. Father Chen's eyes widened. Saul took a step forward, getting close enough to see the sticks of dynamite wrapped around Erika's waist. His pulse rushed when he saw her right thumb reach for a button attached to a detonator. She held it down.

"If anybody shoots me, my thumb goes off the button, and all of us go to heaven, except I don't want any virgin women," Erika said.

"Your husband will die."

"He'll die anyhow as long as your men are outside. But this way, you'll die also. How does it feel, to be on the receiving end of a suicide, bomb? I don't know how long my thumb can keep pressing this button. When will my hand start to cramp?"

"You're insane."

"As insane as you and your killers. The only good thing about what you do is you make sure those nutcases don't breed. For Saul, I'll give you a chance. Get the hell out of here. Take your men with you. Disarm the trap. You have my word. You've got twenty-four hours."

Habib stared, analyzing her rage. He spoke to Father Chen. "If she leaves before the twenty-four hours have elapsed . . ."

"She won't." Father Chen pulled a pistol from behind his robe.

"To help me, you'd risk being blown up?" Habib asked the priest.

"Not for you. For this safe house. I pledged my soul."

"My thumbs beginning to stiffen," Erika warned.

Habib nodded. Erika and Saul followed him along the corridor to his room. Guarded by the priests, they waited while he packed his suitcase. He carried it to the reception area, moving awkwardly because of his wounded shoulder. There, he used a phone on the counter, pressing the speaker button, touching numbers with the index finger of his uninjured right arm.

Saul listened as a male voice answered with a neutral, "Hello." Rain made a staticky sound in the background.

"I'm leaving the building now. The operation has been postponed."

"I need the confirmation code."

" 'Santa Fe is the City Different.' "

"Confirmed. Postponed."

"Stay close to me. I'll require you again in twenty-four hours."

Habib pressed the disconnect button and scowled at Erika. "The next time, I won't allow you to come close to me."

Erika's thumb trembled on the button connected to the

detonator. She nodded toward a clock on the wall behind the reception desk. "It's five minutes after ten. As far as I'm concerned, the countdown just started. Move."

Habib used his uninjured right arm to open the door. Rain gusted in. "I am indeed sorry," he told Erika. "It's terrible that children must suffer to make politicians correct wrongs."

He used his car's remote control to unlock the doors horn a distance. Another button on the remote control started the engine. He picked up his suitcase and stepped into the rain.

Saul watched him hurry off balance through shadowy gusts toward the car. Lightning flashed. Reflexively, Saul stepped back from the open door in case one of Habib's men ignored the instructions and was foolish enough to shoot at an Abelard safe house.

Buffeted by the wind, Habib set down his suitcase, opened the driver's door, shoved his suitcase across to the passenger seat, then hurried behind the steering wheel.

Father Chen closed the sanctuary's entrance, shutting out the rain, blocking the view of Habib. The cold air lingered.

"Is that parking lot past the boundaries of the sanction?" Erika asked.

"That isn't important!" Father Chen glared. "The dynamite. That's what matters. For God's sake, how do we neutralize it?"

"Simple." Erika released her thumb from the button.

Father Chen shouted and stumbled away.

But the blast didn't come from Erika's waist. Instead, the roar came from outside, making Saul tighten his lips in furious satisfaction as he imagined his car and Erika's blowing apart. The vehicles were parked on each side of Habib's. The plastic explosives in each trunk blasted a shock wave against the safe house's doors. Shrapnel walloped the building. A window shattered.

Father Chen yanked the entrance open. Slanting rain carried with it the stench of smoke, scorched metal and charred flesh. Despite the storm, the flames of the gritted vehicles illuminated the night. In the middle, Habib's vehicle was blasted inward on each side, the windows gaping, flames escaping. Behind the steering wheel, his body was ablaze.

The rumble of thunder mimicked the explosion.

"What have you done?" Father Chen shouted.

"We sent the bastard to hell where he belongs," Erika said.

In the nearby hills, shots cracked, barely audible in the downpour.

"Friends of ours," Saul explained. "Habib's team won't set any more traps."

"And don't worry about the authorities coming to the monastery because of the explosion," Erika said.

A second explosion rumbled from a distance. "When our friends heard the explosion, they faked a car accident at the entrance to this road. The vehicle's on fire. It has tanks of propane for an outdoor barbecue. Those tanks blew apart just now, which'll explain the blasts to the authorities. Neither the police nor the fire department will have a reason to be suspicious about anything a half mile farther along this deserted road."

By now, the flames in the cars in the parking lot were almost extinguished as the rain fell harder.

"We had no idea there'd be a storm," Saul said. "We

didn't need it, but it makes things easier. It saves us from hurrying to put out the flames so the authorities don't see a reflection."

Another shot cracked on a nearby hill.

"We'll help clean the site, of course," Erika said. "The Monastery of the Sun and the Moon will look as if nothing ever happened."

"You violated the sanction." Father Chen raised his pistol.

"No. You told us the parking lot wasn't part of the safe house," Saul insisted.

"I said nothing of the sort!"

"Erika asked you! I heard her! This other priest heard your answer! You said the parking lot wasn't important!"

"You threatened an operative within a sanctuary!"

"With what? That isn't dynamite around Erika's waist. Those tubes are painted cardboard. We don't have any weapons. Maybe we bent the rules, but we definitely didn't break them."

The priest glowered. "Just like when you killed your foster father."

Erika nodded. "And now another black-hearted bastard's been wiped from the face of the earth." Tears trickled down her cheeks. "But my son is still dead. Nothing's changed. I still hurt. God, how I hurt."

Saul held her.

"I want my son back," Erika whimpered.

"I know," Saul told her. "I know."

"I'll pray for him," Father Chen said.

"Pray for us all."

Lightning Rider

Rick Mofina

Rick Mofina's *If Angels Fall* introduced the San Francisco crime-fighting duo Tom Reed (a reporter) and Walt Sydowski (a homicide inspector). The book was honored with Arthur Ellis Award from the Crime Writers of Canada as Best First Novel. Mofina put the pair through their paces four more times with *Blood of Others* winning yet another Arthur Ellis Award, this time for Best Novel in 2003. The Jason Wade series appeared then as Reed and Sydowski went on hiatus. The debut Wade series novel, The Dying Hour, was awarded a Thriller for Best Paperback Original by the newly formed International Thriller Writers and Mofina's short story, "Lightning Rider," which appeared in the *Murder in Vegas* anthology, won the 2006 Arthur Ellis Award for Best Short Story.

Jessie Scout tightened her grip on the wheel of the armored car when she spotted her crew members, Gask and Perez, emerging from the casino lobby. Their canvas bags were now empty of cash. Another delivery done.

Relax, she told herself.

Her utility belt and the holster cradling her Glock gave a leathery squeak as she ran a perimeter check of the mirrors around their truck. All clear. *Wait.* A stranger was getting way too close to her.

"Bobby? Hey Bob, check this out, buddy!" A man laughed.

Scout picked them up, distorted on the driver's side convex mirror. A couple of all-night rollers. White guys. Forties. Midwesterners. Mid-management. Suburban. Wife and kids back home. Skip the buffet, Skippy. Bloody Marys for breakfast. Riding higher than the morning desert sun. *Don't come near the truck. Don't you dare.*

"Hey Bob. Get this." The first one is reaching into his pocket.

Scout's right hand brushed the butt of her Glock. Her two crew members were still far off on her right side. They can't see the guy or the flash of metal in his hand. He's *too* close.

"What's the pay-off if I play a dollar here? Ha-ha."

He starts to fiddle with a gunport. Jerk. Scout spanks the horn. He recoils, his reddening face contorting in anger aimed up at her as he passes by the front of the truck, hands up, palms open.

"What's a matter? Can't you take a joke?"

Scout eyeballs him hard and cold from behind her dark glasses.

He's mesmerized. She's a young goddess. Tanned, high cheekbones. Chestnut hair, long and braided. Her face betrays nothing. He concedes he is out of his league. No fun here. The rollers walk away.

She heard keys jingle, then the tap of metal on the steel passenger door. It was Gask and Perez, their faces moist, their shirts darkened with sweat under their armpits. "C'mon, Scout, we're cookin' here," Gask shouted over the idling motor, air conditioner, and the truck's sound-absorbing armor.

Scout unlocked the doors from the inside. Gask heaved himself into the passenger seat. Perez sprung up the step of the side delivery door, into the rear with the money. Both men locked their doors as Jessie eased the truck down the casino's driveway and onto Las Vegas Boulevard.

"What's the problem, you hittin' the horn, Scout?" Gask studied his clipboard, then shouted through the sliding viewer window of the steel security wall separating the cab and the rear of the truck. "Next drop is ATMs, Perez. Got it?"

"Got it."

"I asked you, what's the problem, Scout?"

"No problem."

"I think you still don't know what you're doing, do you?"

Scout didn't answer. Gask's face hardened.

"I swear to God, I don't know why they hire you people."

Scout said nothing.

"My last week on the job and this is what you give me?"

"I said it was no problem."

"You sure? You seem a little tense today. Is it a woman thing?"

Scout rolled her eyes. What a pig. "A tourist was touching the truck. I scolded him. He backed off. No problem."

"Fine. Put it in the log. Time. Place. Description. Incident. I'm retiring with a spotless record. Got it. Christ, you got a brain in there?"

"I know the procedure."

"As long as you're sure," he grunted. "Call in the drop."

Scout grabbed the radio handset and said: "Ten sixty-five."

"Go sixty-five," the radio responded.

"Six clear."

"Ten four, sixty-five."

Gask shifted in his seat. "Damn gun, digging into me." He removed his uniform cap and dragged the back of his hairy forearm over his forehead. "You got the AC on full, Scout? You got it up full?"

"Full."

"You sure you know how to operate that thing. Might be complicated for someone like you."

Scout concentrated on the road. Gask had been her crew chief since she was hired as a driver for U.S. Forged Armored Inc., four months ago. Today was his first day back from a vacation and he was bursting to tell her and Perez about it that morning at the terminal while downing his ritual breakfast of chocolate glazed donuts. They were finishing up coffee, ready to head out on deliveries.

"Know where I went, Scout?" he'd asked.

As if she cared.

"Aryanfest," he sucked on his teeth, working them over with a toothpick. "Up north, near your old reserve. Pretty country. Lots of *white*. On the mountaintops. We burned a cross," Gask smiled. "Once I punch out of this job, I'm going to buy me a lake cabin near the border."

Scout and Perez looked at each other, saying nothing.

Gask did not keep his beliefs secret. Experience taught them to avoid trigger topics like Martin Luther King, the pope, Waco, Ruby Ridge, Oklahoma City, or civil rights. Scout could deal with his insults but despised the way Gask treated Perez, who had three years with the company.

Gil Perez was a quiet, soft-spoken father of two little girls. He was loyal, honest. Hard working. Dreamed of starting his own car wash business, but one day he made the mistake of telling Gask, who'd spit on his dream every chance he could.

"Ain't gonna happen for you, Refried. You just don't have what it takes. Trust me. I know you, your abilities. It exceeds the reach of your people. Scout's too. In both cases, your folks generally lack the *motivation,* the *dedication,* the drive of red-blooded Americans like me to succeed. You'd best invest all your energy in your job here and maybe one day, if you're real lucky, which I doubt, but maybe one day, you'll have your own crew like me."

Like you?

Scout shuddered at the notion of anyone making themselves in the image of Elmer Gask, Forged's most senior guard and legendary asshole. According to the dinosaurs who knew Gask's story, Elmer was Mississippi white trash, whose family moved in the night to avoid debts. Gask's granddaddy was a Grand Dragon who oversaw the firebombing of churches before he died of complications arising from syphilis. Gask was a former bull with the Nevada State prison system, fired for severely beating a black con.

Then he was hired at U.S. Forged where he earned mythic status. Over his twenty-two years on the job, Gask safely moved up to twenty million dollars daily among the casinos and banks of Las Vegas without a single dollar loss. Not a cent. There had been attempts. Three men had died in botched hits on Gask's watch. Two drifters from Minnesota in '88 when they jumped him and his partner making a two million dollar drop at the Nugget. In 1983, Gask shot dead a 24-year-old Brit named Fitz-something, who was AWOL and wired on LSD when he tried to run off with two bags of newly minted one-hundred-dollar bills outside Caesar's Palace.

No one had, or would, win against Gask. He was the money mover king of Las Vegas. He kept the casinos lubricated, kept things humming. In this town, where every move was a gamble, Gask had the edge and he enlightened every newcomer that his greatness was the reason U.S. Forged entrusted him with the heaviest deliveries and rookie staff. He knew the business and its vulnerabilities, how to inventory a casino during a drop. How to scan faces and sense trouble like a county sheriff's bloodhound. Gask had no family. No wife. No kids. He was the job. U.S. Forged profited by his intense dedication and bigoted intimidation. All packaged in a six-foot-two-inch, two-hundred-thirty-pound button-straining frame.

The cost: $33,500 per annum. With a $22,000 retirement bonus coming his way for his twenty-two 'loss-free' years of service.

Moving north along the Strip, they stopped for a red light near the Hacienda. Gask scanned his clipboard. "We gotta load six ATMs at the next drop. Best use the dolly, Refried."

Perez's face appeared at the viewer window.

"Don't call me Refried, Elmer, please."

Gask's eyebrows ascended. "Why's that?"

"Because I don't like it."

"You don't like it?" Gask watched the casinos roll by.

"Call me Gil, or Perez, please."

"Or what? You gonna complain to the ACLU?" Gask bit hard on his toothpick. "You forget who you're talking to?"

"I'm just making a respectful request."

Gask sucked on his teeth. The muscles of his lower jaw pulsated.

"Well, well, well," he said as they passed the mammoth Excalibur with its fairy-tale turrets. "Here I am in 1993, crew chief of *'Gil, please don't call me Refried Perez, and Pocahontas.'* Ain't America the land of equal opportunity. This is what I get for my last week on the job? Attitude from the two of you." Gask shook his head. "And I get this shit-hole truck today, a heavy day. Still no transmitter. How many times have I told Rat to fix the goddammed trans-mitter in this one? Today I get the bottom of the heap."

Gask had deliberately not mentioned that Scout had alerted him to the fact they were skedded to have this truck weeks ago. He couldn't stomach anyone telling him anything, let alone a woman. Even worse, a Native Amer-ican woman. He ignored her. The truck they had was a far cry from the war wagons they usually used. Today they had the company's ten-year-old armor-plated Econoline van. The back up. Each crew used it for one shift every second week while the new trucks were serviced. But Scout thought it best not to debate facts. Let him rant.

"Nothing better happen today on my goddamn watch, right Scout?"

She didn't answer.

He looked at her. "What's with you?"

"Nothing."

"Nothing? I don't think so."

Gask sensed something wasn't right, he was sniffing at something, Something about her was eating at him, something he couldn't quite figure. She was as indifferent as she was on every shift. Maybe it was because he'd been away a week? He kept staring.

"Aren't you embarrassed riding in this tin can today, Scout?"

"I'm embarrassed riding with you today, yes."

Scout knew what Gask was thinking, that she was playing with him and he liked it. She was a challenge to him, an enigma. He knew virtually nothing about her. She said little and rarely smiled. But she knew men like Gask. Knew what they wanted. They told her with their eyes. She knew Gask enjoyed looking at her. Especially now. His eyes had lit on her uniform where a button had come undone, offering a glimpse of her ample breast. Firm and dark, bouncing in her bra until she caught him staring and, without a hint of shame, buttoned her shirt. Gask sucked on his teeth.

"You got a boyfriend, Scout?"

"I don't need one."

"Maybe you don't know what you need."

She said nothing and gazed beyond the glitz of the Strip west to the Spring Mountains, searching for answers. The meaning of her life. Jessica Mary Scout. Born in Browning, Montana. Her mother, Angela Scout, was Blackfoot. Her father was German, a philosophy student on exchange at MSU. He was conducting field research on Native American mysticism at the reserve when he met Angela. He was going to marry her and take her to Berlin. The day Jessie was born he borrowed a truck and was driving to the hospital. He swerved to miss a rabbit, the truck rolled. He was killed. Jessie's mother was never the same. Her heart was broken, and she had buried a piece of it with the man she loved.

Jessie had grown up accepting that her life had brought death.

One of the old women called it the black wind, the bringer of misfortune. And when Jessie was ten, the old woman told her that it would never leave her until the Lightning Rider came for her.

"Grandmother, how will I know him?"

"You will see with your eyes and know in your heart, child."

Until that time, the black wind would always be with her. Whispering. Laughing. Jessie began seeing it. Straw in a black wind. Hearing it in a crow's cry. Felt its presence. She was its harbinger. This was her destiny. Did the mountains know, she wondered, for they reached back to her home.

Jessie had lived most of her life in Browning with her mother. She missed her. Ached for her sad sweet smile, her fragrance, her gentle hands, the way she filled their house with the aroma of bannock. She missed her voice. Was it out there in the mountains? She listened for it, but heard nothing. Jessie yearned at this moment to be with her mother. To ask her. Would it always be true, what the old woman said? Don't think about it. But the black wind was kicking up, making her remember other times.

Several years after her father's death, Jessie's mother had a second child. A baby-girl she'd named Olivia. The father was an alcoholic trucker Angela had met at a bar in Shelby. When Angela was in the hospital having Olivia, the trucker raped Jessie. After he finished, he threatened to kill them all if she told. Jessie was eleven. She didn't tell. Then one winter day, they got word his rig had crashed near Standoff. He was dead. Angela locked herself away to mourn him as the cold winds blew down from the Bitteroot mountains.

As the armored car passed the Stardust, Jessie tried to drive the memories back. It was futile. Even now, a world away in Las Vegas. Please Olivia. Please . . . the wind . . . the black wind was there . . . scattering the snow. Blinding. Biting. The black wind was pushing her, punching her. Jessie was walking as fast as she could. The wind was stealing her breath. Snow melted in her eyes, blurring her vision. Faster. Walk faster. Holding her baby sister to her chest. Olivia naked against her skin. Feeling her tiny warmth. *Growing colder.* Wrapped in her shirt, worn coat, old blankets. Icy wind jabbing at Olivia through the holes. The halo of the car's lights. Snow crunching under its tires as it crept beside her. Warmth spilling from it when the window dropped. "Where you going, there?" asked the Montana Highway Patrol officer. Jessie's face was numb. "My sister's sick." The car squeaked to a halt. The door opened. "You got a baby under there! Let me see. Jesus! Get in. I'll take you to the hospital in Cut Bank!" He was a young cop. Concern on his face. The rhythm of the wipers. He said things into his radio. The smell of his cologne. Her skin thawing, tingling and itching. Olivia is blue. Her eyes are wide open. She does not move. She does not breathe. The black wind is blowing, and the siren was screaming and screaming.

The armored car passed the Mirage. Jessie liked the way

it caught the sun. She shrugged Gask off. People like Gask didn't intimidate her. She feared no one. For the knowledge she possessed could not be measured by the twenty-six years of her life, a life steeped in pain, a life broiling with cosmic forces and ancient truths. Her heart had traveled to regions few could conjure in dreams. It was reflected in her photo ID card clipped to her chest. Her pretty face was a mystery. A glint of arrogance in her eyes that squinted slightly to offer a smile. Or was it a sneer, one that revealed to people like Gask a hard fact they couldn't bear: They were insignificant. Jessie's face was a manifestation of righteous contempt for every injustice that had befallen her. It held a vengeful calm. Because she had purchased secrets. Paid in full with her tears. Her blood. Her life. She had come to Las Vegas, a city of risk, not to gamble.

But to collect.

They had come to the next delivery. The armored car exited Las Vegas Boulevard for the casino's driveway. Gask initialed his clipboard. "Ready back there, Re—Gil?"

"Ready."

"OK, Scout. We got a lot of ATMs here. Going to be thirty minutes inside then we got four more big loads. You know the drill. Drop us at the back and pick us up out front. Main entrance. Think your half-breed brain can manage that?"

She was silent, maneuvering the truck through the casino's parking lot.

"You hear what I said, Scout?" Gask looked at her.

"I know my job." She stopped the truck neatly at the casino's rear entrance, looked at Gask then radioed their arrival to Forged's dispatcher. Gask's jaw twitched. He spat out his toothpick and leaned toward her.

"Before this day is done, Scout, you and me are going to have a talk about your goddammed attitude." Gask's breath smelled of coffee and the celebratory retirement whiskey he mixed with it. "Maybe you fail to realize how close you are to having your Pocahontas ass kicked back to the reserve where you'll be reading numbers off ping pong balls to old squaws with no teeth."

Jessie looked at Gask calmly and said nothing.

Gask stared back hard and cold for a long time, then said: "Let's go, Refried."

Gask and Perez got out. Perez quickly loaded the dolly with delivery bags containing nearly a million dollars in unmarked bills while Gask scanned the area. The casino's security cameras recorded their work while rollers and families slowed to watch, making the old joke about their jackpots having arrived. They wheeled the cash into the casino, Gask glancing at the rear of the truck as Jessie headed for the main entrance.

A black wind was kicking up.

Half an hour after they'd finished loading the last ATM in the casino, Gask savored the air conditioning and decided to take a leak before he and Perez started for the main entrance to meet Scout.

"You're taking part in Las Vegas history, Gil, did you know that?" Gask said at the urinal while relieving himself.

Perez was bent over a sink, running cold water over his face. "No."

"When I punch out at the end of the week, I'll be leaving with a spotless loss sheet, one nobody in this town can touch."

"Didn't Roger Maddison retire from Titan Federal, a few months back? He put in twenty-seven years without a loss."

"No. I don't think so."

"It was in the newsletter. Your record would be second to his. Third actually. Pike Radeaux at Titan packed it in last year. Twenty-five loss-free years."

"No. You're wrong."

"I've still got the newsletter somewhere. I'll show you."

"That newsletter's bullshit," Gask flushed. "What the hell do you know, Refried? Let's go. Jesus. Why do I waste my breath on you?"

The wheels of the empty dolly cart sank in the lobby's carpet as Perez pushed it to the main entrance. Amid the eternal clanking of the slots, Gask strained in vain to locate the familiar colors of the Forged armored car through the glass doors. No truck. No Scout.

"That damned squaw better have an explanation!" Gask's fingers clasped his radio, knowing the instant he called for Scout on the air, a fuck-up attributed to him was exposed fleet-wide.

He held off.

"Perez, quick. Check the back. Maybe she had a breakdown. I'll search the front lot. Meet me back here. Hurry."

Gask shivered as the sun worked on him, his keys chiming as he trotted. No trace of the truck out front.

Perez returned, breathless. "She's gone, Elmer," he doubled over gasping. "Maybe it was the last drop? Those guys touching the truck?"

Gask's stomach tightened. Four days from retirement. Twenty-two years. His twenty-two-thousand-dollar bonus was melting here in a casino parking lot because of that stupid goddammed squaw.

"Better call it in, right, Elmer?"

Gask couldn't believe he was being screwed like this. Why?

"Elmer, she could have been taken hostage. Jesus! Call it in!"

Gask scanned the lot, willing the truck to appear. Goddammit. It was a hit. Had to be. On his goddamn watch. His twenty-two grand.

"Elmer! Call it in!" Perez's hand shook as he ran the back of it across his dried lips. "They could kill Jessie!"

Gask put his walkie-talkie to his mouth. "Sixty-five. Sixty-five. This is three. Radio check?"

"Elmer." Gask was wasting time covering his ass.

"Sixty-five. Sixty-five. This is three. Radio check?"

Nothing.

"Dispatch to three. Is there a problem?"

Perez watched him.

Gask swallowed hard. "There's been a hit."

"Say again three?"

"A hit. We can't raise our driver."

U.S. Forged Armored Inc., immediately activated its loss incident procedure, alerting a Las Vegas 911 dispatcher then Len Dawson, Forged's manager for Las Vegas. He notified Wade Smith, his supervisor at headquarters in Kansas City. Smith warned Dawson he would "have somebody's head on a stick if we lost points." Dawson drove to the scene calculating a multimillion-dollar loss with a severe detrimental impact on the company's insurance rates. Maybe the casino could be nailed for partial liability? Dawson cursed the fact Gask's crew had the truck with no electronic location finder. Scout's well-being did not enter his mind as he monitored Forged's attempts to reach her through the truck's radio and cellular phone.

Unit 1065 was not responding.

Las Vegas Metropolitan Police launched a bulletin across Clark County and the Valley. The Las Vegas FBI and Nevada Highway Patrol were alerted. Within two minutes, four marked Metro units arrived at the casino, followed later by an unmarked sedan and detectives Todd Braddick and Chester King from the LVMP robbery detail. Before they could enter the lobby, a crew from Channel Three and Ray Davis, the *Review Journal*'s crime senior reporter, approached them.

"Chester, you got a second?" Davis opened his notebook. "We hear it's an armored car heist with big numbers?"

King smiled. He was six feet six inches tall, a gentle giant whose confidence came from twelve years as a robbery detective. His partner was another story. Braddick had less than two years as a detective, yet he was a brash cock-of-the-walk. Handsome. Single. His laser-sharp eye for detail was earning him a reputation as fast as his switchblade tongue. He exhausted King. They tried unsuccessfully to blow by the reporters.

Davis said: "We heard three to four million, that right, Chester?" King wouldn't take the bait. Then Seleena Ann Ramone from Channel Three thrust her microphone toward him: "Have you found the driver, yet?"

Braddick shook his head. "Give us a break, Hon."

"Hon?"

"Folks, please," King spread his hands apart. "We just got here. You know more than we do. We'll get back to you. Thanks."

Inside, the detectives were directed to an office behind the main registration desk. Half a dozen people watched as Forged's manager was going at it with Theo Fontaine, the casino's security boss.

". . . this is on you, not the casino," Fontaine said.

"Just answer me. Did you, or did you not, seal the perimeter of your facility once my people reported the theft?" Dawson said.

"Your people never breathed a word to us. It was Metro who called us, sir. Don't be putting this on us."

"Excuse us, gentlemen," Braddick said. "Metro Robbery. Braddick and King. We'd like to interview the armored car crew, please. My guess is that is you two?" He pointed at Gask and Perez. They nodded.

"Theo, could you pull all your recorded security video for us," King said.

"Already on it, Chester."

King nodded to Gask. "Sir, could you come with me. Detective Braddick will interview your partner. Theo, we're going to need separate offices."

"No problem," he led them away.

"Detective," Dawson said. "I'd like a word with my staff first, if I may? I'd like to go over the log and drop sheets."

"And you are . . . ?" King said.

"Len Dawson. Manager of Forged's operations here."

"Mr. Dawson, once we're finished, they're all yours."

Fontaine led Braddick and Perez to a small meeting room. Plush carpet. Floor to ceiling one-way glass overlooking the outdoor pool. Big mahogany table. Thick leather chairs. Dark paneled walls. Gil Perez puffed his cheeks and exhaled as Braddick took his name and particulars, then asked:

"How much was in the truck when it vanished, Gil?"

"Three million seven hundred thousand. Unmarked nonsequential."

"You sure about the number?"

"I'm the money man, the counter."

"OK, tell me about the driver, Jessica Scout."

"Jessie, was—is a good person. She always defended me in front of Elmer. He's our crew chief."

"You needing defending?"

"He called us names. Called me Refried. Called Jessie squaw, Pocahontas. She's an American Indian. She stood up to Elmer. He's good at his job. Never had a successful hit on his watch. Retires this week after twenty-two years. He's a very tough boss."

"Gil, what was Jessie's demeanor today?"

"Same as any other day. She was quiet. Alone in her thoughts, she was a very quiet woman. What if she's dead? What if she's been killed?"

"Gil, we don't have any evidence of anything. We're only one hour into this. Do you remember anything unusual today?"

"Two guys."

"What about them?" Braddick wrote carefully.

"At the drop before this one. Here, I wrote it on my drop sheet," Perez handed it to Braddick, explaining. "Jessie said two rollers got too close to the truck. She sounded the horn to make them back off."

"Maybe a distraction for something else?"

"You think so? What if they killed her, there was three

point seven million left in the load. I was the money man today."

"Yes, you said. And she was scheduled to drive?"

"Yes."

"And the truck without the finder? You knew about that today?"

"Yes. Each crew is scheduled in advance to take it."

"*In advance?*" Braddick continued writing. "How long has Jessie been with the company?"

"Four, nearly five months."

"And you? How long?"

"Three years."

"What do you know about Jessie? You two socialize after work?"

"No. She's shy, quiet."

"Any money problems? Debts? Drugs? Gambling? She living beyond her pay?"

Perez shook his head.

"You know what she does after work? Who her friends are?"

"Like I said, she's very quiet."

"So you really don't know her at all, do you Gil?"

"I—I guess, I, man, I worked with Jessie four months."

"Gil, tell me why you said she was so quiet."

"I figure, by the little she told me, she'd had a sad life."

"How?"

"She started to tell me once how bad things always follow her."

"What bad things?"

"Death."

"Death?"

"Detective Braddick, what if she's dead already?"

• • •

A few doors away, in a dim office, Elmer Gask fished out a stick of gum and a fresh toothpick from his chest pocket, crossed his arms, leaned back hard in his chair and watched King.

"She was a bitch to me all morning, is all I can attest to her 'demeanor.' " Gask's toothpick moved rhythmically with his chewing.

"What do you think happened?"

The toothpick froze as the gum chewing stopped.

"I'll tell you what happened." Gask's eyes widened with cold rage. "I just lost a twenty-two thousand-dollar bonus because of that stupid squaw."

King waited for an explanation.

"I retire at the end of the week. You clock out with a loss-free sheet, you get a grand for every year."

"That's a tragedy. What do you think happened?"

"If I knew that, we'd recover our load," Gask resumed chewing. "She wasn't careful. I told her to be cautious after the incident with the two jerks at the previous drop."

"The two guys who approached the truck?"

"I told her to log it, to call it in to dispatch when we were in here servicing the ATMs."

"Did she?"

"I doubt it."

"What about her past, her personal and career history?"

"Squaw or half breed from some welfare-eating reserve in Montana, or some end of the world state like that. Supposed to have done a good job at security for some faggy antique dealer in New York. If you ask me, she was an equal opportunity hire. Right gender, right race, right useless."

"You don't think she was qualified?"

"I don't hire 'em, Chester."

"What kind of driver was she?"

"Substandard."

"What about her past, any debts, habits, anybody leaning on her?"

"I wouldn't know anything about that shit."

"Tell me about today, what sort of day was it?"

"Routine, we were just making our drops."

"What about the truck? It had no finder?"

"That was her job as driver to deal with that. I told her to get that finder fixed. She ignored me."

"Aren't you her supervisor?"

Gask gave some thought to how he should answer.

"Yes and I supervised her to see the finder was fixed. I was intending to write her up for not following through."

"I see. What do you know about Jessica Scout, her circles?"

"Not a goddamned thing. She never spoke to me. I told you, she was an ice bitch who acted like she was better than everyone."

"Tell me about Gil Perez?"

"He's kind of a shifty beaner."

"That right?"

"Always talking about his dream of going away and starting his own car wash business. Only thing holding him back was lack of cash."

"That so?"

"That's so."

"And what about you, Elmer, what do you talk about?"

"Football and America."

"What about America?"

"She's fucked up real good."

"What really happened to the money?"

"Jessica Scout got herself jammed. Thought she knew it all. Let her guard down, now she's gone."

"That prospect doesn't exactly bring tears to your eyes."

Gask shifted his toothpick to the opposite side of his mouth then leaned to King. "Her stupidity cost me twenty-two grand."

"But you break even."

"How's that, Chester?"

"Scout may have paid with her life."

Later, Braddick and King compared notes at a quiet table at the casino's nearest bar, which serviced a keno lounge.

Braddick started. "My guy fears she is dead."

"Mine hopes she is," King said before his pager went off. He read the caller's number. "Looks like the feds." He squinted, tilting the pager for better light. "Yup. FBI's offering to help. I'll call."

"Three point seven. What do you make, Chester? Inside? Outside?"

"All of the above."

Joe Two Knives's dark glasses reflected the sun, cloudless sky and warehouses of a light industrial section of Las Vegas.

What if something went wrong? He watched the garage one hundred yards away. He did not want to be near it in case something went wrong. Nothing appeared suspicious. Everything had gone smoothly. Every detail of preparation had come off cleanly.

He checked his watch then the cell phone on the seat beside him. His hands were sweating inside the two pairs of surgical gloves he wore. The car's air conditioner kept him cool. He kept himself calm. He had been through this before. Twenty-five years ago. *No one will die this time.* But what if she didn't make it? What would he do? He didn't know. It was the one event he did not plan for.

His phone trilled.

"Yes," he said.

"ETA seven to ten."

"Thank you."

Two Knives drove along a back service alley, stopping at the rear of the garage which bore a small painted sign: AAA Armored Repair. It was a rectangular cinder block building. One story. The garage had three auto bays each with an electronic-door in the front and rear. He unlocked the building, parked his car in one of the bays then closed the rear electronic door. The garage was clean and empty. It had a small office and a bathroom. He went to a work-table, switched on a scanner, listening as Las Vegas police dispatches echoed clearly.

A horn sounded two quick beeps in front of the building. Two Knives hit a switch, the door rose, a motor revved, and a U.S. Forged armor-plated Ford van edged inside, the electronic door closing behind it. Jessica Scout stepped out and studied her watch.

"Nineteen minutes since I left."

He tossed Scout two pairs of rubber gloves. "Every second counts. You know what to do."

Scout unlocked the truck's side door, entered, then slid three canvas bags to him. All together, they weighed about forty pounds, he figured, carrying them to the work table. The cash was wrapped in blue plastic, three packages of one hundreds, fifties, and twenties. They covered the table with the bundles, laying each one flat.

"Three million, seven hundred thousand," she said. "Unmarked."

He then took a metal detector wand and slowly passed it over the cash several times. No transmitters. He took one bundle, pulled up his pants leg and rubbed it against his moist skin. Then he took an ultraviolet lamp and illuminated his leg. Nothing. No chemicals. He carefully packed the bundles into white plastic medical containers, with lids cautioning:

DANGER DO NOT OPEN
MEDICAL WASTE
CONTAMINATED CADAVER TISSUE

He sealed the containers, placed them into three small, black suitcases, then loaded them into the car's rear seat. Then he grabbed a utility knife, a roll of silver duct tape, and a small box. His eyes met Scout's. "Ready?"

She nodded and climbed into the back of the truck. He taped her ankles together, then her knees, then her wrists, avoiding the rubber gloves, then her mouth. Again he looked in her eyes and stroked her hair.

She was prepared. Scout rolled onto her stomach.

Two Knives pulled her Glock from her holster. Examined it. He removed the safety, chambered a round, placed the muzzle against Scout's back, laying it nearly flat while pressing it slightly into the fleshy part of her hip. The bullet would graze her. His finger slid around the trigger. Two Knives saw Scout's pretty half-turned face, blinking in anticipation.

Just enough to bleed, he instructed himself.

She nodded.

He fired the gun. Scout lurched, grunting. A small tear, edges blackened with powder appeared on her uniform. Blood soaked the wound. He examined it. A small charred gash. Her skin was ragged and torn. He cut the tape from Scout's mouth and wrists, making sure some blood was on the remnants. The used tape with her blood, hair and fibers from her uniform would be left in the truck.

"Ok?"

"It burns a little, but I'm fine."

"I'll patch it up."

Two Knives opened the first aid kit. Scout removed her shirt. She jerked when he dabbed iodine in her wound, more so than when she was shot. He dressed her wound.

"We're almost through. Stand up."

Scout undid her utility belt, letting it drop to the floor. Two Knives dropped the Glock in the truck. Scout undid her pants, handing them to him. He ripped them near the zipper.

"We're coming up on half an hour," he said, scooping up the knife, tape and kit, dropping them in the trash as he rushed to the small office. Scout, now stripped down to her bra and panties, gathered her hair as she hurried to the garage's washroom.

In the office, Two Knives changed into new, pressed slacks, pin-striped shirt, Gucci shoes, and a conservative jacket. He combed his neatly trimmed silver hair, then slipped on a pair of wire-rimmed glasses.

Taped to the bottom of the desk was a brown envelope

with several passports, driver's licenses, credit cards, cash. He tucked it into his breast pocket. Then he gathered everything from the worktable and tossed it in the trash, except the radio scanner. That went in the car. He left a window down so he could still hear it. He opened the trunk. A wheelchair was folded inside. Next, he inventoried the entire garage, nothing was left. Nothing. He closed the doors of the Forged truck then unfurled a white nylon sheet that he cast over the van, pulling it down at spots where it was uneven. He checked the printed note he had taped earlier to the window of the front door.

Closed Indefinitely Due to Death in Family.

"Ready," said the old woman who'd stepped from the washroom. She was wearing a light-knit knee-length sweater over a flower print caftan, flat-soled shoes. An emerald scarf hid her neck, her gray hair reached to her shoulders, framing her face, which was sallow and frowning under large, dark glasses. She was wearing rubber gloves and clutching her brown purse. She was hunched as if she were ill or enduring pain as she walked to the car's front passenger seat.

Two Knives grabbed the trash from the washroom, then tied three large garbage bags from the garage and tossed them in the car's trunk. He hit the switch for the electronic door, drove the car outside, stopping to close the garage door before they drove off down the rear alley.

Several blocks away, he stopped to drop the trash bags in a warehouse dumpster. He knew the schedule. This dumpster would be emptied the next morning.

They were well along Interstate 15 southbound, which paralleled the Strip, by the time their portable scanner crackled with the first dispatch of an armored car heist at a casino on Las Vegas Boulevard.

"So far, so good," he said, tossing the scanner out the window as they neared the Exec Air Terminal at McCarran.

Scout said nothing. She was looking west to the mountains.

The clerk at Desert Airstream Services moved from behind her counter to greet the old woman in the wheelchair and her physician.

"Dr. Hegel. Everything's ready. That's a pretty scarf, Mrs. Duggan," the clerk said after summoning the ground crew. They assisted Hegel getting his patient, Heather Duggan, comfortably aboard her chartered jet, for her one-way flight to Orange County.

Duggan, a reclusive casino heiress, had a terminal condition, her doctor had explained a few weeks earlier. It was her wish to die in California where she was born. Hegel had arranged the trip, paying cash in advance.. He'd included large gratuities for respecting the eccentric woman's privacy.

The fresh-cut roses in the jet were a nice touch, Two Knives thought as the small Cessna Citation shot over the Spring Mountains, about ninety minutes after Scout had driven off with $3.7 million in unmarked cash.

That evening after dinner in the restaurant of the Ramada in Santa Ana, Two Knives told Scout that he wanted to do something he'd dreamed of doing all his life and they drove to Newport Beach where they watched the sun set on the ocean.

"I never really knew you Jessie," he said as they walked near the surf. "I was angry at Angela for being with a white man. I'd thought, how could my sister betray her people, her blood. I was consumed with anger. I'd lost my way in the world and ended up in a cell."

Gulls cried above them.

"I never meant for that man, the armored car guard, to die like that in San Diego. It was a terrible mistake. A terrible thing and I paid for it with twenty-five years of my life." The sun painted the creases of his sad, weary face with gold as he searched the horizon. "I did a lot of thinking in those twenty-five years, thinking how I could set things right."

"My mother was angry that I'd written to you in prison. She said you were no good, Joe."

"She has a right to her opinion of me. Especially now. I heard she has less than three months with her illness."

Scout nodded.

"Jessie, your letters kept me alive during my darkest times. Gave me a reason to want to make up for deserting my own blood when they needed me."

"You're the only one who knows the truth about all the things that happened when I was young."

"It hurt me more than you'll ever know, to read of your pain. I knew in my heart you did nothing to deserve it. I believe you were owed a life, and that I could help you get it."

Scout took her uncle's hand and squeezed it.

"Remember, you must never call your mother, or see her. Once the FBI puts everything together, they'll watch. If you're going to survive you must let her spend her last days thinking you are dead. It's better this way. You'll see her in the next world."

Scout brushed a tear from her cheek.

As if reading her mind, he said: "Not even a letter, Jessie."

She nodded. They'd gone over every detail.

"This looks like a good spot." He stopped, pulled a hotel towel from his bag and began to undress. Jessie was surprised. He was wearing swimming trunks. "I've always dreamed of swimming in the ocean," he said.

At fifty-four, he had the firm muscular body of a man thirty years younger, a dividend of keeping in shape during his time in Folsom. Scout noticed a small tattoo over his shoulder that looked like a storm over mountains.

"What's this mean?"

"Ah, that," he said. "I got it from an old chief I met on C-Yard the second year I was inside," he said. "Funny. I wanted an eagle. But he was very insistent that I have this one."

"What is it, what does it mean?"

"He said it was for the entity who delivers calm after the storm. Pretty cool, don't you think?"

Jessie nodded.

"The old man called it, The Lightning Rider."

Two Knives walked into the ocean, leaving Scout standing alone on the beach brushing her tears, feeling the warmth of the fading sun.

Driven to Distraction

Marcia Talley

Through the Darkness, released in 2006, is Marcia Talley's sixth Hannah Ives mystery. Her debut novel, *Sing It To Her Bones* (1999) won a Malice Domestic grant for Best Unpublished Novel and was eveually honored as an Agatha Award nominee for Best First Novel. The next Ives mystery, *Unbreathed Memories,* won the *Romantic Times* Reviewers' Choice Award for Best Contemporary Mystery. Talley has published a number of short stories, including two that were nominated for Agatha Awards. This story, from *Chesapeake Crimes II,* won the 2005 Agatha Award for Best Short Mystery story.

When Harrison keeled over and died I didn't think I'd marry again, but Mama said, "Life goes on, Marjorie Ann. When you fall off a horse, you have to climb right back on."

Given a chance, Mama would have matched me up with

one of Harrison's law partners, right there at South River Country Club as they converged on the roast beef carving station after the funeral, but I have my pride. I waited a respectable year before marrying Stephen, who swept me off my feet with the lean, rawboned, good looks of a Montana rancher, a laid-back wrangler who spoke fluent U.S. Tax Code. The way Stephen handled Harrison's estate was nothing short of dazzling.

Stephen was clever with gadgets, too. In his office at home, he had a desktop computer, a laptop, a scanner, three monitors—one as big as an over-the-sofa painting of the Last Supper—two cameras that scanned the room like disembodied eyeballs, and wires that snaked kudzu-like around the table legs. I pretty much kept out until cleaning day when I'd have to run the vacuum and dust his office myself. Theresa refused. The blinking and beeping unnerved her. She was convinced the machines would steal her thoughts, and to tell the truth, I half agreed with her.

The last thing Stephen needed was another piece of electronics, so for his fortieth birthday, I gave him a fabulous five-course dinner at Northwoods Restaurant and a gift card from American Express. He reached across his crème caramel, gathered up my hand and pressed it to his lips, his green eyes flashing "thank you" in the candlelight. By the way he glanced at his watch, I suspected he wanted to skip the after-dinner glass of Remy Martin and rush straight off to the mall, but, fortunately, it had closed.

I hoped he'd use the card at Nordstrom or Eddie Bauer, but the next morning Stephen left the house early and was probably waiting at Circuit City when the doors slid open.

He came home lugging a box labeled MapMasterIV, and spent the rest of Saturday morning holed up in his office, reading the manual. After lunch, he plopped his new toy onto the dashboard of his pickup and drove off, happy as a clam.

Sunday morning when I eased into the passenger seat of the BMW, I found Stephen balancing the MapMasterIV on his knees. He plugged its cord into the cigarette lighter socket and jiggled what I took to be an aerial up and down. He leaned sideways, so close I could smell his Drakkar Noir aftershave, adjusted the MapMaster on its bean bag base, positioned the whole shebang on the dashboard, and punched a few buttons. Then he backed carefully out of the driveway, grinning. "Just listen," he said.

Drive point two miles west and turn right.

The MapMaster was female and she spoke in a calm, non-judgmental voice, like the 411 information lady.

Obediently, Stephen turned right onto Dogwood Lane. "It'll direct us to church."

"You know how to get to church."

"Of course I know how to get to church, Marjorie Ann, but it's interesting to see how the MapMaster will route us."

Drive one point seven miles south and turn right.

Stephen tilted the MapMaster slightly in my direction so I could see the bright yellow display. He tapped the screen with his index finger. "Here's our route in pink. That's the interstate over there, in red," he explained, as if I were a particularly slow and difficult child.

Continue point five miles and take ramp right.

Stephen flipped on his turn signal and eased the car onto the interstate. "It's fantastic technology," he beamed. "Uses the global positioning system. It gloms onto satellites, figures out where you are, then gives you driving directions." He waved a hand. "It comes pre-programmed with hotels and restaurants, or you can put in a street address . . ." His voice trailed off. "I've got it programmed for St. Margarets."

Drive four point one miles and exit right.

I watched as Allen Parkway, our usual turnoff, receded in my side view mirror. "Why didn't you turn back there, Stephen?"

Stephen stared straight ahead, one hand resting lightly on top of the steering wheel. "I wanted to see where Marilyn would route us."

"Marilyn?"

"MapMaster. M. M. Get it?"

I rolled my eyes toward heaven. Where in the marriage vows did I promise to cherish a guy who names his toys after dead movie stars? I sighed. "Well, I can understand why, uh, Marilyn might be helpful if you're driving in a strange city and don't know where you're going," I grumbled. "But if you already know the way, why waste time fooling around?" I swiveled the screen toward me and studied the buttons: Find, Route, Menu.

"Don't mess with it, Marjorie Ann! You'll screw up the settings."

"Okay, okay." I raised both hands in self-defense. "I won't touch your precious whatzit." I folded my arms across my chest and settled into my seat, wishing I could turn on the radio, but I knew better. Stephen wouldn't be able to hear MM over the sound of NPR.

A few minutes later, MM chirped, *In four hundred feet turn right.*

Stephen pulled off the expressway and, following MM's

instructions, wound through a public housing project and an industrial neighborhood until at last, by some miracle, we turned onto a street I recognized and I could see St. Margaret's steeple directly ahead.

Arriving at destination on right.

"Well I'll be darned," I said.

Stephen eased into the parking lot, switched off the ignition and grinned like a schoolboy. "Ain't technology grand?"

Even Reverend Nelson's interminable sermon on life lessons to be learned from the parable of the Prodigal Son didn't dampen Stephen's enthusiasm. After the benediction, he hustled me out to the car, not even pausing on the chapel steps to shake the good Reverend's meaty hand. "Toilet paper," I reminded my husband somewhat breathlessly. "And milk."

Stephen drove the few blocks to our Whole Foods market and waited while I went into the store. When I returned to the parking lot carrying my purchases, Stephen demonstrated how to set a waypoint. "You just drive where you want to go, Marjorie Ann, and press the Mark button." A number popped up on the screen. "Now you use this rocker pad to rename the waypoint. W . . . H . . . O . . . There. Whole Foods." Looking over his shoulder, I noticed that Stephen had already set up waypoints for his office, Home Depot, Golds Gym, B&B Yachts and our home, of course. He punched the waypoint labeled "Home" and peeled out of the parking lot, tires squealing.

Between Whole Foods and Home, the bypass around the construction site on Truman Street threw MM for a loop. *Off route. Recalculating.*

"Why it'd do that?" I asked.

"It's a new road, Marjorie Ann. Marilyn doesn't know about it."

MM dutifully recalculated and wanted us to go up Route 2 and take the Route 100 by-pass, but Stephen decided not to.

Off route. Recalculating.

The woman was far more patient with my husband than I was.

As soon as possible, make a U-turn, she recommended politely.

"You could make money," I mused. "Designing special voices for this thing."

"What do you mean?"

"You can already select a language," I said. "So why not come up with some alternate voice chips," I suggested, "like the nagging wife. Instead of saying 'off route, recalculating,' she'd say, 'You missed the turn, you idiot! But do you ever listen to me? Nooooh.'"

The corner of Stephen's mouth twitched upward.

"Or," I continued, warming to my invention. "You could punch in a waypoint for your mother. Then every time you by-passed her house it's 'So, Mr. Bigshot. How come you never visit your mother? Make a U-turn. Now!'"

Stephen joined in, dredging up a Beavis and Butthead voice from somewhere in his reckless youth. "Whoa, Dude, Like there's a fork in the road. Huh huh huh. Fork. Get it?" He chuckled, a rare event, and turned to study me over the rims of his sunglasses. "You patent that, Marjorie Ann, and we can both retire to the south of France."

Truth is, Stephen made excellent money as the head of

his own firm. We could retire to the south of France like, any minute, if he wanted, but Stephen preferred to spend his money and his spare time on boating or golfing or off-roading in the Arizona desert. The previous weekend he'd dragged me to the GM dealership to check out a Humvee. As if.

I squirmed in my seat. MM had selected a route home that didn't involve a freeway. If she didn't hurry up, the milk would spoil. "I think you should just go straight up 32," I said, feeling testy.

Stephen ignored me.

"I'll bet this route is ten minutes longer."

"Than?"

"Than going straight up 32."

"Where's your sense of adventure, Marjorie Ann?"

"I don't know, Stephen. I think I lost it back in 1998."

MM was feeling testy, too. *Off route. Recalculating.*

Stephen slapped his palm against the steering wheel. "Damn!"

I flinched. "Why'd she say that?"

"I missed the exit. I was listening to you, Marjorie Anne. Can't you keep quiet even for a minute?"

I turned my head and glared out the passenger-side window, my eyes shooting darts into the trees, my mouth clamped shut, feeling glad that Stephen was leaving town the next day for the annual AICPA tech conference in Las Vegas. He was giving a talk on the paperless office. Paperless, ha! Good thing nobody at the AICPA had to empty Stephen's wastepaper basket or they'd ask for their money back.

I would have gone along—the Venetian Hotel has lagoons with gondolas floating through it, et mind-blowing cetera—but Mama was having an eyelift and I felt obliged to stay home and hold her hand. So while Stephen spent his days holed up in frigid conference rooms and his nights playing blackjack on The Strip, I spent mine fetching and toting for Mama. I bundled up her newspapers for recycling, cleaned out her refrigerator and scoured the shelves at Blockbuster for Russell Crowe DVDs. She invited me to the film fest, but I think it was because she wanted *me* to make the popcorn.

Mid-week, I was taking a break from Mama and getting a pedicure when she rang through on my cell phone. "Can you pick up Elroy in Shady Side?"

Elroy was Mama's handyman. His truck had "broke down" and Mama was too hopped up on pain killers to drive down there herself.

I didn't feel like going anywhere and told her so.

"Do *you* want to pick dead leaves out of my swimming pool, Marjorie Ann? Or mow the lawn?" Without waiting for an answer, Mama started rattling off directions to Elroy's, but I tuned out about halfway through. I had Elroy's address. I had Stephen's MapMaster. Piece of cake.

Stephen had left the MapMaster locked up in his truck, so when I got home from the beauty parlor, I moved it into the BMW. When I plugged it in, MM politely informed me she was acquiring her satellites, then waited for me to press Find, then Addresses. I used the rocker key to spell out, number by number and letter by letter, Elroy's address, then pressed Go To.

MM, bless her little batteries and computer chip heart, got me to Elroy's and back to Mama's without a hitch.

I was backing down her driveway, mere seconds from a clean getaway, when Mama popped out her front door, waving her arms. "Trash bags, Marjorie Ann! I need heavy-duty trash bags. And bug spray!" I waggled my fingers so she'd know I'd heard her, then punched Home Depot into the MapMasterIV.

I hardly ever go to Home Depot, especially from Mama's house, so it didn't particularly surprise me when MM directed me off the freeway and onto a quiet street in Morningside Heights. I *was* surprised when she advised me to turn right into a cul-de-sac and absolutely astonished when MM announced that I was *arriving at destination,* smack dab in front of a cute little Dutch colonial.

I recognized the house. It belonged to Cheryl, from church. She sang in the choir with Stephen. At the Ferguson wedding they'd sung a duet, "One Hand, One Heart," and there hadn't been a dry eye in the house.

Why had Stephen set a waypoint for Cheryl? I felt dizzy, wondering if all the hours they'd spent practicing "One Hand, One Heart" had escalated into Two Hands, Big Breasts.

Deeply suspicious, I selected the waypoint Stephen had set up for Gold's Gym and pushed Go To. MM directed me out of the cul-de-sac, back onto the freeway and through the center of town. Gold's Gym had long disappeared from my rearview mirror when MM instructed me to turn into Foxcroft Acres, a new development on the south side of town.

Arriving at destination on right.

I eased my foot onto the brake and stared at the name on the mailbox: J. Barton. I recognized that name, too. The "J" stood for Julie and she was Stephen's personal trainer.

So, Julie had set up private practice in her home? Helping my husband with his pushups, perhaps? If Stephen hadn't been in Las Vegas, I would have beaned him with one of his own five-pound, handheld dumbbells.

I slammed the accelerator to the floor, and peeled out of there. Mama's trash bags and bug spray would just have to wait.

The waypoints labeled "T&E" and "Russell" turned out to be just that, the Art Deco building housing the city's most prominent accounting firm and the office of Russell Herman, Stephen's attorney, respectively. But when I followed MM's directions for B&B Yachts, she took me miles out of town, down Route 214 and onto a narrow country road that ended in a long wooden pier.

Arriving at destination.

The BMW's tires crunched on the gravel as I eased onto the shoulder and cut the engine. Just ahead, at the water's edge, stood a cluster of summer cottages that had been converted into year-around homes. A child of perhaps three or four rode a tricycle around and around on the blacktopped driveway of a white clapboard rancher adjacent to the pier. I scrunched down in the driver's seat and watched the kid pop wheelies, my head swimming. What the hell was going on?

Almost immediately, the garage door yawned open and a woman appeared, her hair a nimbus of gold against the dark interior behind her. I scrunched down even further. When I dared to peek again, she had hustled the kid into a car seat and was backing her PT Cruiser out of the garage and down the drive.

B&B Yachts? Hah! I knew what was going on. Stephen was leading a double life. He probably had mistresses, maybe even wives and children, scattered all across the city. The county. The state of Maryland. Maybe even the world!

After all I'd done for the SOB! I watched the dust kicked

up by his girlfriend's tires swirl down the road behind me and remembered a moment just before our wedding, at the rehearsal dinner. I had been leaning over the sink in the ladies room, touching up my lip liner, when Mama took me aside and in one of those priceless mother-daughter moments, came the closest she ever came to discussing sex with me. "Remember, Marjorie Ann. Give a man steak at home, and he won't go out for hamburger." Well, I'd been giving Stephen filet mignon twice a week since our honeymoon, so what the hell was he going out for? Tenderloin?

When the dust had settled, I climbed out of the car, hoping that a walk in the spring sunshine might clear the sick visions out of my head. I strolled to the end of the road and stepped onto the pier. To my left, three sailboats bobbed quietly, water chuckling softly along their sleek fiberglass hulls. To my right, a half dozen kayaks were lined up on a narrow strip of sand, each stern bearing a TWHA stencil to show that they belonged to the Truxton Woods Homeowners' Association. If I took one out for a paddle, probably nobody would notice or care.

I reached the end of the pier and sat down on the rough boards, dangling my feet over the water. A soft breeze lifted my hair and cooled the hot tears that streamed down my cheeks. I turned my face toward the afternoon sun. As far as I was concerned, Stephen could take a long walk off a short pier.

I sat up straight. Where had that come from? Perhaps the snowy egret elegantly fishing in the shallows had whispered the suggestion into my ear. *A long walk off a short pier.* I scrambled to my feet, brushed off the seat of my slacks and hurried back to the car to fetch MM.

With the MapMaster tucked under one arm, I returned
to the beach and selected what appeared to be the most
seaworthy kayak. I switched MM to battery power, then laid
it carefully on the bottom of the boat. I plopped down on the
sand, rolled up my pant legs, removed my shoes, and set
them next to MM. When I was confident nobody was looking,
I eased the kayak into the water, climbed aboard, and pad-
dled to a spot about fifty feet off the end of the pier where I
figured the water would be nice and deep. I balanced the
paddle across the gunwales and lifted MM onto my lap, my
thumbs hovering over her array of buttons.

I had been half listening when Stephen showed me how
to set a waypoint; I hoped I wouldn't foul it up. Following
his instructions as I remembered them, I punched the
MARK button to capture my present location, somewhere
in the middle of Calvert Creek. When MM asked me to, I
used the rocker pad to scroll through the letters, carefully
relabeling my new waypoint: "B&B Yachts" and obliter-
ating the old one.

When Stephen came home from Vegas on Friday it was
all I could do to remain civil, wondering with whom he'd
shared his king-sized bed at the Venetian, wondering who
had been his lucky charm at the blackjack tables, wondering who had been his partner for the two-for-the-price-
of-one buffet dinner special at The Mirage. I could hardly
bear for Stephen to touch me, wondering as his fingers
caressed my cheek exactly where those hands had been
lately.

Monday night, no surprise, Stephen called on his cell
phone to say he wouldn't be home for dinner.

"Where are you now?" I asked.

"Just leaving the gym and heading back to the office."

In the background, MM chimed in. *In point three miles take ramp right.*

I paused, doing my own recalculation. *Ramp right.* From his gym to the office was a straight shot down Fairmont. No right ramps anywhere in that scenario. "I see," I said, each word a frozen shard.

"It's tax season, Marjorie Ann. Need I remind you? I'm working late. I have a lot to do."

Drive one point three miles then exit left.

Where had I seen an exit left recently? Ah, yes. On the way to whomever lived at "B&B Yachts".

Inside me, something snapped. "Lies, Stephen. All lies."

"What are you talking about, Marjorie Ann?"

I held the receiver to my ear, silently seething, listening to Stephen pile excuse upon sorry excuse while in the background, turn by turn, MM was confirming what I already knew. In a few minutes, Stephen would be heading down a dark, dusty country road, where a beautiful blonde awaited him in a white clapboard rancher adjacent to a pier.

"Marjorie Ann? You still there?"

"As far as I'm concerned, Stephen, you can go straight to hell!"

"You can't . . ." Stephen began, followed by, "What the—?" and seconds later by the nearly simultaneous explosions of shattered glass and deploying airbags.

And MM's voice, softly reassuring. *Arriving at destination.*

Little Sins

Mike MacLean

Mike MacLean's ethically challenged P.I. first appeared in the *Thrilling Detective* story "Little Holes" and will soon darken the pages of *Ellery Queen's Mystery Magazine*. In addition, Mike is featured in the *Best American Mystery Stories* of 2006, edited by Scott Turow. A teacher of America's youth, Mike lives in Tempe, Arizona with his wife Bobbie and their three lazy dogs. When not teaching or writing, he studies Ja-Shin-Do and watches way too many violent movies.

I'm about to do something very bad.

The car is a Porsche. A vintage red Boxster. Sitting in a parking space like it's any other mortal car. Forty years old, but it gleams like it just rolled out of the factory. I know I'll never own such a beautiful machine.

I pull an ice pick from my sheath and punch a hole in the taillight. I feel like I've defaced the Mona Lisa.

Seconds later, I'm back behind the wheel of my rust-bucket Nova, parked across the lot.

Waiting.

The Porsche almost loses me on the freeway. Then I see the cracked taillight, bleeding white. My beacon in the dark.

I catch up to him on an exit ramp and follow the little car into a residential neighborhood. Once the area was called "working class." Now it's "funky." Track homes line both sides of the street. New paint on old bricks. Green grass instead of weeds.

The Porsche pulls into carport of a renovated bungalow. I do a drive by. Scope out my target. His name is Jason Powell.

Jason has a friend. The two of them are straight out of a Hitler youth dream. Strong, blonde, and white as the sun. But they do something that would've earned them a dose of Zyklon B from the Third Reich. They kiss. Full on the lips.

My dad was no Nazi, but he would've called the men faggots. Would've spit the word out like it was a rancid piece of meat. Tells you what kind of sensitive guy old dad was. Me, I barely wince. Darwin called that evolution.

Before I can get the camera up, they're in through the front door. I curse myself, kill the engine of the Nova, and swing out from behind the wheel. Time to get up close and personal.

I creep around the side of the house. Feels like I've spent my whole life sneaking around in the dark, circling other people's homes, other people's lives.

A light clicks on in the kitchen window. I ready my

camera. Through the glass, I see Jason, scavenging in the fridge. Jason but no friend.

"What do you think you're doing?"

I turn around slowly and there he is, Jason's kissing partner. Blonde guy with the LA Fitness muscles.

Shrugging, I hold my hands up in surrender. "Howdy."

"I asked what the fuck you're doing?" And now he's got this smile on his face. A pit bull's smile. A "trouble" smile.

"Relax," I tell him. "You got me. You won. So, I'll leave you guys alone. Catch you another time."

I try to walk away, but he stops me with a straight arm. Veins bulge, squirming like a snake from his bicep to his wrist. "You're not going anywhere," he says. "Not until you answer some questions."

"What'd you say?"

"You're not going . . ."

That's when I make my move. It's an old trick. Fighting Dirty 101. Ask a man a question then hit him while he's giving you his witty reply.

My first shot is a quick jab. I follow with a hard right to the base of the chin. Then I kick him in the balls like I'm going for the extra point.

The guy's eyes bulge and he doubles over. While he's down, my fingers snake into his hair, and I drive my knee up into his face. Bone crashes with cartridge. That perfect Aryan nose of his goes "crack!" Blood geysers out in all directions.

He sits down hard on his butt, his eyes like window glass. He stays there for a moment then tries to stand.

I shake my head. "Don't be stupid kid. Won't do either us a bit of good."

He listens. Sits holding his ruined nose as I walk past him, glaring at me.

"Nothing personal," I tell him.

I head for the Nova, hoping not to hear sirens coming my way. A voice catches up to me as I'm slipping behind the wheel.

"Wait!"

I look up to see Jason Powell running towards the Nova. When I try to close the door on him, the kid grabs the handle and holds tight.

"Please," he says. "Wait."

"Nothing to say to you." I turn the key in the ignition and the engine rumbles to life. If the kid doesn't let go, I'll give the Nova a little gas, send him tumbling on the black top.

"It's my brother, isn't it?" he asks. "My brother hired you to spy on me, didn't he?"

I rev the engine as a warning, but the kid doesn't let up.

"Whatever he's paying you, I'll match it," he says. "In fact, I'll double it."

I take my foot off the gas and look the kid in the eye. "Double?"

Old man Powell lies in a hospital bed at Saint Joseph's, tubes and wires coming out of him like spaghetti. His eyes are closed tight to the world. His mouth is opened wide in a perpetual yawn. His skin is the color of faded sheets.

Once upon a time, Powell ruled an empire of car dealerships and hotel chains. He owned thoroughbred horses, sailed yachts, and dined with senators. He was one of the richest, most powerful men in the state. Now, the old man needs someone to wipe his ass for him.

"Okay to talk in front of him?" I ask.

"He's out of it right now," says Patrick. He's Powell's son—Jason's big brother. A polo shirt and khaki kind of guy. A sweater vest kind of guy. Handsome in a boyish sort of way. Soft.

"But he's lucid, right?" I ask. "When he's awake, I mean."

Patrick waves his hand in the air like he's shooing away a fly. "Sure he's lucid. I've got a doctor in my pocket that'll testify to it. But there isn't much time left. Five weeks max. So I need those pictures."

The place stinks of ammonia and the constant "beep, beep, beep" of the monitors is working on my nerves. "I've got a few already. The two of them walking around, getting coffee. Nothing incriminating."

"Not good enough," says Patrick. "I need them kissing, or at least holding hands. Fucking would be better. My dad's from the old school, you understand? One look at a photo like that and he'll write Jason out of the will. Won't even think twice about it, the bitter old fart."

"Giving you a bigger slice of the pie."

"And why not?" Patrick says. "My brother's been living his depraved lifestyle since he was sixteen. Pulling the wool over Dad's eyes the whole time. I deserve a bigger slice."

"You'll get no argument from me."

Patrick flashes a perfect smile, the kind that belongs on a toothpaste commercial. "Of course I won't. I didn't forget your bonus. Five thousand on top of your regular rate. But I need those photos, and I need them yesterday."

"You'll get them. Trust me."

I pass the waiting area on my way to the elevators. It's a big room full of overstuffed chairs and old magazines. A line of windows overlooks the grounds, letting in the dusty sunshine. As comfortable as a hospital waiting room could aspire to.

With his money, old man Powell could've gone anywhere in the world. But he owned a chunk of Saint Joseph's and liked to stay close to his investments, even in the end.

I notice Patrick making a pit stop here. There's a woman sitting in the corner, and he leans in to kiss her on the cheek. The woman is his father's second wife; I recognize her from my research. They talk to each other in whispers, their faces close.

Too close.

The woman's a trophy wife. Maybe forty, judging by the smile lines. But nothing else gives away her age. She's tall. Curvy. Blonde from a bottle. She's visiting a hospital, visiting her dying husband, but that doesn't stop her from wearing a skimpy sundress. Showing off lots of tan skin.

She touches her stepson's chest. Lets her fingers linger there.

I look away and catch sight of the youngest of the Powell clan—little Ashley, sitting across the room. Little Ashley's seventeen with a woman's body and long black hair that curtains down over half her face. She stares back at me. Something dark living there in her eyes.

I grab the elevator and leave the happy Powell family behind. In the lot down stairs, I've got Johnny Cash waiting for me in the tape deck of my Nova. I've also got a bag full of camera equipment in the trunk.

A picture, they say, is worth a thousand words. Maybe I can do better than that.

• • •

I wait and watch.

I'm sitting in a rented Pontiac, parallel parked on a hillside overlooking a man-made lake. The car is white with factory everything—about as inconspicuous as a brick wall. It's perfect. I couldn't risk driving the Nova. Couldn't risk Jason Powell recognizing it.

The fake lake has a track around it for morning joggers. Jason is there, running with his little friend Roland, the two of them taking their time. They do a couple of eight-minute miles then stop for a break under the shade of mesquite tree. Roland must be having a hard time breathing through the bandages patched across his nose. I almost feel sorry for the guy.

I pull out the Nikon and screw on a telephoto lens. The boys are just talking, passing a bottle of water back and forth. I snap off a few shots to warm up. Then Jason gives me something I can use. He touches Rolland's face and gives him a quick peck on the lips.

I get the shot and pack my gear up. Pulling away from the curb, I turn up the volume of the Pontiac's radio. Turn it way up. I don't even care what's playing, just so long as it's loud.

I drop the photos on the desktop.

Patrick sits up straight in his executive chair, gazes at the pictures of his little brother then grins so hard his mouth looks like it'll tear.

"Goddamn," he says, flipping through the pictures. His office is all mahogany and plush fabrics. Smells like leather and lemon oil. On the corner of his desk is a tiffany lamp, giving off a soft glow. "You do excellent work."

I say nothing.

Patrick's smile fades slightly. He reaches into his sports coat, produces a checkbook. Before he can find a pen, I shake my head at him.

"I told you on the phone. I take cash. Nothing else."

"You think I'm going to carry five grand around with me?"

"It's seven. The first two covers my rate. The five is my bonus."

Patrick says nothing. Just looks at me, trying to give me a concrete stare. Trying to play the tough guy, but he's too soft to pull it off. I let out a frustrated sigh and lean over to gather the photographs up.

"Fine," he says, "You win." He opens the bottom drawer of that big desk of his and fishes out a bundle of bills. Sets the bundle on the table and rests back in his chair.

I swap the snapshots for the cash and head for the door. No goodbyes. No handshakes. I can hear Patrick behind me, shuffling through the pictures, chuckling to himself. I let him have his moment of victory. Then I turn around, pulling one more photograph from my pocket.

"I almost forgot," I tell him. "Here's another shot you might be interested in."

I lay the photo gently on top of the others. Patrick sees it, and his skin goes milk white.

"What's this?"

"It's you and your father's wife. Or should I call her your step mom? The two of you look to be having a pretty good time together. Wonder what Freud would say about that?"

"This . . ." he stutters. "This was taken at the house. In the bedroom. How did you get inside? We have a security system . . . Dogs . . ."

"You're asking the wrong questions," I say. "What you

should be asking is how Dad will feel about you fucking his trophy wife. Do you think he'll keep you in the will?"

Patrick's soft, boyish face turns to stone. "You bastard."

"Fifty thousand dollars," I tell him. "By noon tomorrow. In cash. I'll call you with the details."

I go for the door again, turning my back on the man. Patrick begins to rummage through his desk. He's breathing hard. Excited. Nervous. Angry. I don't need to see his face to know that he's going to do something stupid.

My veins do a jitterbug beneath my skin. I let instincts take over and spin around to face him. Two quick steps and I'm standing over Patrick's desk. Close enough to see the sweat rolling down his forehead.

Patrick isn't rummaging anymore. In fact, he's not moving at all. His hand is down inside one of the desk drawers, gripping hold of something. His mouth is a hard, flat line across his face.

"Let's just relax now," I tell him. There's an ice pick strapped to my spine in a makeshift sheath. I slip it out. Clutch it behind my back. Out of sight.

The guy doesn't say a thing. His arm, the one reaching into the desk drawer, begins to tremble.

"Don't do it," I tell him. But Patrick doesn't listen.

For a soft businessman, he moves pretty well. The gun comes up in a blur—a short-barreled revolver. I can tell he's practiced this. Probably spent some bored nights alone at the office, jerking the gun out quick, aiming it at imaginary bad guys. If he was a split-second faster, it might've made a difference.

With one hand, I grab hold of Patrick's wrist—stop him from getting the gun around. With the other, I swing the ice pick out from behind my back. It flashes through the air. Patrick's eyes go wide.

I bring the pick down hard. *Thud.* Patrick screams and drops the pistol. His free hand is nailed to the desk, spurting blood.

Circling the desk, I quickly scoop up the gun and tuck it into my waistband. I don't much like the idea of being shot in the back.

Patrick's screams die down into sobbing whimpers. "Close your eyes," I tell him. "You don't want to see this."

Patrick does as he's told, and I yank the ice pick free. He stumbles backward into his big chair. Quietly, he sits there, cradling his bloody hand.

"It was an accident," I tell him. "You cut yourself on some broken glass." I kick the tiffany lamp off the desktop. It crashes against the floor sending shards of stained glass everywhere. "Should be more careful."

"What about the picture?" he asks, nodding towards the photograph of he and his step mom together. His voice is small and distant, like a shy child's.

"You go ahead and keep it," I tell him. "I've got copies."

It's a dark night. A few lamps give the waiting area of St. Joseph's a dim yellow glow. I take a seat in one of the over-stuffed chairs and watch black clouds roll past the windows.

Waiting.

She shows up an hour later. Plops down in the chair next to me, chewing bubble gum. Her long dark hair is pulled back tight in a ponytail. Her legs stretch out from a short skirt, slim and tan.

"How's it going, Ashley?"

Ashley Powell pops her gum at me. "How did the security codes work?"

"Like a charm," I tell her. "Got into the house no problem."

"So you showed him the pictures, right? Did he go for it?"

"Not right away. Your brother's a very stubborn man."

"Half brother," she says. Then she holds out her hand to me.

I pass her a manila envelope full of the photographs— both brothers committing their sins. She looks them over, shaking her head, making little noises with her gum.

"Don't show your father these until tomorrow night," I tell her. "After I collect from Patrick."

She nods, still eyeing the snapshots. "Tell me again how much I owe you."

"Fifty thousand."

"I turn eighteen in a month," she says. "I'll pay you then, out of my share of the inheritance. Which I'm betting will be much larger after Dad sees these."

"A month's a long time to wait. What am I going to do for a month?"

Her hand finds my thigh. I can feel the warmth of her fingertips through the fabric of my jeans. "We'll think of something," she says.

Her gum goes "pop."

Dust Up

Wendy Hornsby

When Wendy Hornsby isn't writing, it's probably because she's teaching history. Educated at UCLA and California State University, Hornsby holds graduate degrees in Ancient and Medieval History and has served as a faculty member at Long Beach City College. Her novels have featured characters Maggie MacGowan, a documentary filmmaker in LA (*A Hard Light, 77th Street Requiem*), and Kate Teague, history teacher in CA (*Half a Mind, No Harm*). In 1992, her short story "Nine Sons" was honored with an Edgar Award.

10:00 A.M., April 20, Red Rock Canyon, Nevada

Pansy Reynard lay on her belly inside a camouflaged bird blind, high-power Zeiss binoculars to her eyes, a digital sound amplifier hooked over her right ear, charting every movement and sound made by her observation target, an

Aplomado falcon hatchling. As Pansy watched, the hatchling stretched his wings to their full thirty-inch span and
gave them a few tentative flaps as if gathering courage to
make his first foray out of the nest. He would need some
courage to venture out, she thought. The ragged, abandoned nest his mother had appropriated for her use sat on
a narrow rock ledge 450 vertical feet above the desert floor.

"Go, baby," Pansy whispered when the chick craned
back his neck and flapped his wings again. This was hour
fourteen of her assigned nest watch. She felt stiff and
cramped, and excited all at once. There had been no
reported Aplomado falcon sightings in Nevada since 1910.
For a mated Aplomado falcon pair to appear in the Red
Rock Canyon area less than twenty miles west of the
tawdry glitz and endless noise of Las Vegas, was singular,
newsworthy even. But for the pair to claim a nest and suc-
cessfully hatch an egg was an event so unexpected as to be
considered a miracle by any committed raptor watcher, as
Pansy Reynard considered herself to be.

The hatchling watch was uncomfortable, perhaps dangerous, because of the ruggedness of the desert canyons,
the precariousness of Pansy's rocky perch in a narrow
cliff-top saddle opposite the nest, and the wild extremes of
the weather. But the watch was very likely essential to the
survival of this wonder child. It had been an honor, Pansy
felt, to be assigned a shift to watch the nest. And then to
have the great good fortune to be on site when the hatchling first emerged over the top of the nest was, well, nearly
overwhelming.

Pansy lowered her binocs to wipe moisture from her
eyes, but quickly raised them again so as not to miss one

single moment in the life of this sleek-winged avian infant. She had been wakened inside her camouflage shelter at dawn by the insistent chittering of the hatchling as he demanded to be fed. From seemingly nowhere, as Pansy watched, the mother had soared down to tend him, the forty-inch span of her black and white wings as artful and graceful as a beautiful Japanese silk-print kite. The sight of the mother made Pansy almost forgive Lyle for standing her up the night before.

Almost forgive Lyle: This was supposed to be a two-man shift. Lyle, a pathologist with the Department of Fish and Game, was a fine bird-watcher and seemed to be in darned good physical shape. But he was new to the Las Vegas office and unsure about his readiness to face the desert overnight. And he was busy. Or so he said.

Pansy had done her best to assure Lyle that he would be safe in her hands. As preparation, she had packed two entire survival kits, one for herself and one for him, and had tucked in a very good bottle of red wine to make the long chilly night pass more gently. But he hadn't come. Hadn't even called.

Pansy sighed, curious to know which he had shunned, an evening in her company or the potential perils of the place. She had to admit there were actual, natural challenges to be addressed. It was only mid-April, but already the desert temperatures reached the century mark before noon. When the sun was overhead, the sheer vertical faces of the red sandstone bluffs reflected and intensified the heat until everything glowed like—and felt like—the inside of an oven. There was no shade other than the feathery shadows of spindly yucca and folds in the rock formations.

To make conditions yet more uncomfortable, it was sandstorm season. Winds typically began to pick up around
noon, and could drive an impenetrable cloud of sand at
speeds surpassing eighty miles an hour until sunset. When
the winds blew, there was nearly no way to escape both the
heat and the pervasive, intrusive blast of sand. Even cars
were useless as shelter. With windows rolled up and
without the AC turned on you'd fry in a hurry. With the AC
turned on, both you and the car's engine would be
breathing grit. If you could somehow navigate blind and
drive like hell, you might drive clear of the storm before
sand fouled the engine. But only if you could navigate blind.

People like Pansy who knew the area well might find
shelter in random hollows among the rocks, such as the
niche where the hatchling sat in his nest. Or the well prepared, for instance Pansy, might hunker down inside a zip-
up shelter made to military specs for desert troops, like the
one that was tucked inside her survival pack. Or navigate
using digital GPS via satellite—Global Positioning System.
Not an environment for neophytes, Pansy conceded, but
she'd had high hopes for Lyle, and had looked forward to
an evening alone with him and the falcons under the vast
blackness of the desert sky, getting acquainted.

Pansy knew she could be a bit off-putting at first
meeting. But in that place, during that season, Pansy was
in her métier and at her best. Her preparations for the nest
watch, she believed, were elegant in their simplicity, com-
pleteness, and flexibility: a pair of lightweight one-man
camouflage all-weather shelters, plenty of water, a basic
all-purpose tool, meals-ready-to-eat, a bodacious slingshot
in case snakes or vultures came to visit the nest, good

binocs, a two-channel sound amplifier to eavesdrop on the nest, a handheld GPS locator, and a digital palm-sized video recorder. Except for the water, each kit weighed a meager twenty-seven pounds and fit in to compact, waterproof, dust proof saddlebags she carried on her all-terrain motorcycle. The bottle of wine and two nice glasses were tucked into a quick-release pocket attached to the cycle frame. She had everything: shelter, food, water, tools, the falcon, a little wine. But no Lyle.

Indeed, Lyle's entire kit was still attached to the motorcycle she had stashed in a niche in the abandoned sandstone quarry below her perch.

A disturbing possibility occurred to Pansy as she watched the hatchling: Maybe Lyle was a little bit afraid of her. A champion triathlete and two-time Ironman medalist, Lieutenant Pansy Reynard, desert survival instructor with the Army's SFOD-D, Special Forces Operational Detachment—Delta Force, out of the Barstow military training center, admitted that she could be just a little bit intimidating.

10:00 A.M., April 20, Downtown Las Vegas

Mickey Togs felt like a million bucks because he knew he looked like a million bucks. New custom-made, silver-gray suit with enough silk in the fabric to give it a little sheen. Not flashy-shiny, but sharp—expensively sharp, Vegas player sharp. His shirt and tie were of the same silver-gray color, as were the butter-soft handmade shoes on his size eight, EEE feet. Checking his reflection in the shiny surface of the black Lincoln Navigator he had acquired for the day's job, Mickey shot his cuffs, adjusted the fat Windsor knot in his silver-gray necktie, dusted some sand kicked up from yesterday's storm off his shoes, and grinned.

Yep, he decided as he climbed up into the driver's seat of the massive SUV, he looked every penny like a million bucks, exactly the sort of guy who had the *cojones* to carry off a million-dollar job. Sure, he had to split the paycheck a few ways because he couldn't do this particular job alone, but the splits wouldn't be equal, meaning he would be well paid. One hundred K to Big Mango the trigger-man, one hundred to Otto the Bump for driving, another hundred to bribe a cooperative Federal squint, and then various payments for various spotters and informants. Altogether, after the split, Mickey personally would take home six hundred large; damn good jack for a morning's work.

Mickey Togs felt deservedly cocky. Do a little morning job for the Big Guys, be back on the Vegas Strip before lunch, get a nice bite to eat, then hit the baccarat salon at the Mirage with a fat stake in his pocket. Mickey took out a silk handkerchief and dabbed some sweat from his forehead; Mickey had trained half his life for jobs like this one. Nothing to it, he said to himself, confident that all necessary preparations had been made and all contingencies covered. A simple, elegant plan. Mickey pulled the big Navigator into the lot of the Flower of the Desert Wedding Chapel on South Las Vegas Boulevard, parked, and slid over into the front passenger seat, the shotgun position. The chapel was in a neighborhood of cheap old motels and auto shops, not the sort of place where Mickey and his hired help would be noticed. In a town where one can choose to be married by Captain Kirk, Elvis Presley, or Marilyn Monroe, where brides and grooms might dress accordingly, wedding chapels are good places not to be noticed. Even Big Mango, an almost seven-foot-tall Samoan wearing a turquoise Hawaiian shirt and flip flops, drew hardly a glance as he crossed the lot and climbed into the backseat of the Navigator.

Otto the Bump, a one-time welterweight boxer with cauliflower ears and a nose as gnarled as a bag full of marbles, ordinarily might draw a glance or two, except that he wore Vegas-style camouflage: black suit, starched white shirt, black tie, spit-shined black brogans, a clean a shave and a stiff comb-over. He could be taken for a mâitre d', a pit boss, a father of the bride, a conventioneer, or the invisible man just by choosing where and how he stood. As he hoisted himself up into the driver's seat of the Navigator, Otto looked every inch like a liveried chauffeur.

"What's the job?" Otto asked as he turned out of the lot and into traffic.

"The feds flipped Harry Coelho," Mickey said. "He's gonna spill everything to the grand jury this morning, and then he's going into witness protection. We got one shot to stop him. Job is to grab him before he gets to the courthouse, then take him for a drive and lose him as deep as Jimmy Hoffa."

"A snitch is the worst kind of rat there is," Otto groused. "Sonovabitch deserves whatever he gets."

"Absolutely," Mickey agreed. Big Mango, as usual, said nothing, but Mickey could hear him assembling the tools for his part of the job.

"How's it going down?" Otto asked.

"Federal marshals are gonna drive Harry from the jail over to the courthouse in a plain Crown Victoria with one follow car."

"Feds." Otto shook his head. "I don't like dealing with the feds."

"Don't worry, the fix is in," Mickey said, sounding smug. "I'll get a call when the cars leave the jail. The route is down Main to Bonneville, where the courthouse is. You get us to the intersection, park us on Bonneville at the corner. We'll get a call when the cars are approaching the intersection. When they make the turn, you get us between the two cars and that's when we grab Harry."

"Whatever you say." Otto checked the rearview mirror. "But what's the fix?"

Mickey chuckled. "You know how federal squints are, doughnut-eating civil servants with an itch to use their guns; they get off playing cops and robbers. A simple, good follow plan just doesn't do it for them, so they gotta throw in some complication. This is it: Harry leaves the jail in the front car. Somewhere on the route, the cars are going to switch their order so when they get to the courthouse Harry will be in the second car."

"How do you know they'll make the switch?"

"I know my business," Mickey said, straightening his tie to show he had no worries. "I got spotters out there. If the switch doesn't happen or the Feds decide to take a different route or slip in a decoy, I'll know it." He snapped his manicured fingers. "Like that."

Otto's face was full of doubt. "How will you know?"

"The phone calls?" Mickey said. "They're coming from inside the perp car. I bought us a marshal."

"Yeah?" Otto grinned, obviously impressed. "You got it covered, inside and outside."

"Like I say, I know my business," Mickey said, shrugging.

"Here's the plan: Otto, you get us into position on Bonneville, and we wait for the call saying they're
approaching. When the first car makes the turn off
Main, you pull in tight behind it and stop fast. From
then till we leave, you need to cover the first car; don't
let anyone get out. Mango, you take care of the marshals
in the second car any way you want to, but if you gack
the marshal riding shotgun, you can have the rest of the
bribe payment I owe him."

"Appreciate it," Mango said. "You want me to take out
Harry, too?"

"Not there. I'll go in myself and get him. Otto, you stay
ready to beat us the hell out when I say. We're taking Harry
for a little drive and getting him lost. Are we clear?"

"Candy from a little baby," Otto said. Mango, in the backseat, grunted. Could be gas, could be agreement, Mickey
thought. Didn't much matter. Mango got paid to do what he
did and not for conversation. With a grace that belied his
huge size, Mango rolled into the back deck of the vast SUV
and began to set up his firing position at the back window.
Quiet and efficient, Mickey thought, a true pro.

The first call came. Harry Coelho left the Clark County
jail riding in the backseat of a midnight blue Crown Victoria. The follow car was the same make, model, color.
After two blocks, as planned, the cars switched positions,
so that the follow car became the lead, and Harry Coelho's
ass was hanging out in the wind with no rear cover.

When the second call came, the Navigator was in position
on Bonneville, a half-block from the courthouse, waiting.

The snatch went smooth, by the book exactly the way
Mickey Togs wrote it, the three of them moving with

synchronicity as honed as a line of chorus girls all high-kicking at the same time. The first Crown Vic made the turn. Otto slipped the massive Navigator in behind it and stopped so fast that the second Crown Vic rear-ended him; the Crown Vic's hood pleated up under the Navigator's rear bumper like so much paper, didn't leave a mark on the SUV. Before the Crown Vic came to a final stop, Mango, positioned in the back deck, flipped up the rear hatch window and popped the two marshals in the front seat—fwoof, fwoof, that breezy sound the silencer makes—just as Mickey snapped open the back door and yanked out Harry Coelho, grabbing him by the oh-so-convenient handcuffs. They were back in the Navigator and speeding away before the first carload of Feds figured out that they had a problem on their hands.

No question, Otto was the best driver money could buy. A smooth turn onto Martin Luther King, then a hop up onto the 95 freeway going west into the posh new suburbs where a behemoth of an SUV like the Navigator became as anonymous and invisible as a dark-haired nanny pushing a blond-haired baby in a stroller.

After some maneuvers to make sure there was no tail, Otto exited the Interstate and headed up into Red Rock Canyon.

10:50 A.M., Red Rock Canyon

The hatchling was calling out for a feeding again when Pansy Reynard heard the rumble of a powerful engine approaching. Annoyed that the racket might frighten her falcons, she peered over the edge of her perch.

The sheer walls of the abandoned sandstone quarry

below her were a natural amplifier that made the vehicle sound larger than it actually was, but it was still huge, the biggest, blackest pile of personal civilian transport ever manufactured. Lost, she thought when she saw the Navigator, and all of its computer-driven gadgets couldn't help it get back to the freeway where it belonged.

For a moment, Pansy considered climbing out of her camouflaged blind and offering some help. But she sensed there was something just a little hinky about the situation. Trained to listen to that quiet inner warning system, Pansy held back, focused her binoculars on the SUV, and waited.

The front, middle, and back hatch doors opened at once and four men spilled out: two soft old guys wearing suits and dress shoes, a Pacific Islander dressed for a beach party, and a skinny little man with a hood over his head and his hands cuffed behind his back. The hood muffled the little man's voice so that Pansy couldn't understand his words, but she certainly understood his body language. Nothing good was happening down there. She set the lens of her palm-sized digital video recorder to zoom, and started taping the scene as it unfolded below.

The hooded man was marched to the rim over a deep quarried pit. His handlers stood him facing forward, then stepped aside. With a cool and steady hand, Beach Boy let off two silenced shots. A sudden burst of red opened out of the center of the hood, but before the man had time to crumple to the sandstone under him, a second blast hit him squarely in the chest and lifted him enough to push him straight over the precipice and out of sight.

"Kek, kek, kek." The mother Aplomado falcon, alarmed perhaps by the eerie sound of the silencer or maybe by the burst of energy it released, screeched as she swooped down between the canyon walls as if to dive bomb the intruders and distract them away from her nest. The two suits, who peered down into the abyss whence their victim had fallen, snapped to attention. Beach Boy, in a clean, fluid motion, pivoted the extended gun arm, spotted the mother and—fwoof, fwoof—she plunged into a mortal dive.

The hatchling, as if he saw and understood what had happened, set up his chittering again. Pansy saw that gun arm pivot again, this time toward the nest.

"No!" Pansy screamed as she rose, revealing herself to draw fire away from the precious, now orphaned hatchling. Binoculars and camera held aloft where they could be seen she called down, "I have it all on tape, you assholes. Come and get it."

Pansy kept up her screaming rant as she climbed out of the blind and rappelled down the backside of the cliff, out of view of the miscreants, but certainly within earshot. She needed them to come after her, needed to draw them away from the nest.

When she reached the canyon floor, Pansy pulled her all-terrain motorcycle out of its shelter among the rocks, gunned its powerful motor and raced toward the access road where the men could see her. The survival kit she had packed for Lyle—damn him, anyway—was still attached to the cycle's frame.

Otto the Bump scrambled back into the Navigator while Mickey and Mango pushed and pulled each other in their haste to climb inside lest they get left behind.

"Feds," Otto growled between clenched teeth as he started the big V-8 engine. "I told you, I don't like messing with feds."

"She ain't the freaking Feds," Mickey snapped. His face red with anger, he turned on Mango. "You want to shoot off that piece of yours, you freaking idiot, shoot that damn girl. Otto, go get her."

The old quarry made a box canyon. Its dead-end access road was too narrow for the Navigator to turn around, so it had to back out the way it came in. Pansy was impressed by the driver's skill as he made a fast exit, but she still beat the Navigator to the mouth of quarry. For a moment, she stopped her bike crosswise to the road, blocking them. There was no way, she knew, that she could hold them until the authorities might arrive. Her entire purpose in stopping was to announce herself and to lure them after her, away from the nest. She hoped that they would think that size and firepower were enough to take her out.

Pansy'd had enough time to get a good look at her opponents, to make some assessments. The two little guys were casino rats with a whole lot of starched cuff showing, fusspot city shoes, jackets buttoned up when it was a hundred freaking degrees out there. Beach Boy would be fine in a cabana, but dressed as he was and without provisions . . . Vegas rats, she thought; the desert would turn them into carrion.

Rule one when outmanned and outgunned is to let the enemy defeat himself. Pansy figured that there was enough macho inside the car that once a little-bitty girl on a little-bitty bike challenged them to a chase, they wouldn't have the courage to quit until she was down or they were dead. Pansy sniffed as she lowered her helmet's face guard; over-confidence and geographic naivete had brought down empires. Ask Napoleon.

Pansy didn't hear the burst of gunfire, but twice she felt the air wiffle past her head in that particular way that makes the hair of an experienced soldier stand up on end. As she bobbed and wove, creating an erratic target, she also kept herself just outside the range of the big handgun she had seen. Still, she knew all about random luck, and reminded herself not be too cocky herself, or too reliant on the law of averages.

Because she was in the lead, Pansy set the course. Her program involved stages of commitment: draw them in, give them a little reward as encouragement, then draw them in further until their training and equipment were overmatched by the environment and her experience. Play them.

The contest began on the decently paved road that headed out of Lee Canyon. Before the road met the freeway, Pansy veered onto a gravel by-road that took them due north, bisecting the canyons. When the road became a dry creek bed, Pansy disregarded the dead-end marker and continued to speed along; the Navigator followed. The canyons had been cut by eons of desert water runoff. The bottoms, except during the rainy season, were as hard-packed as fired clay and generally as wide as a two-lane road, though there were irregular patches of bone-jarring imbedded rocks and small boulders and some narrows. The bike could go around obstacles; the four-wheel-drive Navigator barreled over them.

Pansy picked up a bit of pavement in a flood control culvert where the creek passed under the freeway, and slowed slightly to give the Navigator some hope of overtaking her. But before they could quite catch her, she turned sharply again, this time onto an abandoned service road, pulling the Navigator behind as she continued north.

At any time, Pansy knew she could dash up into any of the narrow canyons that opened on either side of the road, and that the big car couldn't follow her. She held on to that possibility as an emergency contingency as she did her best to keep her pursuers intrigued.

The canyons became smaller and broader, the terrain flatter and Pansy more exposed. Sun bore down on her back and she cursed the wusses behind her in their air-conditioned beast. At eleven o'clock, right on schedule, the winds began to pick up. Whorls of sand quickly escalated to flurries and then to blinding bursts. Pansy pulled down the sand screen that was attached to her face guard, but she still choked on grit, felt fine sand grind in her teeth. None of this, as miserable as it made her feel, was unfamiliar or anything she could not handle.

Always, Pansy was impressed by the skill of the driver following her, and by his determination. He pushed the big vehicle through places where she thought he ought to bog down. And then there were times that, if he had taken more risk, he could have overcome her. That he had refrained, clued Pansy to the strategy: The men in the car thought they were driving her to ground. They were waiting for her to fall or falter in some way. She used this assumption, feigning, teasing, pretending now and then to weaken, always picking up her speed or maneuvering out of range just before they could get her, to keep them engaged. Some birds used a similar ploy, pretending to be wounded or vulnerable as a feint to lure predators away from their nests.

The canyons ended abruptly and the terrain became flat, barren desert bottom. There was no shelter, no respite, only endless heat and great blasts of wind-whipped sand. Pansy could no longer see potholes or boulders, nor could any of them see roadside markers. Though Pansy could not see the road, and regularly hit bone jarring dips and bumps, she was not navigating blind. Three times a year she ran a survival course through the very same area. She had drawn her pursuers into the hollow between Little Skull and Skull Mountains, headed toward Jackass Flats, a no-man's land square, in the middle of the Nellis Air Force Base gunnery range.

"Get her," Mickey growled. The silk handkerchief he held against his nose muffled his words. "I have things to do in town. Take her out. Now."

Mango's only response was to reload.

Otto swore as he switched off the AC and shut down the vents. Sand so fine he could not see it ground under his eyelids, filled his nose and throat, choked him. Within minutes the air inside the car was so hot that sweat ran in his eyes, made his shirt stick to his chest and his back, riffled down his shins. There was no water, of course, because this was supposed to be a quick job, out of Vegas and back in an hour. He had plenty besides heat and thirst to make him feel miserable. First, he thought he could hear the effects of grit on the car's engine, a heaviness in its response. Next, he had a pretty good idea what Mickey would do to him if he let the girl get away.

How could they have gotten so far into this particular hell? Otto wondered. In the beginning, it had seemed real simple. Follow the girl until they were out of the range of any potential witnesses, then run over the girl and her pissant bike like so much road kill. But every time he started to make his move, she'd pull some damn maneuver and get away: she'd side slip him or head down a wash so narrow that he had to give the road—such as it was—his undivided attention. The SUV was powerful, but it had its limitations, the first of which was maneuverability: it had none.

And then there was Mickey and his constant nudging, like he could do any better. By the time they came out of the canyons and onto the flats, Otto was so sick and tired of listening to Mickey, contending with the heat, the sand, and the damn girl and her stunts that he didn't care much how things ended, only that they ended immediately. He knew desperation and danger could be found on the same page in the dictionary, but he was so desperate to be out of that place that he was ready to take some risks; take out the girl and get back up on the freeway and out of the sand, immediately.

Between gusts Otto caught glimpses of the girl, so he knew more or less where she was. Fed up, he put a heavy foot on the accelerator and waited for the crunch of girl and bike under his thirty-two-inch wheels.

Pansy heard the SUV's motor rev, heard also the big engine begin to miss as it became befouled by sand. With the Navigator accelerating toward her, Pansy snapped the bottle of wine out of its break-away pouch, grasped it by the neck, gave it a wind up swing as she spun her bike in a tight one-eighty, and let the bottle fly in a trajectory calculated to collide dead center with the rapidly approaching windshield.

As she headed off across the desert at a right angle to the road, she heard the bottle hit target and pop, heard the windshield give way, heard the men swear, smelled the brakes. The massive SUV decelerated from about fifty MPH to a dead, mired stop in the space of a mere sixty feet. Its huge, heavy-tread tires sliced through the hard desert crust and found beneath it sand as fine as talcum powder and as deep as an ocean. Forget four-wheel drive; every spin of the wheels merely kicked up a shower of sand and dug them in deeper. The behemoth SUV was going nowhere without a tow.

When she heard the rear deck hatch pop open, Pansy careened to a stop and dove behind a waist-high boulder for cover. As Beach Boy, leaning out the back hatch, unloaded a clip in her general direction, Pansy, lying on her belly, pulled out her slingshot, strapped it to her wrist, reached into the pouch of three-eighths-inch steel balls hanging from her belt, and, aiming at the dull red flashes coming from the end of Beach Boy's automatic, fired back. She heard random pings as her shot hit the side of the Navigator.

"She's packing heat," Otto yelled. Pansy continued to ping the side of the car with shot; sounded enough like bullet strikes.

Mango finally spoke. More exactly, Mango let out an ugly liquid-filled scream when Pansy's steel balls pierced his throat and his cheek. Mortally hit, he grabbed his neck as he fell forward, tumbling out of the SUV. With the big back window hanging open, the SUV quickly filled with fire hot, swirling yellow sand.

"She got Mango!" Otto yelled in Mickey's direction. "We try to run for it, she'll get us, too."

Mickey Togs, feeling faint from the heat, barely able to breathe, pulled his beautiful silver-gray suit coat over his head, being careful not to wrinkle it or get sweat on it, and tried, in vain, to get a signal on his cell phone. He didn't know who to call for help in this particularly humiliating situation, or, if he should be able to get a call out—and he could not—just where he happened to be for purposes of directing some sort of rescue.

Otto the Bump heard Mickey swear at his dead phone, and nearly got hit with it when Mickey, in a rage, threw the thing toward the cracked and leaking windshield. Not knowing what else to do, Otto reached for the little piece strapped to his left ankle.

"I'm making a run for it," Otto said.

"Idiot, what are your chances?" Mickey asked. "You got thirty, forty miles of desert, no water, can't see through that damn sand, and a lunatic out there trying to kill you."

"If I stay in this damn car or I make a run for it, I figure it's eighty-twenty against me either way," Otto said. "I prefer to take it on the run than sitting here waiting."

"Ninety-five to five." Mickey straightened the knot in his tie. "You do what you think you gotta do. I'm staying put."

"Your choice, but you still owe me a hundred K," Otto said. He chambered a round as he opened the car door, brought his arm against his nose, and dropped three feet down to the desert floor.

5:00 P.M., April 20, Downtown Las Vegas, Nevada

Without pausing for so much as a perfunctory hello to the clerk on duty, Pansy Reynard strode past the reception desk of the regional office of the Department of Fish and Game and straight back to the pathology lab. Pansy had showered and changed from her dirty desert camouflage BDUs—battle-dress utilities—into sandals, a short khaki skirt, and a crisp, sleeveless linen blouse; adaptability, she knew well, is the key to survival.

She opened the lab door and walked in. When Lyle, the so recently absent Lyle, looked up, she placed a large bundle wrapped in a camouflage tarp onto his desk, right on top of the second half of a tuna sandwich he happened to be eating, and then she flipped her sleek fall of hair over her shoulder for effect.

Eyes wide, thoroughly nonplused, Lyle managed to swallow his mouthful of sandwich and to speak. "What's this?"

"I went back to the nest this afternoon after the sandstorm blew out." Pansy unfastened the bundle and two long, graceful wings opened out of the tarp chrysalis. "I found her in the canyon."

"Oh, damn." Lyle stood, ashen-faced now, tenderly lifted the mother Aplomado falcon and carried her to a lab bench. He examined her, discovered the deep crimson wound in her black chest. Through gritted teeth he said, "Poachers?"

"Looks like it," Pansy said.

"What about the hatchling?"

"He's okay but he has to be hungry." With reverent sadness, Pansy stroked the mother falcon's smooth head. "Another week or two and the baby will be ready to fend for himself. But in the meantime, someone needs to get food to him. Or he needs to be brought in to a shelter."

Lyle sighed heavily. He was obviously deeply moved by this tragedy, a quality that Pansy found to be highly attractive.

"What are you going to do, Lyle?"

"I'll ask for a wildlife team to come out," he said. "Someone will get up there tomorrow to rescue the hatchling.

Too bad, though. We've lost a chance to reestablish a nesting pattern."

"Tomorrow?" There was a flash of indignation in her tone.

"He'll he okay overnight."

"What if the poachers come back tonight?"

Again he sighed, looked around at the cluttered lab and the stacks of unfinished paperwork. Then he turned and looked directly into Pansy's big brown eyes.

"Pansy, I need help," he said. "Will you watch the nest tonight?"

"Me?" She touched her breastbone demurely, her freshly scrubbed hand small and delicate looking. "Alone? Lyle, there are people with guns out there."

"You're right," be said, chagrined. "Sorry. Of course you shouldn't be alone. You shouldn't have been alone last night and this morning, either. It's just, I got jammed up here in the office with a possible plague case in a ground squirrel, Chamber of Commerce all in a lather that word would get out. I couldn't break away."

"Ground squirrels aren't in danger of extinction," she said.

"I am sorry, very sorry," Lyle said, truly sounding sorry. "Look, Pansy, I really need you. If I join you, will you be willing to go back to the nest tonight?"

She took a long breath before responding, not wanting to sound eager. After a full ten count, during which he watched her with apparent interest, she nodded.

"The two of us should be able to handle just about any-thing that comes up," she said. "I'll meet you out front in five minutes."

"In five," he said as be peeled off his lab coat. "In five."

Why'd You Bring Me Here?

Stanley Cohen

Ellery Queen Mystery Magazine has published a number of Stanley Cohen stories, beginning with his first in the 1960s. His stories have also been published in other magazines and anthologies including *The Strand*, *Alfred Hitchcock Magazine*, *Crime Wave*, *Adams Round Table*, and *Mystery Monthly*. Some of his many short stories have been collected in *A Night in the Manchester Store and Other Stories*.

Soaking wet, he emerged from the mouth of the cave into the chill air. Nothing looked familiar. After hesitating a moment, he broke into an exhausting dead run, straight ahead, through the snagging underbrush. His feet were cold and leaden in his waterlogged shoes. He had to get help and get back to the cave. He had to get her out of there, if possible before nightfall. The sun was already down into the tree line, dusk less than an hour away.

"There's just one way out of here," he'd told her. "And that's by swimming. Underwater. We've got to dive in and swim underwater toward that spot of light, and when we come up on the other side of that big rock, we can walk right out."

"Why'd you bring me here?" she'd said.

"It was a mistake. But that's not what's important now. What's important is that there's only one way out: by diving right toward that spot of light and coming up on the other side of the rock."

"You know I can't swim."

"You've got to. Don't you understand?"

"I can't."

"But we don't have a chance of getting out any other way. Don't you understand? It's the only way out. There's no use trying to get back out the way we came."

"I can't swim."

"You don't have a choice."

"It's no use. I can't swim at all, much less dive down there. You knew that."

"We've got to. It's the only way. I'll help you. I'll pull you through it. But we've got to." He'd turned the flashlight into her face briefly at that point and, seeing her expression, knew she'd never make it. For a moment he'd pictured in his mind trying to pull her down through it. And as he did, he experienced the kind of panic he knew must have gripped her. She was right. It was hopeless. You can help a nonswimmer on the surface of water but never, never downward through water. He'd imagined the two of them underwater, upside down, trying to move downward, deeper, toward nothing more than a glow of light, she desperately clutching at him and drowning and he losing control and feeling the cold underground water flowing into his own mouth and nose.

He'd had to give up the idea. It couldn't be done. How deep was the pool? How far down was the pass-through? How large was the pass-through? Could he make it himself? Alone? He thought about getting stuck in it and thrashing helplessly until dead. He imagined her watching his legs as he'd start through, stop, and then kick until he stopped kicking. But that wouldn't happen. Others had made it. Lots of them. He'd make it. But only alone. There was no other way.

He took her into his arms. "Here's what we'll have to do," he'd said, "I'll have to go out through there and go for help."

"Why did you bring me in here? You could have come alone."

"There's no use in talking about that now. Don't you understand? There's no point in talking about anything except getting out."

She remained silent.

"It's the only choice we've got." He knew she was thinking about being left alone in the cave. "There's nothing in here that'll bother you. I'll get back with help as quickly as I can."

She still didn't speak.

He had run probably a hundred yards from the mouth of the cave, ripping and stumbling through the coarse underbrush. He had run hard, which he realized was stupid because he was already exhausted in the wet clothes and shoes. And he'd run straight ahead, which was also stupid, hoping in his desperation for a miracle, someone standing there, waiting to help him. He stopped, turned, and started back toward the cave, jogging. He passed the mouth of the cave, cringed, and started up the side of the hill toward the other entrance, the "lock" through which they'd entered. It wasn't far. The chamber was much shorter on the outside than it seemed within.

He stopped at the lock, leaned against the sign, and looked in. Nothing. Darkness. He shouted down the hole, "Sweetheart, are you all right?" No answer. "I'm out safely. Be back soon with help." No answer. "Sweetheart? Take it easy, now. I'll be right back." Silence. "Sweetheart? Are you okay?" Nothing. She couldn't possibly hear him. It was too far down the sheer, vertical, convoluted drop of the lock, through the twisting passageways, to the gravel beach by the pool with the emerald light source at the bottom.

He glanced around. The sun had set and night was coming on fast. Night would snuff out the emerald glow, the only source of light in the cave where he had left her. Had he made a mistake? A really stupid mistake? He should have stayed there with her all night and left at the first sign of light in the pool. He should have left her alone during daylight, with at least the little green glow in the water. He'd figured wrong again. Stumbled ahead without planning, just the way she said he always did. Should he drop back down through the lock and wait with her until morning? He was already out. The dive had been tough. Real tough. His lungs and ears had nearly exploded. The water was deep. Maybe he'd get lucky and get back with help in a hurry.

He pushed away from the opening and broke into a run, toward the road, he hoped. He had found the cave from the road. He should be able to find the road again. But it was rapidly getting dark.

She was alone in darkness now. She had the flashlight but he had cautioned her against burning it continuously. "It won't last too long," he had said. "I'll probably be back long before it'd burn out, but we'd better not take any chances. Best thing to do is just turn it on for a minute or two and take a quick look around every once in a while. Or if you hear something." What a stupid thing to have said! He'd realized it as soon as he'd gotten it out. "But you won't hear anything because there's nothing to hear. There's nothing down here. Nothing to be afraid of."

"Why did you bring me here?" she'd asked again.

He came to the road. Right at the place where they'd left it, right by the landmark for finding the cave, the big white boulder shaped like a cow's head with one horn. At least he still had his sense of direction.

He looked up and down the desolate road, trying to decide which direction would bring the quickest help. He couldn't see any lights in either direction. It was a cloudy night and was going to get good and dark. To the right was back toward town. He vaguely remembered seeing a few little houses somewhere back that way. To the left was unknown. Just around the curve could be help. Maybe he'd get lucky.

He started down the road to the left, running, but not fast. His clothes were nearly dry but the wet shoes burned his feet. As he rounded the curve in the road, he could make out that the road went straight for a long stretch and there wasn't a light of any kind in sight. This stopped him. He'd be better off going back toward town.

He stopped and started back in the opposite direction, running slowly, more of a trot, hardly faster than a walk. He passed the cow-head rock and headed into another curve. He slowed to a walk because he couldn't run anymore. It was extremely dark. He began to realize that a lot of time had passed since he left the cave. He thought of her alone in total blackness on the rocky beach by the pool, bruised and skinned from the descent through the moss-slicked lock. He walked a little faster for a while and then he saw the pinpoint of light ahead.

The light spurred him into a dead run, and as he pounded toward it, he realized it was much farther away than it had looked. He finally had to stop running and walk because of the pain in his sides. When the pain had let up, he started running again and reached the little frame house with the wooden porch. He ran across the yard, walked up onto the porch, and rapped on the screen door.

The lights went out in the house and then he heard a slide latch on the inside of the front door. "Hey, please," he shouted. He slapped the screen door against the jamb several more times. "You gotta help me. My wife's in the bottom of the cave back down the road." He paused. Hearing no sound within, he hit the screen door again. "Hey, please, help me. Just let me use your phone." He waited again. Still no signs of response. "Call the police," he shouted. "At least do that. Will you do that?"

He looked at the window that had gone dark after his first knock. He thought about kicking it out and going in and getting them to help him. But they might have a gun and decide to shoot him. That's what he'd probably do if he was in the house and somebody came busting in.

He rattled the screen one more time. "Aren't you going to help me? Please! My wife's in the bottom of that cave up the road. Just call the cops for me."

He paused again. They obviously weren't going to do anything. He turned and sat down on the porch step. She was alone in that black cave. How was he going to get her out? He'd really done it this time. He loved her. He really did. Loved her more than he thought possible. She was so great to him. She put up with so much. Sometimes he wondered why she did. He didn't drink and he didn't chase around after other girls. That was probably part of it. And he loved her and she knew it.

But he had to do things. That was the way he was. He heard about things and just had to do them. That was why they didn't have anything. She often said they probably never would. But he couldn't help it. Once he got a bug up his ass, he was off and running. The sky-diving lessons. The flying lessons. That stuff cost big money. And the automatic rifle with the scope. That had cost all of both their take-home pay from the mill for a week.

They didn't need that rifle. But once he'd made up his mind, she went along with it. They'd taken it and hiked out to the old quarry a couple of times and floated bottles and beer cans on the water and sat up on the rim of the quarry and used up a couple of boxes of shells potting away at the stuff, taking turns. Then, she'd heard the ricochet. Since that time, the rifle just hung on the wall in their apartment.

He thought about their apartment. She called it their rat's nest and that was just about right. But he couldn't help it. He'd rather do things than have things. They didn't even have a car. Not even an old one. They walked to the mill and they hitched most everywhere else. They'd had a bike for a while, a Harley, a real beauty, but he'd wiped it out trying to learn to hill-climb. He'd had to let it go and he got off just in time, then sat there watching it head back down alone, end over end, just flying. They made payments for eight more months on something they couldn't ride. Salvage parts covered one payment.

He heard about the cave and how the light coming up through the water was the most fantastic sight anybody ever saw and he had to see it. Clearest and greenest water anywhere, glowing green in the middle of a black cave. A giant emerald. A giant green light. He hadn't listened too carefully to the part about getting out. He remembered that you had to get wet, but he figured you just got down on your belly and crawled through. He didn't get the message that you had to swim straight down maybe fifteen feet. After he decided that *he* had to see it, he talked her into going with him, told her that it was something he wanted to do bad and it wouldn't even cost anything. He'd said they'd just wear old clothes and she'd said that was all they had. And she'd finally agreed to go on a pretty Saturday afternoon when there really wasn't much else to do.

And now it was a black Saturday night and she was in there alone. He wondered if there were any bears in that cave. Or snakes or waterdogs or rats. Or spiders. She was deathly afraid of spiders. Or bats that could see in the dark and fly down and get tangled in her beautiful long brown hair. What if there was another person in there? Maybe somebody hiding out? He had to get her out of there. He glanced back over his shoulder at the window. The lights were still out.

He got up and went back to the door and tapped lightly

on the screen. Maybe he'd been too rough before. "Please listen," he said in a pleading voice. "I've got to get help and get back to that cave back down the road and get my wife out of there. I'm not going to hurt anybody. I just want to get help. Can I just use your phone? Or could you just call the highway patrol? Please, won't you help me?" He waited several minutes. "Please? Can't you see I'm in trouble and need help?"

When he saw they weren't going to answer, he became enraged. "Goddammit! Open the door! Help me! I need help." He waited again. It was useless. He slammed the screen once more and then turned, left the porch, went across the yard and back onto the dark road. He could just make out objects near the road in the darkness. He thought about the level of blackness in the cave and wondered how much she'd used the flashlight. As he did, he tried to figure back how long he'd been gone from inside the cave.

Having rested on the porch, he started running again, his footsteps on the pavement producing the only sound anywhere in the vacuum of the black, windless night. He glanced back over his shoulder and the lights were on again in the window.

He kept moving, and in a few minutes the sounds of his heavy breathing fell around his footfalls as he concentrated on finding a pace he could maintain for a while. How far had he run? How far was he from the big cow-head rock? Two, three miles? That's how far it seemed. Maybe four. The rock was around twenty-six miles from the edge of town. Would he have to get close to town to come to any more houses? He couldn't remember.

Suddenly he saw some light. A car coming toward him. The first one he'd seen since he'd been on the road. It was coming pretty fast. He stepped out into the road in the path of the car and began to wave his arms up and down. The car approached, slowed down as it got near him, steered carefully around him as if he were an obstacle, and then accelerated back up to speed.

He turned and watched it disappear and then dropped to the surface of the road, flat on his back with his knees up, resting, waiting for his body to stop throbbing. He wanted to sleep and closed his eyes for a moment. He thought about his wife in the blackness of the cave and wondered if somehow she might have been able to sleep, or at least rest. Probably not. How would anybody be able to? He had to get help and get back there. Suddenly feeling very rested, he hustled to his feet and started off again, first walking and then in a slow run.

The road curved sharply and he saw another light in the distance. Remembering how he had been fooled before, he didn't rush at the light but held his pace, watching it slowly approach him with each heavy jogging stride. The little house was very reminiscent of the first one—same distance from the road, same setting, same porch on the front with the light coming through the window. The house was on the right-hand side of the road instead of the left. Could it be the same house? Could he have started off in the wrong direction when he got up off the road? Maybe he had slept a minute or two and had gotten up all turned around. This possibility made him feel weak for a moment, but he figured he'd find out as soon as he knocked on the door. He slapped the screen three times and waited.

The lights went out and a strong voice said, "Git going!"

"You gotta help me. I gotta get help. My wife's in the bottom of a cave back down the road and I gotta get help getting her out."

"Git going. Git off the porch and off this land. Git going."

"Please help me. I mean no harm. Let me just use your phone. I'm telling the truth. My wife's in that crazy cave down the road. I gotta get help."

"If I open the door I'm gonna be shootin' to kill. Now, git!"

"Please! You gotta help me. Just let me use your phone. Call the cops. Anything. Please help me."

"Got no phone. Now git moving."

He hesitated a moment. "How far to the next house?"

After a prolonged silence, "A mile toward town."

"Tell me something else," he said to the closed door. "Was I here banging on your door a little while ago?"

A foot kicked the other side of the door and the voice shouted, "Git! Git moving!"

The kick startled him and he ran off the porch into the yard. He stopped, turned, and stared at the house. There was a white earthenware pot with something growing in it on the porch step which looked familiar. He had gotten turned around. He had to get moving toward town. One mile to the next house. He could get there in ten minutes. He was going to get lucky at the next one. He felt assured and took off running down the road.

Another car approached him from behind and this time he was determined to stop it. He turned and stayed in the middle of the road, flagging wildly with his arms. When it became apparent that the car would hit him if he didn't move, he leaped out of the way and watched the red taillights fade.

He started running renewed. Help was a few minutes away. This time he was sure. He was going to get help and get on back and get her out of that black hole. The next house was the one.

He came up over a little rise and the lights appeared, right on schedule. He pounded harder, down the hill, feeling much stronger. Second wind. As he came upon the house, he could see it was much larger than the other one, set farther back from the road, painted white, lots of lights, a nice house, one like she often said she wished someday she could have.

He slowed down as he reached the corner of the yard and then noticed an old pickup truck, a small one with an open bed, parked heading out. He studied the house. They couldn't see him. They were inside in the light. He was outside in the dark and already had eyes like an owl's, used to the dark.

He moved across the yard to the truck, stepped up on the running board, and reached through the open window. The key was in the ignition with a heavy piece of cotton string hanging from it. After surveying the house again, he silently eased the truck door open and slid into it. He clutched, twisted the key, and the old clunker exploded into life. He was on his way to get help.

As he approached the town, things finally started looking familiar. Once in the town he began to realize that a lot of time had passed. Everything seemed quiet, deserted, asleep, even for Saturday night. He went straight for the highway patrol station and as he pulled up to it to park, two troopers got out of a car where they had been sitting and walked over to him.

"Where'd you get the truck?" one of them said.

"You gotta help me. My wife's in the bottom of the cave and we gotta get her out. She's alone out there."

"Where'd you get the truck?"

"This is the fastest one yet," the other trooper said. "We get the call fifteen minutes ago and here he comes, driving right up to us."

"Please, you've got to help me get her out of that cave."

"Taking trucks is serious business, friend. You'd better come inside."

"Please listen to me. My wife's in the bottom of that crazy cave about twenty-five miles out on Fifty-eight. You guys gotta help me. We gotta get her out."

"You want to call a lawyer?"

"I don't need a lawyer. I need help getting my wife out of that cave."

They kept him in a cell for what seemed an endless period of time until they could get the sheriff up and in to see him. He lay on the cot and fidgeted, thinking about her out there in that black hole. He began to think about how much he really did care about her, how much he liked just touching her, seeing her at lunch at the mill, having her go with him when he was off doing something, watching her give in when there was some new wild-ass thing he just had to do.

"How'd you get out there?"

"We hitched."

"What'd you go out there for?"

"I had to see it."

"See what?"

"The green light."

"What green light?"

"The light that comes in through the water under the rock. Some of the guys at the mill told me about it and I had to see it."

"Didn't they tell you about getting out of there after you got in?"

"I guess I didn't figure the water was so deep."

"Didn't you read the sign on the lock, telling you to stay the hell out of there?"

"They went in and saw it and got out okay. I figured I could, too. And I did."

"Why didn't you leave your wife outside?"

"Anything I want to do that bad I like her to get to do, too. Can't we go get her out?"

"In a little while. We need a little more light. We got to get a wrecker over to the hole. We've had to do this a time or two before. You're lucky. We drop a chain down with a little harness on it and strap it around her and snake her back up out of there. We need a little more light to get the wrecker down the hill to the lock."

They dropped off the pickup truck on the way back out to the cave. And he studied the little house with the porch as they passed it. Not much of a place.

He read the sign carefully for the first time as he watched them set up to drop the harness down through the lock. "Warning! Stay out! Do not enter. Once down inside, impossible to get back out." He wanted to be the one who went in to help her out, using the harness. He wanted to be the first to see her. And he wanted just a little bit to see the green light once more. But he was relieved when the sheriff said no, that the man who'd designed the harness and handled the other rescues would go. He was relieved because he wasn't sure what to expect.

She appeared at the mouth of the pit, both feet wedged into the little stirrup and a wide leather strap around her hips, binding her to the chain. She clung to the chain with one arm and held the other arm tightly over her eyes to protect them from the gray morning light and she was sobbing convulsively. They helped her off the chain and onto the ground and she sat, her face against her knees, closed in by her arms, her whole body shuddering. He wanted to go over to her but he was afraid and so he stood back and watched. He felt his own eyes fill up and start sending water down his face. He watched her and he watched as they dropped the chain back in and easily brought out the other man.

A trooper gave her a pair of sunglasses. She walked next to the sheriff back up the hill to the road and he lagged a little behind the two of them. When they reached the sheriff's car, she began to get in front, doing so in such a way that it was clear he was to sit in back. As she was getting in, he finally said, very softly, "You all right, sweetheart?"

She glanced quickly at him. "I'm fine," she said. And as she closed the door, he knew that she would never look directly at him or speak to him again.

She had been moved out for two weeks. He kept watching for her around the mill but she avoided him. He missed her, wanted her back, couldn't get used to being without her. Everything seemed to be falling apart.

Since it was Saturday, he slept an hour or so later. When

he woke up, he lay there, thinking about her and also about the fact that he'd have to make some changes. He couldn't afford even their "rat's nest" without her paycheck coming in, helping to carry it. He'd have to find something cheaper. Lots of things were going to be different.

He got up and looked outside. Pretty day. After some cereal and milk, he left the place, walked to where 58 came through town, and started hitching. The first lift took him all the way. When they reached the cow's-head rock, he got out, hiked into the thicket to the lock, and lowered himself down to the floor of the cave. He made his way to the gravel beach and sat down, rubbing a freshly skinned elbow, to stare at the beautiful green glow and think about how it all had happened.

Chapter 82:
Myrna Lloyd Is Missing

Robert S. Levinson

Robert S. Levinson is a man of "affairs": *The John Lennon Affair,*
The James Dean Affair, The Elvis and Marilyn Affair, and *Hot*
Paint (The Andy Warhol Affair), each a title in Levinson's the Neil
Gulliver and Stevie Marriner series of mystery-thriller novels.
After working in newspapers and public relations, Levinson
formed his own PR company where he developed, wrote, and
produced more than forty comedy, musical, variety and awards
specials including the Annual Soap Opera Awards. He also
helmed the inaugural International Thriller Writers' Awards pres-
entation in 2006 as well writing and producing the 2003 and
2004 Annual Edgar Awards gala of the Mystery Writers of
America. Levinson's stories have appeared in *Alfred Hitchcock*
Mystery Magazine and *Ellery Queen Mystery Magazine* where
his 2005 story, "Death Conquers All," was voted a coveted EQMM
Readers Award, marking the third consecutive year was so honored. His latest release is *Where the Lies Begin.*

I was one card away from a straight flush, hearts, queen high, displaying nary a twitch of emotion to Freaky Bakersfield, who was weighing the possibility I was bluffing like the fate of mankind rested on his bony shoulders. I was on the verge of scoring one of the greatest pots in the history of Los Angeles Police Central press room poker, when the red phone connecting me to the *Daily*'s city desk screamed for attention.

I settled my hip flask on top of my hand, eased up from the table, warned Freaky to have his gluteus maximus in gear before I got back, and fought through the blue haze of chronic cigar and cigarette smoke to my desk.

Eddie Grimm was on the horn, the guy who cost me my exclusive on the L. Faye Tilden murders, but that's for another chapter in *The Life and Crimes of A. K. Fowler.*

"Eddie, this better be good," I said, not trying to hide my annoyance.

"How'd you know it was me, Augie?" Breathing like he had a whistle caught in his windpipe.

"I recognized your asthma."

"I suppose." He cleared his throat. "Augie, got someone on the line says he's an old acquaintance of yours, needs to talk to you urgent-like about somebody by the name of Myrna Lloyd, whoever that is." That got my attention. "He said you'd know."

"A movie star, big, big, before they were called superstars, before you were born, Eddie. Subtract thirty or so years from this year. We're talking late fifties, early sixties." That was all Eddie needed to know. More than he needed to know. That I loved Myrna Lloyd once was none of Eddie's business. "Mr. Urgent-Like tell you his name?"

"No. You wanna hang while I—"

"Just patch him through, Eddie." I glanced over to the poker table. Freaky was pushing a mountain of chips into the pot, adding his raise to mine. Hands were folding around. I covered the mouthpiece and announced to the room I was seeing the raise and bumping it another twenty. Freaky gave me the finger, switched off the nasty ogre face he always made when he was trying to buy a pot, and went back to looking indecisive.

"Fowler here," I said.

"Augie, hello. Long time." Although it had been years since I last heard it, I knew his maple syrup voice at once. I gave it a name even before he spoke it:

Tom Carpenter.

Except for Tom Carpenter, Myrna Lloyd might have married me, and chances are we'd still be together, blowing out candles on her birthday cakes.

"It's Tom Carpenter, Augie."

"Yeah, Tom? What gives?" No way I could pretend I was happy to hear from him. Some wounds heal and disappear with time. Others become scars that are always there to remind you of things you would much rather forget.

"Did he tell you it was me, the chap who answered the phone?" I let the question pass. He unleashed a desperation sigh and said, "Myrna's gone, Augie."

I shook my head at the phone.

I wanted to say something like, Myrna is dead, remember? I held off wondering if maybe Carpenter's memory had deep-sixed.

For several seconds I thought we'd been cut off, then: "You hear what I'm telling you, Augie? I'm over at Hollywood

Memorial Park. Calling you from my car phone. Her crypt's been vandalized. Her coffin's gone. Stolen. Myrna's gone, Augie. She's gone." The words escaped from him in a torrent of emotion that turned into a waterfall of undecipherable weeping.

I let it play itself out, then asked, "Why you calling me, Tom? Let the cemetery people know. They'll get the cops in on this."

"No. No cops. The note said no cops."

"What note?"

"The one in my mailbox, saying to come here and see that she was gone. And not to tell the police that she's missing, but just wait for their ransom demands."

"Myrna's been kidnapped?"

"Help me, Augie. Myrna would want that. Myrna always loved you more than she loved me. We both know that."

I didn't have to think about it.

"Wait there for me," I said. "I'm on my way."

I grabbed my jacket off the rack and one-stopped at the game long enough to grab my hip flask and tell Deke Sparrow of City News Service to play out the hand for me. I could have hung back another five, faked Freaky Bakersfield out of his Jockeys even if my fifth pasteboard came up a clunker, except—

—all these years later, Myrna Lloyd was again working her magic spell over me.

It's a twenty minute drive from downtown L.A. to Hollywood Memorial Park in early rush-hour street traffic on Sunset Boulevard. I made most of the lights heading west past tired buildings and storefronts dominated by signs in

Spanish, across Alvarado Street and through a stretch of weed-filled hillside full of ramshackle homes dating back to the turn of the century. I eased my classic red Rolls Royce onto the Santa Monica Boulevard access curve, tore past more neighborhoods in dire need of a facelift, and soared through the rusted gates of the downtrodden cemetery that backed on the Paramount studio lot.

Not a minute or a mile went by where I didn't have Myrna on my mind, picturing her the way she was the day we met at the studio, on the other side of the cemetery wall, a half mile from where she was ultimately laid to rest.

It was before I became this prize-winning giant of crime journalism, the Rocky Marciano of my craft. 1961. I was in my late twenties, still dancing with the dream of leaping from bit parts to movie-star big and rich.

Paramount was celebrating its ninetieth anniversary year with a party the studio press agents had put together and I had wangled an invitation through Sunset Beaudry, a cowboy star I knew, who was on the lot shooting *The Man Who Shot Liberty Valance* for Jack Ford, playing fourth or fifth fiddle to Duke Wayne, Jimmy Stewart, and Lee Marvin.

Maybe four or five hundred people were squeezed inside a soundstage, elbowing in, out, and around an apartment set for the Blake Edwards movie *Breakfast at Tiffany's,* swilling champagne and grabbing Chasen's-catered delicacies from mile-high platters on sterling silver serving trays.

I spotted Edwards off in a corner, holding court with his stars Audrey Hepburn and George Peppard, and navigated toward him, intent upon making adulatory small talk that would conclude with my handing him my résumé. I always carried copies in the one-button, silk-and-cashmere jacket from Frank Sinatra's swanky tailor, Sy Devore, that set me back a bundle and came out of the closet only for interviews and this kind of see-and-be-seen scene.

Halfway at him, I was brought up short by a hand capturing my arm.

"Slow down, pard," Sunset Beaudry said, shouting to be heard over the din. "I want you to meet someone special."

His other hand was around the waist of Myrna Lloyd, who had been Sunset's leading lady in two of his cheap Monogram movies three or four years ago, before she broke through big time playing the deaf mute who inspires a revolution in Selznick's *Sounds of Triumph.*

She leaned over, made a megaphone of her hands around my ear, and cooed in a voice as seductive as a siren's call, "Actually, I told Sunset I wanted to meet you." She stepped back, her wisp of a smile framed by modest laugh lines.

"Who do you have me confused with?" I said, fumbling over the words, unable to free myself from her bold, mesmerizing stare, her ocean blue eyes the size of boulders.

Sunset answered an invisible someone with a wave and excused himself with a wink for both of us.

Myrna said, "No confusion, Mr. Fowler . . . Sunset's friend, who visited the set one day when we were making *Gunmen of Abilene.* Every time I looked over, I caught you staring at me. You'd hurry-up turn away, but not always fast enough. Why didn't you ever say hello?"

"You were just a kid, playing Sunset's daughter, and—"

"I'm not a kid anymore, Mr. Fowler . . . Augie."

How it began between us, Myrna and me.

Within the hour, we had slipped away and were making erotic love in a garden paradise surrounding the Hollywood Memorial Cemetery lake, on a bed of fertile lawn shaded by twin cypress trees.

I headed there now after parking the Rolls.

The grounds had fallen into decay in the years since I'd last been here, although I'm sure the dead didn't mind. The lawns, the shrubbery, the trees; footpaths that once were lovingly looked after were now sad illustrations of the hard times that had driven the owners to bankruptcy upon the rise in status of Forest Lawn and Hillside Memorial Park among the families of the famous. Some tombstones were broken, others had been bent out of shape by tree roots.

In earlier times, Hollywood Memorial Park had been their cemetery of choice. The old-fashioned headstones and high-rise monuments, the huge mausoleums and the countless lawn plaques bore names that reeked of movie history: Valentino; Fairbanks; DeMille; Huston; Muni; the Talmadge sisters; Charlie Chaplin's mother and son; call girl—starlet Virginia Rappe, whose death doomed the career of comic Fatty Arbuckle; director William Desmond Taylor, whose death was never solved; the notorious "Bugsy" Siegel, who brought Murder, Inc. to Hollywood and Las Vegas; even the great Al Jolson, until his family got a better offer from Hillside and he was dug up and reburied.

I navigated between the grandiose, mud-caked double tomb of Harry Cohn, the foul-mouthed tyrant who had run Columbia Pictures, and the far less imposing grave of

Jeanette MacDonald's singing partner, Nelson Eddy, past the mud-encrusted monument to Tyrone Power, the dashing matinee idol and swordsman nonpareil in *The Mark of Zorro* and *The Black Swan,* to Our Tree, Myrna's and mine, the towering cypress on which I'd impetuously carved our initials the next time she and I shared an indecent hour here.

Parting the tangle of underbrush revealed our brief history, ML + AF. Top billing to her, of course, although she tried to argue me out of it. An X scarring my initials, my handiwork within a day of her news, that she'd taken up with Tom Carpenter and it was over between us.

I exhaled a deep breath of the past and strolled back to the Hollywood Cathedral Mausoleum under an armada of somber gray clouds rolling in from the ocean in advance of a rainstorm the weather boys had been predicting for a week.

Tom Carpenter was sitting on a marble bench by the entrance to the last aisle at the end of the mausoleum's main corridor, slumped forward, with his elbows on his knees and his face buried in his hands.

He reacted to the echo of my footsteps, jumping up with a look of sudden relief on a wrinkled, shopworn face barely suggesting the hypnotic good looks of thirty years ago that I'd never doubted had caused Myrna to abandon my bed for his.

Dark circles rimmed deep set, bloodshot eyes that contrasted starkly with a plain vanilla skin color showing no evidence of the overripe suntan that had been his trademark. Once a sharp dresser, his jacket and slacks looked like they had been bought thirty pounds ago. His posture, once as sturdy as a flagpole, had taken on a fifteen degree angle.

"Tom, it's good to see you," I said, words I never expected to pass through my lips, meaning them more than he'd ever know. "Now, tell me. What's this about Myrna and—"

He cut me off with a gesture, grabbed my hand, and led me halfway down the aisle she shared with Valentino and several minor silent screen celebrities forgotten by time. The marble square that sealed her vault was on the floor, angled against the wall. The vault was empty.

He looked at me helplessly, laced his fingers like he was getting ready to recite a prayer. "You are going to help me, aren't you, Augie?"

"No," I said. Carpenter's jaw dropped and a snap of noise flew from his throat. I said, "Anything I do, I'll be doing for Myrna. Not for you."

He blasted me with his eyes. "Fine," he said, spitting out the word and following it up with a meaningless laugh. "Whatever ransom these rats want, I'm ready to pay them, and maybe someday you'll understand that anything you do for her you are also doing for me." His expression suddenly held a secret he showed no interest in sharing. I wrote it off as an actor acting.

"Not today, though, Tom. Probably not tomorrow, either."

"I did not take Myrna from you, Augie. I know you've always thought so, but it's not true."

I said, "Myrna died in your arms. She should have died in mine."

"Myrna shouldn't have died at all. The bullet that killed her was meant for me."

"Then it's a shame the shooter didn't have a better aim."

"Finally, Augie. At last. We agree on something."

I had a restless night, wrestling with Tom Carpenter's declaration when he caught me in the Police Central press room: *Myrna always loved you more than she loved me. We both know that.*

I'd let it pass without comment at the time, but the truth is I didn't know *that* any more than I knew whether to believe Carpenter believed *that* or used *that* as a sure ploy to get me to the cemetery.

Later, when he asserted, *I did not take Myrna from you, Augie. I know you've always thought so, but it's not true,* I knew Carpenter was flat-out wrong.

What I thought, what I knew: It was every bit Myrna's doing.

She was never one to stay with one man long, or only one man at a time. It was a carryover from her childhood, she confessed once, in a moment of extreme intimacy and rare candor. They were years straight out of Dickens, lower-depths parents who used her as illegal tender to pay the rent, fill the gas tank, replenish their stash, or hand her over to a new trailer trash pal just for the hell of it. She'd finally escaped, using her body to make it from the Midwest to Hollywood, into the movie studios, and onto the silver screen.

I asked her, "Why are you telling me this?"

"So you know what you're getting into, handsome. I don't come with any long-term guarantees. No *Lucy* or *Donna Reed Show* here. Love 'em and Leave 'em Myrna, that's me. Yesterday it was mostly Leo Bennett. Today?" She tapped my nose with an index finger. "Mostly you."

"Tomorrow?"

"Ask me tomorrow."

"What if tomorrow never comes?"

"You do have a way with words, handsome. Maybe you should be writing instead of acting."

"You're saying true love's out of the question for you?"

"I'm saying true love may not be the answer for me. I play the field the way the field used to play me, then move on before the hurt can set in."

"I want to love you, not hurt you, Myrna."

She laughed and got to work on an imaginary violin. "How many times do you think I've heard that tune?"

"What will it take to get you to believe me?"

"How are you fixed for miracles?"

A few months later, she broke the news and my heart by announcing her decision to leave me for Tom Carpenter. I pressed her for a reason. "It's time," she said. "If it's any con-solation, you lasted longer than any of the others, handsome." She nursed me through our final night together, urged me to forget about her and get on with my life, and paused at the front door, a silhouette against the early morning light, only long enough to blow a kiss across the room.

Tom Carpenter.

An Oscar in his trophy case and now Myrna Lloyd.

I aimed all my rage at him, although there were others I might have blamed—the actors, authors, singers, studio grips, politicians, and the occasional counter boy who took up some of the nights she strayed from me without more of an explanation than *I'm busy tonight.*

Tom Carpenter became and stayed my target, I suppose, because he lasted with Myrna longer than me—

—to the day she died.

Because Myrna married him, not me.

Because he, not me, was with Myrna the night she was killed.

Because he never remarried and further mythologized his claim of eternal love for Myrna by visiting her crypt year after year on the anniversary of her murder, the widower in black emulating the "Lady in Black" who annually showed up at Hollywood Memorial Park to shed tears for Valentino.

A question also kept me on edge through the night, as much as Carpenter's words: *Thirty years after Myrna's death, what had motivated parties unknown to steal her coffin and hold it for ransom?*

Was this some cruel prank being worked on Carpenter, was that it?

Or what?

Carpenter's call the next morning came at an indecent hour, in uncertain daylight, the battle of the birdcalls barely underway, his voice terrorized by what he was reporting. The crypt burglars had somehow managed to steal onto his walled Bel-Air estate without setting off alarms and had slipped a new note under his door.

I rolled into a sitting position on the bed, coughed the sleep into my fist, and said, "How much they asking for?"

"Not money," he said. "Myrna's diary. I give them her diary, they return Myrna."

"What's in her diary makes it so special?"

"Augie, damned if I know, damn it. If Myrna kept a diary, she never told me. You? She ever mention a diary to you?"

"I'm drawing a zero as big as my bank balance. What else? The ransom note say anything else?"

"Yes. If I don't hand over the diary, not only will Myrna be gone for good, but I'm a dead man." Sobs began gutting his words. "Why me, Augie? Why the hell me?"

"You were the one who was married to Myrna when she was killed. You inherited her estate. It's reasonable to think it included a diary she kept hidden from prying eyes in a dresser drawer, someplace like that?"

"I don't—I never looked through her . . . I was too depressed. The lawyers took care of everything. Sold the house. Our place in Palm Springs. Took care of the bequests, the donations to her favorite charities. The thrift shop people came in with packing boxes and emptied her closets, her dressers, her—" He seemed to run out of words.

I remembered something he'd said yesterday: *The bullet that killed her was meant for me.* I put the question to Carpenter, suggesting, "Maybe the shooter's been practicing since then?"

He groaned at the concept. "Nothing to do with a diary," he said. "A gambling debt, before I finally squared it away. Money I owed certain people in Vegas, well into seven figures when they came to the house to teach my kneecaps a lesson. The situation got out of hand and—"

"Squared away the debt too late to do Myrna any good."

"That was cruel, a cruel thing to say, Augie." He began milking his tear ducts like he wanted to fill the L.A. River.

My eyes clouded over thinking back thirty years to the caller who brought me the news, a legman for Louella Parsons, Hearst's syndicated queen of Hollywood gossip, up against deadline and fishing for an exclusive quote from one of Myrna's past romances.

The way Carpenter explained it at the time, he and Myrna were returning home from a press screening of *Lawrence of Arabia* at the Cinerama Dome. Burglars were in the process of ransacking the place. Converting the make-believe of his screen image to real life, he charged at the one who'd pulled out an automatic. They wrestled for the gun. It went off, mortally wounding Myrna, while Carpenter was knocked unconscious by a blow to the back of the head. The burglars were gone when he roused. Myrna died in his arms.

I told Parsons's guy, "It's a great tragedy for all her fans, everyone who loved her."

Hung up on him. Got drunk and stayed drunk for a week.

Until this morning, Carpenter had never said anything to anyone about Vegas or a gambling debt.

I reminded him of the burglary story he'd played for the cops.

"Dramatic license. The truth about the gambling, if it leaked to Parsons or Hopper or even Harrison Carroll, it would've cost me a plum role I was up for that had Oscar written all over it. That would have taken me to the next level. Besides, nothing I said was going to bring Myrna back."

"Or now, from the sound of it."

He choked on my words, but recovered quickly enough to say, "What can I do, Augie?"

"No diary and all things considered, relax and wait to be killed."

• • •

The ransom demand hadn't included delivery instructions. They arrived the end of the week, in a note parked under a windshield wiper of Carpenter's Porsche while he was shooting a bit on Wagon Train at "Crash" Corrigan's Corriganville, the two-hundred-acre movie location in Simi Valley, by the Southern Pacific railroad tracks, where the old two-lane Topanga Canyon snaked out of the Santa Susana Pass.

He'd gotten the part after a desperate call to his old buddy John McIntire, who'd replaced the recently deceased Ward Bond as the show's wagon master. It was a job Carpenter needed to sustain his Screen Actors Guild medical benefits.

For all his front and braggadocio—the lavish home, the expensive car, the name-above-the-title demeanor—Carpenter by his late fifties had become a sad reminder of the Old Hollywood, a Trivial Pursuit answer. He had one foot in bankruptcy court to go with the one foot in the grave warning he'd gotten from the crypt robbers.

The new ransom note set a day and time for Carpenter to bring Myrna's diary to Church of the Good Shepherd on Bedford Drive in Beverly Hills.

The name triggered another dormant memory. Myrna's funeral service had been held at Good Shepherd. She wasn't a Catholic, at best a practicing agnostic, but Carpenter wanted a photogenic central location that would be convenient to celebrities on the guest list he had put together and the media he was certain would be massing outside to capture the occasion for posterity.

Me, I wasn't invited, but I went anyway and stood among the fans and autograph seekers mourning the loss of the first woman who had ever meant anything special to me, feeling how James Dean must have felt a decade earlier at Good Shepherd, when his love Pier Angeli was inside marrying singer Vic Damone.

Equally vivid was the memory of trailing Myrna's funeral cortege to Hollywood Memorial Park and burying myself among dozens of gawkers being held back from the mausoleum steps by uniformed studio guards.

I had waited for the mourners to clear out before stealing inside to settle a bouquet of fresh red roses at her crypt. Afterward, I visited the cypress trees where we had first made love and touched a kiss to the carved heart I'd mutilated the day after she destroyed mine with her news about Tom Carpenter.

Then I remembered something that happened in the next two or three—or four—weeks while I was stumbling around in a scotch fog, angry at Myrna for leaving me, for demolishing any hopes I had that she would wise up and come to her senses one day, give Carpenter the boot, and come back to me. I remembered my head splitting at the sound of somebody trying to break down my front door.

Through the spy hole, the fun-house image of a somber-faced gent with tightly knit features overpowered by a mis-shapen salt-and-pepper goatee, a tie completely out of synch with his Brooks Brothers pinstripe. His name was Duberchin, he said. Attorney-at-law. The second Duberchin of Duberchin and Duberchin, L.L.C. Representing the Estate of Myrna Lloyd. The late Miss Lloyd in her last will and testament had specified gifts for certain of her friends and, turning cautious in his choice of words, *certain of her special acquaintances*. Personally delivering mine, pursuant to Miss Lloyd's wishes, was the second Duberchin of Duberchin and Duberchin, L.L.C.

"Where do I fit in the cast, friend or special acquaintance?" I said.

"I'm sure I don't know, Mr. Fowler. There was no indication from Miss—"

"Yeah, fine," I said. I wanted Myrna, the real thing, the genuine article, not some reminder she was dead. I snapped the spy hole shut and went chasing after some hair of the dog.

A few hours later, I discovered the second Duberchin had left the package parked against the door. It was wrapped in the Sunday funnies; neat corners; frizzy gold-colored ribbon; "Augie" written on the gift tag in her elegant script, a tiny heart dotting the "i" in Augie the way she always did; small, about the size and shape of—

A small book.

A small book!

A diary maybe?

Maybe, a diary!

I ripped backward through time, challenging my mind to remember what I had done with Myrna's gift.

I wasn't going to be like some people, who dress a mantle with an urn containing the ashes of a loved one. I wanted to put the past behind me and get on with my life. Out of sight, out of mind, but I couldn't bring myself to discard the package like garbage, so a few days later, moving stealthily under cover of a moonless night, I buried it sight unseen at Hollywood Memorial Park.

And managed to forget about it, rinse it out of my mind with more scotch.

Until now.

Except for camera-bearing tourists wandering the cracked,

weed-riddled concrete pathways, pausing to pose and snap
whenever they recognized a familiar name on a grave
marker, I had the cemetery to myself. I navigated the dense
underbrush to the cypress tree I had shared with Myrna,
gave our desecrated heart a martyr's glance, and started
digging with the small sharp-nosed shovel the nursery store
guy promised was perfect for cutting through hard soil and
roots.

I dug down a foot before admitting this wasn't the
right spot.

I moved a few feet over and tried again.

Again, no luck.

The third try wasn't the charm either.

Thirty-something years ago, had I been so boozed up
that night that I buried the package under the wrong tree?
The theory bore exploration. I angled over to the cypress
tree's twin, picked a spot, and began digging.

Nothing. Not until the next try.

I tossed aside the shovel and used my hands to push
away the wet earth and pull out the book-sized package.
Using the full moon as a flashlight, I saw no evidence of the
Sunday funnies wrapping I remembered or the tag with my
name, but the ribbon hanging limply around a muck-
racked coat of aluminum foil was gold-colored enough to
tell me I'd found Myrna's gift.

I waited until I was back home to peel off the foil.
Through a second inner coat, this one clear plastic, I saw
the word *Diary* on a red pebbled-leather cover with a strap
connected to a silly lock. It was the kind of diary I always
associated with adolescents who needed a place to hide
their innermost secrets, fears, and longings.

Myrna's diary contained all that, but there was nothing childish about anything she committed to the page, beginning with the handwritten letter addressed to me she'd inserted under the cover.

Hey, handsome. If you're seeing this, I'm dead. It won't take you long reading this partial record of my reckless, outrageous, and highly enjoyable life to find the reason they came after me. It'll be as clear as the freckle on your cute butt. I'm entrusting this little corner of dangerous history to you because trust was the one quality I found in you and few others among the multitude of gents it was my pleasure to know, including in the Biblical sense. Hide the diary in a safe place and use it one day when it can do you the most good. By the way, Tom was not a disappointment, ever, but he was never you. XXX and OOO.
Your Myrna.

The entries, bearing only an occasional scratch-out or correction, revealed a My Myrna who more accurately resembled an Everybody's Myrna. Over the years, from her earliest starlet days, she had been generous with the pleasure of her company. Producers, directors, and screenwriters. Singers, athletes, politicians, and scholars. One-of-a-kind one-night stands. Her set-side trailer a frequent rendezvous point for what she cataloged in her diary as either "brain food" or "body therapy."

Myrna saved snapshots and passionate, frequently obsessive notes of thank you and appreciation, the way sportsmen hang elks' heads and hoist marlins, jamming them between pages on which she followed a performance review with a critical appraisal on her personal scale of one to ten, ten being best. Her highest marks were reserved for the conquests who brought a new trick into her boudoir on wheels. I smiled at my ranking. Instead of a number, Myrna had written:

Off the charts, but only one reason I must soon protect myself from falling madly, deeply in love with him, a trap for me with a real human being who deserves better than me. Oh, Augie. Oh, oh, oh, you sweet devil, you.

Her words still had the power to destroy me.

Einstein was a genius for pursuing a theory of relativity, not love.

Love defies definition.

I felt as close as ever to Myrna.

Closer, maybe.

I raised the diary to my nose, inhaled deeply, and convinced myself I'd caught a lingering reminder of her favorite perfume, Diorrisimo, the floral scent that came in a Baccarat flacon.

All those other men—not just Tom Carpenter—they didn't matter.

Except one, and he was calling himself Alek Hidell.

Myrna had met him on a shooting range at Miller's All-Star Shooting Gallery in Northridge. She was practicing for her next picture, a co-starring role in a Universal big-budget Western with Jimmy Stewart and Julie Adams. He stepped over to offer her advice on her stance and did enough fancy showing off with his .38 Smithy and an Italian-made Mannlicher-Carcano rifle to capture her awe and an invitation to a home-cooked meal.

The next morning, she told her diary Alek was a modest, mediocre four by her measure, writing:

He was nothing special in the looks or body departments. Dark, suspicious eyes always on guard. An unsettling smile and a nervous laugh undercutting polite manners and a quiet voice reeking of New Orleans while he talked up Marxism as the one true hope for the future of mankind most of the night. Breathed easy after he split with the friend he phoned to come over and get him. The friend, Cubby, spooky-looking and not as gabby, barked at Alek to shut up when he told me it wouldn't be long before their place in the history books was guaranteed. Cubby apologized for the outburst, said he was a fan, and asked for an autographed photograph. I signed one for him and also one for Alek.

That wasn't the last of Alek Hidell in Myrna's life.

Slotted between later diary pages was an envelope postmarked Fort Worth, with a note from Alek and a photograph. The note thanked Myrna for her kindness and said the photo was in repayment for hers. It showed a somber Alek and Cubby standing shoulder-to-shoulder in a parklike setting, a freeway and office buildings behind them. Inscribed on the back in carefully plotted block letters was, *For Miss Myrna Lloyd. Two comrades-in-arms make ready.*

I didn't have to ask *Make ready for what?* any more than I needed the photo to know Alek Hidell's presence in Myrna's diary defined him as the reason her crypt had been broken into, her casket stolen, and Tom Carpenter threatened with death if he did not meet the kidnappers' demand.

I had stumbled into evidence that could give me the byline of a lifetime, probably a Pulitzer, on a yarn greater than all the prize-winning exclusives I'd scored since making the switch from acting anonymity to the business of deadlines and headlines.

I called Carpenter and told him I'd keep the meeting for him at Good Shepherd. He sounded relieved, but wondered, "Augie, aren't you scared they'll kill you, not just me, when they find out we don't have the diary?"

"You could say that," I said.

There was no reason to trouble him with the truth.

At a quiet hour somewhere between the final mass of afternoon and the first of evening, I settled in the last row of benches in the nave, left of the central portal, and admired the holy majesty bought and paid for over time by the practicing faithful in this grotesquely wealthy community, imagining I had accidentally stepped into a set built for the next DeMille epic. The people scattered around were few in number and caught up in their prayers.

After a few minutes, a priest did an awkward job of crossing himself and slid into the row alongside me. "You're not Carpenter," he said, his voice loaded with bad tidings. He had thirty years, six inches, and daily workouts at the gym on me. A mop of black hair overlapped his ears and hung over the back of his neck like a bargain-basement hairpiece.

"I know," I said. "And I'm betting you're not a priest. Does that make us even?"

"No, smart guy, but get ready to say your prayers if you didn't bring what I'm here to collect." He jammed the business end of a silenced pistol into my side hard enough to win a grunt. "You bring it?"

"You're what? CIA? FBI? Some other set of alphabet soup?"

"YWN—your worst nightmare if I hear otherwise. You bring it?"

"Say I did. What are the odds you don't pop me once I hand it over?"

"Fifty-fifty. Not that good if you keep me on this merry-go-round any longer."

"And Tom Carpenter?"

"The other fifty."

"Now that we have that out of the way—" I dipped inside my jacket and pulled out a folded sheaf of paper. He eased up on the pistol he had shifted to the side of my neck. "Worth reading before you do anything rash," I said, doing my best Bogart. "A little story I banged out on my trusty Corona before heading over."

"Why should I care?" he said.

"In a word, Alek Hidell . . . That's two words, isn't it?"

A voice behind me said, "I care, Mr. August Kalman Fowler. Pass it here."

I looked to see who had joined us.

This priest was closer to my age and made no secret of

his baldness. His face had fallen into his neck and was the salmon pink color of someone who didn't get out into the sun much; pockmarked and acne scarred. It was vaguely familiar. I mentally peeled away thirty years and was willing to wager his friends called him "Cubby."

Cubby scanned the lead and first few paragraphs, contorted his lips into nothing you'd ever see on *Captain Kangaroo*, and said, "Leave us, Figley. I'll take it from here." Figley started to protest. Cubby gave him a look. Figley made the pistol disappear and retreated.

"That confessional there," Cubby said, pointing. It wasn't a suggestion.

"Your story tells me you have Myrna Lloyd's diary, but not everything you write is factually correct, Mr. Fowler."

"Correct enough to cause an earthquake after it appears, Cubby."

"Another error, Mr. Fowler. The Cubby of whom you speak was killed last week in an unfortunate automobile accident."

"About the time Myrna's crypt was broken into and her coffin stolen?"

"Soon after, yes. We continue to mourn Cubby's loss."

"*We.* He work for you?"

"In a manner of speaking. Cubby was an independent contractor, a recruitment specialist, who could be trusted to deliver the desired result on the occasional odd job."

"Like on November 22, 1963, with his friend Mr. Hidell."

Through the confessional window I saw him dismiss the thought with a wave of the hand. "You draw conclusions like a chimpanzee with a crayon, Mr. Fowler. Hidell acted

alone. The finding made after serious and prolonged investigation. Disputed down through the years, but never dis-
proved, as you damn well know."

"Give the chimp enough crayons and time and he may
produce a masterpiece. My story may help to rethink and
reevaluate those findings after it appears."

"The earthquake you mentioned."

"Kaboom."

"Have you filed the story with your newspaper?"

"Not yet, but trust me when I say my death wouldn't
stop it. Or exhibits one and two. A postcard that puts
Hidell in Texas when he supposedly was sopping up the
party line in Moscow. A photograph that connects Hidell to
an agency of the government and puts a second man with
him on a scouting expedition to a certain grassy knoll in
Dallas."

"You have these items?" He saw the answer register on
my face. "What will stop your story?"

"The truth about Myrna. Her safe return. No need for
Carpenter and me to spend the rest of our lives looking
over our shoulder."

"And I get?"

"The diary and its contents. The postcard. The photograph."

All I heard for the next several moments was the chaotic
buzzing of a horsefly loose in the booth.

"How do I know I can trust you to keep your word, Mr.
Fowler?"

"You don't."

Laughter filled the confessional. "Mr. Fowler, any other
answer and I'd have held you immediately suspect," he

said, and proceeded to dish out the past like Thanksgiving turkey without the stuffing or trimmings.

Thirty years ago, Cubby recognizes that the man who calls himself Alek Hidell has a tongue that won't quit and, carrying on about Marxism and the history books, has told Myrna Lloyd enough to possibly link the two of them after their work in Dallas is concluded. Cubby knows he must dispose of her and the threat with extreme prejudice. Her husband, Carpenter, has outstanding markers he can't cover being held by gambling interests in Las Vegas and Cuba who owe favors to Cubby's employer. Cubby enlists the gamblers' help in staging the incident that will culminate in Myrna's death.

The problem is resolved until thirty years later.

Carpenter, his career suffering and desperate for media exposure that might get him a job, tells Jerry Buck of the Associated Press that he is developing a screenplay around his late, beloved wife. The screenplay will be based on a diary Myrna kept more faithfully than she did her marriage vows, in which she detailed her numerous amorous adventures.

I said, "I would have spotted a story like that."

"Buck only gave it a line or two in his column, easy to miss, but we caught it and knew we had to deal with a ghost who'd come back to haunt us."

"Carpenter told me he didn't know about the diary."

"Then clearly, Mr. Fowler, one of us must be lying."

"A better actor than I ever gave him credit. What else?"

"Let's say he knew enough when we put the question to him to trace the diary to his wife's estate lawyers and your gift, and he was most accommodating when we asked his help in recovering it. The graveyard skullduggery was his brainchild. We'd have been far more direct. He also pro-posed excluding from his screenplay what he had once read about Alek and Cubby. For a substantial price, of course, as if we have our own set of keys to the U.S. Mint. Like all chronic gamblers, he has a propensity for betting on the wrong horses with the wrong bookmakers."

I phoned Carpenter when I got home. I told him only what I felt like sharing, that Myrna would be returned to the mausoleum before morning.

The news put a brass band in his voice.

He said, "Man, oh, man, I don't know how you managed it, you old son of a gun, but I owe you my life, don't I, Augie?"

I said, "Keep it, Tom. With my compliments."

I visited Myrna the next day, bringing a dozen fresh red roses as a welcome home present before heading to Police Central.

Freaky Bakersfield looked up from his cards and whis-tled for my attention when I wheeled into the press room. "Check your desk, Aug. Your favorite graft, delivered about an hour ago. Who's the adoring fan with better taste in his scotch than in hack reporters?"

The Glenlivet was a premium '59, hard to find and cur-rently selling at auction for more than a grand. There was a bright crimson bow hanging from its neck and a gift tag, unsigned.

"Something else," Deke Sparrow said. "Eddie Grimm called over looking for you. Said to tell you that movie star you told him about the other day—"

"Myrna Lloyd."

"Her. Eddie said tell you the sheriff's boys have identified the victim of a hit-and-run this A.M. over in West Hollywood. He's been ID'd as her husband, Thomas Carpenter. He was also some kind of actor, right?"

I grabbed the Glenlivet and cracked the bottle heading for my seat at the table. "A damn fine one," I said, as I settled in. "Whose deal?"

Down and Out in Brentwood

Neal Marks

Neal Marks is a law-abiding citizen who pays all his taxes, observes every traffic regulation, and never bets with bookies. Writing crime fiction is as close as he gets to lawlessness. He and his wife live in Encino, California.

Whenever one of Jackie's friends visited L.A., he took them on what he called "The O.J. Tour," starting with Simpson's estate on Rockingham.

"They've torn down the house since then," he'd tell them as he slowed down in front of the home that had replaced it. "But the wall where he dropped his glove?" Jackie would point to the far end of the property. "It was over there." Then he'd smile and ask, "Or was it Detective Fuhrman put it there?" Pausing for effect before adding, "Don't you just love a mystery?"

He'd stop the car at this point saying, "And Kato's guest

house—did I tell you he's a friend of a friend?—it was right in front of the wall. I can't reveal exactly what Kato's told me," Jackie would have a serious look about him now, "but let's just say his advice would be, Never get O.J. pissed off at you."

And so it would go. Four or five minute's worth of this until he'd rub his hands together and say, "Okay. On to the scene of the crime."

To get to Nicole Brown Simpson's condo he'd take the scenic drive—no houses under two an a half million—and they'd invariably ask, "Hey Jackie. So where's *your* place?" They'd say "place," not actually using the word "apartment," not wanting to come right out and say they knew that Jackie was full of shit about owning a house in Brentwood.

"It's up Mandeville Canyon," he'd say. "We'll run by there before dinner. But I gotta be honest. It's not a two-story job like a lot of what you're seeing. By Brentwood standards, it's really pretty low key, trust me."

A quick drive-by past the murder site—it was walled with nothing much to see—and it would be on to the coffee shop that used to be the Mezzaluna restaurant, "Where Ron Goldman served Nicole the 'Last Supper.'" He'd shake his head saying, "Poor bastards," then look at his watch, "Holy shit, we're running late. We got eight o'clock reservations at Mirabelle." Sometimes it would be Spago, or maybe The Palm. "We'll have a drink at my place *after*."

But they never did. Jackie always came up with a reason; and they always let it slide.

From where he stood on the side street, Jackie could see the occasional car pull up to the hotel's Wilshire Boulevard entrance. The drivers would get out to wait for a parking attendant, then they'd notice the freestanding sign at the curb—"Valet Parking In Rear"—and move on.

Jackie liked it: no doorman, not much foot traffic in and out of the hotel. He walked up Wilshire and, without missing a beat, snatched the valet-parking sign as he passed it. He dropped it in the alley, continued to the next corner, and waited.

Less than ten minutes later, a white Honda swerved to the curb—an Accord, the most stolen vehicle in America. Jackie smiled. If he boosted it, he knew one man who'd be happy: the insurance-company actuary. Validate the man's numbers. But why fuck over this poor working stiff? The guy, opening his door now, for sure upside down considering the car was brand-spanking new.

Jackie would prefer an SUV—hopefully a Navigator or Escalade. Or maybe a convertible—a Corvette or Lexus SC. A rich guy finds out his car's been stolen, he takes it more in stride. Probably finds a way to turn a profit. Hey, if you looked at it that way, Jackie'd be doing him a favor.

So he'd take a pass on the Accord. Jackie headed over saying, "Sorry. Valet's in back."

The guy, seeing Jackie in his "uniform" of black pants, white shirt and black vest, said, "What took you so fuckin long?" A little guy, late twenties, wanting to impress his girlfriend. Trying to act tough, but not looking so tough in his Gap khakis, pink Izod shirt, and brown Dockers shoes.

Jackie said, "Maybe you didn't hear me, sir." Saying "sir" as sarcastically as he could. "We'll be happy to take care of you at our *rear* entrance." He turned to walk away but then heard the guy say, "Hey, buddy," and looked back in time to see car keys flying his way, the guy saying the luggage was in the trunk.

Jackie caught the keys, staying calm. He said, "I guess I owe you an apology. I didn't realize you know me." Fucking with the guy now.

The guy said nothing, looking confused.

Jackie said, "I mean, you know my *name*: Buddy."

The guy nodded.

"But I'm a bit embarrassed," Jackie said. "I've forgotten yours."

"Uh, Webster. Alan Webster."

"Okay, Mr. Webster, no problem. I'll bring the car around back." Jackie reached into his vest pocket saying, "Here's a claim check," opening the car door now. "I'll bring your luggage to the bell desk. Just call for them after you get to your room."

The guy tipped him a buck. Big shot.

As Jackie started the car, he heard the cassette player come to life—Britney Spears, holy shit—and thanked God for creating the eject button. He stopped in the circular drive behind the hotel and hit the trunk-release, waving a young bellhop over with a five-dollar bill in his hand.

"Would you please hold my bags at the bell desk until I'm checked in?" The kid took the five. "The name's Webster."

As he was pulling away, Jackie watched the bellhop maneuver the brass luggage trolley through the doorway, the trolley holding four bags. Jesus, none of them matching, Jackie thinking it made him look like he lacked class. But the five hundred he'd get for the Accord was some consolation. It would almost cover his own car payment.

• • •

Jackie sat on his balcony, an evening breeze blowing in from the Pacific, pouring himself an orange/strawberry/banana smoothie. Very California. Adding a shot of Canadian Club. Very Detroit. He heard a cell phone ringing on the balcony below, then the voice of his neighbor Marsha saying, ". . . It's a great listing. The house comps out at a million and a quarter . . . Nice lot, corner Jonesboro and Beckwith, twenty-three hundred square feet . . . The owners are back east already, so they're really motivated and want it listed at a million one. Thing is, with the shortage of inventory, there'll be a bidding war and they'll still get a million and a quarter . . . It'll show beautifully, it's still furnished. The wife says she's over her contemporary phase. Says their new place calls for more of a Tuscan-country look, so they left everything, even the wall hangings . . . And the place has a little bit of local history to it. You know who used to own it? Remember Mickey Cohen, the gangster? Well, his sister used to live there . . ."

Jackie ran the numbers in his head. Six percent commission on 1.25 million was 75 thousand. Say another agent sold it; the listing office would get half of that: better than 37 thou. And Marsha's cut would be about 25 grand, not bad. She was a girl on her way up. He took a deep breath, pursed his lips, and exhaled. Where the hell was *he* going?

Jackie, halfway through his drink and starting to feel a little buzz, heard *his* cell phone ringing now. It was a "guess who?" call and he recognized the voice—Ted Corey. He'd partnered a bit with the guy a while ago—bootlegging cigarettes, paper-hanging at the track—small stuff like that, back in Michigan. Ted said he was in L.A. for his cousin's wedding, staying at the Doubletree Hotel in Westwood. Was Jackie free for dinner tomorrow night? Italian, maybe?

Jackie wondered what was on Ted's mind—the guy was always scheming—but only asked, was seven o'clock good? He knew just the place and could pick Ted up.

Ted said fine. Said he'd bring a bottle of Asti Spumante. When Jackie told him it wasn't necessary— the restaurant had a full bar—Ted said it was to "christen the bar at your house. Celebrate the good fortune you're having in California."

The house. So that's what this was about. His fish story—that's all it was—had reached Ted. A nice enough guy, lots of laughs, but a big-league bullshitter who cut nobody any slack on *their* bullshit. Now wanting to call Jackie's bluff.

Jackie laughed. "Here's how it is. You want to christen my bar, nothing less than Dom Perignon will do." Jackie raising the stakes now, Dom going for one thirty-five a bottle and Ted being a mooch.

Ted asked how do you spell it, he'd look for it. Said he'd be out in front of the Doubletree at seven, ciao.

Jackie powered the phone off and splashed another shot of CC into what remained of the smoothie. The last thing he needed now was someone busting his chops.

Jackie interrupted the O.J. Tour, turning onto 5th Helena Drive, pointing out the Marilyn Monroe house to Ted. "This is where she died, 1962. I was just a baby then." Stopping the car now. "What I know her from, mostly, is the Biography Channel. Her singing "Happy Birthday" to President Kennedy."

"I'm old enough to remember her," Ted said. "Especially in the movie with Tom Ewell. The one where she gets tipsy and he tries to get her in the sack. Except they never really got it on in the movies back then." He was smiling now. "Offscreen she did it plenty. But onscreen, they'd just cut to logs blazing in the fireplace." Then he took a different tack. "Your house is around here, isn't it, Jackie?" Getting right to it. "Why don't we toss back a couple scotches before dinner? Shoot the shit sitting around your pool." Pulling a bottle now—christ, Dom Perignon—from the oversized pocket of his cargo jacket. "Sip champagne chasers."

Jackie shot a glance at Ted, the guy really enjoying himself. "Tell you what, Ted. We'll head over there after we finish up at the Mezzaluna."

But when they wrapped up the tour, Jackie looked at his watch and said, "Holy shit. We gotta be at Matteo's by eight o'clock." Looking over at Ted now. "Did I mention it was Sinatra's favorite?"

Ted said, "Hey, Jackie—"

Jackie waved him off. "We'll run by my place *after*," he said.

As Jackie pulled out of Matteo's parking lot onto Westwood Boulevard, Ted turned to him and said, "You got any Amaretto at home?" The guy was relentless. "I like to mix it with my scotch."

Jackie just shrugged.

"Worst case," Ted said, "we'll have the scotch neat."

On the radio, they were playing "Light My Fire," the long version, neither of them talking until Jackie made the right

from San Vicente onto 26th Street and headed down the
hill. "This part of Brentwood's called the Polo Fields,"
Jackie said. "You know what? The '32 Olympics, the
equestrian events, they took place right here." He hung a
left saying, "In the fifties, when they built homes and dug for
swimming pools, the place smelled of buried horseshit for
weeks. Can you believe that?" Stopping the car now in
front of a beautifully landscaped home, accent lighting
giving the place a resort-type feel. Jackie asking, "Ever
hear of Mickey Cohen?"

Ted shook his head.

"Big outfit guy in L.A. years back. When he lived in this
house, they'd all visit: Lucky Luciano, Meyer Lansky, the
whole bunch."

They walked up the brick pathway to the front door,
Jackie smiling to himself as the previous hours' work ran
through his mind like a Quentin Tarantino flashback: Res-
urrecting his old B&E skills—picking the door lock,
decoding the mechanism, making a duplicate key. Doing a
walk-through—scoping out the place, getting a feel for it,
stashing a bottle of Johnnie Walker Black, Ted's favorite.
Then sweetening the scene eighty-sixing the sales flyers
and agents' business cards. And taking down the "for sale"
sign—late in the day when no one would notice—just
before picking Ted up.

Man, if Ted only knew how much work his fucking bottle
of Dom Perignon had created.

Jackie opened the door now, turned on the lights, and
heard Ted whistle—"Jesus, look at this"—the place combining art deco with contemporary, done in black and
cream, chrome and glass: very Architectural Digest.

Jackie couldn't figure why the homeowners had got tired of this stuff.

Ted said, "Whoa, Jackie. L.A.'s been good to you, huh?"

Jackie played it low key. "I can't complain," he said. "My place up Mandeville was bigger, but I like this layout better." He beckoned Ted with a wave of his hand. "Here, I'll show you around . . ."

A couple hours later as they were leaving, Jackie locking up, Ted pointed toward the top of the door. Jackie thought Ted had spotted the real-estate-agent lock box, shit, starting to figure things out. But, no, it was something else. "Hey Jackie. This little goodie on the doorframe. That's a Jewish doodad, no?"

Jackie was unfazed. "Yeah, I think they call it a "mezuma" or something. It's for good luck." They were heading down the stairs now, Jackie saying, "Can never have too much luck. Can you, Ted?" Figuring it was about time that *his* changed for the better.

The idea came to him that night in a dream, played out in his head like a movie, with Jackie in the starring role. It opened with no credits, jumping right into the action. Jackie duplicating the key to Mickey Cohen's place.

Now the house was becoming much bigger, like a mansion on "Lifestyles of the Rich and Famous." And Jackie was a real estate mogul showing the property to Ted.

Then Ted disappeared. It was Angelina Jolie checking out the house now—flirting with Jackie—until George Clooney walked into the room and she began flirting with *him*. Jackie started to tell George to get the fuck out, get his own dream. But Angelina interrupted Jackie saying she loved the place, five million being no problem, would a two hundred grand deposit—green money—be okay?

In the final scene, Jackie was on a beach in Tahiti counting the cash, sharing a pina colada with a topless island girl; and only a little pissed off that George had probably ended up with Angelina.

When he woke up, everything still vivid in his mind, Jackie decided to rerun the dream. There was some good shit here, some things he could use.

The key to planning a good con, Jackie'd been taught, was to put yourself in the mark's shoes. See the proposition from *his* perspective.

So Jackie—sitting now at his kitchen table, head bowed, eyes closed—pictured a wealthy home shopper. The guy, opening the Times real estate section, sees an ad that grabs him. Gives the agent—that would be Jackie—a call. Then makes an appointment and goes out to take a look. Problem number one: The guy and the missus would expect to see a "for sale" sign with Jackie's name on it. After all, it was Jackie's ad.

Then Jackie pictured the couple taking the walk-through and giving each other little signals. Saying how nice the place was. Then saying they wanted to think it over. Problem number two: How do you get them excited enough to fork over a deposit right away?

Jackie looked up, his gaze fixed on the windowless wall across the way, thinking it through, things getting clearer. The way it would go down, he'd start with a simple bait and switch. The middle part, the pitch, was just bullshit talk—no problem. But the close would be the best part: He'd appeal to their greed. As W.C. Fields once said, "You can't cheat an honest man."

Jackie thought the place looked like an English country estate: ivy-covered Tudor, carriage house, gardens. He imagined James Bond walking out the front door, holding a cigarette and drink in one hand, his free arm wrapped around some babe.

But as he got closer to the couple waiting on the porch, Jackie saw it was a nerdy sort of guy, mid-fifties, clutching a palm pilot. The woman, though, *was* a babe: a ringer for Adriana on the "Sopranos" but without the hard edge. And the two of them weren't arm in arm; Jackie noticed that right away.

The woman spoke first. "Mr. Winston?" A hint of New England Brahmin in her voice, not New Jersey Bimbo.

Jackie said, "Please call me George," handing her his business card: "GEORGE WINSTON, Estate Properties." Jackie liked the sound of it—half George Washington, half Winston Churchill.

He also liked the sound of *her* name when she said it: Sandra Clark coming out as S*ah*ndra Cl*ah*k. Then she said, Please meet Frank Halverson, the guy nodding but not saying anything yet. Jackie noticed the different last names, curious about their relationship.

"Thanks for meeting me here, folks," Jackie said. "And sorry about the other property."

Sandra said it had sounded lovely.

"Well, desirable properties don't last long in this market. But *this* opportunity—" he swept his outstretched arm in a wide arc, indicating the grounds—"is even *more* exceptional."

Jackie was thinking he sounded just like an actual broker. "Your timing is perfect. An associate of mine just obtained the listing."

He gave them the tour and pointed out all the features. The masonry: "Beautiful work, no? What you don't see is the steel reinforcement. Makes the place practically earthquake proof." The floor plan: "More open than your typical Tudor. Imagine yourself entertaining family and friends." The view: "From this balcony you can see all of Westwood. Like a vista from heaven, isn't it?"

Now they were in back, Jackie walking them through the gardens saying, "Notice the blending of color and texture."

"It's beautiful," Sandra said. "Even nicer than the one inside the Bellagio in Las Vegas, and that's going some."

Jackie pictured her in Vegas, heads turning as she walked through the casino; but he couldn't see Frank with her. His guess: she was from a good family and comfortable. And he was filthy rich. Otherwise, go figure.

Jackie led them back into the house, the three of them in the kitchen now. It was time to go for the close. "And all of this, folks, for only three million six."

It got their attention, Frank getting involved for the first time. "Three six? I'd think this would go for at least four and a half. Is there a problem Sandra should know about, Mr. Winston?"

It took Jackie by surprise. So, *she* was buying the house. He said, "It's a foreclosure, an ugly divorce, the bank wants it off their books. You know how that goes."

They both nodded.

Jackie was looking Sandra in the eye now. "So anyone

with the means, such as yourself, can't go wrong. You could flip it right way, actually. Make a profit." Getting down to business now. "Were you thinking of this as a residence, an investment, or both?"

Sandra said, "There's no better investment than your own home, is there?" Thinking a moment before telling Jackie she wouldn't quibble about the price. Would a 3 percent deposit do?

He said an even hundred thousand would be sufficient, the check made out to his firm: George Winston. It would go into a trust account.

Sandra reached into her purse, felt around, then smiled at Frank. "Sorry. I'll need the keys to your car. My checkbook's in my attaché." She rested the purse on the kitchen counter and left.

Jackie told Frank he'd give the listing agent a call. Let him know about the offer. But where was his phone? He had it a minute ago . . .

Frank said, "Not a problem." He patted his front pant pocket, thought for a second, then reached into Sandra's purse for her phone asking, "What's your number?" He punched it in.

From across the room, they heard Jackie's cell phone playing the theme from *The Godfather*—he'd left it on the windowsill next to the French doors—as Sandra returned, checkbook in hand. She laughed and said, "I guess you made me an offer I couldn't refuse."

The fifties-style apartment building reminded Jackie of his own: yellow stucco, two stories built around a swimming pool—the motel look being all the rage back then: L.A., the neverending vacation. He found the name pasted over the mailbox: Huntington, Apartment E. White letters punched on black plastic.

Jackie walked up the stairs, knowing what he'd say to get things started, but not sure how it would play out. She opened the door, looking cute in her little Lakers tank top and sweatpants, a surprised look on her face.

He said, "Deborah Huntington?" and left it at that, curious to see how she'd react.

She nodded and said nothing, waiting to see where things were headed.

"It's funny," Jackie said, "but you're a dead ringer for someone I know. Gal named Sandra Clark. Ever been told that?"

She just shrugged.

"And Sandra is a very bad girl. Wrote a check—a very large check—bounced so high, it hasn't come down yet."

She said, "How the hell did you find me?" New England accent gone. Sounding tough now, just like the girl on the Sopranos.

Jackie thinking she was being pretty cool about it.

He said, "Were you aware that writing an NSF check with intent to defraud is a felony? A violation of Penal Code 476a?"

"I'm not saying anything," she said, "until I speak with my lawyer." Defiant, not scared.

His kind of woman.

Jackie figured it was fate that brought him here. If Ted hadn't visited, Jackie knew he wouldn't have thought up the real estate scam. And if he hadn't run the ad on that particular day, maybe Deborah wouldn't have seen it. Best of all, if he hadn't misplaced his phone at the house, Frank wouldn't have used hers—and her name, number and address wouldn't have ended up on his caller ID.

But here he was. So fuck the "ifs." Some things were just meant to be.

She stepped aside as he moved forward, inside the place now. A small single: sofa, club chair, and entertainment center on one side of the room; kitchenette on the other. Jackie sat down on the sofa, facing her. She was still standing in the doorway.

"As best I can figure it," he said, "you were working some kind of long con on the guy. Making him think you had money, lots of it. Setting him up for something big."

She closed the door and came over to sit on the chair across from him.

Jackie said, "It's strange, isn't it? Once a mark thinks you don't need the money, they can't help but give it to you. You know what I mean."

She nodded, leaning toward him now.

"But when they do," Jackie said, "it's *your* money. And you don't feel the least bit guilty about it. I mean, you earned it. Right?"

She was still nodding.

"Crazy thing, it bothered me when I thought I was stealing your money. I would have done it, no problem. But it would've bothered me."

She was looking him square in the eye now. "George," she said, "just who the fuck *are* you?

"Different times, I'm different people. Whoever I need to be to get things done. Know what I mean?" He extended his hand. "But to my friends, I'm Jackie."

She shook his hand gently, a little longer than she had to, saying, "Where are we going with this, Jackie?"

He smiled. "Not sure. We could talk about it over dinner." He thought for a moment. "Hey, you know The Ivy? Brad Pitt and Jennifer Aniston eat there all the time."

"I've been there once or twice. Don't you just love their Cajun prime rib?" She gave him her cute, devilish look and said, "But it's expensive. Who's going to pay?"

"I don't know," he said. "Why don't we make it a test? See who can outcon who."

Cain Was Innocent

Simon Brett

Simon Brett is the man behind the Fethering series (*Stabbing in the Stables*) which features Carole Seddon, a retired civil servant, and her neighbor, Jude), as well as the Mrs. Pargeter's books (*Mrs. Pargeter's Point of Honor*), and the Charles Paris mysteries (*Dead Room Farce*), as well as several other novels (*A Shock to the System, The Penultimate Chance Saloon*) and collections (*A Crime in Rhyme: and Other Mysterious Fragments*). Brett also produced the first episode of *The Hitchhiker's Guide to the Galaxy* for the BBC and is also an accomplished sitcom writer for BBC Radio.

It was a quiet afternoon in Heaven. This was not unusual. It's always afternoon in Heaven and, by definition, it's always quiet.

Inspector Gabriel was bored. He was still glad he had gone to Heaven rather than The Other Place, but after his first fifty years of Eternity, he was beginning to learn the truth of the old saying that you could have too much of a good thing. O.K., the Big Man had been generous to him. Given him his own precinct, just like he'd had on earth, and put him in sole charge of solving every crime that happened in Heaven. But, though initially gratifying, the appointment carried with it an in-built contradiction. Indeed, it joined all those other jokes about being a fashion designer in a nudist colony, or trying to make it as a straight actor in New York, or being George W. Bush's conscience. There actually wasn't much of a job there.

So Inspector Gabriel had precisely nothing to do. And the same went for his sidekick, Sergeant Uriel. They'd done out the station more or less as they wanted it, though they did have a real problem recapturing in Heaven the essential shabbiness of the working environments they'd been used to on earth. But they lacked cases to work on. They had reached the goal towards which every terrestrial cop aspired. Heaven really was a crime-free zone.

They looked out of their windows—far too clean to have been part of any real-life station—and watched golf. White-clad figures with golden clubs addressed their green balls on the undulating cloudscape. Mostly newcomers—they had to be—who still got a kick out of holes-in-one from every tee.

In the same way, the people sipping vintage nectar on the terrace of St. Raphael's Bar had to be recent arrivals. However good the liquor, the fact that in Heaven no one ever got drunk or had a hangover rather took away the point of drinking.

"Do you reckon I should go and check out the back

alleys?" suggested the Sergeant. "See if there's been a murder . . . ? Even a mugging . . . ? Someone making a rude gesture . . . ?"

Inspector Gabriel sighed. "Uriel, you know full well there aren't any back alleys in Heaven. And no rude gestures either . . . let alone the more extreme crimes you enumerated."

"Yeah, I know." A wistful, shake of the head. "I kinda miss them, you know."

"You're not the only one." The Inspector looked out over the vista of perfect white. A moment of silence hung between them before he vocalized an idea that had been brooding inside him for a long time. "Maybe we should start looking at old cases. . . ."

"How'd you mean, boss?"

"Well, look, we could spend a long time sitting here in Heaven waiting for a new crime to be committed. . . ."

"We could spend Eternity."

"Right, Uriel. Funny, till you get up here, you never really have a concept of Eternity. I mean, you may kind of get a feeling of it, if you've watched golf . . . or baseball . . . or cricket, but up here it's the real deal."

"Yup," the Sergeant agreed. "Eternity's a hell of a long time." He looked shrewdly across at his boss. "You mentioned looking at old cases. You mean crimes that happened down on earth? Like murders?"

"That's right. Most of the victims end up here, and if you wait long enough most of the suspects will also arrive eventually."

"Hm." Sergeant Uriel nodded his grizzled head thoughtfully. "There is one drawback, though."

"What's that?"

"Well, we won't get the villains coming up to Heaven. By definition, the actual perps are going to end up in The Other Place, aren't they?"

"Oh, come on, Uriel. You know how many murder investigations end up fingering the wrong guy. People who're capable of getting away with murder down on earth are not going to have too much of a problem blagging their way into Heaven, are they?"

"I guess not. So you're saying there actually are a lot or murderers walking round up here?"

"Of course there are. Well, there's Cain, for a start."

"The Daddy of all murderers. Yeah, we see plenty of him."

"Constantly maundering on. Complaining about that Mark on his forehead. And insisting that he was stitched up for the case, that he never laid a finger on Abel."

Sergeant Uriel let out a harsh laugh. "Still, you hear that from every villain, don't you? They all claim they're innocent."

"Yes." Gabriel gave his white beard a thoughtful rub. "Mind you, it is odd that he's up here, though, isn't it? I mean, the Bible says he did it. The Word of God. There's never been much doubt that he did. And yet here he is in Heaven, boring everyone to tears by constantly saying he didn't do it. Why? The Big Man doesn't usually make mistakes on that scale."

"No. I'd always assumed that Cain came up from The Other Place in one of the amnesties. You know, when they redefined the crimes that you had to go to Hell for. I mean, way back everyone who got executed went straight to The Other Place—never any question about whether they were guilty or not."

"I heard about that, Uriel. All those poor little Cockney kids who'd stolen handkerchiefs."

"Right. Well, I figured Cain got a transfer up here as a part of one of those amnesties."

"Yes. Except his crime was still murder. That's about the biggest rap you can take." There was a gleam of incipient interest in Inspector Gabriel's eye. "I definitely think there's something odd about it. Something worthy of investigation. If we could prove that Cain was innocent. . . ."

Uriel was catching his boss's enthusiasm, but still felt it his duty to throw a wet blanket over such speculation. "It'd be a very difficult case."

"We've cracked difficult cases before. What makes this one so different?"

"It's all a long time ago."

"A very long time ago. In fact, by definition, about as long ago as it possibly could be."

"Yeah. Then again, boss, we've got a problem with lack of suspects. We start off with Adam and Eve, then they have kids, who are Cain and Abel. Abel gets killed so he's kind of out of the equation, unless we get into the suicide area. . . ."

"Don't go there."

"No, I don't want to."

"I've been thinking about this for a while," said Gabriel, "and doing a bit of research. The obvious thing to do, of course, would be to ask Abel, but the funny thing is, nobody up here seems to know where he is. Which is odd. I mean, he wouldn't have gone to The Other Place, would he?"

"Unless he *did* commit suicide."

The Inspector dismissed the idea with a weary shake of the head. "I'm sure we'll find him somewhere up here."

"So, boss, going back . . . we've just got the three suspects. Cain, who took the rap for it. . . ."

"Not just the rap. He took the Mark too. Don't forget the Mark."

"Could I? The Mark's the thing he keeps beefing on about. But the fact remains, given our current level of information, we've only got three suspects. Cain, Adam and Eve."

"And the Serpent. What happened to the Serpent?"

"I don't know, boss. He probably just slipped away."

"Like a snake in the grass. But he's important, Uriel. I mean, with any list of suspects, the first thing you ask is: who's got form? Adam, Eve—just been created. Cain—just been born. When have they had a chance to mix with bad company?"

"And how do you *find* bad company in Eden?"

"Ah, but remember, they weren't in Eden when it happened. Adam and Eve had been kicked out by the Big Man."

"For eating the Apple. Yeah, that was a crime. So they've got form too."

"But not form on the scale that the Serpent has. God recognized him straight away, knew the kind of stuff he got up to. I mean, come on, this guy's Satan! Also, he's in disguise, which is not the kind of behavior you expect from the average denizen of Paradise. And, second, he was responsible at that time for all the evil in the known world—though, granted, not much of it was known then— but this Satan was still one nasty piece of work. So far as I'm concerned, the Serpent's definitely on the suspect list."

"And he'd have been clever enough to frame Cain and make him take the rap."

"Be meat and drink to him, that kind of stuff."

Sergeant Uriel nodded agreement. "So what do we do? Go after the Serpent?"

"Call him by his proper name. He's Satan."

"A.k.a. Lucifer."

"Yeah, but that was a long time back."

"O.K. So we go after Satan? That's going to involve a trip down to The Other Place."

"Not necessarily, Uriel. He comes up here for conferences and things, you know, ever since the Big Man got more ecumenical and He started reaching out to embrace other faith groups."

"Yeah. I'm afraid that still sticks in my craw—the idea of Satan coming up to Heaven."

"Now you mustn't be old-fashioned. We've got to try and build bridges towards these people. Maybe they aren't so different from us."

"Huh." The Sergeant's hunched body language showed how much the idea appealed to him.

"Anyway, Satan's not our first port of call in this investigation."

"No? So who is?"

"Cain, obviously. As you say, he's always maundering on about how he didn't do it. Now, for the first time, we'll actually *listen* to what he's saying. Let's go find him."

"O.K." Sergeant Uriel eased his massive but weightless bulk up off his white stool. "And when we talk to him, boss, what . . . ? We use the old Good Cop, Good Cop routine?"

"Do we have any alternative, Uriel?"

Cain was sitting in a white armchair in the corner of

St. Raphael's Bar. Alone. He was nearly always alone. His one-track conversation tended to drive people away.

As ever, in front of him stood a bottle of the finest two-thousand-year-old malt whisky, from which he constantly topped off his chalice. The conventional wisdom in Heaven was that, however much you drank, you never got intoxicated. Cain didn't buy that. He reckoned that somewhere in infinity was the magic moment when the alcohol would kick in and do its stuff. He drank like he was determined to find that moment.

The two cops idled up to the bar. They didn't want to make a big thing of their entrance. Inspector Gabriel ordered the first lot of drinks. Even though no payment was involved in St. Raphael's Bar, there was a strictly observed protocol as to whose round it was.

Sergeant Uriel asked for a beer. Gabriel ordered it from St. Raphael, adding, "And I'll have an alcohol-free one, thanks." It didn't make any difference, but it did make for variety.

They stayed leaning against the counter and looked across the bar toward Cain. It was the mid-afternoon lull, but then it always was the mid-afternoon lull in St. Raphael's Bar. Knots of newcomers at a few tables enthused about how great it was to be there, how relieved they were not to be at The Other Place and how really nice Heaven was. They all looked white and squeaky clean against the white and gold furniture.

The only bright color visible in the room was the Mark on Cain's forehead.

The sight would have settled a lot of ancestral arguments amongst biblical commentators and freemasons.

The Bible remains tantalisingly unspecific about the nature of "The Mark of Cain." Some authorities maintain that it was the name of God etched across the miscreant's forehead. Others thought that it was dark skin and that Cain was the father of all the world's people of color. Some rabbinical experts even identified it with leprosy. (And it is also, incidentally, the name of an Australian rock band.)

But all the theorists would have been silenced by the neat red cross tattooed above Cain's eyes.

"I never understood," said Uriel, "why he didn't have that removed in C & P."

"C & P" stood for "Cleansing and Purification." It was a service offered to all new souls as soon as they had finished their Pearly Gates paperwork. The nature of the dying process meant that few arrived looking their best, but C & P gave them the chance of a complete makeover and the opportunity to select their "Heaven Age," the stage of their lives at which they would like to stay for all Eternity.

It was hardly surprising that a lot of souls—particularly the women—chose to look a good few decades younger than their death age. Not Gabriel and Uriel, though. They'd opted to stay the way they'd looked just before the car-chase crash which had brought them up to Heaven—though they'd had their actual injuries tidied up. They reckoned the grizzled look added gravitas to their image as cops.

"I mean," Uriel went on, "those C & P boys can do wonders with facial blemishes. And some of the stuff they've done with reassembling organ transplant recipients with their donors . . . it's just stunning. For them, a little thing like Cain's forehead wouldn't present any problems."

"You're missing the point, Uriel. Cain wants to keep it."

"Yeah?"

"Sure. Until his innocence is proved, it's part of his identity. And it's a conversation piece. I mean, anyone incautious enough to ask, "What's that Mark on your forehead? . . . ?"

"Gets the full spiel."

"Exactly. And that's what we're about to do."

"I mean, how many more times have I got to say this?"

Not many more—please, thought Inspector Gabriel. They'd been talking to Cain for three-quarters of an hour and he'd already said his bit at least a dozen times. Trouble was, the bit he'd said lacked detail. When you stripped away the grievances about the millennia he had spent with a Mark on his forehead, being shunned by all and sundry, Cain's monologue still consisted of just the one assertion: "I didn't do it."

Inspector Gabriel tried again. "Can you be a bit more specific? We have it on good authority that—"

"What authority?"

"The best authority available. The Bible. Holy Writ. The Word of God."

"Oh, forget that. The Word of God has never been more than just a whitewash job. Public Relations. Spin."

"According to the Bible," the Inspector persisted, " 'it came to pass, when they were in the field, that Cain rose up against Abel his brother, and slew him.' "

"I was never in the damned field!"

"Ah, but you were. Only just before the incident you had 'brought of the fruit of the ground an offering unto the Lord.' " Gabriel was rather pleased with his logic. "How could you have got 'the fruit of the ground' if you were never in the field?"

"It was a different field! Abel was killed in the field from which he took his offering, 'the firstlings of his flock and of the fat thereof.' It was a different kind of field, a different kind of farming. I was arable. Abel was 'a keeper of sheep.' I was just 'a tiller of the ground.' I never went into his field. I'm allergic to sheep!"

"It doesn't say in the Bible which field Abel was slain in."

"There're a lot of things about the case that aren't mentioned in the Bible. The guys who wrote the Old Testament, these bozos who claimed to be transcribing the Word of God, all they wanted was everything neat—nice open-and-shut case, no loose ends. 'Cain slew Abel,' that's easy, isn't it? They'd rather have that than the truth."

"So what is the truth?"

"I didn't do it!"

Inspector Gabriel had difficulty suppressing his exasperation. "So why didn't you say that when God challenged you about the murder?"

"Cause I was taken by surprise, that's why. Suddenly He's asking me where Abel is. I don't know, do I? I haven't seen him for a while. We're not that close and, apart from anything else, he always smells of sheep, and, like I say, I'm allergic to—"

"Yes, yes, yes. But why didn't you tell God you didn't do it?"

"He didn't give me the chance! He asks me where Abel, my brother, is, and I say, 'I know not: am I my brother's keeper?' And at this stage I don't even know anything's happened to the guy, so why should I be worried? But immediately God's saying that 'the voice of thy brothers blood crieth unto me from the ground' and then that that I'm 'cursed from the earth, which hath opened her mouth to receive thy brother's blood from thy hand.' I mean, when do I get the chance to tell my side of the story?"

There was a silence. Sergeant Uriel, who'd been feeling a bit left out of the conversation, was the one to break it. "But you don't have anything else? You haven't got an alibi for the time when the homicide took place?"

"I was in my field. The field where I grow 'the fruit of the ground.' That's what I do. I'm a tiller."

Uriel looked bewildered. "I thought he was a Hun."

"Who?"

"Attila."

Inspector Gabriel tactfully intervened. "Don't worry. We have a slight misunderstanding here. So, Cain, nobody actually saw you in your field at the relevant time? Nobody could stand up in court and give you an alibi?"

A weary shake of the head. "Only the vegetables."

"I don't think they're going to be much help. After all this time, maybe the best thing would be," the Inspector went on, "for us to have a word with Abel. Except nobody seems to have seen him recently. Do you know where he is, Cain?"

"Oh, don't you start!" And he shouted, "I know not: am I my brother's keeper?"

"Sorry. I didn't mean to do that."

"I should bloody hope not."

"But Cain," asked Uriel urgently, "if you don't have an alibi, maybe you saw someone? Someone who might've been the perp? Someone who went into that field with your brother?"

"I tell you, I was nowhere near Abel's field. I didn't see a soul."

The two cops exchanged looks. The Sergeant's long experience read the message in his superiors eyes: we've got all we're going to get here, time to move on.

"Yes, well, thank you Cain, this has been—"

"Have you the beginning of an idea what it's like going through life with a thing like this stuck on your forehead? Everyone convinced you're guilty of a crime you didn't commit? It wreaks havoc with your family life, for a start. You know, after I was framed for Abel's death, I went into the Land of Nod, and I knew my wife, 'and she conceived and bore Enoch . . . And unto Enoch was born Irad: and Irad begat Mehujael: and Mehujael begat Methusael: and Methusael begat Lamech. And Lamech took unto him two wives: the name of the one was—' "

"Yeah, we get it," said Inspector Gabriel. "You have a big family. What exactly is your point?"

"Just that they're all up here and, because I got this Mark on my forehead, none of them ever comes to visit."

"Cherchez la femme," said the Inspector as they wafted back to the station.

"I'm sorry. I don't speak foreign."

" 'Look for the woman.' Old-fashioned bit of advice, but sometimes old-fashioned is good."

"What, boss? You're suggesting we check out Cain's old lady? The one who conceived and bore Enoch?"

"No, no. We may get to her eventually, but she's not where we go next."

"Then who?"

"Look, Uriel, Cain and Abel were brothers. Bit of sibling rivalry there, I'd say. In fact, if Cain did actually do it, the ultimate sibling rivalry. And who's going to know those two boys best? Who was around all the time they were growing up?"

"Eve? You mean Eve?"

"You bet your life I do."

Officially, there wasn't any pecking order in Heaven. Everyone was entitled to exactly the same amount of celestial bliss. That was the theory anyway, but some souls, by virtue of the profile they'd had on earth, did get special attention. Gabriel and Uriel were made well aware of that as they entered Eve's eternal home.

The décor was very feminine. Clouds, which are by their nature fluffy, had never been fluffier, and Eve herself moved around in her own nimbus. She had selected for her body image the moment when she first sprang from Adam's rib and, although she was now clothed, the diaphanous white catsuit, through which a fig-leaf *cache-sexe* could be clearly seen, left no ambiguity about the precise definition of her contours. The two detectives could not repress within them a vague stirring which they distantly remembered as lust.

Eve was surrounded by other female souls, similarly dressed. Their main purpose was apparently to worship her, but there seemed little doubt that, if the need arose, they would protect her too.

She was one of the souls whose position in Heaven had undergone radical reassessment. After Cain and Abel, Eve had given birth to Seth. "And the days of Adam after he had begotten Seth were eight hundred years: and he begat sons and daughters. And all the days that Adam lived were nine hundred and thirty years: and he died." So, though Eve did slightly predecease her husband, she had had a busy life and, at the time of her death, she was very tired.

And then, when she arrived at the Pearly Gates, there had been a rather unseemly altercation. St. Peter, a Judaeo-Christian traditionalist, blamed Eve for Original Sin, and was not about to let in a soul who, to his mind, had corrupted the purity of humankind for all Eternity. The Big Man himself had to intervene before the newcomer was admitted, and for a good few millennia, Eve suffered from a certain amount of misogynistic prejudice.

It was only when Sixties feminists—particularly American ones—started dying that her status changed. The new generation of female souls entering Heaven saw Eve as an icon. Her eating of the Apple and persuading Adam to do the same was no longer a shameful betrayal of the human race; it was now viewed as an act of female empowerment. Eve had resisted the phallocentric dictates of the traditional male establishment and asserted herself as a woman. So far as her newly arrived acolytes were concerned, she could do no wrong. For them, she was an Earth Mother . . . in every sense.

Uriel may not have been, but Inspector Gabriel was aware of this recent reassessment, and accordingly circumspect as he began his questioning.

"I'm sorry to go into ancient history, Eve. . . ."

"It's not about the Apple again, is it?"

"No, no. Nothing to do with the Apple, I promise."

"Thank the Lord! I've done so many interviews on that subject that I'm totally Appled out."

The expression was greeted by a ripple of sycophantic appreciation from her acolytes.

"The Apple won't be mentioned."

"Good." She gave Gabriel a shrewd, calculating gaze. "So does that mean it's sex?"

"No, not even sex."

She started to look interested. "There's a novelty. I tell you, the number of times I've had to talk about sex to *OT Magazine* or *Halo,* well, you just wouldn't believe it."

"No, I want to talk about your kids."

"Which ones? There were quite a few of them. Remember, for over nine hundred years Adam was a serial begetter."

"It's the first two we're interested in. Cain and Abel."

"Ah." Eve looked thoughtful. "Those two boys have a hell of a lot to answer for."

"Not least giving Jeffrey Archer an idea for a novel," Sergeant Uriel mumbled.

His boss ignored him. "The thing is, we all know the official story. As printed in the Bible. I just wondered, Eve, what with you having been on the scene at the time, do you agree with what's written there?"

"It's the Word of God. That was there in the beginning. Holy Writ. Doesn't pay to argue with the Word of God."

"I wasn't asking you whether it paid." Inspector Gabriel's voice took on the harder note he'd used to employ in interrogations. It sounded pleasingly nostalgic. "I was asking whether you agree that Genesis, Chapter Four, is an accurate account of what took place in that field."

"I was never in the field."

"No. Cain says he wasn't either."'

"Oh."

"I mean, when he was growing up, was Cain a truthful kid?"

"Yeah, I did my best to teach all of them the value of honesty."

"The knowledge of right and wrong?"

"I thought I made it clear, Inspector Gabriel, that the Apple was off-bounds."

"Oh, sure. Sorry. Listen, Eve, what were Cain and Abel like? What kind of kids? Did they have similar personalities?"

"No way!" She grinned wryly at the recollection. "No, no, no. Abel was very anal. You know, the way he kept those sheep, all neat in little folds, clearing up after them all the time with a pooper-scooper. Whereas Cain was more laid-back, bit of a slob really. O.K., he'd occasionally till the fields, but not like his life depended on it. Tilling—he could take it or leave it.

"I mean, when they presented God with the offerings, that was typical of their characters. Abel got all 'the firstlings of his flock' groomed with little bows round their necks 'and the fat thereof' in neat little packages. That's Abel all over. But when Cain comes up, well, for a start he's late, and 'the fruit of the ground' is a few root vegetables still covered in earth, like they'd just been pulled up that morning, which of course they had.

"So it was no wonder the Big Man went for Abel's offering rather than Cain's . . . as Abel had planned He would."

"But did the incident cause dissension between the two boys?"

Eve shrugged. "Not that I was aware of. Cain knew

Abel was always going to be the arse-licker, he was cool with that."

"And yet, according to the Bible, he still slew his brother."

Eve looked uncomfortable. "Yeah, well, he must've had a rush of blood to the head." She fell back on the old formula. "It's the Word of God. You can't argue with that." Her manner became brusque. "Now I'm afraid I really must get on. Another feminist historical revisionist has just died and we girls are organizing a Welcome Party for her at the Pearly Gates."

"Yeah, just a couple of things before you go. . . ."

"What?" Her patience with him was wearing thin.

"I wondered if you knew where I could find Abel?"

"No one has seen him since he came up here, assuming, that is, he did come up here."

"Doesn't that seem odd?"

Another shrug from the archetypal shoulders. "I've found it doesn't do to question too many things that happen up here. The Big Man knows what he's doing. We get very well looked after. Doesn't do to rock the boat. Just trust the Word of God."

"And what about Adam? Will it be easy for me to find Adam?"

She let out a sardonic chuckle. "Oh yeah, easy to find him. Probably not so easy to get any sense out of him."

"Why? What's he—!"

But Inspector Gabriel had had all the time Eve was going to allot him. She looked round at her acolytes. "Now let's get this party organized."

Her words were greeted by an enthusiastic simpering of dead American feminists, through which Inspector Gabriel managed to ask, "One last question. Did Cain have any allergies?"

"What?"

"Was there anything he was allergic to?"

"Oh, we're talking a long time ago now. A long, long time ago. You're asking a lot for me to remember that. I mean, after all those kids. . . ." Eve's heavenly brows wrinkled with the effort of recollection. "Yeah, maybe there was something, though. . . ."

"Can you remember what?"

"No, I. . . . Oh, just a minute." A beam of satisfaction spread across the original female face. "Yeah, there was one thing that used to bring him out in this really nasty rash, not helped of course by his clothes being made of leaves, and there weren't any antihistamines around then or—"

"I'm sorry, I must interrupt you. What was the thing that Cain was allergic to?"

"Sheep," said Eve.

"It sounds to me like he was telling the truth," said Sergeant Uriel, suddenly loquacious after taking a back-seat during the interviews with Cain and Eve. "I mean, his own Mom's confirmed Cain had this allergy, so he's not going to go near Abel's field, is he? Not if it's full of sheep."

"I wouldn't be so sure." Inspector Gabriel shook his head solemnly. "I've dealt with enough murderers to know how strong the urge to kill can be. A guy who's set his mind on topping someone is not going to be put off by the thought of getting itchy skin."

"Maybe, boss, but I'm still having problems seeing Cain as our murderer."

"Me too. But we don't have any other very convincing scenario, do we? I mean, if only we could prove that Cain had an alibi. But there once again we're up against one of the big problems of the time period we're dealing with."

"How'dya mean?"

"It's like with the suspects, Uriel. Not a lot of people around, either to commit the murder or to give someone an alibi to prove they didn't commit the murder."

"Yeah. We're back to Cain, Eve and Adam."

"And the Serpent. Never forget the Serpent, Uriel."

"I won't." The Sergeant shrugged hopefully. "Oh well, maybe we'll get the vital lead from Adam."

"Maybe. I wonder what Eve meant about it not being easy to get any sense out of him."

It soon became clear why his former rib had lowered their expectations of coherence from her husband. Adam was seriously old. When he grew up longevity was highly prized, and he got a charge from being the oldest man to have died in the world (though, had he thought about it, he would have received the same accolade by dying at ninety-eight, or forty-three, or seventeen, or one week). So he had selected the moment of death as his Heaven Age . . . and no one looks their best at nine hundred and thirty.

He was, of course, very well looked after. Some deceased nurses, who'd really got a charge out of their caring profession on earth, were in Seventh Heaven with Adam to look after.

But, as a subject for police interrogation, he left a lot to be desired. All he did was sit in a wheelcloud and chuckle to himself saying over and over again, "I'm the Daddy of them all."

Gabriel and Uriel didn't bother staying with him long.

Back at the station a pall of despondence hung between them as they yet again went through the evidence.

"Every minute I'm getting more convinced of Cain's innocence," said the Inspector, "but I just can't see who else is in the frame."

"There's still the Serpent."

"Yes, sure. I checked. Satan's coming up here for an Interfaith Symposium in a couple of weeks. He's giving a paper on 'George W. Bush and the Religious Wrong.' We could probably get a word with him then, but . . ." Inspector Gabriel's lower lip curled with lack of conviction.

"Why have you suddenly turned against Satan as a suspect? Come on, he's the Prince of Darkness. He's responsible for all the bad things in the world. Slaying one keeper of sheep here or there isn't going to be a big deal to a guy like that."

"No, but that's why I'm going off him. It's too small a crime. There's no way Satan would bother with killing Abel. Or if he did it, he'd certainly claim the credit."

"Yeah, but his old boss God had just started His big new idea—Mankind. Satan wants to screw that up, so he kills Abel and makes it look like Cain did it."

"But if he wanted to destroy Mankind, why did he stop there? Why didn't he slay the other three humans?"

"Erm, well. . . ." Theological debate had never been Sergeant Uriel's strong suit. He'd always been better at splaying hoods across their automobiles and getting them to spill the beans. "Maybe he slays Abel, because that way he brings evil into the world?"

"He'd already brought evil into the world by making Eve eat the Apple."

"But . . ."

"No, no, quiet, Uriel." Inspector Gabriel scratched at his grizzled brow while he tried to shape his thoughts. "I think we've got to go right back to the beginning."

"The beginning of the case?"

"The beginning of the world. What's the first thing that happens in the Bible?"

" 'In the beginning God created the heaven and the earth,' " quoted Sergeant Uriel, who had been to Sunday school.

"O.K., that's Genesis. But we have another description of the beginning."

"Do we, boss? Where?"

"First verse of The Gospel According to Saint John. 'In the beginning was the Word, and the Word was with God, and the Word was God. The same was in the beginning with God.' What does that sound like to you, Uriel?"

"I don't know. It's kinda neatly written." The Sergeant thought about the words a bit more. "Sounds kinda like an advertising slogan."

"Yes." Gabriel nodded with satisfaction. "That's exactly what it sounds like. And what did Cain say? 'The Word of God has never been more than just a whitewash job. Public Relations. Spin.' "

"Yeah, but he would say that, wouldn't he? If he was the murderer, he'd say it."

"But if he wasn't the murderer, why would he say it then?"

"Because, but for the Word of God, he wouldn't have had to go through life with something on his forehead that makes him look like an ambulance."

Inspector Gabriel tapped a reflective finger against the bridge of his nose. "That might be a reason. Other possibility is that he said it because it was true. . . ."

"Sorry?"

"That it all was just whitewash. P.R. Spin."

Obviously, though there were no secrets in Heaven—that would have gone against the whole spirit of the place— some things weren't particularly advertised. Where the Big Man lived was one of them. The precise location was never defined, for security reasons of course. Though He wouldn't have been at risk from any of the usual denizens of Heaven, there has been considerable slackening of border controls in recent years, and the increase of Cultural Exchange Programmes with The Other Place brought its own hazards.

In the same way, the whole administrative apparatus of Heaven was, well, not overt. This was for no sinister reason. Most people had spent far too much of their time on earth organizing things, and longed for an Eternity which was totally without responsibilities. Too much evidence of the stage management of Heaven would only have brought back tedious memories for them.

But everything was, of course, above board, and totally transparent. Any soul who wished to find out some detail of the celestial management would instantly have been given the information required. It was just that very few people ever bothered to ask.

This was borne in upon Inspector Gabriel when he first began enquiring about The Word. Most of the souls he talked to claimed ignorance of where he'd find it, so he went to ask Raphael, who heard all the heavenly gossip in his bar. But the Saint was uncharacteristically evasive. " 'The Word of God?' That's always been around. The 'Logos,' from the Greek, you know."

"But you don't know where it actually is?"

Mine Heavenly Host shook his head. "I've always thought of it more as a metaphysical concept than a concrete one." You did get a high class bar room chat at St. Raphael's.

But it was in the bar that Inspector Gabriel found the clue. There was a list of regulations pinned up on the wall. They weren't there because they were likely to be infringed, but for a lot of souls a bar didn't feel like a bar without a list of regulations. So there were a few prohibitions like "Thou shalt not spit on the floor," "Thou shalt not wear muddy boots in the bar" and "Thou shalt put thy drinks on the nectar-mats supplied." At the bottom of the list, though, as Gabriel pointed out triumphantly to Uriel, was printed: "A Word of God Publication," followed by an address many clouds away.

It was a huge white tower block, with "The Word of God" on the tiniest, most discreet gold plate by the front door. The receptionist wore smart business wings and a huge professional smile. "How can I help you, gentlemen?"

"There's something we want to inquire about the Word of God," said Inspector Gabriel.

"May I ask what is the nature of your inquiry? Is it Purely

Factual, are you looking for an Informed Commentary on the text, tracing your family history through the Begetting Lists or Challenging the Accuracy of Holy Writ?" Her voice contained no disapproval of any of these possibilities.

"I guess it'd be the last."

Sergeant Uriel spelled it out. "Yes, we're Challenging the Accuracy of Holy Writ."

"Very well," said the girl, with another omnicompetent smile. "You'll need to speak to someone in Doctrinal Spin." She leant forward to the keyboard in front of her. "Let me see who's free."

The man who was free had chosen thirty-five as his Heaven Age. He was neat and punctilious, and his character was reflected in a neat and punctilious office. Pens and papers were laid out on his desk with geometric precision.

"Cain and Abel," he said. "Goodness, you are going back a long way."

"Nearly to the beginning of time. I hope your records go back that far."

"Don't have any worries on that score," he said with a small patronizing laugh. "Remember, 'in the beginning was the Word.' These offices have been here right from the start."

"Even before 'God created the heaven and the earth'?" asked Sergeant Uriel.

"Oh yes. Long before that. It was here that the whole development strategy for the creation of the heaven and the earth was devised."

"So this was where the Big Man did the planning?"

"This is where He was advised on the most appropriate ways of planning, yes. And, incidentally, in these offices we still refer to Him as 'God.' The 'Big Man' initiative was only developed in the last century to make him sound more approachable and user-friendly."

"O.K." said Gabriel. "So you're kind of strategic thinkers and advisers to God?"

"That's exactly what we are."

"Right then, can you tell us the strategic thinking behind the Cain and Abel story?"

The young man pursed his lips unwillingly. "I won't deny that I'd rather not tell you. My personal view is that some secrets should be kept secret. In the same way, I can't claim to be an enthusiast of all these Interfaith Dialogues with The Other Place."

"Maybe not, but since the Freedom of Heavenly Information Act, you are obliged to—"

"I am fully aware of my obligations, thank you," he snapped. "Yes, the new buzz word in Heaven is transparency. All records are available to whoever wants to see them."

"And presumably," said Inspector Gabriel, "it was God who brought in that policy?"

"Goodness, no. God doesn't bring in any policies. The Think Tanks here at The Word of God recommend policies to Him. In the past those policies have been extremely sensible. But in recent years there has been a younger element recruited here"—his lip curled with distaste—"who have brought in these modern notions of transparency and accountability. I was always more in favor of keeping some mystery about Heaven. Nothing wrong with a bit of ignorance, you know. But these new, so-called Young Turks have no respect for tradition and keep trying to make God trendy, and I'm afraid to say He listens to them in a way that—"

Inspector Gabriel stemmed this flood of bitchy office politics. "Can we get back to Cain and Abel, please?"

The young man's lips were tightened as if by a draw-
string. "Very well." Unwillingly he summoned up a file to his
computer screen. "What precisely do you wish to know?"

"Whether Cain was the perp or not," Uriel replied.

"You have to set this in context," said the young man
primly. "The creation of the heaven and the earth and light
and the firmament and the waters and the dry land and
the seeds and the fruit and the sun and the moon and
every living creature after their kind and man was a very
considerable achievement—particularly inside a week. But
obviously it wasn't perfect. Corners had been cut so
inevitably shortcomings were discovered, and in the
ensuing weeks and years a certain level of adjustment was
required.

"The really big problem was that of good and evil."

"But I thought that was sorted out in the Garden of
Eden. Adam and Eve got the knowledge of good and evil
after the Serpent had persuaded her—"

"Inspector Gabriel, will you please let me finish! Having
the knowledge of good and evil was not enough. Even outside the Garden of Eden, Adam and Eve's lives were still
pretty idyllic. The Think Tanks here reckoned a more vivid
demonstration of human evil was required. So a rather
brilliant young copywriter had the idea"—

"Copywriter? You have copywriters here?"

"How else do you think the Word of God got written? Of
course we have copywriters. Anyway, this rather brilliant
young man had the idea of creating a really archetypal
act of evil."

There was an inevitability about it. "The murder of Abel by Cain."

"You're ahead of me, Inspector," the official said sourly. "Yes. If this murder was recorded in Holy Writ, then it would serve to all mankind as an example of human evil. And we had to get more evil into the world somehow. The people in this building had to look ahead. George W. Bush was going to need people to bomb. How can you bomb people unless you can convince other people that they are evil? Paradise—even the Paradise that Adam and Eve found after they'd been evicted from Eden—was just a bit too good, not viable in the long term, you know." He snickered smugly. "Setting up an apparent murder solved that problem at a stroke."

"You say an 'apparent murder.' "

"Yes, and I say that quite deliberately, Inspector."

"You mean"—Sergeant Uriel pieced things together—"Abel wasn't actually killed?"

"His death was recorded in Holy Writ. That was all that mattered. There was no need for him actually to die."

"So Cain didn't do it?"

"No," the man agreed smugly, "but everyone thought he did it, so the aim of that rather bright young copywriter was achieved. The world now contained evil, which in the future could provide a justification for . . . absolutely anything."

"So what happened to Abel? Adam and Eve and Cain would have noticed if he was still around, wouldn't they?"

"Yes, Inspector. The people here at the Word of God did a deal with him. They offered him an early exit from earth and a good job up here, where he could keep to himself and wouldn't have to mix with all the other riff-raff. Who's going to turn down that kind of package? And all this was the work"—an even more complacent smile spread across his face—"of one very bright young copywriter."

"I get it," said Inspector Gabriel. "You're that bright young copywriter, aren't you?"

"No," came the reply. "I'm Abel."

The cops were surprised by Cain's reaction to the findings of their investigation. They thought he'd be ecstatic finally to have his innocence proved.

But no, he asked them to keep quiet about the whole business. Take away his claim not to have killed his brother, and he wouldn't have anything to talk about.

Besides, he was getting rather fond of the Mark on his forehead.

A Temporary Crown

Sue Pike

Canadian writer Sue Pike's stories have appeared in *Ellery Queen Mystery Magazine, Storyteller, Cold Blood,* and five *Ladies' Killing Circle* anthologies. Her short story "Widow's Weeds" won the Arthur Ellis Award for Best Short Story in 1997, and "Boarding School Reach" was co-winner of the first Bony Pete Award from the 1999 Bloody Words mystery conference.

Dolores shuffled into the Solarium looking for the paper cups the nurses used to distribute the meds. It was a hobby of hers, collecting the tiny, fluted cups. She liked to put treasures in them and line them up on the windowsill of her hospital room.

Leonard was slouched on the sofa watching TV and scratching his head. Leonard was always scratching his head. It was sort of a hobby of his, Dolores thought. She spotted four abandoned cups on the card table, but just as she was gathering them up her attention was caught by an image on the TV. She sucked in her breath as Bryce and a young woman drove onto the screen riding a huge black motorcycle, the pink sand of the Nevada desert glowing behind them in the evening sun. They skidded to a stop, pulled off their helmets and waved at the camera. The woman shook her head, catching Bryce full across the face with a sheet of long blond hair. Bryce brushed the hair away, threw his arm around the blond girl's shoulder and laughed. Then Leonard started laughing and Dolores had to flap her hands to shush him so she could hear the commentary.

"Bryce Campion, best known for his role in *Worlds Apart,* and Marie-France Lapin, of Jazz Hot, the all-girl band from Paris that's been making waves all over the country, announced their upcoming nuptials today in Las Vegas. Bryce is currently headlining a brand new show at the Three Crowns. . . ."

Her knees wobbled and she dropped into a chair, sending the paper cups skittering to the floor. That made Leonard laugh some more, but when she started to shush him again she caught herself. His eyes had that glittery look that meant something crazy was going on in his head and she'd better watch out.

She leaned closer to the screen. "The wedding will take place next week in the Little White Wedding Chapel, a Las Vegas landmark."

Dolores began to hum two notes over and over. It was something she did when she could feel her heart beating too fast. She was going to have to decide what to do but she couldn't think in here with the TV and Leonard scratching his head and laughing too loud in all the wrong places. She grunted as she leaned over and picked up the cups from the floor and then she pulled herself to her feet and shuffled away as fast as her swollen legs would carry her.

Back in her room, she tore a sheet from the steno pad Dr. Bradford gave her at their first session. She was supposed to be using it for a journal, writing about all the times she felt angry and all the times she felt sad. But the pages were mostly empty and every time he asked her about it she just hummed a bit and stared at the floor while he gripped the desk so hard his fingers went white.

She reached between the mattress and the box spring and fished out a silver pen she'd found on Dr. Bradford's desk one day when he was looking at something in her file. After scribbling a few words on the paper, she reached into the crevice under the radiator where she'd hidden the blank stamped envelope she'd found a few weeks ago at the nursing station when the matron had gone to the bathroom. She addressed it to Bryce Campion, Three Crowns Hotel, Las Vegas, Nevada, and then tucked it into the zippered compartment of her bag. They were releasing her to the group home tomorrow and she'd be able to slip out and mail it once the social worker was through talking to her. She sat on the edge of the bed for a minute or two and then reached behind the radiator again to check the money hidden in there. She liked to think of it as her nest egg. That's what her grandmother had called the money in the cookie tin she kept high up on the shelf over the icebox. Dolores had stood on a chair and reached for the tin one day when she thought her grandmother was lying down in the next room. It slipped out of her fingers, and the coins had clattered to the floor. Her grandmother had shot into the room and yanked the chair right out from under Dolores making her crack her head on the table as she fell. The social worker had asked how she'd hurt herself, but she never said. Not that time. Not ever.

Dolores stepped out of the cool of the Greyhound Bus Terminal onto South Main and caught her breath. The noise and heat and brilliant sunshine jumbled together inside her head and made it hard to think clearly. She shuffled a few blocks before she dropped her pack onto the sidewalk and leaned against the wall of an office building. She put both hands behind her and pushed hard against the wall, feeling the stucco bite into her fingers, trying to read the bumps as if they were Braille. She took a deep breath and tried to think about the mantra Dr. Bradford had taught her, but sounds and images were jittering around in her mind so fast she couldn't remember how it began. After a while she rummaged in her bag for a jam jar of water and with a few sips she felt strong enough to push away from the wall and pick up her pack again. She stood for a moment and tried to get her bearings. In her letter she'd described the donut shop where he should meet her. It was one she'd discovered last year when she'd come here to be with him. But she didn't want to think about that time and had to hum very loud to keep it out of her head only the trouble with that was it kept the location of the donut shop out of her head as well. But it was on the Strip, that much she could remember, so she set off again humming even louder to take her mind off her heartbeat and her sore ankles.

When she'd gone to the group home the social worker had watched her unpack her bag and fold things into the dresser drawer. Dolores smiled, remembering how easy it had been to push everything back in the bag and drop it from the window the next day. When she walked out the front door she'd called to Stella, who was in the kitchen making lunch, and told her she was just going for a walk and then she'd gone around back, picked up her pack and walked to the bus terminal. It took most of her nest egg to buy the one-way ticket.

Dolores walked on, stumbling a bit every once in a while, holding onto the walls of buildings when she was afraid she might fall. She thought about Dr. Bradford and how he made everything he said sound like he was talking to a child. "Doris," he'd said, always calling her Doris even though she'd corrected him so many times. "Doris, sometimes people think they have a connection to people they've never met. Especially celebrities. Some even believe they're married to well-known men like Bryce Campion." He'd looked sad when he said it, like it was one of the big tragedies of the world. "You understand you're not married to him, don't you?" He'd twisted his pencil between his lips, making it squeak and then he'd pulled it out with a wet popping sound and leaned forward, trying to catch her eye. "You can get rid of this obsession, Doris. You have the power to make yourself better." She'd had to hum hard into her pillow that night, remembering the little frown between his eyebrows that made an upside-down V like the pitched roof on her grandmother's hen house. But she didn't really blame Dr. Bradford. He didn't know any better. He hadn't seen the look Bryce had given her that night in the movie theatre. He hadn't been there the night Bryce had asked her to marry him. She could still remember it as clear as day. She was sitting in the second row and he was looking down at her from the shiny, pebbly screen. There was a hurt look on his face, as though afraid she'd refuse. "Dolores," he'd said, "Marry me, Dolores. Please." She'd said yes right there, out loud. Some people in the audience laughed, but she didn't care. He'd said the words she'd been waiting to hear all her adult life. After that she'd watched every movie he ever made. And she'd gone to the library and looked through all the movie and entertainment magazines in hopes of finding a photo of him. When they stopped making musical films he'd taken a job in Las Vegas, singing in one of the smaller hotels. And she'd gone along last year to be with him. But it hurt to think about that right now.

She'd managed to make her way to the area known as the Strip with its confusing jumble of moving lights and jangly music that hurt her head. The pack was scraping against her so she put it down on the sidewalk and slumped on to it, splaying out her legs.

"Hey, watch it." A young girl veered around her, her roller blades screeching on the sidewalk just inches from Dolores's worn plastic thongs. The girl flipped her hair and a barrette dropped to the sidewalk.

"Watch it yourself," she shouted back, scooping up the barrette and running her fingers along its surface. It was just the right size to fit into one of the fluted paper cups she had stacked in her bag. She shoved it into a side pocket and struggled to her feet again. She had to find the donut shop fast in case Bryce was waiting for her. She stared along the Strip, humming to keep her heart from pounding. It was packed with people looking in shops and restaurants, but they weren't looking at her so that was okay. She walked on, stumbling a bit with fatigue and confusion and then she spotted it, just a little way down a little side street, nestled between an adult video store and a newspaper shop.

It was wonderfully cool inside. She dropped her bag into a booth and peeled a couple of dollars from what was left of the nest egg in her pocket. A young man with acne and a tattoo of an alligator on his left arm took her order for three chocolate glazed and a large coffee and then, balancing her meal in both hands, she squeezed between the moulded chair and table and began the serious business of eating. Dr. Bradford would have a fit if he saw her. He'd handed her some diet sheets at one of their last sessions and made her promise to read them. Easy for him to eat all those fruits and vegetables, half of which she'd never even heard of. He didn't have to live on the little bit of money she got from welfare.

"Mind if I share your table?" A young woman with black hair swept back into a wide red ribbon made Dolores jump. She looked around the restaurant but almost all the other tables were empty.

She shrugged and chocolate crumbs cascaded to the white plastic table.

"Man," the woman giggled. "Is it ever hot today." She tossed a couple of parcels onto the bench beside Dolores's pack and threw her cotton jacket on top.

"Looks like you could use another coffee." The woman was still standing, the smell of perfume wafting about her, "can I get you anything else?"

Dolores shrugged again without looking up and the

woman strode away leaving her jacket and parcels behind. Dolores sneaked a peek at the top one. Neiman Marcus, it said. Well, well. All right for some, she thought, resentment pinching her lips together.

"Here you go. I picked up a couple more donuts as well." She giggled again. "I'm Jennifer, by the way. What's your name?"

Dolores pulled the new bag of chocolate glazed toward her and counted four. They would have cost a fortune, she thought toting up the total in her head. "Dolores."

"Well, *bon appetit,* Dolores!" Jennifer smiled brightly while she dusted the bench and perched gingerly on the edge. She stacked a pile of napkins onto the table and placed a carrot raisin muffin in the exact center. She turned the napkin pile around a couple of times before breaking off a tiny portion from the top and popping it into her mouth. A couple of miniscule crumbs dropped onto the table. "Mm mm," she said, and giggled again while she touched the corners of her mouth with the longest, pinkest, nails Dolores had ever seen. She pushed her own hands with their gnawed nails into her lap while she examined the woman across from her. Jennifer had one of those smiles that made her nose scrunch up, the kind the girls in high school used to try on in front of the restroom mirror until they caught her watching and made her leave. It was definitely the kind of smile for girls who giggled a lot.

"So," Jennifer studied her largely undamaged muffin and then looked up. "Where are you from?"

Dolores hesitated wondering if this was a trap. "Why? What makes you think I'm not from here?"

"Oh I don't know. Nobody you meet around here is actually from Las Vegas. Most people are tourists." Jennifer leaned toward her conspiratorially. "I'll bet you flew here, right?"

Oh sure. On her budget. "Huh uh. Bus from Chicago."

Jennifer flapped her hand with its pink nails in front of her mouth indicating it was full, but the muffin sitting on the tidy pile of napkins appeared almost whole. "Chicago?" she said after she swallowed. "I love Chicago!"

"Um . . ." Dolores looked into the donut bag and selected another chocolate glazed. She didn't want to talk about Chicago, it made her think of Dr. Bradford and the little roof-shaped frown.

"What did your mother call you, Doris?" he'd asked at their last session.

"I told you, I don't have a mother."

"Grandmother, then. What did she call you?"

"You know," she'd mumbled. She wished she'd never told him about the Doris Doolittle rhyme.

"Huh?" she looked up at Jennifer, realizing she'd missed a question.

"I asked if you had a place to stay."

Dolores shrugged.

"I could help you find a nice motel room and give you a lift, if you'd like."

Dolores scanned the seats in the donut shop again. "No, thanks. I'm meeting someone."

"Oh!" Jennifer beamed at her. "A boyfriend, I'll bet." She looked around herself at the mostly empty tables. "Is it a boyfriend, Doris?"

"My name's Dolores." The familiar anger bubbled up, pricking her eyes with tears.

"Oops. Sorry." Jennifer grinned. "I'll bet he's gorgeous. Is he gorgeous?"

Dolores shrugged. "He's not all that young any more."

"A sophisticated older man. They're the best kind. I'll bet he's nice. Is he nice?"

Dolores thought about the last time she saw him. She remembered the restraining orders and the policeman who'd yanked her arms behind her back and bent her over the hood of the squad car. "I dunno. Not nice exactly."

"Men, huh?" Her frown looked a lot like Dr. Bradford's. "Well, he should be here to meet you. That's for sure." She rummaged in her purse and produced a cell phone. "Why don't we call him and tell him to get on over here." The long pink nails hovered over the keypad like butterflies waiting to land. "What's the number?"

"I . . . I don't know the number. It's probably unlisted." Dolores could feel her breathing getting fast again. She wanted to hum but thought she'd better not. "Anyway, he's probably just busy." She wanted to tell Jennifer about Bryce's act at the Three Crowns and that he couldn't just drop everything at a moment's notice but she was afraid, afraid she'd get that look on her face like Dr. Bradford's. She was afraid Jennifer would talk about obsessions and stalking and all those things people said when they didn't understand about Bryce and her.

But Jennifer wasn't even looking at her. She seemed to be looking at something inside her own head and her eyes had gone all glittery, like Leonard's did when he had his scary thoughts. "Men need to be taken down a peg, don't you agree? Think they can walk all over us." Her laugh was a little bit like Leonard's too. "My own so-called boyfriend tells me the other day he's going to marry someone else. Didn't want me to see it first on TV, can you believe it?" The pink fingernails were drumming the table so hard the tip of the middle one snapped off, but Jennifer didn't seem to notice. "I've been his secretary, his lover, even his laundress." She made a disgusted snort. "I've answered thousands of letters from his retarded fans. And now he tells me he's knocked up some blond bimbo and he's going to marry her. Can you believe it?"

"Um . . ." Dolores wanted to tell her about the fingernail but Jennifer suddenly sniffed and then giggled again. "Well enough about me. I'm just a teensy bit angry." She crumbled a corner off her muffin, popped it into her mouth and bit down hard on it. Suddenly her eyes widened and she grabbed her jaw. "Oh shit." She fished around inside her mouth with the thumb and forefinger of her left hand, withdrawing something white.

Dolores was alarmed. It looked like a tooth. She'd had enough teeth yanked out of her head to know how painful it was, but when she looked at Jennifer's face the woman seemed more furious than wounded. She sucked the thing once and then dropped it into the ashtray and got to her feet. Dolores stared at it.

"Is that your tooth?"

"That piece of shit is a temporary crown. I'm not getting the real thing installed until tomorrow." She rolled her tongue around inside her mouth and then turned away. "I'm going to the washroom to rinse out my mouth."

Dolores stared at the thing, tipping it this way and that in the ashtray, amazed at the contours, trying to imagine where it had come from and if this one was temporary what the real crown would look like.

Jennifer reappeared and gathered up her parcels from the bench. The muffin lay abandoned on the table. "Okay. I think we need to take you to your boyfriend's place."

"Um. That's okay. I'll wait here a while."

"He's never going to come." The giggle and the scrunched-up smile had vanished but the eyes were still glittering. "You need to have it out with him, Doris. Once and for all." She grabbed her parcels and the duffle bag and headed for the door. Dolores sat for a moment, humming softly and when she looked over and saw the woman and her bag disappearing out the door she scooped the temporary crown into a napkin and shoved it in her pants pocket. The tip of the pink nail was harder to find, it had slipped under the pile of napkins holding the scarcely touched muffin. Dolores gathered the whole thing together and put it in the pocket of her shirt.

She pushed through to the heat and confusion of the street and found Jennifer standing beside a black convertible, holding the passenger door open. Dolores sank with difficulty into the seat and then had to pull her swollen legs in after her.

She peered at the console once they were moving. "What is this thing?"

"You're kidding, right?" Jennifer frowned at her. "You've never seen a Jaguar before?"

"Um . . ." Dolores found she could hum under her breath and the sound of the motor masked it.

Within minutes they were pulling up to the shipping entrance to Three Crowns. The woman reached across Dolores's stomach and pushed the passenger door open. "Out you get. I'll go and park this thing and then I'll get the key for you from the front desk." She checked over her shoulder watching for an opportunity to pull out, but then she appeared to change her mind and reached across again, this time to open the glove compartment. Dolores was stunned. Inside was the biggest pile of quarters she'd ever seen. Jennifer scooped up two handfuls and thrust them into her lap.

"You can play the slot machines while you wait." She gave Dolores a little shove. "Off you go. But stay in the lobby, okay? That way I can find you again."

Dolores stumbled out of the car, shoving coins into her pant's pockets. Several quarters dropped to the sidewalk and she had to stoop down to retrieve them. When she looked up again the car and the woman and all Dolores's possessions had disappeared.

She stood still for a full minute, trying to make sense of what had happened, feeling the pockets of her yellow knit pants stretch under the weight of the coins. She wanted to sag against the wall and close her eyes but she hadn't liked that glittery look in Jennifer's eyes so she pulled herself together and shuffled around to the front entrance of the hotel.

She gasped. A big poster advertising Bryce's show took up most of the front of the building. He seemed to be looking right into her eyes and she ran her fingers through her hair trying to tidy it. She didn't want him to see her looking like she'd just stepped off the bus. There were little trees in cement boxes lining the drive and she stood behind one for a moment watching the doorman in his red and black uniform. A limousine pulled up to the curved driveway and the man tugged at his tunic and ran over to open the driver's door. Dolores could hardly believe it. Jonathan

Finn from *Las Vegas Nights* stepped from the car and handed the doorman the keys. He took the stairs to the entrance two at a time and just before he pushed through he turned and smiled at Dolores. She thought she saw his lips move, saying, "I love you, Dolores." She had to hang onto one of the little trees for a minute and take a deep breath. What would Leonard say about this? It was his favorite TV show. She waited another minute until the doorman got into the limousine and began to drive it off, and then she sidled through the revolving doors and into the lobby of the Three Crowns. Jonathan Finn was nowhere in sight, but she knew what she'd seen. He loved her. She hummed to herself, hugging this new knowledge to her heart.

She wanted to stop and stare at the colors in the carpet and the impossibly soft sofas and chairs but she knew from last year that if the management noticed her they'd ask her to leave. She spotted banks and banks of slot machines lining the walls and found an unoccupied one tucked away behind a huge potted plant. She watched a man put his quarters into the machine next to hers and listened to the jangly sounds. She was astounded. They sounded a lot like the notes she hummed when she tried to get calm.

Dolores had no idea how long she'd been standing there sometimes shoving quarters into the machine and sometimes staring at the flashing lights. Once she was surprised by a shower of coins but was afraid of the noise the machine made when she won, fearing people would be drawn to it and ask her what she thought she was doing in such a fancy place. Hunger pangs and worry about

Jennifer and her duffle bag made her eat the muffin in her pocket and now she was hungry again.

Suddenly Jennifer was there, standing beside her, just as she bad been in the donut shop. Only this time she was wearing a scarf, dark glasses and black leather gloves and she was holding out a plastic card with a strip on one side.

"Here's the key to your boyfriend's suite." She pushed her sunglasses onto her head for a moment and her eyes glittering even more than Leonard's when he was about to do something crazy. "I think you'd better get right up there. Tell him how you feel about things."

Dolores took the card and ran her finger over the surface. It wouldn't fit in the little paper cups but she'd keep it anyway. "My bag . . . ?"

"It's still in the car. I'll go and get it while you're going to the room."

"Where do I go?" Dolores was confused about so many things; all she really wanted to do was lean against the wall and close her eyes.

"He's on the top floor where the big suites are. The elevators are over here." She put the sunglasses on and took Dolores's elbow, pushing her across the thick carpet, past the gorgeous sofas and into a marble foyer with elevators along both walls. "It's straight ahead when you get out of the elevator." She seemed to remember something. "You know how to use this key?" Dolores stared at the floor.

"Okay, you shove it into the slot above the handle with the strip away from you. Bring it out again and when the little light turns green, you can open the door."

"But my bag? Where'd you say my bag was?"

"I'll be waiting right here with your bag." Jennifer was

talking very softly now, almost whispering. "When you've told him . . . well, whatever you want to tell him, come back here and I'll give you your bag." She pushed something with her gloved finger and the elevator door slid open.

Dolores hesitated but Jennifer pushed her in and reached behind her to push a button inside the elevator.

When the elevator stopped, Dolores peered out, making sure there was no one in the hall. She held the card that Jennifer had called a key but the door across from the elevator was already ajar. She pushed it farther open and stuck her head in, humming the two notes as loud as she could. When no one stopped her she stepped into a light green vestibule with a huge painting of cactus and desert sand on the right wall. She hesitated and then called out softly, "Bryce?" She wished she'd rehearsed what she'd say to him but there was no answer. She walked into a living room, with another of the scrumptious sofas on a pale beige carpet. Two glasses half full of some kind of liquid and melting ice cubes sat on the coffee table. She glanced at the kitchen but it was empty. There was another half-open door leading off the living room. She walked over and pushed it fully open.

At first she thought they were sleeping, Bryce on his back, his naked torso partly covered by a sheet and the girl with her long blond hair spread out on the pillowcase. But then she saw the blood and the hole in Bryce's forehead where no one should have a hole. And when she leaned over to get a better look, she noticed the girl's hair was covering a section of her cheek that was red and pulpy and leaking blood.

A gun lay on the counter. She thought for a second

about picking it up, but it was much too big for her treasure collection so she left it where it was. She felt sad about Bryce and about the pretty girl too. But she knew in her heart that what Dr. Bradford had said was true. She and Bryce weren't really engaged. It was just a kind of dream of hers.

She heard a siren and then another and when she looked out the window she saw several police cars pulling up to the hotel's entrance. The doorman was tugging on his tunic and flapping his arms around.

Dolores decided to take the stairs down. She could stop at each floor and see if there was any sign of Jonathan Finn. He might be wondering where she'd got to and she didn't like to keep him waiting.

Before she left she looked again at the couple on the bed. She'd like to leave a gift for them, some sort of memorial like people left her when her grandmother died, but all of her treasures were in Jennifer's car. Then she remembered the temporary crown in its little bed of napkins in her shirt pocket. She pulled it out and dropped it near Bryce's hand. She noticed the little pink fingernail was caught in the folds, but it looked so pretty against the white sheet she decided to leave that as well.

Sanctuary!

Peter Tremayne

Peter Tremayne has published nearly forty-five books and a number of short stories. Under his real name, Peter Berresford Ellis has published an additional forty books and more stories, several pamphlets, and numerous academic papers and as well as a number of signed articles in over twenty foreign languages.. He has also been a regular columnist for the *Irish Democrat*, and *The Irish Post*. Writing as Peter Tremayne, he has been writing supernatural fantasy, mainly based on Irish folklore, which has won him international recognition, and the Sister Fidelma mystery series. He has also published eight thriller novels as Peter MacAlan.

"Fidelma! Do you have a moment?"

Fidelma had been crossing the quadrangle of the law school of the Brehon Morann when she was halted by the voice of the Ard-Ollamh, the chief professor, himself. She turned and smiled nervously as Brehon Morann approached.

She had been studying at the famous law school for six years now and had recently passed her examination for the degree of *Clí*, which meant she was now able to practise law in most courts in the land but with limitations as to the cases that she could undertake. However, she was ambitious to become a fully qualified advocate, able to practise defence or prosecution in all fields of the law, and that would mean at least another two years of study.

Even with her present qualifications, she was still in awe of the distinguished figure of the chief professor of the school.

"I understand from the Ollamh Neit that you have recently been studying the laws relating to sanctuary with him?" Brehon Morann said as he halted before her.

"I have," she acknowledged cautiously.

"Excellent. Then you will be interested in accompanying me to my chambers to hear some questions that a visitor has come to put to me. It seems he seeks advice on this subject."

"He wishes to consult you on the law of sanctuary?" asked Fidelma, before she realised that her question had already been answered, and Brehon Morann hated repetition. The chief professor did not bother to answer her. Fidelma bowed her head slightly. It was something of an honour to be singled out by the chief professor and given such an invitation.

"I will be most interested," she responded contritely.

A man was waiting in Brehon Morann's chambers. A tall, pleasant-looking individual, with sandy-coloured hair whose clothing and accoutrements pointed to the fact that he was a man of some rank.

"My steward, Adnaí, informs me that you are Faichen Glas, an *aire-deise* of the Uí Echach Cobo," Brehon Morann greeted him.

Fidelma realised from this introduction that Faichen Glas was a noble of some wealth and his people dwelt in the northern kingdom of Ulaidh.

The chief professor then introduced Fidelma and indicated that they should all be seated.

"What is the matter that brings you hither, Faichen Glas?" he prompted.

"I need advice, Brehon Morann. For a week I have been chasing a killer. A man who killed my own cousin. I have sworn an oath to capture him and take him back to my own people for trial. He has eluded me until now. I tracked him to a place not more than a day's ride from here. However, I have found that he has taken refuge in a chapel where the priest in charge claims that he has been granted sanctuary. I have come to ask you, what can I do?"

Brehon Morann sat back with a sigh.

"The Laws of the Fénechus, our own laws, have very strict rules about the concept of refuge, and these predate even those on sanctuary brought in by the New Faith of Christ." He paused. "I think you should tell us your story first and then we will come to the law in a moment. Who exactly is this killer that you seek?"

The noble of the Uí Echach Cobo grimaced.

"He is a man called Ulam Fionn, a drover without fixed land, who has long been suspected of taking cows from the local farmers among my people. He was never caught. It was noticed that he made a good enough profit at markets but nothing could be proved about the provenance of the livestock he sold there. Nine days ago, my cousin, Nessán, and his wife were awoken by the lowing of their cattle herd. It was in the morning, about first light. My cousin went out to see what ailed the cattle. The thief was caught in the act but he turned on my cousin and slew him before escaping."

Fidelma coughed nervously.

Brehon Morann glanced at her.

"You have a question?"

"How was this man, Ulam Fionn, identified if your cousin was slain and he escaped?"

"Easy enough to answer," replied Faichen Glas. "My cousin's wife was the witness to the evil deed."

"She was the only witness?"

"Only she, apart from her husband, saw Ulam Fionn."

"Then why was she not attacked?"

Faichen Glas frowned, trying to understand the question.

It was Brehon Morann who explained Fidelma's thinking.

"If she was the only witness to this deed, then this Ulam Fionn might well have contemplated silencing her—the silence of the grave."

"From what she told me, the killer did not see her," the noble replied. "She observed the killing from the window of the farmhouse and was too horrified and fearful to emerge before he left."

"There is no doubt of her identification? She had a clear view of this man, Ulam Fionn?"

"She did. There is no question," Faichen Glas assured her. "And his flight confirms his guilt. I have pursued him for nine days now in order to bring him back to my chief for justice."

Brehon Morann looked thoughtful.

"He has taken refuge in a church here, you say? How did you find him?"

"It was known that he had a cousin named Ulpach who dwelt in this area. I do not know the man, but I was told that they are each as bad as the other, in so far as their morals are concerned. I thought that he might seek refuge with Ulpach but I could not trace either of them. I found a shepherd that had heard a rumour that someone had sought refuge with a religieux in the chapel of St. Benignus . . ."

"That's about half a day's ride from here," mused Brehon Morann. "I do not know the religieux who has charge of it. He is fairly new to the area, by all accounts."

Faichen Glas nodded in agreement.

"I rode there and this man, Brother Mongan was his name, told me that he had given Ulam Fionn sanctuary. I came to you, learned Brehon, to ask whether there is any way that I can take this murderer from the sanctuary and return him to Ulaidh for trial?"

Brehon Morann sat back for a moment and then turned with a smile to Fidelma.

"My young colleague here will tell you of the rights of sanctuary."

Fidelma coloured, feeling ridiculously proud to be called a colleague of the chief professor. "Well," she began hesitantly, "our laws provide for a place of asylum for those fugitives who seek refuge. And the rules of the New Faith are fairly similar to our concepts. Those of our scholars who have travelled abroad find the same system common in many lands."

Faichen Glas was obviously impatient at the preamble

but a frown from Brehon Morann checked him as Fidelma continued.

"In our law we have an area called the *maigen,* a precinct in which a fugitive may claim sanctuary surrounding any chieftain's home. Its extent ranges from that of a minor chieftain, where it is reckoned as the extent of one spear cast from the central house, to that of a chief of the entire clan, where it is reckoned as the extent of sixty-four spear casts from the house. In the *maigen,* a fugitive can claim safety from all who seek to harm him.

"With the coming of the New Faith, the abbeys, churches, and monasteries have assumed the same role as the chieftain's *maigen* in our law. The place of the fugitive is confined to what they call Termonn Land." She glanced at the Brehon Morann. "The word is borrowed from the Latin word *terminus,* the limit or extent of the church lands. In these areas, for a pursuer to kill or injure a fugitive is to commit the crime of *díguin,* the violation of protection. For that there are prescribed punishments. A fugitive cannot be captured or harmed in these areas . . ."

"Unless?" It was Brehon Morann who prompted her when she hesitated.

Fidelma thought for a moment. "There are three conditions that must be met. The owner of the *maigen,* whether secular or ecclesiastic, must have given the fugitive permission, having been given a truthful account by the fugitive of the need for asylum. Thus the owner of the *maigen* becomes legally entitled to act for the fugitive. The next condition is that any pursuer must be clearly informed by the owner that this place is regarded as a sanctuary. The last condition is that while the fugitive remains in the *maigen* he cannot use it to profit from his alleged crimes, going forth from the asylum area and attacking people and then returning to claim asylum."

Brehon Morann nodded approval and turned to Faichen Glas.

"I presume that all three conditions have been fulfilled in the matter we are discussing?"

The northern noble looked troubled. "I know nothing of the law here. It is true that when I approached the church Brother Mongan came forward and forbade me to enter with hospitality, declaring that it was a sanctuary . . . what you said—a *maigen dígona.* That is why I came here to find out what I could do."

Fidelma leaned quickly toward Brehon Morann. "Of course, it is not lawful for even a cleric to give protection to certain classes of fugitive, especially a murderer, indefinitely."

Brehon Morann grimaced. "My young colleague speaks truly. But the *snádud,* that is, the legal protection, can be extended until guilt or innocence is made certain."

Faichen Glas looked from one to the other with a frown.

"What can I do, then? How can his guilt be proved before he is brought to trial? Ulam Fionn is hiding in this church and I am powerless to bring him to justice. I am minded to go with my men and take the man by force."

"Do that," Fidelma quickly commented, "and it will be you that will stand trial. The fugitive, whatever his alleged crimes, is under protection of the law."

"We must act in accordance with the law, Faichen Glas," added Brehon Morann firmly.

He paused for a moment and then rose with a smile.

"Faichen Glas, you will accept the hospitality of this

college—you and your men will stay here while we investigate this matter further." He picked up a handbell from a nearby table and rang it.

Adnaí, the elderly steward of the college, entered almost immediately, as if he had been waiting outside the door for the summons.

Brehon Morann instructed the man to see to the needs of the noble of the Uí Echach Cobo and his men and provide them with food and beds in the college hostel.

When they had gone, Fidelma stood nervously wondering whether she, too, should leave, but Brehon Morann gestured her to be seated again.

"This is a fairly simple case," he began thoughtfully. "Provided the sanctuary has been granted in the legal form, then our friend Faichen Glas will have to return to the land of the Uí Echach Cobo. He must then bring his witness and his own Brehon before the abbot in whose jurisdiction the church of St. Benignus lies. I happen to know Abbot Sionna and he is a fair man. If Faichen Glas can present a just case as to why the sanctuary should be withdrawn, then the abbot can instruct that Ulam Fionn be handed over for trial."

Fidelma waited politely. Her recent class on the law of sanctuary had taught her this much.

"Before I can inform Faichen Glas that this is the course of action he must take, we will have to ensure that the sanctuary has been properly given. I have no reason to suspect otherwise but, Fidelma, in law you can never assume anything. Assumption without verification can lead to great miscarriages of justice."

"I understand," Fidelma replied, not really understanding why he was emphasising what she had already learnt.

"It will be good experience for you to go to this church of St. Benignus and speak with Brother Mongan and ensure that all has been done in legal form," went on Brehon Morann.

"Me?" Fidelma's ejaculation was one of surprise.

"It is only a half-day's ride there and a half-day back again. It doubtless means that you will have to stay overnight in a public hostel. There is no one from the college staff who can afford this time. You, on the other hand, are qualified to take this deposition and can be spared from your studies . . . rather this is part of your studies, for this matter of sanctuary may well occur in your future career when you begin to practise law."

"Of course," responded Fidelma nervously and then added weakly, "but I don't know where this church of St. Benignus is."

"I will give you instructions to the abbey of Sionna and he will instruct you further. You may take one of the college horses. Once you have returned, having ensured that all is satisfactory under the law, then, we can instruct Faichen Glas on the appropriate action." Brehon Morann glanced through the window at the darkening sky. "It is too late to begin today. You should leave at first light tomorrow." He smiled in gentle rebuke as Fidelma rose slowly and reluctantly. "The practise of law is not all about solving puzzles or clearing up mysteries. Often it is very boring and pedestrian work, checking and rechecking simple facts and making tiring journeys to do so."

Fidelma was contrite again.

"I apologise, Brehon Morann, if I seem to display a lack of enthusiasm for the task. I will, of course, carry it out."

It was noon on the following day when Fidelma found herself sitting before Abbot Sionna. He was a chubby-featured man who was well past his middle years. His silver hair and wide blue eyes gave him an almost cherubic look.

"The chapel of St. Benignus?" he was saying thoughtfully, after she had explained her mission. "It is not far from here and it is only recently that Brother Mongan was sent to administer there. You will find him most helpful. He is a thoughtful man, a good scholar. He entered our abbey as the poor son of a farmer and achieved his scholarship by his own diligence. He worked in our library for a while, where he copied most of the Pauline texts from the scriptures. I was loath to see him go but he wanted experience in administering a small chapel. Don't concern yourself, young lawyer. He will have obeyed all the laws governing the granting of sanctuary."

"But he has not informed you of the matter yet?" Fidelma asked, picking up on the tense used by the abbot.

Abbot Sionna shook his head.

"Brother Mongan would probably have to wait until he could find someone to bring me a message. The chapel is two hours' good riding from here and off the main highway. As he is alone at the chapel, he could not, in law, leave the fugitive there by himself. However, I will leave this matter in your hands. Report back to me as to the situation on your return."

• • •

It was midafternoon when Fidelma spotted the oblong shape of the chapel of St. Benignus. The five kingdoms of Éirinn were abounding in vast forests, so it was usual for most of the small churches to be built of wood, although in the western parts, such as Fidelma's own homeland of Muman, many abbeys and oratories were constructed of local stone. Here, in Midhe, the middle kingdom, it was unusual to see a limestone church building, strong like a fortress. Such, however, was the chapel of St. Benignus. It was strongly built, six metres wide and twenty-five metres in length. Its roof towered upwards, and the jambs of the main door—the only door so far as she could see—were inclined so that it was wider at the bottom than the top.

The grounds around it were planted with yew and ash. Fidelma knew that this was often called the *fidnemed* or sacred grove covering the area of the *nemed* or *termonn,* the sanctuary's limits.

She approached on horseback, slowly and deliberately, but she was already some way from the gates to the sanctuary area when the door of the chapel swung inward and a thin figure in badly fitting religious robes stepped out.

"Halt, stranger!" the figure called in a harsh voice. "I have to warn you that you are approaching sanctuary land and may not enter if you seek harm to one who has claimed sanctuary here."

Fidelma smiled inwardly. At least the religieux seemed to know the legal requirement of informing everyone approaching the church. She drew rein and sat for a moment regarding the man from her horse.

He seemed young, fair-haired with pale blue eyes. In spite of his slight build, he was pleasant-looking. He came slowly down the short path from the chapel to the gates into the *fidnemed*.

"What do you seek here, daughter?" he asked in a softer tone of voice.

Fidelma tried to control her smile. Daughter! The young religieux was hardly older than she was. But the New Faith was importing a lot of new phrases and concepts to their language. Priests of the New Faith were now being called *Athair* or Father, which was an affectation brought in from the Faith in Rome. A few even preferred the term *Rúinid*, confidant or counsellor.

"Are you Brother Mongan?" she asked.

A frown passed the young man's brow.

"This is my chapel," he acknowledged in reply.

"My name is Fidelma. I am . . ." she hesitated slightly, "I am a lawyer from the college of the Brehon Morann, which lies not far from here."

"I know of it," the young man replied, the frown deepening. "What do you seek here?"

"I would have thought that obvious." Fidelma could not help her automatic retort. "I have been asked to come here to verify that the sanctuary you have given to the fugitive who now resides in your chapel has been accorded in strict adherence to the law."

Brother Mongan sniffed slightly. "Had it not been, I would not have given it," he replied with equal curtness.

"It is a legal requirement that this be checked," Fidelma responded, trying not to make her voice sharp, as was her inclination. She did not wish to irritate Brother Mongan, realising that impatience was one of her faults.

"And I confirm it," replied the religieux.

"I am glad to hear it," smiled Fidelma, and swung down from her horse so that she could stand facing him. "However, there are still formalities to be gone through."

Brother Mongan was clearly unhappy.

"Formalities?"

"Of course," she replied, tethering her horse to a nearby bush and glancing around. There were two other horses grazing nearby among the trees. "I suppose one of those belongs to your fugitive?"

Brother Mongan glanced in the direction she was looking and nodded quickly. "But what formalities?" he pressed again.

"Sanctuary has to follow certain legal requirements," she replied. "When the fugitive came here, did he properly identify himself?"

"He said he was Ulam Fionn of the territory of the Uí Echach Cobo. That he sought protection because he was being pursued and sought to escape impending harm."

"That harm coming in what form?"

"He said that his life was in danger. He was falsely accused of murder. He told me that he had caused the death of someone but in self-defence. He said he was attacked by this person and had to defend himself. Those chasing him would not listen to reason and meant him harm."

Fidelma regarded Brother Mongan thoughtfully. It was a different side of the story from that told by Faichen Glas.

"So you offered sanctuary to Ulam Fionn and accepted that you were legally entitled to act for him?"

Brother Mongan nodded but did not speak.

"You are prepared to confirm and guarantee that Ulam Fionn will not take advantage while dwelling in this sanctuary, that he will engage in no unlawful activity? That he will not use this as a base to ride out to bring harm or loss to anyone?"

"Of course."

"And, as in the manner you have already informed me, all who come here are informed that the chapel has become a sanctuary and they must abide by the laws appertaining to that provision?"

"Yes," agreed Brother Mongan impatiently.

So far, Fidelma thought, it seemed straightforward enough.

"Then I simply need to see this Ulam Fionn and speak with him."

Brother Mongan hesitated and seemed about to protest. Then he shrugged.

"Wait here. He is nervous, so it is best that I speak with him first."

He turned and made his way into the church. Fidelma turned and absently patted her horse's muzzle. With a thoughtful frown she turned to where the other two horses were grazing.

Brother Mongan's voice called from the door of the chapel.

"You may come in, my daughter."

She walked up the path and entered the doorway of the chapel, halting for a few moments to get used to the darkness of the interior. There were a few high windows and the place was lit with candles, but it was still gloomy; shadows danced everywhere in accordance with the dictates of the flickering flames.

"You want to see me?"

Ulam Fionn was a short, thin man with close-set eyes and a beak of a nose. His voice was sharp. Fidelma could not help disliking him and then she felt guilty. She was allowing her personal prejudices to form judgments. Brehon Morann had long taught that those practising law should be free of forming such ridiculous intolerant bias.

"Ulam Fionn, I am sent here to ensure that the proper laws relating to sanctuary have been observed. I understand from Brother Mongan that they have."

The fugitive stood without movement. He did not reply.

Fidelma sighed. She glanced around quickly.

"You have come seeking sanctuary for yourself only?"

"I am alone here."

"So what do you intend to do?"

"Intend to do?" a slight frown crossed the man's face.

"Sanctuary cannot be granted indefinitely. Faichen Glas, who has pursued you here, can now appeal to the abbot in whose authority this chapel comes for permission to plead your case before him and his Brehon. . . . You cannot stay here forever."

"What . . . ?" Ulam Fionn shot a startled look at Brother Mongan. Fidelma saw the religieux was looking bewildered.

"I thought the Faith guaranteed that no person could violate sanctuary," he said stubbornly.

"Faichen Glas has to bring his witnesses and his own Brehon to argue his case in the presence of the abbot. Abbot Sionna," explained Fidelma. "The abbot has to decide, together with Faichen Glas's own judge, whether there is a case to be answered. He can set a time limit to the duration of the sanctuary or hand you over to Faichen Glas for trial immediately."

"Then I am done for," Ulam Fionn said with bitterness. "I have no witness to support me. I will be condemned on the word of the widow of Nessán, whom I killed in self-defence. And it is Nessán's own cousin who pursues me."

"You killed the man in self-defence? Tell me your story," Fidelma said.

"I was taking a shortcut across Nessán's lands, near his farmhouse, when he suddenly appeared and started to attack me. I sought to defend myself and in doing so Nessán was killed. I heard his wife start screaming 'Murder!' I hid, for I knew Nessán had many friends in the area and I did not. Then word came that Faichen Glas said he would cause me to pay for what I had done. He was a rich and powerful noble. I fled south."

"But why would Nessán attack you?"

Ulam Fionn shrugged indifferently. "Give a dog a bad name. He and his kind have always disliked me. They accuse me of all sorts of things of which I am innocent. The whole world is against me."

Fidelma had a slight feeling of guilt that she could dislike the man simply because of his looks. If she was going to be successful as a *dálaigh*, a pleader before the courts of the Brehons, when she left Brehon Morann's law school, then she would have to curb any emotional prejudice such as judging on people's looks. Looks were no measurement. What was it Brehon Morann often told his students? The tree that has handsome foliage often has a bitter fruit. The reverse was also true.

"The law is not there to take sides but to seek the truth," she placated, feeling sorry for the man. "You should be able to find an experienced lawyer to represent you."

"The nobles of the Uí Echach Cobo are powerful," complained the fugitive. "They will not rest until they have taken vengeance on me."

"The law says that a killing in self-defence is not murder," Fidelma reminded him.

Ulam Fionn laughed sharply. "And I must prove self-defence?"

She shook her head. "Your accusers must prove murder," she pointed out.

"Well, I prefer not to fall into their hands to argue the matter."

Brother Mongan coughed sharply. "That is not the way to look at things, my son," he intoned somewhat piously. "You are safe here for a while but you must heed the counsel of this learned lawyer. When you are in a more reflective mood, you may consider what course you must follow."

Fidelma turned to the religieux. "Thank you, Brother Mongan. I am sure that you will add your voice in advising that the best course is for Ulam Fionn to resort to the law and put his case before Abbot Sionna and his Brehon."

"I will advise him, my daughter," agreed the religieux. "Is there anything else that I can assist you with?"

Fidelma thought for a moment.

She had carried out the legal requirements, but she had a strange feeling of dissatisfaction. She did not really want to leave. She wondered if it was because, should Ulam Fionn be truthful in his claim, and it was certainly a possibility, then she ought to help him resolve the matter. After all, she knew some powerful families could find ways to thwart justice, and if it was a case of self-defence then she did not wonder that the man was afraid to seek resolution in the law.

She glanced round the interior of the chapel.

"Are you comfortable here?" she suddenly asked. "It must be cold and draughty living in this old chapel."

"I get by," replied the fugitive, curious at her sudden concern.

"Do not bother yourself on that account, daughter," began Brother Mongan. "There is a small cellar below the altar where there is warmth and comfort. We . . ."

He suddenly cut off and dropped his eyes.

"I am comfortable enough," Ulam Fionn added quickly.

"Then I need hear no more," Fidelma said, as if making up her mind. "Everything seems in order."

Brother Mongan accompanied her to the door of the chapel.

"Is this the first time that you have had to offer sanctuary to a fugitive?" she asked at the door.

"It is," replied the other, seeming relieved by her approval.

"It is difficult to know what to do, to make sure we follow the law," she went on. "I suppose you have read the *Cáin Snádud?*"

Brother Mongan frowned slightly. "The what?"

"The law of legal protection."

He shook his head. "I am no scholar, my daughter. I leave interpretation of the law in the hands of good people like yourself. I am merely concerned with issues of the Faith."

"Of course," Fidelma replied. "But you did seem to know and obey the legal requisites."

"I knew the basic rules, of course," replied the religieux. "What one of us in authority over a chapel or an abbey would not know those?"

"Indeed. And you are fortified by the fact that the Faith also offers such sanctuary so that it does not conflict with the civil law."

"Just so, just so." Brother Mongan smiled.

"What is it that Scripture quotes that gives the foundation for the bestowal of sanctuary? *Nescitis quia templum Dei estis et Spiritus Dei habitat in vobis . . . ?*"

"Just so, just so," agreed Brother Mongan again.

"From Paul's letter to the Hebrews, I think."

"You are very learned, my daughter," Brother Mongan agreed gravely. "I wish you a safe journey back to the school of Brehon Morann."

Fidelma raised a hand in farewell, then mounted her horse and rode away.

Two days later she was seated before the fire in the chamber of the Brehon Morann and sipping a glass of mulled wine, which the chief professor had offered her.

"I congratulate you, Fidelma. But how were you able to resolve this matter?"

Fidelma examined the fire pensively for a moment, as if the dancing flames would help her clarify her thoughts.

"It was not hard." She spoke slowly. "Mostly, I suppose, it was merely a guess."

Brehon Morann snorted sceptically.

"A guess? Do you realise what might have happened if your guess had been wrong? There should be no guesswork in law."

"I did not think it was wrong at the time," she said calmly.

"You have a legally trained mind. Take me through the process that produced the result."

"I first went to see Abbot Sionna, as you told me. While speaking to me, he mentioned in passing that Brother Mongan was a scholar. A copyist of the Pauline letters, among other works."

"And so?"

"When I arrived at the chapel, I saw that there were two horses tethered outside. As you know, a religieux does not own or ride a horse unless he's of special rank or privilege. Brother Mongan had no such rank. The abbot told me Brother Mongan was the son of a poor farmer. So I wondered why two horses were there. Ulam Fionn said he was there alone. Then I recalled Faichen Glas saying he suspected Ulam Fionn had fled in this direction to join his cousin, Ulpach. I began to suspect that the other horse was that belonging to Ulpach.

"Having cleared up the matter of the legality of the sanctuary, I thought I would take the matter a step further and ask to see Ulam Fionn, to see if Ulpach was also sheltering in the chapel. He was not. Only Ulam Fionn and Brother Mongan were there. They swore that Ulam Fionn was the only one seeking sanctuary there. But what made me even more suspicious was when I asked about the comfort of residing in the chapel. Brother Mongan was about to talk about the cellar under the chapel and how comfortable it was. He caught himself in time, and Ulam Fionn tried to pass over his mistake quickly enough. I went along with it. My guess was that there was something in the cellar that they did not want me to see."

Brehon Morann looked at her carefully.

"Suspicions only? Guesswork only? You needed more than that to do what you did."

Fidelma smiled softly.

"I needed only the confidence of my interpretation of what my ears heard and my eyes saw. Abbot Sionna said that

Brother Mongan was a scholar. When I congratulated him on his knowledge of the law and said he must have read the *Cáin Snádud* he replied that he did not know it and that he was no scholar at all. So I quoted a line that is to be found in Paul's first letter to the Corinthians—the line that says "Know you not that you are in the temple of God and that the Spirit of God dwells in you?" I quoted the line in Latin. It is the scripture that is often used to support the concept of sanctuary, for one cannot use violence in the temple of God. But I said it was from the letter to the Hebrews. Brother Mongan congratulated me on my knowledge."

"Ah, and were he a scholar and copyist of the letters of Paul, he would have known better."

"Exactly so."

"So you rode back to Abbot Sionna?"

"And he sent the abbey's Brehon and half a dozen stout members of the abbey. They went into the chapel, took hold of Ulam Fionn and his companion, and found in the cellar below the trussed-up form of the real Brother Mongan."

"With the fake Brother Mongan turning out to be . . . ?"

"Ulam Fiona's cousin, Ulpach," she ended triumphantly.

"A sad tale. Had Ulam Fionn and Ulpach sought genuine sanctuary, it probably would have been granted and they would have been safe."

"Unfortunately, they trusted no one other than themselves. They were liars and thieves and could not conceive of having confidence in the good intentions of others, let alone depending on them. They did not even bother to ask Brother Mongan to grant them sanctuary."

"I presume that Brother Mongan told Ulpach the rudiments of sanctuary law."

"Ulpach forced Brother Mongan to confirm the basic

requirements, but it was obvious to me that Ulpach did not know those things he should have known. He did not know that there is a limitation on sanctuary that applies to those accused of taking a person's life, nor that the abbot has eventually to resolve the granting of sanctuary given by one of his clerics. That surprised the fake Brother Mongan and confirmed to me that it was Ulpach."

Brehon Morann was thoughtful.

"So Faichen Glas will be taking Ulam Fionn and his cousin Ulpach back north to the lands of the Uí Echach Cobo?"

Fidelma grimaced. "There is, of course, the attack and imprisonment of Brother Mongan to be dealt with, and the New Faith will doubtless have something to say on that before they hand the culprits over to Faichen Glas."

Brehon Morann smiled indulgently at his young pupil.

"You have much promise, Fidelma. Indeed, you have promise of becoming a fine lawyer. But you relied on guesswork. Consider this . . . you might have been wrong in your interpretation of these events."

Fidelma shrugged. "Yet as it turned out, I was not. I was confident in my own ability. I have heard it said, 'The confident person may succeed, but the person who hesitates may lose all.'"

Brehon Morann knew that he had often quoted the proverb to his students. He smiled sadly.

"Proverb for proverb, Fidelma. 'The end of the day is always a good prophet.'"

A Matter of Honor

Jeremiah Healy

Jeremiah Healy, a graduate of Rutgers College and Harvard Law School, was a professor at the New England School of Law for eighteen years. He is the creator of the John Francis Cuddy private-investigator series and (under the pseudonym "Terry Devane") the Mairead O'Clare legal-thriller series, both set primarily in Boston.

Healy has written eighteen novels and over sixty short stories, fifteen of which works have won or been nominated for the Shamus Award. Healy's later Cuddy novels include *Rescue, Invasion of Privacy, The Only Good Lawyer,* and *Spiral.* His Devane/O'Clare books from Putnam/Berkley are *Uncommon Justice, Juror Number Eleven,* and *A Stain Upon The Robe.*

A past Awards Chair for the Shamus, Healy also served as president of the Private Eye Writers of America for two years. In October, 2004, he concluded his four-year term as president of

the International Association of Crime Writers ("IACW"). Books of
his have been translated into French, Japanese, Italian, Spanish,
German, and Turkish. Healy has spoken about mysteries at the
Smithsonian Institution's Literature Series, *The Boston Globe*
Book Festival, the Sorbonne in Paris, and at conferences in Eng-
land, Holland, Spain, Germany, Austria, Iceland, and the Czech
Republic.

1.

The woman sitting in a client chair across my desk from
me laid her handbag in her lap and said, "First thing, I
come to Boston now from Iceland."

I had to admit, it was an attention-getter.

Then again, so was she. About twenty-five, her eyes
shone a pale, haunting blue and her hair a steely blond,
drawn back into a pony-tail. The facial features leaned to
the handsome side of pretty, but to the smart side, too. Her
clothes seemed a little summery for even a sunny October
day, though. And when she'd entered through the door
stenciled with "JOHN FRANCIS CUDDY, CONFIDENTIAL
INVESTIGATIONS" and I'd stood to greet her, the top of her
head was even with my brow, and I go nearly six-three.

"My names I will spell for you."

I drew a legal pad toward me and let a pen hover in my
hand above it.

She nodded solemnly, as though about to start a prayer.
"F-R-E-Y-D-I-S is the first, pronounced *fray*-dees. In Ice-
land, we are most named for our father, and so K-A-R-L-S-
D-O-T-T-I-R is the last, pronounced *karls-dot*-tur."

Simple enough: Karl's daughter. I wrote down the
names, and, since it seemed important to the woman for

me to get them right, I read both back to her as well. Then, "Ms. Karlsdottir, what can I do for you?"

She shook her head. "In my country, we have many traditions. One is to use first names and perhaps middle names, so please: If you can call me 'Freydis,' and I can call you 'John Francis'?"

"That would be fine."

Another nod. "Iceland, you have been there?"

"Never."

"You should. There is a direct flight—Icelandair—from here to our airport, Keflavik, near to our capital, Reykjavik. Which is aid to a second tradition, from the Vikings of ancient days. Our people will—the word we use is 'sail': to go away and come back with skills from job for the enriching of our island, yes?"

"I understand."

"My father did just so, to England, and his younger friend the same, but the friend, Hogni Ragnarsson, came here."

"Can you spell that one for me, too?"

Karlsdottir did, and I felt slightly pleased with myself that I'd gotten it right without her, phonetically.

She reached into her bag. "Hogni lives in not so good neighborhood in your Boston, John Francis, so all we have is postal box for address." Rummaging now. "But when we send him letter, it returns with no delivery."

Karlsdottir sighed heavily and looked at me with those Alaskan Husky eyes. "Sorry. The 'jet lag,' yes? I cannot find the envelope."

"And, I take it, you cannot find Mr. Ragnarsson, either."

A bleak smile. "That is true."

"Freydis, is there a reason you came all this way to look for him?"

She gave me a third solemn nod. "My father is now dead."

"I'm sorry."

"No need, please. He was sick with the prostate cancer that went to his bones."

I'd had an older uncle who'd suffered that particularly cruel and painful passing. "A difficult way to die."

"There is no easy way, I think. But my father left as— 'inheritance'?"

"In his will or estate documents?"

"Yes, John Francis. An inheritance to Hogni."

"And you want to get that to Mr. Ragnarsson."

"I must. My sister and I are the only family to do this duty, and she is younger and sick herself, in hospital." Karlsdottir swiped her right index finger under both eyes, like a miniature squeegee for escaping tears. "So, I have the obligation. As a matter of honor."

I put down my pen. "Freydis, have you tried the Icelandic Consulate here in Boston?"

"There is not one."

"Our police, then?"

A firm shake of the bead now. "When Icelandair woman tells me we have no consulate here, I ask her, what I should do? She tells me police in the United States are not like ours, who function as 'guides' for tourists and do not carry with them guns."

My turn to nod. There wouldn't exactly be an avalanche of help from the Boston department if Karlsdottir didn't even know where the guy lived in terms of our police districts.

She said, "The Icelandair woman tells me to find a private investigator. Like you, John Francis."

"She knows me personally?"

"Oh, no. Sorry. You are the most close one to my hotel."

I've received more ringing endorsements. "Look, Freydis, this could become expensive for you."

"My father was not a rich man, but with my own inheritance from him, several thousand dollars is not the problem."

"Have you looked in a telephone directory for metropolitan Boston?"

"At your airport. The directory is odd to me, because it has the last names, not the first names, in sequence of alphabet. But no Hogni."

If our White Pages threw her . . . I picked up my desk phone. "Let's see if I can save us some of my time and your money."

For a change, Karlsdottir didn't nod, but she did wait politely as a buddy of mine at Verizon confirmed no number for Hogni Ragnarsson, landline or cell, listed or unlisted.

I cradled the receiver. "Do you have any idea where your father's friend might work?"

"No, John Francis. And I am worried true for Hogni. We have not heard from him in many months now."

"And that's unusual?"

"Impossible. Icelanders always maintain contact—with families, with friends—forever."

Family, duty, honor. Quite a trifecta.

"Okay." I quoted Karlsdottir my daily rate, which didn't make her blink. She dipped back into the handbag and found her cash right away.

As Karlsdottir slid two days' worth of retainer across my desk, though, she fixed me with those haunting eyes. "One more thing, please?"

I took, her money. "Yes?"

"I will come with you."

"With me, Freydis?"

"Just so. In your vehicle, or the trains. The ways you will seek for Hogni."

"Wouldn't you rather play tourist?"

Finally, a smile that wasn't bleak, and pushed her back over the line from handsome to borderline beautiful. "The air flight was on my cost, the hotel is on my cost, and you are on my cost. The weather is good, and if the police cannot guide me in your city, I will go with you."

I thought, there are far worse ways to spend your day, John Francis.

2.

Outside a state office building blocks from mine on Tremont Street, Freydis Karlsdottir said, "We have walked this far, and I cannot enter with you?"

"It's not that you can *not* enter. It's more that my expert inside will get nervous if somebody's with me."

Karlsdottir pawed the concrete with her shoe like a bridled horse unhappy to be restrained. "What you do, John Francis, it is perhaps not . . . 'legal'?"

"Not exactly. But it's very efficient, and no one gets hurt."

She glanced around. "Then I will go back to the small place of graves by the church you called King's Chapel."

"I'll meet you there, Freydis."

"So, Jimmy, how're you doing?"

"I'd be doing a lot better, I didn't think you're gonna ask me to do what I think you are."

I rested my rump on the edge of his computer hutch. It's

never been entirely clear to me exactly what Jimmy's real job is, nor which agency of the Commonwealth he actually works for. But he has a genuine talent for finding all sorts of things via the computer. A good thing, too, because at six-one, one-thirty, and with a dress code like Jughead in the old Archie comics, Jimmy doesn't make the sort of first impression that would have private companies vying for his services. And he also loves to bet the greyhounds at the Suffolk Downs dog track, which means fresh cash—in this case, some of Freydis Karlsdottir's retainer—is always welcome.

Jimmy quickly scanned the room—probably for the unlikely presence of a supervisor actually at work—and then cut to the car chase. "All right, Cuddy, what do you want from me?"

I set down a sheet of legal pad, the name "Hogni Ragnarsson" block-printed on it and a fifty-dollar bill beneath it.

Jimmy glanced down. "Screwy name. Swedish?"

"Icelandic."

"You mean, like the Vikings?"

"Some of them, anyway."

"What's this particular Viking done?"

"Nothing, far as I know. But I need a residential or business address for him."

Jimmy palmed the fifty from under the sheet and swung around to his keyboard. "See what I can do."

After clacking and tapping for a while, he said, "No record of a driver's license or car registration."

"I think Ragnarsson came overseas to work."

More clacking, the screen on his monitor zipping images left and right and up and down like a video game. "Let's try the Department of Revenue, then, see if he filed—damn it!"

"What's the matter?"

"Shut up a minute, let me cover my tracks here."

I'd never seen Jimmy upset with his computer before. It was like watching ice dancers at the Olympics when one seemed to blame the other for a spin-out.

"Jesus," he said finally. "That was close."

"Can you explain it in English?"

"At your level of software comprehension? Let's just say that the Commonwealth's tax collectors put in a new burglar alarm, and it almost caught me climbing in their back window."

"Can you keep going?"

"Yeah, but not with Revenue. You say maybe the guy worked, let's try the Eye-Ay-Bee."

As in IAB, or Industrial Accident Board, the state agency that processes employee claims for injuries suffered on the job.

More clacking and tapping, but slower this time around, as if Jimmy didn't want to trip another alarm.

"Ah," he said, "now we're cooking."

I bent over his shoulder toward the monitor's screen. "Construction-site accident."

"Four months ago."

Which might explain the incommunicado status that worried Karlsdottir. "I don't see an address for our boy."

"No," said Jimmy with a smug edge in his voice, "but here's one for the construction company's headquarters, the construction site itself, and even the poor Viking's lawyer."

Jimmy doesn't like to print things from his computer for me, so I began taking down the information on the sheet of legal paper. "You're worth your weight in gold, my man."

Jimmy sniffed. "You don't mind, I'll take my height in gold."

When I returned to the cemetery outside King's Chapel, I didn't see Freydis Karlsdottir, so I went through the massive, fortress-like doors and into the stark little church itself. I spotted her about six rows up, just sitting as opposed to kneeling, so I moved alongside her pew.

She looked up, but not startled. "It is like a church in Iceland, this."

"How so?"

"White, clean. And . . . simple. A place to be reminded that one person is perhaps not so important in the world."

"Interesting observation."

Her eyes changed focus. "You found data about Hogni?"

"Indirectly. We need to go for a drive."

The beaming smile as she rose from her bench. "I like you for my guide, John Francis."

3.

From the passenger's seat in my old Honda Prelude, Freydis Karlsdottir said, "I do not understand why we go first to construction place and not to lawyer?"

I maneuvered around some orange traffic cones, which, since Boston's "Big Dig" road-and-tunnel project began, have become as much a part of our local scenery as the cobblestones at Quincy Market. "Even my computer expert couldn't find a residential address for Mr. Ragnarsson in the Massachusetts official records. Before I approach a lawyer who might be suspicious of us, I'd like to have a little more background on your father's friend."

In my peripheral vision, I caught a frown. "Hogni's inheritance would he 'suspicious' to his lawyer?"

Now I looked over, noticing that her English was improving as she used it more with me. "In this country, Freydis, people are wary of unexpected gifts. Not in Iceland?"

The bleak smile. "So many of us there know each other—are 'related' by distant blood *to* each other—that we have few surprises." Even the bleak smile faded now. "An expression on our island is, 'Who are his people?' which means the man's family history. We are much guided by our history."

I dredged up what I could from a college course on European History. "Here in the United States, we learned about your Leif Ericsson discovering North America before Christopher Columbus."

A grunt, which took me a moment to realize stood for Karlsdottir's laugh. "Only a very small part of this history, John Francis. Iceland held its first parliament, avoided civil war over religions, *and* discovered North America, all before the year one thousand after Christ."

Deciding my own heritage didn't pose a real comeback to that, I concentrated on my driving.

Karlsdottir warmed to her subject. "We have our sagas, books of ancient days in an institute of culture, to tell the stories of such things, the pages to be read through boxes of glass. Our men of Iceland left to explore in their ships, with *atgeir* and *sax.*"

"Sorry?"

"Ah, no. I should be sorry. The '*sax*' is a sword, short with only one side made sharp."

I thought of a pirate's cutlass.

"And the *atgeir* is . . . when you put the blade of the hatchet on a short-also spear?"

"Halberd, I think, is the word in English."

A nod. "Hal . . . berd. Good. But when our men are away, the women must grow strong to work the farm, even to become war chieftains to defend the home."

"Makes sense."

Karlsdottir nodded. "If in ancient days someone did a crime of violence, the family of the victim takes the blood vengeance. Later days, the criminal was made 'outlaw,' to receive no food or water, horse or aid from any other Icelander. Three years for less crime, forever if bad crime. But now, even for beating of wife or taking of children for sex, no real punishing for 'outlaw.' "

I thought about Boston's horrendous priest-rape scandals, somewhat resolved by recent settlements totaling nearly a hundred million dollars. "Modern civilization has a blind spot about some things, Freydis, but eventually, justice kicks in."

"Justice." She turned to me, then turned back. "Perhaps, John Francis."

"Hey, you can't come through that gate without a hard hat. *And* a pass."

There was a slight Southern lilt to the man's words. Outside the open gate in the chain-link fence, Freydis Karlsdottir turned to me, a confused expression on her face. "What is . . . 'pass'? Like for the entering of airplane?"

"Stay here, and let me handle it."

I walked halfway to the burly black guy who'd challenged us, in a hard hat himself. Despite the dusty bluejeans and a torn flannel shirt, he held a clipboard in one hammy hand, and I drew the impression of a foreman, not a laborer. "This young lady and I would like to ask some questions."

"Don't have time for questions, man." He waved the clipboard at the skyscraper-in-progress behind him that was producing one hell of a symphony. Assuming jackhammers, welding equipment, and nail guns were your idea of orchestral instruments. "Got an 'unparalleled tower of luxury condominiums' to build."

If the guy was cynical enough to quote company hype, a bluff might work. "Look, it's about one of your workers who got injured here. You can answer my questions now, conveniently, or traipse into a lawyer's office for a few days of depositions. Your choice."

A disgusted expression for me, then an appraising one as he looked to Karlsdottir. "It's the guy from Iceland, right?"

"Good guess, Mr. . . . ?"

"Monroe. Lionel Monroe."

I took out my leather ID holder and showed him the laminated copy of my investigator's license.

Monroe shook his head. "Mr. Cuddy, anything like this is supposed to go through the office folks first. They say okay, then I can talk to you."

Seemed a reasonable policy, though not very helpful for my purposes. "It's not about the comp claim. We're just trying to locate Hogni Ragnarsson."

"Hogni," with a grunted laugh, nearly like Karlsdottir's. "All the whites on this site who make fun of Afro first names like 'Latrell' or 'Deoncey,' and this guy's is 'Hogni.'" Another look at Karlsdottir. "She family of the man?" "No. Just trying to give him something from a friend of his."

Monroe used the thumb of his free hand to push back the cuff of his shirt. "Watch says I got five minutes, but outside the gate, or the boss'll have my ass for a 'significant safety violation.'"

We moved shoulder to shoulder back to where Karlsdottir waited.

I said, "This is Mr. Monroe, and—"

He cut me off with a sidelong look as he spoke to her. "Hogni, he told me you Icelanders like first names, right?"

The beaming smile from my client, and I sensed we had Monroe won over.

She said, "Yes. And Freydis is mine."

Karlsdottir stuck out her right hand, and, after slapping his palm, against a bluejeaned thigh, he shook with her.

"Then I'm Lionel. Now, what can I tell you?"

"Where Hogni now lives in your city?"

Monroe continued ignoring me to focus on her. "Don't know, Freydis. I recollect that he used a post-office box," another wave of the clipboard back toward the building, "but I never ran into him outside the site here."

The P.O. box might at least indicate Ragnarsson's local neighborhood. "Lionel, do you—"

He snapped his head toward me this time. "I told Freydis she could use my first name, not you."

Didn't want to lose him. "Sorry, Mr. Monroe."

"I mean, like, it's their custom to use first names, not ours, right?"

"Right."

"Okay." Monroe huffed out a breath and returned to Karlsdottir. "Let me tell you all I know about Hogni, and then you both be on your way."

"Yes?" she replied, in a tone that implied she was also trying to keep him talking.

"We're not a union shop here, and your Hogni was big and strong enough, I thought we could use him. Went fine for maybe a week. Matter of fact, he went on about how in Iceland everybody works, account of it's your way. Two, three jobs even, stuff being so expensive on an island because everything's got to be imported. Hogni told the boys stories about eating horse steaks and smoked eels and—what did he call it? Oh, yeah: 'wind-dried puffin,' that cute little bird looks kind of like a duck crossed with a penguin."

"Our tradition from ancient days."

Another huff. "Then one morning I hear him on our coffee break, asking the other guys questions about what happens, you get yourself hurt on the job. And, what do you know, next afternoon, Hogni takes himself a fall. I saw it, would have hurt anybody, but before the end of the week, man's filing for workers' comp, claiming he can't move on his leg."

Like a huge pigeon, Monroe bobbed his head forward. "Freydis, I'm sorry if he's a friend of yours, but I don't think that 'work ethic' stuff from back home sunk into Hogni too well." Now to me. "Okay, that's it."

"Not quite, Mr. Monroe."

"Say what?"

"Do you remember the local post office where Mr. Ragnarsson rented his box?"

A final huff. "No. You can call the company office and ask, but I'll tell you now, they won't give it out." Lionel Monroe turned away from us. "'The privacy rights of our employees are paramount.'"

• • •

Back in the car—and the bumper-to-bumper traffic—I said to Karlsdottir, "You must be pretty tired, the jet lag and all."

She blinked a few times, then rubbed the heels of her hands over both eyes. "For true, but also we must see Hogni's lawyer, yes?"

"We're a little late in the day for that, Freydis. Can I buy you dinner—or whatever other meal your body clock's telling you it wants?"

"My body . . . clock?"

"Do you feel like lunch instead of dinner?"

"Ah. No, John Francis. My . . . body clock makes the sound for dinner."

" 'Chimes.' "

I sensed the confused look without turning toward her. "The sound a clock makes on each hour. We say it 'chimes.' "

The silhouette in profile of her solemn nod. "A lovely word. It is to the ear as the sound it describes."

I agreed, though I thought we might save "onomatopoeic" until the morning.

"You are a good guide for restaurants as well, John Francis."

I'd brought her to Silvertones, a restaurant and bar roughly halfway between her hotel and my office, so I could leave the Prelude in a parking space I rent behind the building. Silvertones is in a cavernous basement and serves mainly comfort food, but it's well prepared by the husband-and-wife team who run the place, and not knowing much about Icelandic fare beyond "horse/eel/puffin," I'd hoped Karlsdottir could find something on their menu that she'd like.

Over a second glass of wine, and halfway through our meals, my new client hooded her eyes, I thought at first from fatigue. Then she said, "The African man at the construction fence. He stood . . . above you?"

I recalled the "first-name" exchange. "Stood *up* to me, Freydis."

"Just so." A sip from her glass. "Confrontation. But what made him offended?"

How to provide her a short version? "Africans first came to this country as slaves, kidnapped from their villages over there."

"This I know of."

"Their white masters here would give them first names, but broke up—separated—families to sell them. At auction."

Karisdottir's eyes grew wide. "As in a . . . place of market?"

"Yes." Fast forward. "More recently, there were many aspects of discrimination, and one was for a white person to call a black person by a first name instead of 'Mr.' or 'Ms.' and the last name."

"As though still the black person, is a . . . slave?"

"Or that would be the insult the black person would assume." I tried to lighten things a little. "Different in your country, eh?"

"As to the tradition of first name, yes." The bleak smile, and she seemed to really be crashing on our differential in time zones. "About the slavery and the race, not so different, perhaps. In ancient days of the Vikings, my people raided and pillaged in their boats to the south, bringing women—and girls—of Ireland back to our island, as slaves and forced wives. And my father told me that when NATO first came with an Air Force base at our Keflavik just fifty years past, the Iceland government required no black soldiers be sent to us. But we have grown. One family in twenty in my country—the word is 'adopt,' yes?—the Vietnam people who leave by boat after your war there is over."

And it had been *my* war, all right. But one in . . . ? "Freydis, five percent of your population adopted those children?"

"I tell you before, John Francis: We believe in family. And courage, to do the right thing. I carry the name of a woman from the Saga of Eirik the Red. That Freydis was pregnant but joined battle with her men against the Native Americans who fought us in your 'new world,' yes? When the natives attacked her, she lifted the sword of a killed Viking, pulled her clothing down to display one of her breasts, and hit the side of the blade against it." Karlsdottir mimed smacking herself there with the palm of her right hand. "The natives run away from Freydis then."

The things you learn. But Karlsdottir now used her hand to stifle a yawn, and I thought it was time to call it a night. "Can I walk you to your hotel?"

A tired, but beaming, smile. "Please, yes."

I settled our tab, and we climbed up Silvertones' internal stairs to the street. Two more blocks, and we were at the entrance to her hotel.

Karlsdottir turned to me and said, "In the duty-free shop, I purchased a bottle of brandy. Would you share some with me?"

"In your room?"

"Just so, John Francis."

"I don't think we should."

The eyes hooded again, though differently. "My name is Freydis, but I am not pregnant, and I will not defend myself with a sword." Now the trace of her beaming smile. "Also, I am not so tired as you may think."

"I'm flattered. And honored, Freydis. But even if you were not a client, I lost my wife to cancer, and I still grieve for her."

Those ghost eyes welled with tears. "Grieve I know of, John Francis." She turned halfway to the entrance. "So, I go to my bed, and you go to yours."

Yes, but not yet.

The cemetery staff is pretty good about leaving the gates open at night, so that people with demanding work schedules can still visit. I walked up the hillside to her row and then to her stone, knowing I could find it even on a starless night.

No flowers, John? I guess the honeymoon really IS over.

I looked down at the etched letters that would forever form "MARY ELIZABETH DEVLIN CUDDY," even though the absence of light made them unreadable. "I tried, Beth. The florist shops were all closed."

What made you so late?

I told her.

The woman comes all the way from Iceland to find this "Hogni," but she doesn't have the envelope with his P.O. box on it?

"She couldn't find it, and besides, there are other ways."

I don't know, John. Doesn't feel right somehow.

I looked down at the harbor. A police boat was out with

its distinctive blue running lights, but otherwise a quiet autumn evening.

"Well," I said, "worst thing, I'm helping a stranger keep a promise to her dad."

My poor widower and his sense of "promise."

I thought back to Freydis Karlsdottir's "brandy" offer, and now it was my turn to nod solemnly.

4.

"What's that?" I said the next morning, still behind the wheel, Freydis Karlsdottir not allowing the teenaged doorman outside her hotel to help with a rectangular wooden case—about long and wide enough to hold a croquet set—that she clutched to her chest.

"Part of Hogni's inheritance." Karlsdottir inclined her head to the trunk of the Prelude. "We can put this in your boot?"

I'd long ago disabled the lid release next to the driver's seat, so I had to get out to open it, the doorman doing his best to keep a straight face over the old fart in the old car picking up this exotic beauty of a hotel guest.

After Karlsdottir laid the case carefully into the trunk and we were on our way, she turned to me. "If you have the mobile telephone, John Francis, we call Hogni's lawyer first?"

I slipped my right hand into the side pocket of my suit jacket and flashed the little Nokia at her. "We could. However, I've generally found that it's best to surprise people."

"Surprise." The beaming smile as she turned forward again. "Perhaps not in Iceland, but in America, 'surprise' works good, yes?"

• • •

The lawyer's office proved to be a flat-faced storefront in a four-story building on the main drag of East Boston, a traditionally Italian-American neighborhood that had become a mixing pot—if not melting pot—of first-generation immigrants from a number of different countries, even continents. As I parked on the opposite side of the street and we got out of the car, a Delta airliner on its landing path roared low enough over our heads that you could almost expect tire tracks on the roof of the Prelude.

Karlsdottir reflexively ducked and blurted out something that wasn't recognizable. Then, "I hope we are near to your airport."

"Very close."

She looked around at the evident, if modest, apartments above the commercial level. "How do the people sleep with such noise?"

I thought about smaller, slower planes rattling the window frames of my family's rowhouse in South Boston when I was growing up. "It's an acquired skill."

We crossed the street to the Law Offices of Michael A. Nuzzo. His picture windows were pasted with decals reading *"SE HABLA ESPAÑOL"* and what I guessed were similar messages from several other languages. Inside the doorway stood three desks and as many young women behind them forming their own miniature United Nations. The placards in front of them were printed with "ITALIAN," "SPANISH," and "CAMBODIAN," small cribs of clear plastic holding business cards nearby. Ringing the floor space around the reception area were four-drawer file cabinets. Lots of them.

The first two women were on the telephone, leaving the

third—staffing the Cambodian station—to look up at us from a computer screen.

A professional smile before, "May I help you?"

I said, "We'd like to see Mr. Nuzzo, please."

"Is he expecting you?"

"No," I showed her my ID, "but he'll want to see us nonetheless."

The smile wavered, but she took my license holder in one hand while she hit a number on the telephone pad with her other. Swinging in the swivel chair away from me, she spoke softly into the receiver, then nodded and turned back. "That door."

There were only two at the back of the reception area, and one had the familiar symbol for a unisex restroom. Karlsdottir followed me to the second, and I knocked just as its handle turned.

The door swung inward, showing a background of manilla files stacked in teetering towers on the floor and against two walls. The short man looking up at me was about forty, with black hair beating a retreat above his temples, leaving a little tuft of wayward strands at the crown and a moat of scalp around it. Nuzzo wore a dress shirt and suit pants, but no tie, and his belly sagged over his belt. In his hand he had a cell phone.

"What's this all about?"

"Sorry," I said. "You on a call?"

He looked down at the cellular. "No, the damned thing's not working. Won't even tell time."

I stuck out my hand. "John Cuddy."

He shook it without obvious enthusiasm. "Michael Nuzzo."

"And this is my client, Ms. Freydis Karlsdottir."

He seemed to appraise the tall woman whose shadow loomed over him. "Well, come on in."

Nuzzo had to move another pile of files from one of his own client chairs to give both of us places to sit. As we did, he moved around his desk and dropped the useless cellular on top of it. "What can I do for you?"

"We're looking for a friend of Ms. Karlsdottir's father."

"What makes you think I know him?"

"Him," not "this person" or other ambiguity. "You represent the man on a workers' compensation claim."

"Hey," gesturing toward the files, "you got any idea how *many* comp cases I do a year?"

It seemed a bit of a non sequitur, but I've always felt you learn more by letting attorneys in any speciality talk. "You want to tell us?"

Nuzzo gave me a sour look. "When I got out of law school fifteen years ago, you could make a good living off comp. Hell, in 'ninety-five, there were over forty thousand claims filed with the Commonwealth statewide. Then Governor Willie may-he-burn-in-hell Weld, a blueblood who never did manual labor a single day in his life, got the legislature to cut benefits from sixty-seven percent of the weekly wage to sixty, and the benefit period from five years down to three. And now there's less than half as many claims filed as back in 'ninety-one."

Karlsdottir broke in with the question I was about to ask. "But you must keep a list of all workers you help and the place they live, yes?"

Nuzzo stared at her. "Confidential."

That seemed a little overprotective, since we'd already told him we knew he represented our boy. "Hogni Ragnarsson."

The lawyer didn't flinch or even squint at the unusual name. "Confidential."

Karlsdottir leaned forward in her chair. "I have from my father an inheritance for Hogni."

Nuzzo perked up. "Inheritance?"

I said, "The reason we're trying to find Mr. Ragnarsson."

"Well—" a pursing of the lips—"you could make out a check to me, and I could pass it on to him."

"If you represent the man," I said.

Nuzzo shot me another sour look.

Karlsdottir shook her head. "I must give this to Hogni for my family. It is a matter of honor."

Nuzzo stood up. "Then I guess this conference is over."

My client started to speak, but I squelched her by rising also. "Thanks for your time."

"Don't mention it."

As we left his office, I put a finger to my lips so that Karlsdottir would hold her peace. On our way past the Cambodia desk, I thanked the woman while plucking one of Nuzzo's business cards from its plastic crib.

Out on the sidewalk, Karlsdottir tugged on my coat sleeve. "John Francis, why did you not—"

I motioned her to move with me beyond the angles of sight allowed by the picture windows. Then I took out my cell phone and dialed that buddy of mine at Verizon again while crossing the street toward the Prelude.

"Who do you call?"

I shook my head as I heard my friend pick up. "It's John Cuddy."

"Twice in one day?" came back from a transmitting tower somewhere.

"Another favor, yeah. Right about now, there's a call going out on—" I glanced down at Nuzzo's card and read off the ten-digit office number—"and I need to know the address it's going to."

"Cuddy, you make a better enemy than a friend."

"I'll wait patiently."

As I did, we reached my car, and Freydis Karlsdottir treated me to her beaming smile.

5.

It took us less than five minutes to reach the address, also in Eastie, that my friend gave me. The number belonged to the pay phone in a rooming house, one that had seen better days, that we were pulling up outside now.

"Hogni is like me," said Karlsdottir, giving another solemn nod. "He goes to the professional most close to him."

I set the parking brake as my client said, "Please, to open the boot?"

As we both moved around to the back of the car, Karls-dottir added, "John Francis, already you have been such a good guide to me. I should see Hogni alone, yes?"

I keyed the lid, but she reached in before I could help her take the wooden case out. "Hey, Freydis, we've come this far together, I'd like to meet the guy."

Karlsdottir clutched the case to her chest, nodding uncertainly now.

We began walking up the path to the rooming house's front door. About halfway there, it flew open, and a tall, redheaded man burst onto the stoop, looking down at the steps and limping down them, too, with a duffel bag in his left hand. The door—maybe on a spring—slammed behind him as he hit the path and looked up to see us.

And to freeze.

Which is when I found myself on my knees, registering that I'd been struck over my right ear, the pain expanding geometrically through my skull. As I lost even that precarious balance and pitched forward, I managed to get my palms out in a modified push-up to break the rest of the fall, ending up on all fours and low to the ground.

Karlsdottir's voice above me said, "John Francis, I am so sorry."

The redheaded man yelled her first name, then a string of what I guessed to be Icelandic.

With that, Karlsdottir strode around and in front of me, tossing a short, broad sword toward his feet and brandishing an axe on a short handle with a spear point at its business end.

In English, "cutlass" and "halberd."

Karlsdottir yelled back at Ragnarsson, "Hogni," and then her own indecipherable statement.

He dropped the duffel bag, but made no move for the sword, instead limping backward with his hands up in "stop" signs and baying in Icelandic.

She advanced on him in a herringbone pattern, first angling left, then right, the halberd held with both hands like a batter in baseball stalking a pitcher who'd just plunked him at the plate.

Ragnarsson, cringing and babbling now, tripped over the last step of the stoop and fell backward, his head nearly at the closed door, crying out in pain but also, I thought, pleading.

It did him no good.

Karlsdottir arrived over him and brought the axe down as if she was felling a horizontal tree, the blade, on impact, making a sickening *thock* as Ragnarsson fell silent.

I closed my eyes, thinking I'd just witnessed an example of what "smote" means.

When I opened my eyes again, Karlsdottir was kneeling in front of me, her hands empty, but Ragnarsson's blood spattered over them as well as over her face and clothes.

"Freydis . . . ?"

"John Francis, true I am sorry. But Hogni in Iceland did rape on my young sister while he was to be caring for her in his house, as I was caring for my father in ours. My sister is in mental hospital forever from the attack of Hogni, yet the courts ordered him to jail for no time. And so he comes here, to escape me." Karlsdottir's eyes drifted northeastward. "I promise to my father as he dies I will take blood vengeance for my sister, because I am the only one of our family who can do just so."

I shook my head, the consequent pain nearly blocking my words. "But the inheritance . . . ?"

Freydis Karlsdottir's bleak smile. "In our tradition, inheritance and vengeance are two sides of the same road, John Francis."

I think I said, "A matter of honor," just before blacking out.

Low Drama

Kim Harrington

Kim Harrington lives in Massachusetts with her husband and son. Though she's currently writing mostly crime fiction, she's also had over thirty horror stories published in anthologies and magazines under a pseudonym. She has a B.S. in marketing and an M.B.A., and lives in New England with her family. Her work has also appeared in *Shred of Evidence, Crime Scene Scotland, Hard-luck Stories,* and the anthology *Best New Noir.*

I gazed at the red oozing glob sliding up and down my line of vision.

"You like it, don't you," Donna said. "At first you thought it was dumb, but now you like it. I catch you watching it all the time."

My roommate at medical school, Donna, was nice enough, though she cared altogether too much about my opinion. We shared a small two-bedroom apartment in university housing, which she insisted on decorating in retro-style. Her bedroom had no door, just beads. She installed an orange shag carpet in our living room. On the rare occasion that we had people over, she hung a disco ball over her record player. I thought it was a little fun and quirky at first, but it quickly became annoying and that shag carpet was a bitch on my allergies.

But I have to admit I dug the lava lamp.

"Yeah, I like it. Happy now?"

"Happy as a dog sniffing an asshole." She waltzed over and sniffed me. "You wearing perfume?"

"Yeah, I've got a hot date."

She feigned cardiac arrest, pumping at her chest with her fist. "Polly Prissypants, the all-study, no-play, little chemist is sticking her toe in the water again after her string of failed experiments with dating. Oh me, oh my."

I swear if she called me Polly Prissypants one more time, I'd fucking slap her, then drive one thousand miles to slap my mother for naming me Polly in the first place. And I was getting sick of her little digs about chemistry as if I was less of a person for not wanting to be a surgeon like her. "Yes, it's true. Don't faint, though, it's only dinner."

"How did you meet him?"

I knew I should lie, but didn't. "One of those Internet dating sites where you take a long-ass questionnaire and then they match you up with a bunch of guys based on their secret compatibility quotient. You read all their ads and pick the ones you like. Go ahead, laugh."

"I'm not gonna laugh."

Now it was my turn to show shock. "Huh?"

"The last guy you went on a date with was convinced the

end times were coming in four weeks and wanted to save your soul so you could be together in the afterlife. The guy before that seemed cool until he asked you to tie him up and attach jumper cables to his nipples. You don't seem to have good people radar, Polly. No offense. Maybe this dumb website can do a better job. It couldn't possibly do worse."

I stood up and smoothed my blouse. "You've got me there. I gotta go. We're meeting at Falconi's."

"The townie restaurant? He couldn't take you to a nice place in the city?"

"Neither of us has cars. It's walking distance, it's easy."

"Wait, he's a grad student here, too?"

"Yeah." I inched toward the door. I didn't want to be late.

"What's his name?"

"Gerry Spindle."

Donna's face paled, then her eyes darkened, and she grabbed my arm. "You cannot go out with him."

"Why?"

"He's, he's, he's too intense."

"Intense is good. I like intense."

"Not good intense. More like 'Hello Clarice' intense. He's a psycho."

My stomach clenched. I'd felt good about this one. Figures. "How do you know him?"

"I went to undergrad with him. He's crazy."

"He seems fine to me. We chatted online for hours the other night. His ad was exactly what I'm looking for."

"What did his ad say?"

I felt like I was sixteen again, in the kitchen with my parents, begging to go out and be a normal teenager. "I didn't memorize it. Something about how he's fun-loving with a sense of humor, but he's a serious student and can balance work and play. He's not into games, he's low maintenance and low drama. That's what I want. Low drama."

Donna crossed her arms and tapped a manicured fingernail on her elbow. "Dating a serial killer will give you a lot of drama."

"So now he's a serial killer."

"I told you I went to undergrad with him. His girlfriend from back then disappeared."

"Maybe she dropped out, went home."

"Or maybe he cut her up into 32 pieces, folded her in a tarp, and dumped her in the river."

"Donna, you're being ridiculous. He seems nice. We're in a public place. I'm not going to be anywhere alone with him until I know him much better anyway."

She twisted around and stormed into her room. Luckily, she didn't have a door to slam. She called out as I left, "Don't come crying to me if you find yourself tied up in the boiler room!"

The restaurant was only five minutes away, but by the time I got there I was nervous. What the hell did I know about Gerry anyway? Yeah, he seemed nice but so did the last two guys and they were batshit crazy. I obviously had no intuition.

I found Gerry sitting at a booth with his hands around a mug of beer. His face lit up when I walked in, and I felt better already.

"You look just like your picture," I said, and I was happy about that. He was boyishly cute with a tossed up mop of black hair, wire-rimmed glasses, and dimples on either side when he smiled.

"I hope you don't mind that I ordered a drink already. To be honest, I was a little nervous and needed to take the edge off."

"I was nervous, too." Nervous you were going to tell me to put the lotion in the basket.

"But I feel better already just sitting here with you." He smiled again, and I was smitten like a schoolgirl gazing at *TeenBeat* magazine.

Dinner went great. He was everything I wanted him to be: smart, funny, ambitious, intellectual, interesting. He held my hand as we walked back to graduate housing, and I walked slow and took deep breaths and stared at the stars and noticed all the beautiful things I usually walk right by with my head down. He was different than the other guys; he truly had nothing up his sleeve, no games.

Donna's words echoed in a dark little corner of my mind.

I glanced over at him, a little miffed at myself for falling so hard so quick. If I found out he lied to me about anything, I'd gouge his eyes out.

We stopped at the door to my building, and he was a gentleman. He didn't ask to come in and when I kissed him lightly, he didn't force his tongue into my esophagus. He said he'd call me tomorrow, and I believed him.

Until I let myself in the building and what felt like a concrete block slammed into my head and my vision faded to black.

I opened my eyes into a world of hurt. My head throbbed and as I turned my head to try to figure out where I was, my stomach lurched and I threw up onto my lap. I was tied to a chair, bound at the waist and ankles with my hands tied behind my back. A low growl hummed behind me. My eyes adjusted to the darkness and I figured it out.

I was in the boiler room.

"That would be the concussion. Vomiting, it's a symptom. But, don't worry, soon enough after I start cutting you'll go into shock and you won't feel anything."

Someone drifted out of the blackness of the corner, a shadow with a voice I recognized. "You weren't out long, only five minutes. I don't even have all my tools sharpened yet."

Donna.

I gasped.

She laughed. "You really have no grasp on people, Polly. You never even suspected."

"You . . . you . . . help him do this?"

"Help him? God, you're stupid. Gerry has nothing to do with this."

The furnace roared behind me, and I winced as it echoed in my head. Through the pain, it took me a moment, but the truth finally sunk in. "So, the other girl that dated him, the one who disappeared—"

"I lied about that. Gerry didn't cut her up into thirty-two pieces. I did, and it was thirty-three pieces."

She inched closer to me, sizing me up. "You're a little taller than she was. I can probably make an even forty out of you."

"Why do you do this? What, did he dump you, break your heart, and now you kill his girlfriends out of petty jealousy?"

She frowned. "You really think that little of me? Sure, jealousy's a part of it, I've got to be honest, but it's not just about keeping Gerry away from other women. It's about being the best. There is no better way to practice my craft than on real, live people. I'm going to be the best fucking surgeon this school has ever created."

The boiler was clanging now, a metallic consistent bang

that made me think my head would explode. I puked again, violently retching, heaving and choking. I opened my eyes and my shirt was covered in blood.

But not mine. Donna stood in front of me, eyes wide in shock, a metal pipe sticking out of her stomach. I felt hands at my hands, then my ankles, then my waist and I was free, standing up and falling down and crawling backward out of the room as a pool of dark crimson leaked from Donna's body onto the floor.

Gerry pulled me up and into his arms. "I'm so sorry. I went back to get another kiss, maybe see if you wanted to invite me in, and saw what Donna did to you. I followed you two down here. I was scared shitless at first but when I heard what she had done to Jessica." He shook his head. "This whole time I thought she just ran off."

I pushed him away. "I don't care."

He grabbed for me, eyes pleading. "I didn't have anything to do with this! I haven't dated Donna since I was twenty. She's just a stalker that's always in the background. She followed me to medical school, leaves me notes, prank calls me, but I thought that was it. I never meant for you to be in harm's way. Please don't push me away."

I closed my fist and smashed it into his nose. Then stormed off and called the police from a neighbor's phone. No second chances for liars. After all, his ad said low drama.

Jury Duty

Kristine Kathryn Rusch

Kristine Kathryn Rusch is an award-winning and bestselling mystery, romance, science fiction, and fantasy writer. The former editor of *The Magazine of Fantasy and Science Fiction*, Rusch has been honored with the Ellery Queen Readers Choice Award, the John W. Campbell Award, the Herodotus Award for Best Historical Mystery Novel (for her Kris Nelscott Series), and the *Romantic Times* Reviewers Choice Award for Best Paranormal Romance. Her story, "Echea," won the Homer Award and the Asimov's Reader's Choice Award, and was nominated for Locus, Nebula, and Sturgeon awards. In 1999, she also won the Ellery Queen Reader's Choice Award and the Science Fiction Age Reader's Choice Award, making her the first writer to win three different reader's choice awards for three different stories in two different genres in the same year. Rusch is also the only person in the history of the science fiction field to have won a Hugo award for both editing and fiction. Her short work has been reprinted in six Year's Best collections. Her fiction has appeared in *EQMM*, *AHMM*, *Asimov's*, *Rosebud*, SciFi.com, and in numerous anthologies. Currently, she is working on pieces in several series: the Retrieval Artist series in Science Fiction; the Smokey Dalton Series in Mystery (written as Kris Nelscott); and the Fates series in Romance (written as Kristine Grayson).

Pamela sat in the center of the courtroom, not too close to the front because she didn't want to call attention to herself, and not in the back because she didn't want people to think she was hiding. She had done everything she could to blend in: she wore no make-up, and her clothes were Northwest business casual—a pair of brown slacks with an off-white sweater. With her left hand, she fingered her juror number—267—thoughtfully provided on a little wooden key chain so that she wouldn't lose it.

The court clerk pulled numbers out of a box and handed them to the judge. He was balding, and the top of his head shone in the fluorescent lights. His nasal voice boomed through the courtroom without the aid of a microphone, "Five-hundred-and-eighty-one. Five, eight, one."

As the unlucky man rose from his seat on the left side of the courtroom, the remaining members of the jury pool swiveled to watch him walk toward the jury box. Six people sat there already, hands folded, heads down, waiting.

The judge had said they would pick twenty-seven, enough for two juries and three extras. Both juries would listen to the case, although one jury would be designated as "alternate." The remaining three people were alternates also, added protection for a death penalty case that could last over a month.

Pamela had been called up two weeks ago, along with 1,000 others out of this county of 50,000, and she had stood in her kitchen, clutching the letter, feeling an uncomfortable sense of irony.

When she had come to Rickets Rock, a town so small that it seldom showed up on any map, she had decided that she would live as quietly as she could. She didn't want to draw attention to herself, good or bad. That meant getting a driver's license, registering to vote, being a good citizen. It meant concocting a history, and trying to smile at the locals. It meant lying, each and every day.

The jury summons had caught her in the lie: she couldn't back out because she had used a false name on her voter registration form. She had to go along with the fiction that she was Pamela Jackson, and hope that something about Pamela would keep her off the largest and most notorious jury the county had seen in decades.

"Juror thirty-four," the judge said. "Three-four."

A woman two seats from Pamela stood, and nearly tripped as she tried to get out of the row. Pamela kept turning her number over and over, the hard wood edges catching on her fingertips.

She had decided, when she had gone to orientation and received the outrageously long questionnaire, that she wouldn't lie if at all possible: she knew that trying to remember too many lies had tripped up more than one person.

So she had placed her personal views on the pages, thinking that they would disqualify her. Particularly the carefully-worded questions on pages 10 through 13, the ones about law, the death penalty, and murder.

Question 33: *Do you believe that some acts are so heinous that they can only be punished by death?*

To which she had replied: *Yes.*

Question 50: *Have you known or are you related to anyone who was murdered?*

To which she had replied: *Yes*

And Question 117: *Do you believe Raymond Northrup is guilty of the crimes of which he has been accused?*

To which she had replied: *I could care less.*

She had felt certain that the defense attorney, going through the questionnaires, would demand she be taken out of the jury pool, especially when she had had to explain her answer to question 50 on a later questionnaire. (*How was the deceased related to you?* Husband; *Explain the circumstances of the death:* He was a jackass. Of course, she didn't write that. Instead, she made up a lie about a beloved uncle who died in a convenience store robbery.)

"Two-sixty-seven," the judge said. "Two, six, seven."

Pamela's hand clenched around the number. She touched her round juror button, pinned to her sweater, and cursed silently. Her luck had abandoned her.

Now her goal was to be dismissed in the voie dire.

She grabbed her book—Patricia Cornwell's treatise on forensics and Jack the Ripper—and slung her purse over her shoulder.

Then Pamela eased out of the row, past the loggers and the truck drivers and the waitresses, and walked, head down, shoulders slumped forward, to the jury box.

Her heart was pounding. She had often pictured herself in a courtroom, but not here, not among the jury.

Instead, she expected to be at the tables, an attorney

beside her, defending what was left of her miserable little life.

Another half hour went by before the rest of the twenty-seven victims were chosen. Then the questioning began, starting with the first juror picked, a dapper man who was the only person in the room, besides the attorneys, to wear a suit. Fifteen minutes into his voie dire, he was dismissed for claiming he did not have a strong stomach.

As he stepped down, the clerk drew a new number from the box, and another prospective juror took the first juror's place.

Pamela noted the excuse, and apparently so had the second juror. He made the same claim, which caused the judge to issue a gusty sigh.

"If we dismiss everyone with a weak stomach, we'll have no one left." He faced the defense attorney, who had posed the question. "If you believe these crimes are too graphic, we'll make sure there'll be no crime scene photos after lunch and we'll provide sickness bags, just like the airlines. Now, move on."

Pamela was the first up after the luncheon break. She returned to the courtroom loggy from the personal pan she'd had at the nearby Pizza Hut, and exhausted by a morning of listening to other people's lives.

During lunch she had toyed with changing her strategy, possibly saying that she did not approve of the death penalty or that she did not believe a person was innocent until proven guilty. But all of those answers would have contradicted her juror's questionnaire, a questionnaire that had informed her on the top of every page that her answers had the force of answers given under oath.

A new answer would call attention to her. If she was lucky, she would escape without much attention being paid to her at all.

Finally, the attorneys reached her. She had to repeat her name and her address.

"You own a bookstore, Ms. Jackson?" The prosecutor, Daphne Sullivan, stood in front of the jury box. She was a middle-aged woman who wore a stylish black suit that seemed out of place in this small county.

"Yes." Main Street Books, the new-and-used bookstore she had opened in what passed for Rickets Rock's down-town. When she had first received her jury letter, she had hoped that being a small business owner would disqualify her, but the clerk of courts had quizzed her, found out that she had a part-time assistant, and that the store some-times closed when Pamela planned a day off, and decided that the store could afford to lose Pamela for a few weeks with little or no hardship.

"Do you enjoy reading?" Sullivan asked.

"Yes."

"Do you often read books like that one?" Sullivan nodded at the Cornwell.

"Yes." That was a deliberate lie, one concocted to get Pamela off the jury.

"Would you hold the book up so that everyone can see it?"

Pamela did. Her copy, a hardcover with a shiny dust, looked black and official.

"We won't have to worry about a weak stomach with this one," the judge muttered, even his soft words echoing throughout the courtroom.

"Do you watch *C.S.I.*?" Sullivan asked.

"Sometimes," Pamela said.

"*Cold Case Files?* The forensics programs on The Learning Channel?"

"Sometimes," Pamela said.

"So you feel you have a grasp on the forensic side of police procedure?" Sullivan asked.

Pamela shrugged.

The judge said, "We'll need a verbal response for the record, Ms. Jackson."

"When you say 'a grasp,' I don't know what that means," Pamela said.

"Do you understand it?" Sullivan said.

"It's just science," Pamela said.

"And you understand science?"

Of course, you fool. I have more advanced degrees in biology and chemistry than you can dream up.

Pamela had to bite back the response. She wasn't a scientist now. She owned a bookstore. She was a mousy woman with mousy clothes who tried to disappear when people looked at her.

"I try to understand it," she said, which was as close to the truth as she could come.

"I have no problem with this juror," the prosecutor said, and turned toward the defense attorney, Jake Chivara.

He was too slick for this part of Oregon. His suit had the shine of silk, and his hands were manicured. His black hair had a layered cut that cost more than Pamela's entire outfit, but his eyes shone with an intelligence that she recognized as a match for her own.

He adjusted his suit coat as he walked toward the rail. "Do you consider murder your hobby?"

Her fingers clutched the book, its hard edges biting into her palm. "My hobby?"

He nodded toward the book she held. "You read about it. You watch television programs about it. You obviously think about it a lot."

True enough. She didn't like how perceptive he was. "I watch television programs about politics and biography and history, too, but I don't consider them my hobbies. I live alone. I run a bookstore. I read almost everything that comes through the door."

"But you brought that book for a reason, didn't you?" Chivara asked.

"To read while I waited," she said.

"You could have brought a romance novel," he said.

She shrugged. "I would have finished it in the time allowed. I wanted something that would last me all day."

"Be honest, Ms. Jackson. You brought that book so that we'd assume you know police procedure. You wanted to force us to kick you off the jury."

She looked at him in surprise and knew, at that moment, she had been caught. She had never been caught before, at least, not in her manipulations. It was a strange sensation.

Chivara smiled at her. "I don't like being manipulated, Ms. Jackson."

Pamela's hands slid on the book's cover. She was sweating.

"Your questionnaire says you believe that some crimes should be punished by death," Chivara said.

"Yes." She swallowed hard. This was the first time, in all of the questioning, that someone had mentioned the questionnaire.

"Does that mean you believe in the death penalty?" he asked.

"I haven't given it any thought." At least not in that way. The law was the law and she had nothing do with it. She didn't plan it nor could she change it. Human laws weren't immutable like scientific ones, but they existed and nowadays she did her best to live within them.

"Do you have a problem sending a man to his death?" he asked.

"Not in the right circumstances." Her answer had too much of an edge to it. She wished she could take the words back the moment she uttered them.

Chivara smiled again. "What sorts of circumstances, Ms. Jackson?"

Her mouth was dry. "I thought we were talking about the death penalty."

"We are. What circumstances? *These* circumstances?"

"If he did it," she said.

"Do you think he did it?" Chivara asked.

"I could care less," she said, repeating her answer from the questionnaire.

"Really? You don't care one way or another?"

She didn't like this attorney. He was irritating her. "Unless you put me on this jury, this crime has no impact on my life. I don't really care what that man did. I don't really care what the President does either, and he has a lot larger impact on my life than some petty murderer."

"Petty murderer," Chivara repeated softly. "You're quite interesting, Ms. Jackson. You know science and read about the law, but you say this case doesn't concern you. If we put you on the jury, would you care then?"

"Not really," she said. "I'd just be doing this because you're making me."

Chivara's smile became broad. "At least you're honest."

He walked back to his table, examined his notes, and then leaned over the railing, clearly speaking to his jury consultant.

Pamela's heart pounded hard. She tried to keep an impassive expression on her face, but she found it difficult. For the first time since she'd shown up in this courtroom, she was frightened.

After a moment, Chivara looked up.

"Ms. Jackson, do you know my client?" Chivara swept his arm toward the defendant. Until this moment, Pamela had refrained from looking at him.

She had seen his photograph on the county newspapers and once on the front page of the *Oregonian,* but she hadn't really looked at him. Nor had she looked at him the one or two times he waited on her.

"We've never formally met," she said.

"But you have met," the attorney said.

"He waited on me once at the Sneaker Wave," she said. "And at the Italian Noodle."

"Did you have a conversation?"

She shrugged, then added for the record, "Probably not."

"Probably not?" Chivara repeated.

"I go out alone with a book," she said. "I usually don't have conversations."

Truthful again.

Chivara's eyes narrowed, and she had the sense that he thought she was holding something back.

Chivara turned away, and she hoped he would dismiss her for cause. Instead, he said, "I have no problems with this juror."

The judge turned to her. "Is there any reason you believe you should not sit on this jury?"

Dozens. She had dozens of reasons, but none she could admit to. Neither attorney had given her a way out.

"I don't know if I can be impartial," she said, "given that I've met him."

The judge let out another of his gusty sighs. "The interactions you've had with the defendant are no different than sitting across a courtroom from him day in and day out. So give it a try, Ms. Jackson."

"Your honor," Chivara said, "this is why we wanted the trial moved."

"You made that motion and I dismissed it," the judge said. "If you want to try this case for the court of appeals and not for the jury, go ahead, Mr. Chivara. Otherwise, get over the loss and move on."

Pamela's cheeks were warm. Her ploy hadn't worked, might even have backfired.

"Juror two-six-seven," the judge said, "you'll be sitting on this case."

Since it was the off-season, the cut-rate hotel that the court used to sequester juries was happy to have them. The jurors even got to have their own rooms, a luxury for which Pamela was grateful. She didn't like company in the best of circumstances, and this certainly was not the best of circumstances.

That first two days in the courtroom were difficult, especially for the other jurors. The prosecution laid out its case, and the defense gave its own theory of the crime. Most of the jurors were already familiar with the crime, but the details made them squeamish.

Pamela didn't mind the details, but she had trouble wrapping her mind around the crime at all.

Apparently, the defendant, Raymond Northrup, arrived home one afternoon in a rage. He shot his wife, his two daughters, and his infant son, supposedly planning to kill himself as well. In the end, he chickened out (or "came to his senses," as Prosecutor Sullivan said), and called 9-1-1 instead. The paramedics arrived to find a house filled with blood, and Ray Northrup sitting on the couch, watching reruns of *The Simpsons* as if nothing were wrong.

The prosecution promised pictures and the tape of the 9-1-1 call; the defense promised experts showing how the police botched the investigation, figuring that they already had the killer when, of course, the defense claimed, they had not.

Pamela listened with—she thought—clinical detachment, picturing both versions of the crime: a man pushed to his limits by bills, sick children and a nagging wife, hauling the shotgun out of the front closet and turning it on all of them; and the same man pushed to his limits, who arrived home after a hard day's work as a waiter (he could get nothing else in this small town) to find his entire family slaughtered.

But the clinical detachment didn't take, or perhaps it was a façade, designed to fool even herself. For that night, and two nights thereafter, Pamela had the nightmare, the one she had fled when she had come to Oregon.

The images were jumbled: Jason stumbling backwards, his hand up; Jason on the floor, his face gone; Jason's blood staining the wall beside their stove. She started to grab things—her ring, his watch, their checkbook, and then she set them down.

She knew better—even her dreamself knew better—and instead, she took the cash from the drawer, and the bike leaning against the old Billingsly house next door.

More images from before: the water from the shower

draining pink; her clothing in the wash machine, the smell of bleach in the air; the half-eaten ham sandwich that had started it all.

She had been clutching it, trying to force it down, when he had walked in. *You can't do anything right,* she had said to him. *I wanted hot mustard, not sweet. Don't you ever listen?*

His voice, meek and soft, infuriated her, and at that moment, she woke up, covered in sweat, shaking, uncertain where she was, figuring at first it was some anonymous hotel on the trip west, then remembering how she had gotten herself into this new predicament years after the fact.

The hotel looked the same as the others: a double-bed barely bigger than the single she'd had in her first apartment; end-tables so cheap that if she leaned on them, they'd crack; a television set bolted to the dresser, and a double-size window with a single pane of glass so thin that it could shatter with the pressure of a determined fist.

Pamela got up and paced, her feet cold against the worn carpet. She was glad she was alone—who knew what she had cried out, what she had actually said?

That first night, she didn't go back to the bed, sleeping instead on the scratchy sofa, an equally scratchy blanket pulled over her scrunched-up form. She didn't sleep much and when she did, she dreamed of being uncomfortable, not of the past.

And she returned to that couch after every day of difficult testimony, after every photograph and replaying of the 9-1-1 call, until the clinical detachment she thought she had achieved that first day became an actual reality.

She could listen, store facts, theories, and opinions in one side of her brain, and kept them separate from the other side.

The emotion side.

The side that had always given her too much trouble.

Three-plus weeks of testimony, arguments, breaks and confusion. Three-plus weeks of "retiring" to the jury room to wait while the lawyers and the judge worked something out. Three-plus weeks of small talk with people who probably never would have entered her store, people who probably hadn't voluntarily picked up a book in their lives, people who—with the exception of the transplanted Californian—had never lived anywhere but here.

Small minds with nothing but television and the trial to occupy them. Talk of the trial was off-limits until the testimony was over, so the Small Minds discussed the previous night's *Frasier* or the *Buffy* rerun or the late-night movie they were given on tape so they wouldn't watch the local news and talk shows.

She didn't watch any of it. She didn't discuss any of it either, preferring to read. The guards—at least they felt like guards—let her assistant deliver books, sometimes four and five a day, and Pamela read rather than socialized. So long as her mind was busy, her body remained calm.

The guards would paw through the bags, of course, verifying that everything Pamela's assistant brought were books, verifying that her assistant hadn't hid a newspaper article about the trial as a bookmark, verifying that there was no note advising her how to vote at the end of the trial.

But no one looked at the titles either. She finished the Cornwell, moved onto a history of the fingerprint, then followed that with a history of the corpse. A few tomes on forensics, a study of ballistics, and of course, dozens and dozens of novels—all shapes and sizes.

She read and thought and listened, and wished she had known all of this years ago, before she had come west. She would have done things oh so very differently. How easy it would have been to make it seem like *he* had gotten angry over the sandwich, *he* had hit her repeatedly, *he* had grabbed the gun.

But she hadn't known any of it. She had done the best she could with the little bits of knowledge she had, and she had managed to escape.

She lived here now, a new life she mostly enjoyed, and saw no use re-evaluating every second of the past.

Then, finally, the moment arrived. The closing arguments ended, the jury instructions were repeated *ad naseum,* the defendant staring at jurors as if he were trying to fathom what each and every one of them were thinking.

This time, when they went into the jury room, there was a palpable sense of relief. The restrictions were off: they could discuss anything now, and the Small Minds all started to talk at once, offering opinions, offering advice, discussing what an ordeal they'd been through, how they couldn't stand the pictures.

Pamela couldn't stand the voices. Middle-class, grating, most of them with that slightly dulled speech she'd learned to recognize from locals. She sat in one of the upholstered chairs nearest the door, and wondered how she would get through this.

The jury room itself was small with two exits—one leading back into the courtroom, the other into the hallway. The room had no windows. Whoever had designed this room had certainly visited and obviously enjoyed the ambience of hell's anteroom, because even the temperature was correct: hot enough to make the already small space seem unbearably stuffy.

"Right, Ms. Jackson?"

She heard her name and looked up. The transplanted Californian was looking at her. He was a wiry blond with a scraggly mustache whose rope-thin body and denim shirt made him look like a man who belonged outdoors, not trapped in a room furnished with modular office chairs and a cheap fake-wood conference table.

"I'm sorry," she said, peering at his name badge. Z. Wilson. She should have learned his name in the past few weeks. She should have learned all of their names, but of course, she hadn't.

"I said, I think we should get around to electing a foreman first, then talk about the case. What do you think?" His blue eyes studied her with an openness she didn't like. Obviously he expected her to be on his side.

"Looks like you're already doing a fine job," she said. "We don't need a vote."

"We'll vote." His voice had that irritated edge Jason used to get when she didn't give him the answer he liked.

She leaned back in her chair, deciding to give Z. Wilson some distance.

The woman who wore the giant silver cross on the front of her blouse each and everyday reached to the center of the table and took twelve little pieces of paper from a notepad. Then she grabbed pencils and handed them out as if she were a school teacher.

She gave Pamela her paper and pencil last, smiling at her. Pamela did not smile back.

"Perhaps," said the Silver Cross, "perhaps we should say a small prayer so that God will guide our work."

"A small prayer?" Pamela asked, unable to keep silent in the face of this new irritation. "What kind of guidance do you want? Dearest God, please let us know if you want this killer to go free or if you want the state to fry him. Amen."

"Ms. Jackson," said the Californian. "That's enough."

She shrugged and pressed her lips together, but she had made her point. Two of the Small Minds who hadn't said anything yet—the first man chosen, and one of the other women—glared at Pamela as if she had killed the three children and the namby-pamby wife.

The wife, quite frankly, sounded like she deserved it, but the kids, well, Pamela didn't believe in killing kids. Kids couldn't be blamed for the situations they found themselves in. Only the parents were responsible for that.

"Write down the name of the person who you think most suited for jury foreman," the Californian said. "Then put your paper in this little bowl next to the notepad. Don't sign your name."

"Why don't we just have a real election?" Pamela asked, clutching her pencil. "You and whoever else is enough of a control freak to want this idiot job?"

"You mean you?" another Small Mind asked.

"I don't want it," Pamela said.

"Vote for whomever you'd like," the Californian said.

Pamela sighed and shook her head. Then she wrote down *Z. Wilson: Because I believe in validating power grabs,* folded the paper into tiny squares and set it in the bowl.

Hers was the sixth. One Small Mind—a twenty-something man who was already going bald—chewed his pencil and looked from person to person before writing on his paper. He was the eleventh to put his vote in the bowl. The Silver Cross lady was the last, and she looked spooked.

"Mr. Acenan," the Californian said to yet another Small Mind, "would you mind reading the results? Mrs. Dunbar will tally them."

The Dunbar woman took another sheet of paper from the stack and held her pencil poised. The man dug inside the bowl, removed a piece of paper and read the results aloud.

Pamela wished she could take the book out of her purse. Who would've thought that average citizens would take this job so very seriously?

The Small Mind reading the papers had finally gotten to Pamela's. He glanced at her, his face flushed, and only read the name, not the commentary.

"You know," Pamela said mildly, "censorship is against the law."

"And you're a disgrace," the Small Mind said, still clutching her paper. "Can't you be serious about this?"

She thought of answering him honestly, but she knew the word "no" would piss him off. So she said, "I just want to get down to business. I've already lost a month of my life to this mess. I don't want to lose another one because you people dither."

"An election isn't dithering, Ms. Jackson," the Californian said.

"You've already taken over," Pamela said. "Why do we have to bother with the election?"

"Because," the Californian said, "it's part of the instructions. See? Item four. Elect a jury foreperson."

"You said foreman before. Can I change my vote?" Pamela asked. "I didn't consider any women."

Someone made a sound of disgust. Mrs. Dunbar said loudly, "We already have a majority for Mr. Wilson. So he is our foreperson, unless there's an objection."

Pamela almost objected, just out of spite. She had to entertain herself somehow. But she was beginning to realize that her own antics might prolong this already painful situation, so she said nothing.

She crossed her arms and listened to Mr. California-Wilson read the jury instructions that the judge had already read to them, then ask if there were any questions that needed discussion or clarification before they got down to the "nitty-gritty."

Everyone said no, except Pamela, of course, who really didn't like the grade-school way this deliberation session was turning out. But she had decided to be quiet, and so she would be. She listened, or pretended to, while the jury discussed the rules, then reviewed the rules, and then discussed them even more.

Finally, at four o'clock, Mr. California-Wilson suggested that they take a preliminary vote—gosh! Just like the instructions suggested!—to see how far apart they all were. The vote would be anonymous, of course, and all the little pieces of paper would go into that damn bowl again.

She put her little piece of paper on top of her book, a novel called *A Certain Justice* which Pamela had chosen more out of irony than interest, and then paused.

She really hadn't given the fate of Mr. Raymond Northrup much thought, although she had done her part. She had listened, without prejudice and with that hard-won clinical detachment, to days and days of repetitive testimony, to

argumentative lawyers and bad judicial rulings, to witnesses who hadn't known a damn thing and to witnesses
who believed they had.

She had listened, she had absorbed, and she had come
to no conclusion.

Yet they were asking her for one now. And if she was
going to be the good citizen she was pretending to be, she
had to give a real opinion. She supposed finding him guilty
would get her out of here the quickest. After all, that was
what the Small Minds seemed to believe, if their post-trial
conversation was any indication.

But she couldn't write *guilty* on her piece of paper. Her
hand froze over the page every single time. She was stunned
to discover that the decision really did matter to her.

After all, she could have been the person sitting next to
Chivara. She could have been pacing some jail cell right now,
wondering if twelve disparate people would sentence her to a
lifetime of imprisonment. She owed Northrup as much consideration as she had, mostly because she hoped someone would
give her the same consideration if (when?) her time came.

She bit her lower lip, then glanced up at the bowl. It
looked full. A number of the Small Minds were staring at
her again.

Her hand shook over the paper. She gripped the pencil
tightly and wrote *Not,* leaving off the guilty. She didn't want
Mr. California-Wilson to misconstrue her intent.

She folded her piece of paper in half this time, just like
everyone else had, and then she shoved it into the bowl. The
Silver Cross woman grabbed it and handed it to California-
Wilson as if he weren't capable of grabbing it himself.

He nodded toward the Dunbar woman and she got out yet
another piece of paper so that she could tally the results.

Pamela expected more than one not-guilty vote. After all, it was pretty obvious that Northrup didn't have the balls to kill his entire family, no matter how angry and frustrated he got.

But she was the only not-guilty. California-Wilson tried not to ask for names, but she knew they'd find out, so she admitted it.

And that was when the clerk of the courts arrived, and told them to break for the night.

The next morning, the Small Minds had a game plan ready. They were going to review the evidence to convince her.

"Don't you want to know why I think he didn't do it?" Pamela asked.

"It doesn't matter what you think," Silver Cross said. "You obviously didn't care enough to listen."

"I listened," Pamela said. "I even made notes every evening. Did you people bother doing that?"

No one answered her. No one even looked at her.

"Look," she said. "I could change my vote so that we could get the hell out of here. Lord knows, I don't ever want to see you people again. But I don't think this guy did it, and I'm not going to send him to jail just because I want to sleep in my own bed tonight."

She was rather proud of herself. She sounded like a Real Citizen, like someone who cared about her fellow man.

"So," Mr. California-Wilson said with a notable lack of interest, "why do you think he didn't do it?"

"Because," Pamela said, careful to keep her tone respectful and polite, "he didn't run."

"Most people know better than to run," Wilson said.

"Most people know better than to kill their families," one of the Small Minds muttered.

"What?" Mrs. Dunbar asked.

The man shrugged. "I'm just saying if you're going to apply that kind of logic, then the whole case all falls apart."

The Small Minds argued among themselves for a long time, apparently forgetting that Pamela was the one they had to convince to change her mind. For a while, she thought she had convinced a few of them, but no.

They simply liked arguing.

And another day went by without any progress at all.

The week blurred into a series of questions and answers, followed by arguments.

"Ms. Jackson," someone asked at one point, "how can you think he didn't do it? He was covered in blood."

"So was the house," she said. "Didn't you look at the pictures? He sat on the couch, by his own admission. It was soaked in blood. Maybe he even hugged one of the kids like the defense attorney said. What would you do if you came home to your entire family dead?"

Of course, during the ensuing argument, she didn't say that she wouldn't have hugged a dead kid. But the arguments were never really about her, anyway.

"Ms. Jackson," one of the Small Minds said long about day three, "he told everybody at work that he was on edge, that he felt like he was going to explode. It's pretty clear that he did."

"Hell," she snapped. "I'm on edge. Does that mean I'm going to go on a rampage and kill you all to calm myself?"

It sounded tempting, but she knew better. She hadn't hurt anyone—deliberately—since she washed her husband's blood off her skin five years ago.

"Ms. Jackson," the Silver Cross idiot said to her on day five, "who else could have killed that family? Nothing was stolen and no one else even knew them, so no one else had a reason to kill them."

"You mean someone has a reason to kill an infant?" Pamela snapped. She ignored the wife. The wife bothered her. Pamela would have killed the wife given half a chance. Just because the woman hadn't been happy with her reproductive choices and her husband's inability to earn a living didn't give her the right to whine all the damn time.

Like these people were doing. The room really had to be bigger, much bigger, so that Pamela could pace.

She was alone and remained alone on this not-guilty thing. Even when she convinced the entire jury to go back into the courtroom and listen to the read-back of some testimony about the way that Northrup was found. His voice on the 9-1-1 tape, filled with emotion (she knew from personal experience that after killing someone, the emotion drained away), and the way he sat on that couch—as one cop put it—like he had nothing left to live for.

Ten days. Ten days they argued and fought and screamed at each other. (She didn't scream. She hated raised voices.) And they couldn't make her change her mind.

Ten days and three hours. The lunch break was when Mr. California-Wilson, whom she'd taken to calling the remaining Beach Boy to his face because he irritated her, knocked on the courtside door, and told the clerk that the jury was hung.

Fascinating word, hung. Past tense of "hang," an active but unhappy word which meant to suspend or to die by hanging or to deadlock. All of those meanings had a little murder in them.

Just a little.

She had committed a killing after all.

And like the one she had committed before, she hadn't given it much thought until she actually completed the act. By then, the deed was done and she had to deal with it. It simply felt wrong to change her mind, as if she had lost a principle or something.

So when the judge polled the jurors—all of them, including her—and asked if there was any way to resolve the deadlock, she had spoken a forceful no.

The judge had no choice but to release the jury from its duty. The case was over, and the prosecutor had lost by one vote. The defense didn't cheer, although Northrup had looked for someone—anyone—to hug and got no volunteers.

Pamela filed back into the jury room with the Small Minds, happy she would never see them again, collected her things, and left the courthouse.

She had to go to the hotel to pack, and then she would be able to go home. Packing took longer than she expected—she had lived in this dive for nearly two months—and when it was over, she found that she would actually miss the place.

She'd learned to sleep in the bed, finally feeling like the ghost of Jason and his hideous death were behind her. The nightmare, completely gone.

It was almost as if she had been on trial and had forgiven herself.

The drive from the hotel to Rickets Rock took her past the courthouse. The cameras and crowds were gone. The place looked almost deserted. She was nearly past it when she realized that she had left her book inside.

She almost thought of donating it, then changed her mind. She had donated enough to this stupid cause already.

She parked in the lot, just like she had on that very first day, and went inside by the front door. The anteroom was empty except for one of the court employees, sitting behind a counter.

The employee looked up, and clearly didn't recognize her. Pamela had taken off her juror button the moment they had been excused.

"May I help you?"

"I was on the Northrup jury," Pamela said, "and I left a book in the jury room."

The employee swiveled her chair, looked behind her, and reached down, lifting *A Certain Justice.* "This it?"

It was. Pamela had never summoned enough energy to read it. She thanked the woman, took the book, and turned.

"Ms. Jackson?"

The familiar voice sent a shiver through her. She looked over her shoulder. "Mr. Chivara. I thought you'd be off celebrating with your client."

Chivara smiled. It wasn't that predatory smile he used in court, but a rather wistful one. "I had a few things to get out of the courtroom. I see you did too."

She nodded, tucked the book under her arm, and started to leave. He kept pace with her.

"I understand you're the one who hung my jury," he said.

"So?" she asked.

"So," he said as he pushed open the door leading outside, "it surprised me."

"I'm sure it didn't, counselor," she said. "You picked me for some reason and it wasn't my good looks."

He laughed. The sound echoed across the empty street. "That's true. I thought you'd help my client, but not in this part of the case."

She stopped. "What does that mean?"

"It means, Ms. Jackson, we found that you lied on your jury questionnaire."

She felt cold. She knew better than to say anything. If she confirmed or denied, she would play right into his little game, whatever it was.

"And since we found that out, we figured we could use you as the basis for our appeal."

"You planned an appeal?" she asked.

"Every good defense attorney keeps one eye on the current case, and one eye on appeal. You were my ace-in-the-hole."

"I was your ace-in-the-hole when you picked me?"

"Now that wouldn't be quite right, now would it?" This time he gave her the predatory smile. "Of course, no one can prove when we learned that you didn't have a murdered uncle. Nor can they prove when we discovered that Pamela Jackson isn't your real name."

Her chill increased.

"Lying on a jury questionnaire is perjury, Ms. Jackson," Chivara said, "and I'm an officer of the court. Technically, I can't let you get away with that."

She forced herself to breathe. Then she turned around. "I can't say anything to you. You're accusing me and doing it in a do-you-beat-your-wife fashion."

"Am I?" he asked, his arms crossed.

"Besides," she said because she had to, because she couldn't keep silent, "if I did lie, and you discovered it, are you going to serve your client by reporting it? After all, I did hang your jury."

Chivara studied her for a long moment. "If I were still prosecuting, I'd already have you for identity fraud, and perjury. If I keep digging, what else would I find?"

A trail of temper, which had ceased. She had found her own kind of peace here in Seavy County.

"I like fiction, Mr. Chivara," she said. "We established that on the day of jury selection."

"You like crime dramas, Ms. Jackson," he said. "We never established that you liked only fiction."

She remembered the feeling she'd had that first day in the courtroom—that he was the only worthy adversary she had ever found. He was as smart as she was, which was a problem.

"We never established what lengths you'll go to in order to win a case," she said softly. "Looks like we'll learn that one today."

Then she turned around and headed down the steps to her car, feeling his gaze on her back. She half-expected to hear his footsteps following her, to feel his hand grab her arm, to pull her back and take her into that courtroom.

She'd be the one going to jail, and then she'd be the one going to trial, defended by someone like Chivara. Just like she'd imagined.

Just like she'd feared for the past five years.

But Chivara didn't follow her down the stairs. In fact, when she got into her car, and looked out the window, he was still watching her.

He had to choose between letting the client he had clearly thought guilty (after all, why else scheme for the appeal?) go free or letting a woman who had changed her identity and committed at least two small crimes that he knew of go free.

Poor Mr. Chivara. Such choices he had.

Such choices she had. Did she stay and pretend like nothing happened, trust the bastard to do what was in his best interest? Or did she run, again, losing all the money she'd put into her store and her home?

She clutched the key to her car. People who ran were guilty: she had argued that in the jury room, and her argument would come back to him. He'd know she'd done something.

But if she stayed, he'd have only his own conscious to wrestle with.

As a good defense attorney, he did that each and every day.

She put the key in the ignition and started the car. Chivara was still watching her.

She waved at him as she drove out of the parking lot.

Away from the courtroom and juries and the law.

Screw Chivara and his suspicions. She was going back to her store, her home and her life, her solitary life as a model citizen, a woman who did her duty and nothing more, just like everybody else.

The Last Interview

Craig McDonald

Craig McDonald is an award-winning journalist and editor. He is a contributor to the 2004 *New York Times* non-fiction bestseller *Secrets of the Code.* One of his short stories will appear in the anthology *Dublin Noir,* edited by Ken Bruen. *Art in The Blood,* a collection of interviews conducted by McDonald with twenty crime writers, is forthcoming from PointBlank Press.

More than a thousand miles from Lake Michigan to the borderlands—this hellhole of red dust and terra-cotta tile roofs.

The Las Cruces sun tumbles down legless drunk behind Picacho Mountain, making the reporter squint. Jug-eared LBJ is yammering on through the radio's static: more lies about Vietnam.

The last three hundred miles are a shock-absorber punishing, pothole-peppered agony. The '65 Ford Galaxie's been making new noises since somewhere south of Santa Fe. Expensive-sounding noises.

The rolled-down windows and strategically angled wings do little but push around the fidgeting journalist's beads of sweat.

But the struggling Ford delivers the interviewer to his destination: A posh hacienda in La Mesillia—two stories of stucco with a wrap-around second floor porch, hard by the Rio Grande.

The author's English wife greets the journalist . . . leads him to a first-floor guest room. "Sleep," she says. "Tomorrow you two talk."

Hector Lassiter: burly, unshaven, brindle hair askew, lays in his deathbed, contemplating the stinging stump of his truncated right leg. The leg was lost last month to gangrene borne of diabetes . . . diabetes borne of alcoholism . . . alcoholism borne of living the life that feeds the books that pay for the life, and the liquor, that cost him the leg.

The doctor has lately eyed Hector's tingling left leg with intent.

Or so the dying novelist believes.

Hector's also taken to sleeping with a loaded antique Colt '73 Peacemaker hidden under his pillow, preparing to take himself out—do it before they can amputate his throbbing hands . . . take those critical, increasingly-tingling trigger fingers.

The doomed author listens to his caretaker, or fifth

"wife," as she regards herself, reading this likely last-journalist-come-to-interview-him the riot act: no smuggling in liquor . . . no loaning of cigarettes.

A promise she'll be back in three hours' time. She tells the reporter she means to take advantage of her husband's company to venture out with Carmelita, their long-suffering Tarahumara-born servant for some goddamned misbegotten, budget-busting shopping spree.

Now the door opens, and the reporter—gaunt, straw-haired and bespectacled . . . perhaps vaguely tubercular—shoulders in, lugging a big black leather bag. Can't be more than 22. He's sporting thick-lensed glasses that probably spared the poor bastard the draft.

Lassiter spreads his arms, smiles . . . those famous dimples, nearly buried under his hoary beard. "Holy Jesus," the last of the first-wave *Black Mask* writers says out of the side of his mouth, in full Texas drawl, "a thousand fucking miles to record the last ruminations of a fitfully lucid, one-legged hack writer. How empty must your life be, eh lad? Fuck on a bicycle: Hope I live down to expectations. Who's this one for?"

The reporter smiles crookedly, revealing crooked teeth. *"Esquire."* He plugs his reel-to-reel recorder in and lays the microphone on the pillow by Hector Lassiter's head. He presses the "record" button with a nicotine-stained thumb.

"If you don't mind, thought we'd start with some impressions regarding your peers," the reporter says, extra loud for the recorder.

"Peers? Yeah . . . shoot," Lassiter says, already disappointed.

"Right: Dashiell Hammett?"

"Pussy-whipped communist."

"Raymond Chandler?"

"Unwitting homosexual."

"Cornell Woolrich?"

"Overtly queer." Lassiter winks. "But I feel a gimpy affinity with old Corny . . . he's a fellow cripple now . . . same circumstances. Or so I hear."

"Agatha Christie?"

The writer's brows knit. "Faker. Fucking *mystery* writer."

The reporter scratches his head. "You're a mystery writer."

"I'm a crime writer. She's a 'mystery' writer. It's different."

"You sound resentful."

Hector smiles, shakes his head. "I out earn her. And her stuff is shit . . . stupid puzzles solved by a daffy old bitch or an effete fucking Belgian. Fuck that. Ever meet a loveable old bitch or effete fucking Belgian who could do more than rub you the wrong way? They'll still be reading me long after the worms have done with Dame Christie. Her audience is nearly as old as her."

Hector Lassiter gestures at his side table with a hairy, shaking hand, pointing to a haphazard stack of hardcovers and softbound galleys in danger of falling. "Look at those damned things. Pretty high pile, eh? Cocksuckers all still crave jacket comments from me. Crap, most all of it. Fucking book about a detective cat in there somewhere. No shit, an actual fucking pussy detective. Holy pleading bleeding Jesus. It'll probably win the Edgar. If I'm not dead when it happens, some dipshit will come after me to write an introduction for the reprint for the Limited Editions Club. Mark my words."

The reporter smiles; crosses one leg over the other. Hector thinks: *Six weeks ago, I could do that, too.*

The reporter tugs at his shirt's sleeves . . . Hector thinks he sees needle scars, just peeking under the cuffs. He frowns. Hector thinks: *Another fucking junkie.*

The reporter says, "How about Rex Stout?"

"Another lefty."

"Estelle Quartermain?"

"Fucking *mystery* hack of the first water. Bad as Christie. Hell, worse—her stupid 'locked room mysteries.' " Lassiter waves a hand. "Ever hear of anyone really getting whacked in a locked room?"

The reporter shrugs . . . he's got those telltale nervous hands and feet. And he's sweating out of proportion to the undeniable heat. Hector knows the signs. He thinks, certain now: *Junkie.*

Lassiter snorts. "Exactly. No damned way. People die over a $10 drug deal. They kill over a dumpy woman in some peanut-shell-strewn, cigarette smoke-laden cantina. They cuff their wife 'cause she won't shut up during Carson's monologue. Her head hits the bedpost, and she falls to the floor, her neck at some impossible angle. I've written those scenes. Scenes I've lived or witnessed. Fucking Dame Quartermain dismisses me for those scenes. Says I only write about whores, drunkards and bottom-feeders. Of course, she doesn't use those terms. But I know what she means. Says I'm sordid. Says I'm seedy. All because I don't have some hump-backed dowager with some shaking, beloved Chihuahua solving murder cases in vicarages . . . murders involving exotic poisons. All that dainty dialogue and 'action' in service to some fretted-over puzzle plot. Know what, scribe of mine? When you have to run to the reference books, you're not writing. Use that windy passage as a pull-quote, eh lad?"

Bouncing one leg, the wired reporter says, "I interviewed Estelle Quartermain a couple of months ago. She's a nice lady."

Lassiter grunts and says, "And that should matter to me—her being 'nice'—that should matter to me as a reader? Why should that be, exactly? There's a letter on the nightstand over there from her somewhere. Arrived last week. She's still nursing a grudge over something I said to her at a party 10 years ago. Writes religiously, about once a month, stubbornly pushing for an apology to her husband. I said something in my cups, or so she says . . . I don't remember what. Her husband left early. Do remember that. Ruined her night, or so the purple-haired bitch says . . . stewing under that fucking beehive. Estelle says I hurt her man's pride . . . in a 'lingering' way." The writer waves it away with a thick-fingered hand. "She says I 'don't have the brains' to write the kinds of books she writes. The point is, I have the brains not to write the kinds of shitty books she writes."

The old writer's big bed is bracketed by double-doors. The doors open onto the upper porch. There is heatlightning on the horizon now. Black clouds roil either side of Hector Lassiter's head. The old writer smiles crookedly, says, "My witchy warden's words of warning aside, got some smokes?"

The reporter smiles and roots around in his jacket pocket; passes Hector a virgin pack of Pall Malls. The crime writer slits the pack with a long, yellow thumbnail and the reporter fires him up with a battered silver Zippo. Hector's cheeks hollow once, twice. He blows some smoke rings, says, "Who do you read, son? When you read for yourself, I mean."

"Some Hesse. Burroughs."

"Skinny Billy. Junkie. Fucker shot and killed his wife playing William Tell, ya know. And Hesse? He's a fuckin' kraut. What about crime fiction—who do you read?"

"Uh, been reading some Kenneth Robeson."

"Kenneth Robeson? Ain't no such beast, boy. You reading those fuckin' *Doc Savage* paperback reprints?"

The reporter squirms. "A few here and there . . . good camp. And Robeson's stuff is—"

Hector Lassiter draws deep and blows smoke out both nostrils, like some paunchy, mutilated dragon. " 'Robeson' was a house pen name, invented by Street & Smith so they could fire the real hard-working pulp writer on a whim if need be. Same shitty joint that published *Black Mask.* 'Maxwell Grant,' who wrote the bulk of *The Shadow* novels, he was really a guy named Walt Gibson. Buddy of Houdini's. Wrote two novels a month for more than a decade for old S&S. Had a battery of typewriters; the keys all stained with blood. No shit: Old Walt typed his fingers bloody. All the time. Let's see your affable Mrs. Quartermain match *that.*"

Hector turns his mouth down. "Anyway, nine times out of ten, your 'Ken Robeson' was a fella name of Lester Dent. Great guy. Born out west, like me. Lonely childhood to stoke that imagination. Just like me. Used to hang with him in Florida. Good as Hammett and funny to boot— when he wrote his own stuff. Look for the books under his own name, sonny . . . look for a short story—'Sail.' Good as anything the best of us have done."

The reporter nods and smiles. "Will do. Florida: You lived there for a few years, in the Keys. Knew Hemingway. You two had a falling out."

"Old news, boy. Put it this way, my Florida P.I. novel, *Wandering Eye,* was ten times the novel *To Have and Have Not* was . . . and published the same year. Outsold Papa, in those early Depression days. Hemingway dismissed me as a 'mystery' writer. Still, he knew his shit in the 1920s . . . those great short stories. His notion of 'one true sentence.' Too bad he forgot all he knew, down there on Bone Key."

Lassiter chews his lip, considering the junkie journalist. He weighs angles. Decides to play with a notion, just a bit . . . probably never go the whole course . . . just flirt with it a bit. Keep himself interested.

Hector reaches over to the sidetable for a legal pad and pen. He hands them to the reporter. "Game I used to play with Hemingway. We'd challenge each other to top one another's one true sentence. Write this down, eh?" Hector recites:

"I killed him because. . . ."

He says, "Okay kiddo, finish it. Make it the truest sentence you can, but keep it fucking short."

Smiling crookedly, the reporter nervously bounces the point of the pen on the paper. He weighs the words: "I killed him because. . . ."

". . . he was bitter and used up"?

No. Might piss the old man off.

". . . of what he said to me"?

No. Too weak.

The reporter searches, sensing the old man's eyes on him . . . on his wrists, sending him off, tugging down his sleeves. He thinks of what Hector Lassiter has said about Estelle Quartermain. He remembers what Estelle told him about the used-up old one-legged man laying before him now. With his left hand, the reporter writes:

"I killed him because of what he did to her."

Hector Lassiter takes the notebook back, reads. He beams. Still has a pretty solid set of teeth. "Good, son. Perfect, really. Short, simple, evocative. And it's gotta all come down to a woman in the end, eh? Always does. Even for Woolrich . . . at least in his books. *Cherchez la femme.*" He hands the notepad back to the reporter. He says, "I feel like a proud teacher. Sign your work for the old man, huh?"

The reporter smiles crookedly again. Under his "one true sentence" he scrawls "Andrew Nagel." He passes the legal pad back to the old writer. Hector looks at it again and smiles, shaking his head approvingly. "Good fucking start, Andrew. You get back to Chicago you write what comes after, yeah? Send it to me. Deal?"

"Sure, Mr. Lassiter."

"Hector. We're fellow writers now, Andy."

The old author is seized by a thought. He abruptly asks: "Andy, what have you read of mine, huh, kid?"

"Read *Rooster of Heaven.* And I really loved the film."

"That was a novelization, sonny, not a novel. I wrote a straight-to-paperback treatment just to put back the parts of my story that that one-eyed fucker Sam Ford tore out for his fucking waste of a film. In the land of the blind, the one eyed man might be king, but in the land of the two, or, even the three-eyed? Well, he's just another myopic dumbass. What else of mine have you read? Anything? Tell the truth."

The reporter shrugs. *"Inside Job."*

"Famously—some would say infamously—done for money. I had a daughter born with a hole in her heart. Needed the cash for a surgery that killed her. My baby girl was named Dolores. She hung in until the age of three. Her first—and last—word, was 'Daddy.' Quote that, Andrew."

The reporter searches the old man's filmy blue eyes. Hector's cataracts look like some inept impressionist painter's notion of drunkenly dispersing clouds.

Well, it's a line Andy is toying with . . . maybe needs work.

Lassiter grunts and points a shaking finger at the reporter. "You drew this assignment, didn't you boy? You didn't come all this way because *Rhapsody in Black* rocked your world? Never read *The Shortest Story,* and so experienced no revelations, right?"

The reporter straightens his shoulders; feels his sweaty shirt peel loose in a few places from his acne-dappled back. He says softly, "I drew the assignment, sir . . . like you said."

Hector credits the reporter's candor. At least the scrawny fucker has that going for him. "Hell . . . doesn't matter," Hector says, resigned now . . . sadly settling on his scheme. "What do you want from me, Andy?"

"There was a hotel in El Paso. It was May 13, 1956."

The old writer tips his head on side. And so it comes. As it always does.

The eternal question.

The one he has never answered.

Hector Lassiter says, "Now that's a locked room, boy. That's my private mystery. The pain too private to trot out."

"You might never get another chance to go on record, Mr. Lassiter."

Hector bites his lip, sighs. " 'There was a ship.' "

The reporter catches that one on the first bounce. "Coleridge . . . right?"

"Just so. So you do read more than just bad pulp fiction and my toss-offs."

"It's a classic."

"Sure it is, Andrew." The bearded writer puffs his cigarette and gestures at his missing leg. " 'It was that accursed white whale that razed me; made a poor pegging lubber of me for ever and a day.' "

"Ahab," the reporter smiles.

"Like old Melville, do you?"

The reporter shrugs again. With two fingers, Andy stabs his slipping glasses back up the bridge of his damp nose. "So long as you don't start regarding me as your Moby Dick . . . sure, why not?"

Hector winks and shakes his head. He reaches to the sidetable for a box. "Only 'Moby Dick' I regard lately is the one between my one-and-a-half legs, and he's not breaking surface much these days." The old writer roots through the box, pulls out a hypodermic and a little vial of liquid. "Insulin," Hector explains. "You'd think three years of heroin addiction back in the late 1950s,"—a damnable lie—"would have given me some facility with this damned rig." He looks for a reaction from the reporter and doesn't get much . . . the kid licks his lips and averts his eyes. "Don't suppose you'd be able to help me out with this, huh Andrew?"

The reporter says, with little conviction, "Wouldn't know how." He shoots his sleeves again.

Lassiter snorts and spikes his remaining leg and grimaces. He sits back and retrieves his Pall Mall. He feels himself leaning harder into his dark notion. "Don't suppose," Hector says, "you smuggled in anything to drink?"

"Couldn't be good for you, Hector."

"Think I'm going to bounce back from this? Naw. We enjoy the moments left us. Solid advice, Andrew."

The reporter grins and reaches in his bag. He holds up the Jim Beam bottle. Andy Nagel smiles wider—meaner—at the dying writer's hungry smile and cracks the seal. Lassiter points to a sideboard across the room. Five glasses sit on a serving tray there, gathering dust. The reporter rubs clean two glasses on the untucked tails of his shirt and pours two generous doses. He passes one to the dying novelist.

Hector savors the delicious bite and burn. He sighs: That warmth infusing his chest . . . fucking sublime. He settles back into his pillows.

"Now," the reporter says. "It's 1956. Your wife dies . . . some say suspiciously. You're a fleeting suspect before it's reluctantly ruled a heroin overdose. The case remains . . . inconclusive. What really happened, Hector?"

The old writer stubs out the butt of his cigarette. He snags the soft pack and shakes out another; leans in for the reporter to light him up again. "No. Not like that Andy. You want the story? The story nobody has ever had? Well, a couple of favors, Andy my boy. 'Cause, ya know, I have to go on living this shitty excuse for a life after you've gone on to your next 'assignment.' "

There's a languishing writing desk in the northwest corner of the room. Hector gestures at a straight-back wooden chair. "For starters, tuck that sucker up under the doorknob," he says "—can't have the she-bitch and her taco-bending sidekick finding us with the booze and coffin nails, can we?"

The reporter winks and rises. He wedges the chair's back up under the brass knob and nudges it tight with his toe.

The old man gestures at the windows next. It's raining now, and the rain is blowing in. "Best close and lock the windows, too," Hector says. "Won't be able to do much about the scent of the cigarette smoke . . . but wet walls and floors—*trés* more suspicious. And the heat? Well, it's a dry heat, right?"

The sweating reporter closes and secures the doors on either side of the author's bed. He sheds his jacket and is about to sit down when the old man says, "Last favor. Grab another glass over there, eh? Might need to go two-fisted for this . . . dark waters my boy, dark fucking waters."

The reporter sets the spare glass down on the nightstand and then holds up a finger. "Hold on a minute—need to flip the tape." The reporter plays with the spools; tightens them. He hits "record" again. "Okay. It's 1956. It's your wife's last day on earth."

How do you tell a man why you murdered a woman you loved?

How to start?

How do you give it context? Not to alibi yourself or excuse what you did. How do you show why you were driven to do that bad evil thing to her?

Your baby's Mexican mother's secret drug addiction . . . that's at the dark heart of it all.

Your woman's heroin Jones: It weakened your unborn daughter's frail body, condemning her to death before she was even born.

It was an addiction that was well hidden by Maria. She

injected through the soles of her callused feel. She kept it hidden through your courtship . . . a year of marriage . . . and through nine months of pregnancy.

She hid it well, through three years of your daughter's short life.

Then it comes: These perplexed words from a doctor, chewing his lip over your daughter's death bed . . . hints of congenital birth defects perhaps caused by . . . well . . . perhaps some narcotic influence. For there were other things wrong with your little girl . . . things only just being discovered . . . or suspected. A welter of birth defects.

Dolores dies in your arms, whispering "Daddy."

Unable to face your house, or your daughter's empty bedroom, her absent voice and laugh, you booked yourselves into a hotel room—paid up two weeks in advance.

You feel sorry for Maria for a time, until when, confronted, she confesses her addiction a week after your daughter's funeral. Drunk, scaring yourself with your thoughts about killing this woman who bore/murdered your child, you reluctantly let her shoot you up.

Once.

It's shitty strategy on Maria's part . . . drug monkey logic. She stares at you with the addled echo of your dead daughter's dark eyes, lips parted, watching for signs of your capitulation to the heroin.

But the drug that mellows her makes you go dark and cold. You let the resentment fester—let the poison stoke your darkest impulses. Let it build on the hate you feel for Maria for letting her worthless devotion to this wired short ride cost you your black-haired, black-eyed baby girl.

Maria condemned your little girl to a slow death that

dragged on for three years—three years to let you grow to achingly love the poor little girl born with no future. Three years of hollow hoping that age will grant her frail body the strength to swamp her damaged heart—render that fierce fucking hole irrelevant.

But your love and hope, your fame and talent, can't fill the hole in your baby girl's heart.

Little Dolores dies whispering "Daddy."

You ride that one and only heroin high—free-associating. Plotting.

You scope the room . . . assess angles.

In the end, you go the easy route.

As Maria lays naked on the bed, black hair spread on the pillow, luxuriating in her high, begging you to fuck her—to make a new baby—you instead berate her . . . leave her alone to her tingling trip. Soon enough, she's asleep. You grab the hotel ice bucket . . . 25 trips . . . and the tub is sufficiently full of cold cubes.

Holding it through a handkerchief, you pick up her hypodermic, surveying the bottoms of her feet. Their soles are covered with scabbed-over punctures, like the scars of a thousand scorpions' stings.

Fuck it—go for her arm. Three shots . . . of air. Give the junkie bitch an embolism of epic proportions. You follow that with a massive injection of heroin.

You carry her naked body into the bathroom and drop her in the ice, spreading it over her. You lay the needle on the closed toilet lid by the bathtub, next to the empty vial.

You write an angry note to her . . . all the expected words. You lay out in the letter your disgusted discovery of her drug addiction . . . what it did to your dead daughter. Now you're

*leaving her . . . and you wish your wife in hell. You date it
yesterday. You stick the note in her dead hand, flung out
strategically over the side of the tub.*

*You pack your stuff, and, still using a handkerchief, drop
the Do-Not-Disturb sign on the doorknob. The air conditioner
is full up: May take twelve, fifteen hours for the ice to melt.
You'll be buying drinks and slapping backs—conspicuously—
in Ciudad Juárez in less than two.*

Tell this junkie reporter the truth?

You do. Baldly.

Andrew Nagel stares out at the storm raging on the
horizon, says, "Jesus, this could make me."

It could indeed. Lassiter says, "That's your last one true
sentence, Andrew."

Then Hector Lassiter reaches under his pillow, grasps
the well-worn butt of the Peacemaker, and, cocking,
reaches over and presses the barrel to the reporter's left
temple. He tugs the hair trigger.

Adios Andrew.

Alone again . . . as he always seems to be.

Alone at the typewriter.

Alone in his own head.

Only time Hector didn't feel alone—those scant
moments spent with his baby girl.

Two more shots—fired through each spool of tape . . .
reduced to magnetized confetti. The ruined recorder kicks
twice.

Andrew Nagel was a southpaw—Hector was careful to
note that when Andrew wrote his first true sentence. Using
the edge of the bedsheet, Hector grabs the legal pad from

the bedside table and tears off the top sheet of paper with its signed, unwitting confession. He slips the note into Andrew's dead right hand. He gingerly raises the reporter's sleeve—a welter of needle scars . . . several of them look fresh. *Worthless junkie.*

The old one-legged writer grabs a pen and Estelle Quartermain's languishing letter. Hector annotates it with lies. He scrawls vile notes in the margins—a punched up version of that night of the supposed big slight he can't recall. At the top of her letter, Hector Lassiter writes, "Estelle, you clapped up cunt, I'm *so* fucking grateful I slept with you that night. Fond fucking memories . . . so to speak."

The crime writer—the last of the first wave *Black Mask* writers—surveys the room. It's a plausible enough murder-suicide scene for these backwater environs.

But now for the vexing nuance—drive that old mystery writing bitch up a wall.

Fox those cops.

Reaching to the other side of the bed, Hector Lassiter picks up a tube of his wife's lipstick. He applies it to his dry lips, careful to avoid the stray hairs of his moustache and beard. He picks up the derelict bottle of whiskey and the virgin glass, pours four fingers and downs it, leaving a glass rimmed with lipstick. Then he smokes two cigarettes, stubbing out the lipstick-smeared butts in the empty tumbler.

Enter the mystery woman.

He rubs the lipstick from his mouth with his fingers and licks those clean, washing away the taste with swigs of whiskey straight from the bottle.

Now, reaching again to the sidetable on his wife's side of the bed, Hector Lassiter grabs a bottle of perfume. He breaks it on the edge of the table and slathers perfume on his gun hand and arm—voiding any possibility of a paraffin test that could reveal Hector fired a weapon. He tosses his arm across his wife's sidetable—feigning the spastically flung arm of a dying man. Glass breaks . . . costly cosmetics fly.

Satisfied with the effect, Hector wedges the Peacemaker in Andrew Nagel's dead left hand, finger on the hair trigger . . . barrel pointed at a one-legged pulp novelist. Hector reaches for the never-used cane that his fifth "wife" has hopefully placed by the headboard. He positions Andrew's dead hand . . . scoots himself in place. With the rubber stopper of the cane, he pushes the dead reporter's dead index finger back against the hair trigger.

Jesus fucking Christ.

That burn.

Like a thousand shots of whiskey, received at once.

That sound.

The Peacemaker tumbles to the tile floor.

Groaning, Hector returns the cane to its former position.

Gut shot.

A bad way to go.

Call it half-assed penitence.

And his remaining leg . . . there's no feeling left. Must have nicked his spinal chord. Maybe severed it.

So: Paralysis to boot.

Dipping his finger in his own wound, light-headed now, Hector grimaces and twists, reaching up over his head-board. He writes above his bed, wincing with the pain:

FOR

EQ

For a moment, he frets, thinking of pillow-biting Cornell Woolrich . . . fearing the "EQ" might be misconstrued—suspected of standing for "Ellery Queen" . . . hinting of sodomistic shenanigans.

Then he remembers Estelle's newly annotated letter.

Hector gingerly rubs a little blood from his gut on Andrew's dead trigger finger.

Lassiter sucks his blood from his own finger. Then the dying crime writer lays back for a last time on his pillow.

Hector lets that old whore death settle in with him, warm and slow.

Death with imagery: Scenes from his books in montage . . . a melodramatic mélange the punchy pulp writer confuses for his own memories:

His lonely office.

Guttering light from a neon sign pulses through slanted shades.

A slow-turning ceiling fan stirs old dust.

Enter the woman: at first, just a busty silhouette through stenciled pebbled glass. Then, she's standing before him in silk stockings with seams up the back. Raven hair and ruby lips. He'll learn she likes to bite his shoulder while peaking. Betrayed, tricked, played for a fool, he'll shoot her during a last shared orgasm. . . .

Mean streets: It's Chicago. It's 1936. He's sent to settle a union strike. He settles that strike. But there are casualties. Talk about a killing floor. . . .

A sibilant homosexual lackey (Street & Smith will balk at that . . . so call him "a Nancy boy") comes calling. Nancy boy is in thrall to an endomorphic European of indeterminate origin (adapted for film, the part will be played by Sydney

Greenstreet). The pair slays his partner, seeking some elu-
sive bronze statue of a wolf with a treasure map stowed
inside. A man owes his partner . . . even if he is banging his
dead partner's dipsomaniacal wife. So he sets off again
down those mean streets. . . .

From his far off place, Hector can dimly hear screams now
. . . screams from somewhere. Fists pounding on a door.

The screams grow closer and he thinks he hears
breaking glass in the distance . . . someone shouting for
him. But it's too late . . . and now drowned out by music
. . . some march maybe, played on a hammer dulcimer . . .
drums, tiple and accordion . . . "Tramps & Hawkers."

Hector reaches out his hand and the little girl takes it
and smiles. He towers above Dolores, beaming, standing
there on his two solid legs.

They march up the side of the hill somewhere near
Creel, half-walking half-running through prickly pear,
maguey . . . sage and heather.

There's a dark-haired woman at the top of that hill,
astride a strawberry roan, silhouetted against some bloody
sunset.

Lost Causes

Anne Perry

Anne Perry's lived a varied life, penning her first words not far from Hadrian's Wall, being reared in a kind of Swiss Family Robinson environment in New Zealand and the Bahamas, and working as an air stewardess, limousine dispatcher, and insurance underwriter before finally settling down to write mysteries set in Victorian London. *The Cater Street Hangman,* published in 1979, was the first Perry novel and the first of twenty-four books to feature Inspector Thomas Pitt. *The Dark Assassin,* published in early 2006, marked the sixteenth mystery featuring another of Perry's popular characters, William Monk. Additionally, Perry, recipient of an Edgar Award and nominated for the Macavity and Agatha awards, began yet another series, set during World War I.

The court was so packed they had had to close the doors on more people trying to wheedle or push their way in. But of course I had known it would be, how could it be anything else, in the circumstances? Alan Davidson was being tried for the murder of his brother. I was sitting in my appointed place, very smart in my black suit with high-necked white blouse, single pearls on my ears, and my wig itching like a hat that didn't fit.

My name is Judith, and some of my friends call me Jude, very appropriate—St. Jude is the patron saint of lost causes, and if ever there were a lost cause, defending Alan Davidson was it!

What on earth had made me accept?

Counsel for the Crown, Sir Peter Hoyle, was questioning the police witnesses who had found the battered body of Neil Davidson on the living room floor of his house. They were making a good job of the horror of it. It was all quietly understated, no melodrama, no playing for effect, and above all, no exaggeration for me to find fault with. Not that it would have made any difference. It would alter none of the facts that mattered, and they were all there in hideous detail.

As I sat increasingly uncomfortably, I remembered the message asking me to go to Lord Justice Davidson's office. At the time I had had no idea what it was about. I did not connect it with the crime in every newspaper headline. My first thought was that I had committed some solecism of legal behavior of which I was unaware, and I was preparing a suitably profound apology. After all Lord Justice Davidson V.C. was one of the most senior judges in England, a man renowned for his wisdom, his heroism and his justice, even toward those who had been his enemies. And he certainly had those! Success such as his breeds envy.

And it had come to him young. During the darkest days

of the war in 1942, aged barely twenty, he had taken a
German gun position almost single-handed and saved the
lives of a score of men. He had won the Victoria Cross for
it, one of the highest decorations in the world for gallantry
on the field of battle.

From then on it had been up all the way. Even his wife
was a legendary beauty! And he had had two fine sons,
and a daughter, by all accounts a beauty also.

I had knocked on his door five minutes early, and been
told to enter straightaway. I had only ever seen him in the
distance before. A couple of yards from me, in his late
fifties, he was still one of the handsomest men I have ever
seen. Many a woman would have paid a fortune for a head
of hair like his, or eyes! Even the dark hollows around
them and the ashen pallor of his skin could not mask the
vigor of life within him.

"Yes sir?" I had said haltingly, only beginning to realize
that whatever it was he had called me for, it was to do with
him, not with me.

"As you will know, Miss Ashton," he said gravely, "my
elder son, Neil, was murdered four days ago. This morning
they charged my younger son, Alan, with the crime.

"I would like you to defend him."

For a moment I had had no breath to reply, no words
even in my mind. My awe of him vanished, the distant,
excited respect I had felt ever since I had been called to the
bar was obliterated by my overwhelming human pity for
him as a man, a father who in one terrible blow was losing
both his sons.

"I . . . I . . ." I had stammered, knowing I sounded like
a fool.

"Please?" he had said simply.

I am a good barrister, sometimes very good, but there are still a score of people better than I, longer established, and with far more respect within the profession. He could have asked any of them and they would have been honored to accept.

I had drawn in my breath to say "why me?" but I hadn't said it. I had been flattered. I wanted to do it. He must have heard something about me, some brilliant defense I had made, perhaps of the Walbrooke boy last spring. I was proud of that. Maybe this was my reward?

I had not argued or made excuses or protests of mock modesty. I had simply accepted, and promised him I would do everything I could to help Alan.

Of course that had been before I had met Alan Davidson, or knew the facts of the case.

Now here I was listening to Peter Hoyle asking the police surgeon to describe Neil Davidson's injuries, and watching the jury's faces as the pity and revulsion spread through them, and then the anger. I saw how they looked across at Alan, sitting motionless, his face frozen in misery. He refused to defend himself even by a second's shame or remorse in his expression, or the softening in the angles of his body. He sat as if already condemned, and I have never felt so helpless in my life.

I hated looking at Lord Davidson where he sat on the front row of the public seats, his face stiff and pale, his shoulders hunched. Beside him his wife had her face turned away from me.

The surgeon was waiting for me to say something, but what could I ask? The facts were incontrovertible.

Someone had beaten Neil Davidson to death. There were bruises and abrasions all over his body, and one final blow had broken his neck. He was a strong man, not yet in the prime of life. His knuckles were bruised and raw. "Whoever had done that to him had to be badly marked themselves. And there was Alan with the scars on his cheek and the purple not yet faded from his brow and jaw.

"Miss Ashton?" the judge prompted and I could hear both the impatience and the pity in his voice.

"No thank you, my lord," I declined. The last thing I wanted was for the surgeon to say anything further!

Peter Hoyle glanced at me, and called his next witness. I have never liked him much, and at that moment I suddenly found him almost intolerable. He looked as if he were secretly enjoying all this misery.

Of course I understood now why Lord Davidson had chosen me. He would not embarrass any of his friends by asking them. No matter what passions of rage or love tore through his heart, the lawyer in his brain would know that there could be no defense. Perhaps only God understood the reasons why Alan had killed his brother, but the facts were being unrolled relentlessly in front of us as I sat there, and I was helpless to argue against any of them, or even to reinterpret them in any kinder light.

"And was there any evidence whatever of forced entry?" Hoyle was asking.

"No sir, none at all," the police sergeant answered.

"And was anything missing, as far as you could determine?" Hoyle pressed.

"No sir. According to the insurance records, and they were pretty detailed, there was nothing of value taken. All his ornaments and pictures were accounted for. His coin collection, which is very valuable, was all around in class cases, and untouched, and there were nearly two hundred pounds in notes in the desk drawer."

"Then it would be reasonable to conclude that robbery was not the intention of his murderer," Hoyle said with a glance at me, and then at the jury. "Thank you, Sergeant, that is all I have to ask you. But perhaps Miss Ashton can at last think of something?" He left the rest unsaid.

I only wished I could, but every time my brain scrambled furiously in the jumble of facts, I remembered Alan Davidson's white face and blank eyes filled with fury and despair, but no will to fight. No matter what I said or did, or how I pleaded, he would barely talk to me. Even the little he did say was of trivia, small duties he wanted done for him as if he expected to die and needed an executor rather than a defense. They were waiting for me . . . again. Not only could I not help Alan Davidson, this was likely to be the end of my own career. Memory of this would wipe out all my past successes.

"No thank you, my lord."

There was a faint titter somewhere in the body of the court, stifled almost immediately, but I heard it and I knew what it meant. It was a mixture of nervousness for the reality of pain, and pity not for Alan, but for me, because I was a failure.

Hoyle next called the elder of the two friends who had gone to the airport to meet Alan on his return from abroad. "And what date was that, Mr. Rivers?" he asked politely.

"The twelfth, sir," Rivers replied. He was a tall man, a little thin, although that might have been exaggerated by the pallor of his face and the pinched look around his mouth. I would have guessed him to be in his middle thirties, but today he looked more like fifty, and yet also oddly vulnerable.

"At what time?" Hoyle enquired.

"Half past eight in the morning. It was an overnight flight from New York."

"Alan Davidson had been in New York?"

"No. He'd been doing botanical and ecological research in the Amazon Basin," Rivers corrected with sudden asperity. "He simply returned via New York."

"I see," Hoyle said, as if he saw nothing at all. "And you met him at one of the London airports?"

"Yes, John Eaves and I met him at Heathrow."

I looked across at Alan, but as almost always, he avoided my eye.

"Will you please tell us where you took Mr. Davidson," Hoyle asked.

Rivers clenched his jaw. Even from where I sat I could see the tightening of his muscles. He was obviously loathing every word he was forced to say, but there was no escape for him. Oddly enough, the transparency of his emotion made his evidence the more powerful. "To the hospital at St. Albans," he replied.

Hoyle opened his mouth, a slightly sarcastic expression flashing across his face, then he changed his mind. "Why was that, Mr. Rivers? Did he ask you to?"

"Yes." His voice was so quiet the judge directed him to raise it so the court could hear him. "Yes!" he repeated, staring at Hoyle with such misery in his eyes that for the first time since the trial had begun I had a sense of some real and intense personal tragedy far deeper than sibling rivalry turned so sour it ended in murder.

"And the reason?" Hoyle pressed.

Rivers looked once at Alan in the dock, then spoke quietly but every word was distinct. "He was very close to his sister, Kate. He'd been abroad for a long time with no way to send letters from where he was, or to receive them, I suppose. Almost the first thing he did was to ask after her." His voice shook a little. "He didn't know . . ." he stopped, blinking his eyes several times, and looking at Hoyle with such loathing I had a sudden vision of how he would look at me when I failed to do anything to help his friend. I dreaded that day, just as I knew it was inevitable.

"And you answered him?" Hoyle said after a moment.

"I had to," Rivers mastered himself again. "He had to know. I just wish to . . . to God . . ." he took a deep breath, "that I'd done it later! Or stayed with him . . . or something."

In spite of himself Hoyle was suddenly gentle. "What did you tell him, Mr. Rivers?"

Rivers's whole body was tight. "That Kate had . . . had some kind of mental breakdown. Nobody knows what caused it . . . and . . . and she was in the hospital, and there was no real hope of her ever coming home."

The court was silent. Hardly anyone moved, even in the public gallery. I knew the story, of course, but told again like this it was still horribly jarring. It was so easy to imagine the joy of homecoming, the reunion of friends, and then suddenly everything had changed, broken. The heart of it was gone. I could see their faces as they turned to look at Alan sitting blank-eyed in the dock.

Lord Davidson put his arm around his wife and she moved a little closer to him.

Rivers went on with the story, how he and Eaves had

taken a shocked Alan to the hospital in St. Albans and waited for him, pacing the floor, talking in snatched sentences, drifting from desperate hope into silence, then fractured words again, and more silence.

It had been nearly two hours before Alan had emerged, ashen-faced, walking so blindly he stumbled into the doors. They had taken him home where he had asked them to leave him, and reluctantly they had done so, not knowing what to do to help. Of course Hoyle made the most of Alan's state of mind, making him appear to have been planning murder even then.

"I thought he needed time alone," Rivers said in an agony of apology. It was Alan he looked at, not Judge Davidson or Barbara beside him, her face at last turned toward me so I could see her features, still exquisitely chiseled, her hair barely dimmed from the russet beauty of her youth, only a little softer, like autumn leaves as the year fades. I could not bear to see the pain in her, it was palpable, like a storm in the air. In a sense she had lost all her children, but in a slow and hideous fashion, worse than disease.

The following day Hoyle called more police witnesses to show that Alan had tried to cover his crime. When questioned he had denied any guilt, then when the net inevitably closed around him, he had fled, making him both a liar and a coward.

As I sat watching Hoyle close his case, without my offering more than a token resistance, I felt utterly beaten. I have never prayed to saints asking for miracles. It is not part of my faith, and to be honest I did not think any form of intervention, divine or otherwise, would help Alan

Davidson now. There was no shred of doubt, reasonable or otherwise, that he had gone straight from the hospital in St. Albans to his home, and a few hours after Rivers and Eaves had left, he had gone to his brother's house and fought with him so savagely and relentlessly as to leave him dead. To escape so lightly himself he had to have taken Neil by surprise. He had not been larger or heavier, simply possessed by a rage which lent him superhuman strength.

Hoyle rested his case. Thank heaven it was too close to the end of the day for me to begin. I had nothing but character witnesses, for any real good they would do.

I left the courtroom. I had to see Alan and try one more time to persuade him to speak to me. I could not argue the facts, I must try the reasons behind them, if only he would trust me. There had to be more than the few bitter details Hoyle had brought out.

He was alone, staring at the small square of sky through the high, barred window. He turned as he heard the door unlock and the very slight squeak of the iron hinges.

He stared at me as the warden locked us in.

I was there for nearly an hour and a half. I tried every argument, every plea I could rake out of my imagination. I begged him, but he would tell me nothing. He just sat patiently on the stool waiting for me to exhaust myself, then spoke in his quite voice, denying me anything at all. I left again with not a single weapon in my hand to defend him, and I had to begin tomorrow morning.

I thought of Judge Davidson and how I would face him when it was all over. I felt that the largest, most vital part of my own life was also going to be consumed in this apparently meaningless tragedy.

And yet I had spent hours with Alan and had had no sense of a psychotic personality, and perhaps that was the most frightening part of it. "Where *was* my own judgment? I used to think I was good at understanding people, that I had a sensitivity, even some kind of wisdom!

It was that moment that I decided to go to the hospital in St. Albans for myself, and see if I could learn anything more as to what happened the night Alan had gone to see his sister. Of course I had questioned each of the witnesses Hoyle would call, but all they did was prove that Alan had been there, and had left white-faced and almost as if walking in his sleep. It hardly seemed possible he could hate Neil so passionately simply because he had not told Alan of Kate's illness. He had been in the Amazon jungle and unreachable to anyone except by the most primitive means. And that was not the sort of message to give except face to face, and when you could be there to explain all you knew, and assure them that everything was being done for her. He could not have helped, and a fractured wireless communication would hardly make him feel better.

Perhaps they had not handled it in the best possible way, but it was a genuine mistake, not worth a quarrel, let alone a murder!

I took the train, and sat thinking about it all the way. It was not a very long journey, just under an hour on the express. By seven o'clock I was in a small side room where one of the doctors patiently explained to me that Kate Davidson would not be any assistance to me as a witness, even were she able to leave the institution and appear in court, and that was out of the question.

"I am afraid nothing she said would carry any weight." He

shook his head ruefully, pushing his hand through his hair and leaving it sticking up in long, wavy strands. "She's completely delusional. Sometimes she is very depressed and we have to restrain her, in case she were to damage herself. At other times she simply sits and stares into space. I'm sorry.'

"But when she does talk?" I insisted.

"I'm sorry, Miss Ashton, but as I said, she is delusional. She wanders from past to present. She's very confused even about her own identity some of the time."

I had nothing else to cling to. "May I speak to her?" I asked.

He looked doubtful, his tired face puckered with lines of strain. "She doesn't know about her brother's death, or that Alan has been charged with killing him," he answered me. "I'm afraid that news might be more than she can deal with. I'm sorry."

I refused to give up, I don't really know why. I had no clear ideas. "If I promise not to tell her?" I insisted.

He still looked dubious.

"You can be there with me," I went on. "Stop me, throw me out, if you need to for her sake. I'm at my wits' end, Dr. Elliot. I have no idea how to defend Alan Davidson, and I have to start tomorrow. She and Alan used to be very close, she would want me to try everything I could, wouldn't she?"

He stood up slowly. I thought it was a refusal, but he opened the door and said "Come on, then," almost over his shoulder, and I followed his white-coated figure, a little stooped, sleeves too short, all the way up three flights of stairs and along what seemed like miles of corridor to a sunny attic. Inside a young woman sat stitching a piece of white linen. There were two other women there, also working at something or other, but no one needed to tell me which was Kate Davidson. She had the same beautiful, passionate features as her mother, and the glorious hair, except that her face was marked with grief of such an intensity it caught my breath in my throat, and even in the doorway I almost wished I had not come.

"Kate, I have someone who would like to see you," Dr. Elliot said gently. "You don't have to speak to her if you'd rather not, and I'll stay here all the time, if you wish." That was a statement rather than a question, as if he already knew the answer.

She raised her eyes from her linen to look at me, and I felt a sense of her mind as sharply as if she had reached out physically and touched me. I did not see insanity, and certainly not any kind of foolishness, only a pain and a fear so profound that she had to shelter from it by removing herself from reality.

"Kate?" Dr. Elliot asked gently.

"If you wish," she said, her voice low, a little husky. Looking at her I had an overwhelming sense of what Barbara Davidson must have been like thirty years ago, and why the judge had fallen so passionately in love with her.

"Thank you." I walked in and sat on the chair opposite her. I had already changed my mind about how to approach her. All idea of treating her like a child had been swept away the moment I met her eyes. It was not a retarded woman who faced me, but one hiding from an unbearable wound. Only one question beat in my brain— did I need to know what that wound was?

By the time I left three hours later I knew at least what

she had told Alan the night he visited her. I was not certain whether I believed it myself. Surely it was too bizarre,
too dreadful? But the only question that mattered was had
Alan believed it? If he had, it would explain both his
actions and his silence now.

I left her weeping quietly, but I thought with some kind
of inner peace beyond the pain, because I had listened,
and I had seemed to believe her. Or perhaps the truth was
that in spite of its horror, its apparent impossibility, in my
heart I had believed her, and she knew that.

Dr. Elliot walked with me as I stumbled into the street
and the glare of the lights and the noise of traffic.

"What are you going to do, Miss Ashton?" he asked me.

"The only thing I can," I replied. "Try to prove that Alan
believed her."

"You won't succeed," he said, biting his lip. "And she
can't testify. She was more lucid with you than I've seen
her with anyone else. You might not find her like that
again for weeks, even months. I wish I could tell you she
was getting better, but she isn't."

"I haven't got weeks or months," I answered. "Anyway,
they don't call me Jude for nothing. It's what I do—increasingly often lately."

He looked confused.

"St. Jude—the patron saint of lost causes?" I explained.
"My name is Judith."

He smiled, making him look younger. "I got there rather
before you," he said. "With the lost causes, I mean."

I smiled at him, and thanked him. I had a lot of work to
do and it would take me all night, and I'd be fortunate to
be ready for the court to open in the morning.

• • •

My first witness for the defense was the Davidsons' cook. I had dug her out of her bed in the middle of the night, but I had asked her only the briefest questions. She had very little idea why she was now on the stand testifying, and she kept glancing from me to Lord Davidson where he sat on the public benches. I could hardly blame the poor woman for being unhappy. She was confused and her loyalties were torn.

"Mrs. Barton," I began. The room was totally hushed. I don't really think anyone imagined I was going to get Alan Davidson acquitted, but they were all curious to know what I was going to try. The mixture of embarrassment and pity was about equal. "Were you employed as cook in the house of Lord Justice Davidson on September ninth last year?"

"Yes, ma'am," she said steadily, staring at me as if I were trying to hypnotize her.

"Was Mr. Neil Davidson living at the house then also?"

"Yes, ma'am."

"What was the state of his health, do you recall?"

There was a slight stir in the court. Lord Davidson shifted in his seat.

Mrs. Barton swallowed. "That weekend he was taken very poorly with the flu," she replied.

"Was the doctor sent for?" I questioned.

"Oh yes, and he came. But there really isn't much you can do for it. Just stay in bed, and drink all you can."

"Did anybody look after him?" I pressed. Please heaven she was not going to go back on her testimony now!

"Yes, ma'am," her voice dropped to barely more than a whisper. "His valet did, and then Miss Kate, his sister."

I let my breath out slowly. "How do you know that Miss Kate did?"

"Because she came into the kitchen and cooked something for him herself. Seemed Mr. Neil asked her to. Said she was the only one who could cook egg custard just the way he liked it, and would take some up to him on a tray."

Hoyle rose to his feet. I knew he was going to object that this was all irrelevant, but in the event he did not bother. With a patronizing smile he shrugged and sat down again, as if nothing I could do would harm his case anyway and he might as well be generous to me.

"And did she cook the egg custard, and as far as you know, take it to him?" I asked.

Judge Davidson stiffened.

"Yes, ma'am," Mrs. Barton replied. "She certainly left my kitchen with it."

"Thank you." I turned to Hoyle and invited him to question the cook.

He stood up and spoke with elaborate weariness, adjusting the front of his gown very slightly. "Mrs. Barton, has this touching story of sisterly affection nearly a year ago got anything whatever to do with Neil Davidson's death . . . by any stretch of your imagination, or ours?"

"I don't know, sir," Mrs. Barton answered. "That was the night Miss Kate was took ill herself, an' I never saw her again."

Suddenly the courtroom was alive, the ripple passed through the public benches like a shock of electricity before a storm. Davidson looked startled. Beside him Barbara was close to tears. In the dock Alan was rigid, glaring at me with panic in his face.

Hoyle for once looked as if he had bitten into an apple and found a worm in it.

The judge leaned forward. "Miss Ashton?" He did not put words to a question but it was there in his face.

"I have no redirect, my lord," I replied.

He sighed and sat back. I had not answered him, but he had understood that there was a story I was going to draw out, and he was prepared to wait.

I called Neil's valet. This was going to be the most difficult. He was a lean, dark young man with a troubled face, as if anxiety sat heavy on his shoulders, and he never once looked toward Lord or Lady Davidson.

"Mr. Clark, were you valet to Mr. Neil Davidson while he was living in his parents' home last September?" I began.

"Yes." I already knew what he had done, and why, from the few words we had exchanged in the small hours of this morning but this was still going to hurt, and I was sorry for that.

"Do you remember his illness on the ninth?" I asked.

"Yes," he answered very quietly. For a moment I was afraid he was going to lose his courage.

"Of course," I agreed. "It is not something a competent manservant would forget, far less a good one, and as close as a valet. Did you look after him during this time, fetch and carry for him, help him in every way he needed?"

There was only one reasonable answer he could give.

"Yes," he agreed.

I smiled and nodded. "And were you there when his sister Kate brought the dish of egg custard she had prepared for him?"

Now he looked confused, but if anything, less frightened than before. "No."

I knew he had been on duty that night. I did not want the trouble of having to call other witnesses to prove that. But if at this last moment his nerve failed him, I would have to. I could not succeed without him. I raised my eyebrows as if mildly surprised. "You were off duty that evening? I must have misunderstood my other witnesses."

His eyes narrowed and he turned even further away from Barbara Davidson. "I was on duty," he said miserably. "I just wasn't in the room when he asked for her or when she came."

"Do you know who was?" I said quickly.

This time his hesitation was so long that the judge intervened. "Mr. Clark, you must answer the question."

"Yes," he said at last. "Lord Davidson.'

"Both times?" I pushed him. "Or just when Neil asked for her?"

"When he asked for her," he said grimly, "it was he who told her to go."

I felt a fraction of the ache ease inside myself, and a different kind of pain take over. "Did you see her go in with the custard?"

"Yes." Now it was a whisper, but in the utter silence of the room everyone must have heard him, even though they had no idea what they were waiting for, I prayed that none of them knew how much I also was feeling my way.

"Was anyone else in the room then, apart from Neil himself?"

"No."

"And when she came out?" That was the question on which it all turned.

The man was ashen, and there was a sheen of sweat on

his skin. Now at last he looked at Lord Davidson, but Davidson was sitting with his body forward, staring at Alan as if he had recognized him for the first time.

Barbara looked at her husband, then at her son, then at me, and I was twisted inside with guilt for what I was going to do to her, but I could not pull back now.

"Mr. Clark?" the judge prompted.

The valet stared at a space on the wall somewhere ahead of him. "Yes, I was there."

"Would you describe it, please?" I requested.

"My lord . . ." Hoyle began. "Miss Ashton is an actress of considerable skill, not to say ambition, but the tragedy of Lord Justice Davidson's daughter is not part of this trial, and ordinary decency requires . . ."

The judge was miserable.

Davidson himself had not said a word, but his distress, and that of his wife, was a presence in the court so powerful there can have been no man or woman unaware of it.

His voice cutting like acid, the judge adjorned the court and requested me to see him in his chambers immediately.

"Miss Ashton," he said the moment the door was closed behind me and I stood in front of him, "I will not permit you to exploit the tragedy of Katherine Davidson's illness to divert the jury's attention from her brother's guilt. For God's sake, have you no sensitivity at all to her family's agony?"

I had been expecting him to say something of that sort.

"My sorrow for their grief does not allow me to conceal facts that are relevant to a murder case, my lord," I answered. "No matter how much I may regret the additional pain it causes, it isn't my right to judge between one person and another, whose feelings may be spared and their sins hidden, and who has to have their wounds exposed."

"You say that so easily," he replied, and for a moment there was a flash of anger at what he saw as my blundering ignorance. "You're, what—thirty? Have you any idea what Davidson, and men like him, did for this country?" He leaned forward over the desk. "You have no concept of what we endured during the war, what fear there was under the masks of courage we put on every day, or what that cost. Davidson's heroism gave us hope, and belief in ourselves and the possibility of victory, if we could just hold on."

I did not interrupt. I knew he needed to say it, and it was probably true.

"You look at him now with honor and prosperity, and you assume it was all easy for him," he went on, now thoroughly consumed in his own emotional memories. "But Barbara was married to Ernest Upshaw when she and Davidson met. It was passionate and total love at first sight, at least for him. He saw her across the street, and from that moment on he could think of no other woman." There was a softness in his eyes, as if vicariously he tasted the fire and the tenderness of that long ago love story.

His voice dropped. "They had to wait. In those days you did not divorce. It ruined a woman." He was staring, soft-eyed, far beyond me or anything within the room.

"Ernest Upshaw was a hero too, in the same regiment as Davidson. He was seconded to a raid across enemy lines. He didn't come back. As soon as a decent period of mourning was over, Davidson and Barbara married." Suddenly his eyes focussed sharply on me again. "They've lost their eldest son, but I will not have you drag their daughter's tragic breakdown into public. Do you understand me, Miss Ashton?"

"Yes, my lord, I understand you," I answered without wavering my gaze from his. "I am sure you will not allow me to overstep the boundaries of the law, but within them, I am going to do everything I can to help my client—"

"Your client is beyond help, Miss Ashton!" he said bitterly. "You know that, and so do I. We'll go through the motions of the law, as we must, but he is guilty, and we can't redeem that. I will not permit you to crucify his father as well by exposing that poor young woman's mental or emotional collapse for the public to pore over and speculate about, and the newspapers to make money out of." His face was hard, his lips tight, exaggerating the deep lines from nose to mouth. "No ambitious young lawyer is going to save her own career, or rectify the mistake of having accepted an impossible case, at the expense of one of our greatest families, which has already suffered more than its share of tragedy." It was not even a threat, just a statement of fact.

I felt a flicker of real fear in the pit of my stomach, like an awakening sickness, but I had believed Kate Davidson, and I still did. It was belief, it was certainly not knowledge, and that doubt was like a needle in my side. I knew what I was risking. But to back away now, to run from the battle because victory was not sure, would be a cowardice that would cripple me forever.

"Of course, my lord," I said steadily. "If the case could be heard in private it would be the easiest, but since there is no question of national security involved, I don't think that will be possible."

A dull flush spread up his cheeks. "Are you attempting to mock me, Miss Ashton?"

My knees were suddenly barely strong enough to hold

me up. "No, my lord. I deeply regret the fact that evidence I may elicit from witnesses will be distressing to the Davidson family—and that is not just words—I do mean it!" I did, more than he could know. "But my feelings are not the point. The truth is, and the nearest to justice that we can come."

"Then you had better get on with it," he said grimly. He seemed to be about to add something else, then changed his mind.

We returned and I resumed questioning the valet. The judge reminded him that he was under oath, and faced me with a spark of hope in his eyes. I killed it immediately. I hated doing it.

"Did you see Kate Davidson when she came out of her brother Neil's room?" I asked bluntly. He must have seen in my face that I knew the answer and that all the power of emotion in me was bent on dragging it out of him, whatever the cost to either of us, or to anyone else. He did not even look to Lord Davidson for help, or to the judge, and I refused to look at them either, in case it robbed me of my courage.

"Yes," Clark said very quietly. But there was not a sigh or a rustle in the room and every word was as dense as a scream.

"Describe her," I ordered. "Tell us exactly what you saw, what you heard, and what you did, Mr. Clark."

He was a man defeated by a weight too vast for him and finally he surrendered to it. He spoke in a tight, almost colorless voice, as if to add emotion to it would be unbearable. "I heard Mr. Neil shouting for me and the dressing room door swung open so hard it crashed against the wall, and he stood there in a rage like I've never seen him before. His face was red and he had scratches on his cheeks and one eye was already swelling up. 'Throw that garbage out!' he shouted at me, gesturing behind him."

Lord Davidson started up in his seat, and then stood frozen, staring first at me, then slowly and with horror darkening his eyes, at Alan.

Barbara looked as if she were confused, like a lost child, growing more and more frightened with each moment.

Clark rubbed his hands slowly up over his face, digging the heels of them into the sockets of his eyes. I did not prompt him to go on, I knew he would.

Even Hoyle was silent.

"I didn't know what he meant," Clark said hoarsely.

I was afraid for an instant that he was going to break down, his voice was so thick, so choked. But he mastered it, lifting his head a little and staring at me, as if I were the one person in that whole room who already knew what he was going to say, and somehow that reality helped him.

"Then I saw Miss Kate lying on the floor. Her hair was over her face and there was blood on her clothes. Her skirt was torn and up around her waist. . . ." He took a deep, shuddering breath. "And I knew what had happened. God . . . I wish now I'd done something different!" The pain in his voice was so sharp it cut the mind. "But I was a coward. I was afraid of him, and . . . what he would do to me. I did as he told me. God forgive me, I put her out."

I was sorry for him. He must have been in hell, the real hell of guilt. But I could not afford pity there or then.

"You knew she had been raped by her brother, and you picked her up and put her out? Is that what you are saying?" I asked.

He looked at me as if I had struck him, and that he deserved it. I admit even now that I can still feel the twist of guilt in my stomach I did at that moment.

"Yes," he whispered. "I did."

I gave him his chance. "Why?" I asked. "Why did you not help her? At least tell her father or mother what had happened?"

His voice was not much more than a whisper. "Because a couple of months before that I had taken some money from Neil's dresser, just a few pounds. My mother was ill. I got something special for her, to help. Neil knew, and he told me he would fire me if I said anything about Kate. My mother's worse now. I can't afford to be without a job. There's no one else."

"So you were blackmailed?" I wanted the jury to be sure of that.

"Yes."

"And what happened to Kate?"

"She locked herself in her room for several days, until they broke the door and the doctors took her away," he said hoarsely.

It was even worse than I had expected. I don't know why. I had believed Kate when she told me. At least I think I had. I looked across at Alan. He sat in the dock with his head bowed and his hands over his ears, as if he could not live through hearing it again.

I meant to look at Lord Davidson, but it was Barbara's face I saw as she stared up at him, and in a dawn of horror more intense than anything I could have imagined before, I realized that he had known! I saw it just as she did. It opened up an abyss in front of me. It must have hurled her into one so deep she felt as if she would never escape the darkness again. He had known and he had done nothing!

She was so white she looked as if she must be dead! Perhaps in that moment something inside her did die.

I thought of the great love story of their meeting, her first husband, Ernest Upshaw, in Davidson's regiment—sent on an impossible raid—to die a hero! So his exquisite widow could marry Davidson?

Was that also the understanding I saw in her face as she stared at him now, as if she had never truly seen him before?

Lord Justice Davidson V.C. looked at the judge, then to the dock and the son who had avenged his sister because no one else would. Then at last, slowly, like a man mortally wounded, he turned to his wife. I can't ever know, but I believe that in that moment at last he began to understand himself, and what he had done, what manner of man he was, and what it had cost him.

His elder son also felt that if he wanted a beautiful woman badly enough, then he could take her. He was cut from the same cloth—handsome, passionate, selfish at heart. The world had loved his father! Why not him too?

The court was still silent, like people who have witnessed something too terrible for speech. I don't know how much they understood, but they felt it.

Davidson turned to me. I expected to see hatred in his face. No man could ever forgive what I had done to him! And I had done it in public, in a courtroom, the realm where he was all but king.

But it was not hate that brimmed his eyes, it was the first white dawn of understanding of what sin truly is, and the hunger above all else in existence, to tear it out of his soul.

Defending Alan from conviction was a lost cause, it always had been, he would have to serve something, even if the court accepted my plea for him of diminished responsibility—but perhaps I had saved another cause no one had even known was lost, until that moment? The path back from such a place as Lord Davidson had gone to is very long indeed, but it is not impossible. It takes more courage than facing an army's guns because the enemy is within you, and there is no armistice.

Thank you, St. Jude, for a miracle after all.

I turned back to the judge, my voice hoarse, but all uncertainty fled away.

Permissions